INVASION OF PRIVACY

Also by Christopher Reich

The Prince of Risk

Rules of Betrayal

Rules of Vengeance

Rules of Deception

The Patriots Club

The Devil's Banker

The First Billion

The Runner

Numbered Account

INVASION OF PRIVACY

A NOVEL

CHRISTOPHER REICH

DOUBLEDAY

New York   London   Toronto   Sydney   Auckland

Copyright © 2015 by Christopher Reich

All rights reserved. Published in the United States by Doubleday, a division of Penguin Random House LLC, New York, and in Canada by Random House of Canada, a division of Penguin Random House Ltd., Toronto.

www.doubleday.com

DOUBLEDAY and the portrayal of an anchor with a dolphin are registered trademarks of Penguin Random House LLC.

Book design by Michael Collica
Jacket design by Michael J. Windsor
Jacket photograph © WK1003mike/Shutterstock

Library of Congress Cataloging-in-Publication Data
Reich, Christopher, 1961–
Invasion of privacy : a novel / Christopher Reich.—First edition.
pages ; cm
ISBN 978-0-385-53157-3 (hardcover)—ISBN 978-0-385-53156-6 (eBook)
I. Title.
PS3568.E476284I58 2015
813'.54—dc23   2014027364

MANUFACTURED IN THE UNITED STATES OF AMERICA

1 3 5 7 9 10 8 6 4 2

First Edition

To Laura, with love

MAGIC

It would be nice to think that everything was perfect before.

The past always appears rosier than it was. A little happier. A little funnier. The girls were prettier. The boys were more handsome. We were all healthier. Time does that. It fades the bad and polishes the good.

But not always. Sometimes things really were as special as we remember. Sometimes we were happier. The jokes were funnier. The girls were prettier and the boys were more handsome. And we all really were healthier.

Sometimes life is magic.

Mary was thinking about Thailand.

Two years. Another lifetime. Or at least another life. A different one from what she lived today.

Koh Samui.

There, on the rugged island in the South China Sea, the ocean was colored a dozen shades of blue and the sand was like warm velvet. Perfumed winds dashed down forested hillsides. And always the hint of smoke and incense, evidence of man's war with himself. Mary loved all those things. But what she loved most was the sky at dusk.

So close to the equator, day turned rapidly to night. As the sun dipped below the horizon, the sky bled darkness, blue yielding to plum. Stars popped into sight like faraway bulbs. The wind calmed. The air grew exceptionally clear. The world was still. And for a few fleeting minutes, she reflected on all that was good about the day gone by, and all that the night ahead promised.

Magic.

That's how the sky was that last Christmas before everything changed.

Mary stepped off the veranda of their hotel room onto the beach and jogged across the sand to join her family for the lighting of the lanterns. She saw them fifty yards ahead, bathed in that special light. Joe, tall and muscled, his legs as dark as those of the natives who offered rides in their motorized longboats, black hair cut so short he could be back in the Corps all over again. Jessie skipping next to him, cargo shorts hanging too low, hair a tousled mess, even now looking at something on her phone. And Grace, slight as a pixie, trailing behind, her strawberry-blond hair and pale legs making her a ghost in comparison to her suntanned father and sister.

"Wait for me," Mary called as she reached them. "And be careful with the matches."

"Don't worry, honey," Joe said, turning and shaking the box of blue-tips. "I think the girls are old enough to light a candle by themselves."

"Just saying."

Mary grabbed Joe's hand, intertwining her fingers with his. They walked at the water's edge, the surf rushing up to their ankles. It was just five o'clock, and the ocean felt as warm as a bath. Music drifted from the open-air hotel lobby, the mysterious and melancholy tones of the *ranat ek*, a kind of Thai xylophone. "Thank you," she said, nuzzling his shoulder.

"For what?"

"For this."

"Still have six more months in big bad Bangkok."

"I can do six months standing on my head."

"Wise guy, eh?"

"The toughest. Married you, didn't I?"

Joe stopped and looked at her. "You sure you made the right decision?"

Mary answered without hesitation. "I'm sure."

"I haven't made it easy."

"No," she said. "You haven't. But that's okay. It's done, right?"

"Right."

"And you're good?"

"Solid."

"That's all I need to know." Mary looked at the girls skipping through the water, then dropped her husband's hand and ran up the beach.

"So you're sure?" he called after her.

"Yeah," she said, turning, running backward a few steps. "I'm sure." And she was.

The past six days had passed in a riot of swimming and sunning and excursions up the coast in Thai longboats. The girls had their hair braided and their nails painted; they made thatched skirts and collected shells. She and Joe took walks up and down the beach and ate lunch, just the two of them, and played tennis and even sneaked away for more adult-themed activities. At some point she'd forgotten that this was the first time she'd seen her husband for more than three days running in the past year, and that they had another move coming, to an as yet to be determined city, and that wherever it was, the FBI would still be the FBI, more of a spouse to her husband than she'd ever be.

"Got ya!" Joe grabbed her waist as he caught up and splashed water on her legs.

"Daddy, stop," said Grace. "You're getting Mommy all messy."

"Mommy likes being messy," said Joe, pulling Mary to him and nuzzling her neck.

"No she doesn't," said Grace. Then: "Do you, Mommy?"

"Dad, stop," said Jessie. "No PDAs. Gross."

"You girls go get your lamps," said Mary.

"They're called Kongming lanterns," said Grace. "People light them to celebrate."

"Whatever, suck-up." Jessie looked at her parents and rolled her eyes. "When did she get so smart? She doesn't have a brain. She has a hard drive."

"Look who's talking, Billy Gates," said Grace, making a face. "Geeka-zoid."

"Forget Bill Gates. Call me Rudeboy."

"Who?"

"Rudeboy. He's only the best hacker in the world. He won Capture the Flag at DEF CON five years in a row."

Grace threw up her arms. "What are you even talking about?"

"Never mind," said Jessie. "If it's not a vampire or a mermaid, you wouldn't know."

"You guys are both wicked smart," said Joe, his nasal Boston twang coming through loud and clear. "Just like your daddy."

He was a Southie, born and raised in the South End of Boston, and forever proud of it. His family had come to America in the 1920s as the Gianninis, but somewhere back a few generations it had been decided to change the name to Grant.

"Hey," protested Mary. "I'm the chem major." Once upon a time she'd dreamed of being a doctor—a pediatric surgeon, to be specific.

"And so are you, Miss Einstein." Joe gave Mary's butt a squeeze, and she told him to watch it, or he might get coal in his stocking and not that other thing he'd wished for. Romance was not his strong suit.

"Hurry along, girls," said Mary. "And make sure you get a lantern for me and your dad." Chem majors don't learn no english?

Jessie looked at her, suspicious brown eyes narrowed, contemplating rebellion. The glance was enough to let Mary know that the years ahead were not going to be easy ones. To her surprise, Jessie took Grace's hand, and together they ran off toward the group of hotel guests gathering twenty yards up the beach.

"Did you see that?" asked Mary.

"I did," said Joe. "Must be the Christmas spirit."

"Must be." Though even discounting that, Mary knew she was seeing something special.

Grace and Jessie.

Chalk and cheese.

Grace was their baby, eight going on eighteen. Quiet, kind, polite, and much too empathetic for her own good. Grace was the girl who plopped down on your lap and gave you a hug exactly when you needed it most.

Then there was Jessie. Jessie did not sit on your lap or give hugs. She was taciturn, quarrelsome bordering on surly, and seemingly happiest on her own. To look at, she was all Joe. Dark hair, brown eyes, a build that borrowed a little too much from his Sicilian ancestors. Grace called her a "geekazoid," and it was true. Jessie loved math and computers and spent all her time conspiring how to separate Mary from her smartphone. At age twelve, she was already five feet five inches tall, and if her shoe size was any indication, she was going to give Joe, who stood a proud six feet, a run for his money.

"Got some news today," said Joe.

"Oh?" Mary studied her husband's face, trying to guess: good or bad? "Didn't know the shop was open on Christmas Eve."

There was only one matter up in the air, and that was where they were to be stationed next. So far his career had taken them to Baltimore, Richmond, and, for the past two years, Bangkok, where Joe worked on an antipiracy task force with the Thai police. She knew that he desperately wanted to be sent to Headquarters FBI in Washington, D.C., to head up the legate program. For a boy from the South End, running the Bureau's network of liaison agents, or legates assigned to foreign embassies, was as far from Boston as you could get, Bangkok notwithstanding.

"Sacramento," he said finally, breaking a crooked grin.

Mary swallowed. Sacramento was a backwater. It was not the Christmas present either of them wanted. She did her best not to scream. "How long?"

"Two."

"Two years? And then D.C.?"

"Heck, yeah," he said with feigned optimism. "They can't keep me away forever."

Mary smiled back at him. She knew he was crushed, far more disappointed than she could ever be. "Bring it," she said. Then an afterthought: "Sacramento have a hoops team?"

"The Kings. They suck."

"Then the seats'll be cheap. We'll get down close for the Celtics."

"That's my girl." Joe smiled harder, and she saw a glint of something in his eye.

"Come on, let's go. We don't want to miss the big moment."

Ahead, twenty or so guests had formed a loose circle at water's edge. Most had already assembled their lanterns and stood holding the large white frames, anxious to be given the go-ahead to light them.

"You guys doing okay?" Mary asked.

"Jessie already finished," said Grace.

"It was simple," said Jessie, holding hers up for examination.

The lanterns were tall rectangular boxes fashioned from oiled rice paper. It was necessary to insert bamboo struts into each corner to expand them to their full height. A strut wide enough to support the candle held the bottom open. Once the candle was lit, hot air rose and was trapped inside the paper until enough accumulated to lift the lantern into the air.

"Let me help, mouse," said Mary.

Grace surrendered her lantern, and Mary quickly realized that the task was harder than she'd expected.

"Mom, let me do it." Jessie took Grace's lantern and had it finished in a jif. "You want me to do yours and Dad's, too?"

"We'll be fine," said Joe.

The hotel manager waved his arms and called the guests to attention. "It's time," he said. "Please light your candles."

The sky had darkened considerably in the past few minutes. An azure belt stretched across the horizon. A multitude of stars danced overhead. Jessie struck a match and one by one lit the candles. The four stood facing one another, arms outstretched, fingertips cradling the lanterns.

"Ladies and gentlemen," said the hotel manager. "I wish you all a Merry Christmas."

Behind them, a cry went up as someone released the first lantern. All eyes turned to the masked light as it crept into the sky. Another lantern joined it, and then another, and soon a dozen pale lights were floating upward, a timid band of souls ascending to heaven.

"Now?" asked Jessie.

Joe looked at Mary. She nodded. "Now," he said.

They released their lanterns simultaneously. For a moment the translucent boxes hung before their eyes, neither rising nor falling, and Mary bit her lip, hoping that they hadn't let go too soon. But then each began a steady, twirling ascent into the sky.

"Go," said Jessie.

"Away," said Grace.

A hush fell over the assembled guests. No one spoke. The only noise was the rhythmic brush of the ocean across the sand. Mary took Joe's hand. He grasped Jessie's, and she took Grace's. Grace grinned and took her mother's. They were connected. One circle. One family.

Mary thought, This is everything I ever wanted. And, How did I get so lucky? And, Please, God, I don't want this moment to end.

They held hands as the lanterns floated higher into the sky, ever farther out to sea, and the flickering lights grew dimmer, until one by one they blinked a last time and were gone.

Somewhere close, a firecracker exploded. And then another. The sharp noises broke their trance. All at once the beach came back to life. Men and women hooted and cheered and shouted "Merry Christmas!" Everywhere there was activity and merriment.

Mary looked at her family, but no one said a word. It was as if they all were transfixed, or, as she came to believe later, after so much had come to pass, that in some indefinable way they knew that this was the last time they would share such a moment. That the world as they knew it was coming to an end, and that somewhere over the horizon a shadow lurked, and it was coming their way.

"Merry Christmas," said Mary.

"Merry Christmas, Mommy," said Grace.

"Love you," said Jessie.

"Love you," said Joe. "All my girls."

The last lantern disappeared from view. Finally they dropped hands. It was magic.

MONDAY

1

"Felix will be there in ten."

"All clear?"

"Nothing out here but tumbleweeds and horseshit."

"Welcome to Texas."

Special Agent Joe Grant of the Federal Bureau of Investigation stared out the window of the Chevrolet Tahoe. The ground was barren, scrub sprouting here and there out of the dirt. Across the yard stood an old windmill, the kind with the tiller and the spoked wheel. Farther down the road he spied a telephone pole strung with wires. Beneath it sat the rusted carcass of an ancient tractor. He sighed. The place had probably looked the same in 1933.

"Stay back a ways once he pulls in. Don't want to spook him."

"Now you're even talking like a cowboy," said Fergus Keefe, a supervisory special agent from the Cyber Investigations Division and his colead on the case. "That ought to go over big in D.C."

"Ain't there yet."

"If half of what Felix says is true, this is your ticket to the show."

"I'll believe it when I'm holding the plane ticket in my hand."

Sacramento's the last stop, they'd promised him. You'll get to D.C. straight after that. But that was before Semaphore came around. Semaphore threw a wrench into everything. If he wasn't so good at his job, Joe thought, he'd be in Washington right now, looking at the dome of the Capitol Building and giving briefings on the Hill. Instead he was parked in the questionable shade of a cedar tree on an abandoned cattle ranch smack dab in the middle of Texas Hill Country. D.C. might as well be on the far side of the moon.

"Felix is turning onto RR 3410," said Keefe.

"Roger that. Wait right there. He sees that dust behind him, there's no telling what he'll do. He's nervous enough as it is."

"Felix" was the confidential informant's code name. For Felix Unger, the OCD half of the Odd Couple.

"I'm pulling over," said Keefe. "He's all yours. And don't take any chances."

"You think he's packing? Felix? A PhD from MIT? The guy's annual 401(k) contribution is bigger than my entire salary."

"I prefer to think of him as a pill-popping drunk with two DUIs and a reckless endangerment under his belt."

"Point taken." Joe laid a hand on his Glock. Tell an agent to be careful and he's going to check that his piece is where it should be—in Joe's case, holstered on his waist, butt facing out for the cross draw. He forgot about the weapon and switched off his phone, staring at the picture of Jessie and Grace on his wallpaper. He ran a fingernail over their faces, but it didn't bring them any closer. *Getting so big.* He said it every time, just like he said he'd be home more often and he'd stop letting "the job" take precedence over his job as a father.

Someday . . .

Joe drummed his fingers on the steering wheel. The exterior temperature gauge read 102, but it felt hotter. Across the yard a clump of tumbleweed rustled. He leaned forward, eyes glued to the windmill. Come on, he whispered. Give us a breeze. The windmill shuddered but did not turn.

Times had changed. You didn't need a windmill to pump water out of the ground. And you sure as heck didn't need wires to send a voice from one person to another. Joe knew all about phones and cables and all things telecommunication. He knew more about digital technology than he'd ever wanted to. Semaphore had taken care of that.

Officially it was Operation Semaphore, and it had brought him to Austin two months earlier. For the record it was a routine transfer, a lateral move from Sacramento to shore up the Austin residency's glaring manpower shortage. He came billed as an agent who knew his way around municipal corruption cases, with a stint overseas policing piracy of intellectual property.

But the record didn't say everything.

There were rumors about a chronic inability to follow orders. People said that Joe Grant was a cowboy who left a trail of wreckage in his wake. They said that Austin was his last watering hole and that he couldn't retire soon enough. And whatever you do, don't partner up with him.

The rumors were bullshit—disinformation designed to give him leeway to act on his own. No one knew about Semaphore except Joe, Keefe, and the task force in D.C.

The sound of an engine made him sit up straighter. He caught a flash of red in the rearview. It was Felix's Ferrari. Joe believed the model was called a LaFerrari, and it retailed for a cool million five. It was also the most conspicuous car on the face of the planet. He felt certain the boys up in the space station could see it right now with just their eyes.

Felix parked close behind Joe's car. A scrawny man with a mop of dark hair climbed out and hurried over. The door opened and Felix slid into the seat, eyes bugging, sweat rolling down his forehead. "You're going to need a bigger boat," he said.

"Relax," said Joe. "We're safe here."

"Safe. Yeah, right. You got no idea." Felix spun and peered over his shoulder. His eyes were red-rimmed and sagging with fatigue. He might have just pulled an all-nighter banging out code at the office, but Felix didn't bang out code anymore. Felix's real name was Hal Stark, and Stark was senior vice president for special projects at ONE Technologies, the biggest tech company in the United States. ONE was a player in everything: software, hardware, online sales, wireless communications; a gargantuan cross of Oracle, Google, Cisco, and AT&T.

"Why don't you take a breath, chill for a second. Then you can give me an idea." Joe pulled a pack of Juicy Fruit from his pocket. "A stick of gum makes you hum."

"What's that from?"

"What movie? I don't know. My wife says it sometimes. Have a stick."

Stark pulled out two and folded the chewing gum into a double-thick square before ramming it into his mouth. A moment later he was checking over his shoulder again.

Joe lowered both windows. "Hear that?"

"What? I don't hear anything."

"Exactly. This is Dripping Springs. Austin is twenty-five miles in the other direction. No one's on your tail. We've been watching you the whole way out. You didn't bring your phone, did you?"

"What do you think?"

"Okay, then. We checked your car earlier. It's clean. As far as anyone knows or cares, you left the office for a doctor's appointment. You're safe."

"All right, then. I believe you. I'm safe."

Joe put a hand on Stark's shoulder. "You have any problem getting it out?"

Stark pepped up. "They didn't take a second look. The security guard had it right there in his hand. He had no idea he was holding the crown jewels."

"What did I tell you?" Joe looked at the Ferrari's nose in his rear-view mirror. "Is there anything about that car that's inconspicuous?"

"That's the point," said Stark. "Nothing's run-of-the-mill on that car."

"Anyway, thank you, Hal. On behalf of the United States government, we are grateful. Now give me the goods, let me tape you swearing that you downloaded the information of your own free will, and we'll cut you loose. No one will ever learn about your cooperation."

"My ass," said Stark. "What about you? You get the DUIs off my record?"

"*Expunged* is the word," said Joe. "And yes, both have been expunged from your record."

"That was cheap," said Stark. "Preying on a man's weaknesses like that."

"A guy like you can't afford to hire a driver? That's the second time you were popped in the past twelve months. And next time make sure your date isn't a minor." Statutory rape?

The DUI was their way in, the chink in the enemy's armor. Stark was right. It was cheap, but Joe had to use what he was given. He'd yet to meet an informant who volunteered his services of his own free will.

"The pressure," said Stark. "You have no idea. He's relentless. Always more. Always better. Always faster. He's not human, I swear it. He's some kind of superman. No . . . a *supermachine*. Men have feelings. He says he's beyond feeling. He's proud of it. He says he's 'becoming.' Can you believe that? Becoming *what*?"

"Okay, Hal. Let's calm down. Just begin at the beginning. You'll feel better once it's off your chest."

"And you expunged the felony, too?"

Yes, Joe said. He had.

Hal Stark sat up straighter. "All right, then, the first thing you need to know is that you don't know the half of it. What you guys found—the reason you came after me—that's the tip of the iceberg . . . no, no . . . the tip of the tip."

Joe took this in without comment. He felt the hackles on his neck stand up as they always did when he was about to get the goods. "Go on."

"The incursion . . . well, you know that wasn't the first time, don't you?"

The incursion referred to a hack of the FBI's mainframe eight months earlier that had triggered the red flags and gotten Semaphore off the ground.

"Of course," Joe lied. "Exactly how long has it been going on?"

Stark laughed. "You didn't know. Well, like I said, he's a supermachine. Amazing you found it in the first place."

"We're no slouches ourselves."

"You might want to reserve comment until I'm done."

Joe looked away, drawn by the rustling of the large tumbleweed. Finally a breeze. He glanced at the windmill, but the wheel didn't budge. He looked back and the tumbleweed was still.

"What is it?" asked Stark.

"Nothing," said Joe. "Keep going."

"It's all about the company we just bought. The one that caused all the headlines."

"Merriweather," said Joe.

"Yeah, it builds the fastest supercomputer in the world, called Titan. He's got plans for it." Stark shook his head. "You won't believe it."

"We're going to need a bigger boat."

"You sure as hell are," said Stark.

Joe kept his eyes on the tumbleweed. He decided the heat was playing tricks on him. Nothing moved without wind pushing it. There was no wind, so the tumbleweed couldn't have inched closer. He razzed himself for being paranoid. Once a sniper, always a sniper. Dripping Springs was not Iraq. Smiling, he looked back at Stark and saw it: a thin column of dust rising into the air five hundred yards behind them. Someone was approaching on the inbound road.

"Everything okay?" asked Stark.

"Shut up." Joe picked up his phone. "Boots, that you?"

"Boots" was Keefe's nickname, earned God knows how or when.

No one responded.

"Boots, come back."

Stark turned halfway around in his seat to peer out the back window.

"Get down," said Joe, as he drew his weapon and thumbed the safety off.

"What's going on?" asked Stark, eyes locked on the pistol. "I thought you said no one followed me."

Joe started the car. "Buckle your seat belt. The ride may get a little bumpy."

Stark muttered something, then elbowed the door open and threw himself out of the car.

"Get back here," said Joe.

"I can take care of myself."

"Get inside."

Stark looked around the clearing. "Government never protected anyone. I can take care of myself."

"Give me the drive."

"Go screw yourself. I was an idiot to trust you."

"Hal!"

"I'm out of here." Stark took a step toward his car, then hopped back toward Joe. "Hey," he said, "I got it. Where that line about the gum came—"

Stark's head exploded in a spray of blood and brain and he dropped to the ground.

Joe caught a muzzle flash from inside the tumbleweed. No rifle report. A sniper like him.

Desperately he slammed the Tahoe into drive. The windshield shattered. He threw himself flat onto the seat and a second bullet struck his headrest. He drove blindly for a few seconds, then raised his head. A bullet hit the steering wheel, cracking it. Another hit the engine block. Steam escaped from beneath the hood. The car ground to a halt.

Joe lay still. His phone had fallen into the footwell. He picked it up and dialed. "Answer," he whispered feverishly. "Pick up. Please."

He heard a car stop behind him. Doors opening. Male voices. The unmistakable metal crunch of a clip being loaded into an automatic weapon.

Joe held the phone to his ear. "Come on. Pick up."

The phone answered. "Hi. This is Mary. I can't take your call right now, but if you leave a message, I'll get back to you as soon as possible. Have a great day."

Joe closed his eyes. "Babe . . . where are you?"

2

"Not today," Mary Grant whispered, grasping the steering wheel harder. "Do not make me late today."

It was four o'clock, and traffic on Mopac was blocked solid as far as she could see. Rush hour started early in Austin.

"Everyone doing okay?" she asked, looking over her shoulder.

Grace gazed out the window, sipping her Sonic limeade, her thoughts a million miles away. Jessie sat beside her, headphones on, eyes glued to Mary's phone, fingers ferociously tapping away.

"Jess, hon, what are you doing with Mom's phone?" asked Mary.

Jessie didn't answer.

"She can hear you," said Grace. "She just doesn't feel like answering."

"What's she doing?"

"I don't know. Probably Instagramming."

Mary watched Jessie's fingers go *pat-pat-pat* on the glass surface. More like writing an article for the encyclopedia, she thought. She could feel the throbbing bass of the music assaulting her teenage daughter's eardrums, an angry voice shouting something she knew she'd rather not understand. "Jessie?"

The cars in front of them began to move, and Mary forgot about the phone. She drove fifty yards before traffic came to another halt. At this rate they'd be lucky to make it home by five.

Today was her and Joe's seventeenth anniversary. Mary couldn't quite believe it. All those clichés about the years going by too fast turned out to be true. She glanced in the mirror. Her eyes were a little more tired, her skin not as taut as it once was, but if she smiled and kept her features alive, she did a pretty good job of keeping the years at bay. She'd even managed to lose six pounds so she could fit into her favorite little black dress. One hundred twenty-five pounds wasn't bad for a five-foot-four-inch, thirty-nine-year-old mother of two. *Perfect.*

She began to think about the night ahead. A dirty martini at the hotel bar to get things started. Dinner at Sullivan's. There was no stopping her once she set foot in a good steakhouse. She couldn't just have the steak. She needed all the trimmings. Creamed spinach, garlic mashed potatoes, and a big ol' wedge of chilled iceberg lettuce with plenty of blue cheese dressing. She wondered how she would fit into her dress after eating a bone-in cowboy rib eye.

After dinner they'd head back to their room at the Westin, overlooking Lady Bird Lake, a reservoir on the pretty green river that snaked through downtown. She and Joe needed the night. He'd been preoccupied with work lately and away even more than usual. There hadn't been any arguments, at least not any big ones. Still, the tension that came from not being able to share each other's lives adequately was building between them. Tonight was for remembering why they were meant to be together. Joe had promised to be on time and on his best behavior, which meant no phone, no work talk, just them. The little black dress would do the rest.

The car in front of her inched forward. Mary saw her prompt arrival going up in smoke.

It was her fault, trying to pack in so much when she knew she had a big evening planned. She had to make dinner for the girls, shower, dry her hair, do her makeup, then drive right back downtown by seven. Not gonna work.

Mary started revising her plans. Chicken strips instead of spaghetti. Fries instead of broccoli. Maybe her hair would be fine without a shower. She caught Gracie looking at her in the mirror. Was her anxiety that obvious?

"We'll be home soon. You can lie down and take a nap."

"I want to go to the park and play soccer."

"It's a little warm to play outdoors, don't you think?"

Grace shook her head.

"You can take your medicine, then rest a little before going out. I'll make you a milkshake."

"I don't want a milkshake. I want to play soccer. I don't care about the bruises."

"You'll be able to play next year. You wait and see."

"Promise?"

"Promise." Mary's white lie was rewarded with a broad smile. "Anyway," she added, "you have another two weeks of vacation."

"Two weeks," said Jessie. "BFD."

"No cursing, Jess," said Mary.

"BFD isn't cursing."

"You know what I mean."

"I told you she could hear," said Grace.

"Shut up, brat," said Jessie.

The fingers went *pat-pat-pat* on the glass.

"Jess, my phone."

"Just a minute. I'm almost done."

"Done with what?"

"Can you turn up the radio?" asked Grace.

Mary upped the volume a notch. A young woman sang mournfully about lost teen love. Grace sipped her drink and looked out the window

"I hate Taylor Swift," said Jessie, leaning over the seat and switching the radio station.

"You're not even listening," protested Grace. "You have your Beats on."

"I can still hear her. She sucks."

Mary shot Jessie a mean glance. "That's enough, young lady."

"You always take her side," said Jessie.

A phone rang. "Is that mine?"

"I don't feel good," said Grace.

Jessie made a face and moved away from her sister. "Mom, I think she's going to be sick."

"Mommy, I need to get home." Grace's complexion had gone from pale to translucent.

The phone rang again. "Jess, is that your dad?"

"I can't tell."

"What do you mean? It's there on the screen."

"Yeah . . . but," said Jessie.

"But what?"

"Mommy," said Grace plaintively.

As if someone threw a switch, traffic began to move. Slowly at first, but then faster, leaving a gap in front of Mary.

"Mom, go!" said Jessie.

Mary returned her attention to the highway and accelerated. The car jumped. Grace moaned. There was a retching sound.

"Mom!" said Jessie. "She's being sick."

"No, I'm not," said Grace.

The phone rang again. "Is it . . . ," Mary began. "Oh, forget it."

Like that, they were cruising at sixty-five, the freeway was as open and uncluttered as a Sunday morning. Mary relaxed a notch. "You okay, mouse?"

"Maybe," said Grace. "I want to be home."

"Got it!" Jessie shouted. "I unlocked it."

Mary jumped in her seat and Grace squealed.

"Unlocked what?" Mary asked.

"Your phone. Now you can use whatever carrier you want to."

Mary caught Jessie's wide-open grin. From grim to giddy in two seconds flat. "Is that legal?"

"It's your phone," Jessie explained. "Who says you have to use one of the big phone companies? Now you can hook up with one that's like a hundred times cheaper. Isn't that great?"

"Is it? If you say so, hon. Does it still work?"

"Of course. I'm saving all the settings. Oh, and that call was from Dad. He left a message."

"He did?" Mary felt a pang of worry. Joe wouldn't cancel. He knew what it meant to her. If it was important, he'd have called back by now or texted. He was probably just letting her know that everything was fine and that he'd see her at seven. "Give me the phone," she said pleasantly.

Jessie crossed her arms. "You can't listen and drive. Do you want me to listen to it?"

Mary knew what kind of messages Joe liked to leave. Definitely NSFW, which meant "not suitable for work." Or, in this case, children. "I'll wait till we get home. Just put the phone on the seat."

Jessie laid it on the front seat, a proud smile firmly in place.

"Thanks, sweetheart," said Mary. "You can tell me exactly what you did later."

"Mom, the exit!"

Mary saw the sign ahead, checked the rearview mirror, and yanked the car into the right lane, barely managing to make the exit ramp. "That was close," she said, laughing it off.

"Why don't you pay attention?" said Jessie. "We've lived here for two months and you still always miss it."

Mary bit back a stinging rebuke. If she'd said something like that to her mother, she'd have received a slap across the face. She had sworn when she had Jessie to be as kind to her children as her mother was mean to her. Getting angry only brought her down to Jessie's level.

She made the turn onto Spicewood Springs. In a minute they were driving through their new neighborhood. The houses were big and bold, each on an eighth of an acre. She turned onto Pickfair Drive and zipped into their driveway. She loved their home, a two-story Spanish-style with a stately live oak shading the lawn and a terracotta fountain next to the front door. "Home again, Finnegan," she said, as she put the car into park.

Jessie jumped out as if the car were on fire. Grace remained in her seat, her cheek pressed to the window. Mary got out and opened her daughter's door. "You okay, mouse?"

Grace mumbled something and vomited.

Mary jumped back, then immediately felt guilty for having done so. She put an arm behind her daughter's back and helped her from the car. "There, there. Let's get you inside and all cleaned up." At the front door, Mary craned her head and yelled up the stairs. "Jessie, get some towels."

"Did she puke?"

"Please, Jessie." Mary led Grace into the laundry room and helped her take off her shirt and jeans, then stuffed them straight into the washer.

"Here." Jessie stood in the doorway, holding out a dishcloth.

"It's in the car, sweetheart. There's not much."

Jessie didn't budge. "I don't do floors or windows."

"Come on, sweetheart. It won't take long."

Jessie shook her head. "N. O."

Mary yanked the towel out of her hand and without a backward glance took Grace upstairs. Jessie followed, pounding up the stairs and slamming the door to her room.

It took thirty minutes to get Grace settled. The doctor hadn't mentioned that the new medication would cause nausea. Either the drugs were stronger or Grace's system was growing weaker. Cancer sucked.

The clock read 5:30 when Mary walked into her bedroom to change after cleaning the car.

Joe's message. How could she forget?

She snatched the phone from her dresser. Just then it vibrated in her hand and began to ring. Joe, she said silently, I'm sorry.

But it wasn't Joe. There was no name on the screen, just a number she didn't recognize. She didn't have time right now to take a call from someone she didn't know. The phone rang again, and she realized that the first three digits were the same as Joe's.

A premonition flashed through her. A cold streak that rattled her spine for the briefest of instants. She hit the Answer key. "Hello."

"Mary, this is Don Bennett. Joe's been hurt. You need to come to the hospital right away."

3

Mary rushed out of the parking garage, following the signs to the emergency entrance. She walked crisply, chin up, shoulders pinned back. Stressful occasions were to be handled calmly and without excessive emotion. She was the daughter of a rear admiral and a lifelong member of the Junior League. She'd been born with a rule book in her mouth.

"What happened?" she asked.

"Hello, Mary." Don Bennett, special agent in charge of the FBI's Austin office, stood outside the emergency room doors. He was stocky and humorless, twenty pounds overweight, with brown eyes and a motorcycle cop's mustache. "Let's go inside."

"Right here is fine. How is he?"

Bennett put a hand on her arm. "Joe's in a bad way. Let's go inside and sit down."

"I don't want to sit," said Mary, pulling her arm clear. "Is he alive?"

"Yes," he said. "He's alive."

It was a hesitant yes, and Mary was too afraid to ask anything more. She followed Bennett through the automatic doors into the waiting room. A cluster of Joe's fellow agents had staked out a corner for themselves. Ten capable, clean-cut men in dark suits and two women who looked even more capable. All eyes turned to Mary. The suffering spouse. The weaker vessel. A civilian. She hurried past them, determined not to let them see her worry.

Joe's been hurt.

Mary had imagined the words, or something similar, a thousand times. And a thousand times she'd dismissed them. Not Joe. He was a specialist in electronic surveillance. He bugged phones and got warrants for wiretaps and spent days inside vans, watching and listening. His targets were mayors and city councilmen and treasurers who siphoned off money from public coffers. Joe didn't do dangerous. He'd promised her after they had Grace, and he'd renewed his promise after she got sick.

But the truth was, she didn't know what he did every day.

Bennett led her to a quiet corner. "Here's how it is," he said. "Joe's been shot. He lost a significant amount of blood. He's in surgery right now. That's all I can tell you."

"How bad?"

"Bad. The bullet may have nicked his heart. He was in cardiac arrest when they got to him."

"He was dead?"

"Clinically."

"Is there another kind?"

"I'm sorry."

"How long had his heart stopped before they were able to get it going again?"

"I don't know. The paramedics or the surgeon may be able to tell you. Joe was brought in on a STAR Flight from Dripping Springs."

"Where's that?"

"Twenty-five miles west on 290."

"He told me he was working a case in Bastrop. That's southeast of town."

Bennett averted his eyes. "Come on, Mary. You know the rules. I can't talk about an investigation."

"Why was he there?" Mary shouted. All faces turned toward them.

"He was meeting a CI," said Bennett, aware of the attention, leaning closer. "A confidential informant."

"I know what a CI is."

"Joe was working alone. I don't have the details, but from all appearances it looks like the debriefing went sideways. The informant was armed and—"

"Stop," said Mary. "We're talking about Joe, not some greenhorn fresh out of Quantico. He'd never let a man he thought was dangerous near him without checking if he was armed."

"All I know is that Joe got into a car with an informant and neither of them got out."

"So the informant is dead, too?"

"Jesus, Mary." Bennett looked away angrily, as if he'd been tricked. "I've said too much already. I'll tell you more when I get the all-clear. Right now let's concentrate on getting Joe through this."

But Mary was in no mood to wait. She looked at Bennett, at his tired brown eyes, which wouldn't quite meet hers, at his perfectly tied necktie and his lovingly shined shoes. She knew when she was being brushed off. "Who's giving you the all-clear, Don?"

"Mary, please."

"Who?"

"That's just an expression. I can't tell you about something I don't know. Joe is my friend, too."

Mary closed her eyes and drew a breath. She was thinking about the call. "He knew before."

"Pardon me?"

"Joe knew something was wrong."

Bennett shifted on his chair, alert. "I'm not sure I understand what you're getting at."

"He called me. He let me know he was in trouble." Mary began to cry. There was no stopping it. No amount of will or anger or shame or anything could arrest her tears. "I missed the call, but he left a voice-mail. I think he wanted me to help him."

"He called you to say he was in trouble?"

"It's my fault. I didn't take the call."

"Don't say that. You're not to blame."

"I could have—"

"Joe knew what he was doing."

The comment offended Mary. Six words to transfer the blame onto her husband's shoulders. Six words to wipe the FBI's hands clean of all culpability. "Yes," she said. "He did. And he'd never put himself into a compromising position with someone who was armed. Not when he was alone. Would you?"

Bennett started to answer, then bit back his words. "This isn't the time."

"Who was his backup?"

"He didn't have one."

"So who called the ambulance? Who found him? What aren't you telling me?"

Bennett ignored her question. "What did the message say?"

"Listen for yourself." Mary looked inside her purse but didn't see her phone. "I left it in the car."

But she didn't need the phone to recall the message. Snippets of Joe's words still rang in her ear.

Mary. It's me. Pick up. Please. You there? Oh, Christ. It's my damn fault. It never made sense coming all the way out here. Listen to me. Every-thing's copacetic, baby. You hear me? If you get this, call Sid. Tell him I didn't get it. Tell him it's key that he keeps trying. He's one of the good guys. He needs to know. I love you, Mary. I love you and the girls more than anything. Tell the girls. Tell them . . . ah hell—

The message ended abruptly and without a goodbye.

"Mary?" Don Bennett stood closer, his gentle voice unable to tem-per his demanding glare.

"He said that it didn't make sense coming out there, that he didn't get it, and that he loved me and the girls."

"Get what?"

"He didn't say."

"That's it? You said he knew something was wrong."

Everything's copacetic, baby.

Copacetic. It was their secret word for when everything was going wrong, when things were not what they were supposed to be, when everything was, as Joe liked to say, FUBAR. Fucked up beyond all recognition.

Mary laughed, a bubble of joy punching through her sorrow as she remembered when he'd first used the term. It was on their honey-moon, a three-day high-speed adventure in Jamaica. They'd arrived at their hotel only to discover that Joe's reservation had vanished, and so had his wallet, somewhere between the airport and the hotel. Mary had her debit card, but it was good for only $200. They'd ended up at a rundown B&B in Montego Bay, sharing a single bed and a bathroom without towels and dining on mangos and papayas from the roadside vendors, with a few Red Stripes thrown in to help them forget their hunger. Instead of sun there was rain. Halfway through their second day, the manager kicked them out for making too much noise . . . laughing, not the other kind. She had a picture permanently framed in her mind of Joe standing by the highway next to their pile of bags, thumb out, hitchhiking to the airport in a driving Caribbean down-pour. And his words accompanied by a big ol' shit-eating grin. "Every-thing's copacetic."

Mary's smile faded. There were other times he had used the expres-sion. Times when things hadn't been copacetic for either of them.

She came back to the present. There was no mistaking his meaning this time. Fear. Desperation. Anxiety.

"Do you know anyone named Sid?" she asked. "Or Sidney?"

"Did Joe mention that name?"

Mary didn't like the eagerness in Bennett's eyes. "I'm confused. It's something else. I'm sorry."

"You were saying," prodded Bennett. "He knew he was in trouble. How'd he know?"

Mary decided that she'd said enough. "I could just tell," she fibbed. "He sounded scared. That's all."

"He didn't say anything specific?"

"No," said Mary. "You can listen for yourself later."

"If it's not too much of a problem, I'd like to listen now." Bennett shifted his eyes over her shoulder. "Well, maybe after. The doc's here."

Mary turned to see a tall man wearing surgical greens approaching from the hall. There was a splash of blood on his lower leg.

"Mrs. Grant?"

"Yes."

The doctor looked at Bennett for a second too long, then returned his attention to Mary. "I'm Dr. Alexander. Come with me."

4

Mary followed Dr. Alexander down the hallway and into the elevator. She listened carefully as he spoke to her of Joe's injuries and the surgery and his chances for survival. She asked questions. She was the calm, rational wife even as the horizons of her life shrank and her prospects grew bleak, for while she was listening, she was thinking of herself, her past, and how she'd prepared for this moment.

"Mountains don't get smaller for looking at them," the admiral had said.

Shying away was not an option. But Mary had never shied away from a challenge in her life, or from anything else, for that matter. Her mother liked to brag that Mary lived "with her elbows out."

Her youth was a record of plucky survival or divine miracles. She fell off her first pony at age seven. The pony's hoof caught her in the head, slicing her forehead from port to starboard and leaving her unconscious for God knows how long. When she stumbled into the kitchen, her mother screamed so loudly that the neighbors called 911, certain that someone was being raped, robbed, or tortured with a sharp instrument.

In the hospital afterward, the admiral pinned one of his Purple Hearts on her hospital gown and admitted he'd never seen so much blood in his life, and that included his time running PT boats up the Mekong Delta in Vietnam.

Mary's next brush with mortality came at twelve. While sailing the family Razor on Chesapeake Bay, she misjudged a change in the wind and was knocked clean off the boat by a wild boom. It was December. The ocean was 42° and the current was running strong. By the time she hauled herself back into the boat and returned to the dock, her body temperature had plummeted to 94° and she was shaking like . . . well, like she was shaking right now. A bout of double pneumonia followed, accompanied by a 106° fever. At some point a priest was brought to her, though Mary had no recollection of any of it. She only remembered the Bible she found at her bedside when she woke up, the ribbon placed at the Twenty-third Psalm.

Later there was a bike accident, a broken leg playing soccer, and concussions playing lacrosse. Mary never considered any of them a big deal. The gash on her forehead was a scratch. The two weeks spent in the hospital, a cold. The priest who came to administer last rites, parental hysteria. She lumped them all together as proof of her invincibility. She'd suffered so much and overcome so many obstacles that she could no longer summon up any situation that might frighten her.

Queen Mary the Lionheart.

All that changed with Grace. The past two years had used up all that confidence and then some. There were only so many nights a mother could spend by a bedside, only so many prayers she could utter. Sooner or later even the most stalwart faltered.

And now Joe.

This was one challenge too many. One mountain she was not equipped to climb.

She was not ready to be a widow. Not now. Not with Grace and her illness and Jessie and her attitude, not with so much of life still in front of her requiring her efforts, so many days to be gotten through.

Stand fast, girl. One hand for the boat and an eye on the horizon.

The elevator reached the fifth floor. The door opened, but Mary didn't move. She remained where she was, her father's baritone loud in her ears.

Order refused, Admiral.

Mary was no longer invincible.

Queen Mary the Lionheart was ready to give up her throne.

She saw Joe through the window—the sole patient in the ICU, eyes closed, respirator protruding from his mouth, more tubes than she could count running in and out of his body. An army of machines monitored his vital signs. There was a heart monitor. An automatic sphygmomometer to measure blood pressure. An electroencephalograph for brain function. And many more, all of which Mary knew by name.

"Do I need a gown or mask?" she asked, eyes never leaving her husband's inert form.

"That won't be necessary," said Dr. Alexander.

Mary stepped inside the room and approached the bed. "Joe," she said softly, as if there were others there she might disturb. "It's me. I came as soon as I heard. You doing okay?"

Dr. Alexander had been forthright in his explanation of Joe's injury and his prognosis for recovery. He'd been shot in the chest by a high-caliber weapon. The bullet missed his heart by an eighth of an inch, nicked an artery, then struck the spinal cord before exiting his back. Paralysis below the neck was a foregone conclusion. The bigger issue was loss of brain function because of oxygen deprivation from the prolonged cardiac arrest.

"The paramedics estimate that your husband's heart had stopped for thirteen minutes when they found him. It's a miracle he's alive at all."

To every profession a code, thought Mary. The FBI had its own vocabulary. Debriefings went sideways. Snitches were CIs. And families didn't have a "need to know." Doctors were no better. They spoke of prolonged cardiac arrest and cerebral oxygen deficiency and significant tissue damage. Mary spoke their language, too. She knew the doctor meant that Joe was brain-dead, unable to breathe on his own, and that he had a hole in his back the size of a softball.

What were you doing in Dripping Springs? she inquired silently as she ran a hand through his hair. *Why did you call me instead of Don Bennett? Who's Sid?*

A married couple has its code, too. *Everything's copacetic, baby.* Meaning "I'm in deep shit and need your help."

Mary pulled a chair close to the bed and sat. "I'm here, baby," she whispered in Joe's ear. "Me and the girls, we know you love us. Take your time. Rest and get better."

In the elevator she'd asked Dr. Alexander a question: "How many patients have ever come back after being dead for thirteen minutes?"

"None that I'm aware of."

Mary didn't like the answer, but at least there was no BS.

She threaded her arm through the protective railings and took her husband's hand. She looked at the EEG. The gray line ran flat. Pulse: 64. Blood pressure: 90/60. She listened to the wheezing of the respirator.

"But if you need to go, I understand," she went on. "I'll make sure Jessie gets to MIT or Caltech or wherever geniuses like her learn all that stuff. You know, she unlocked my phone on the way back from the hospital today. Where does she learn that? And I'll take care of Gracie. The doc said the spike in white blood cells was just temporary. The blasts haven't come back. He's not sure why, but he said we shouldn't worry. She threw up on the way home. It might have been carsickness. Jessie wouldn't help clean up. She said she didn't do floors or windows. That girl knows how to push all my buttons. You two couldn't be any more alike. Anyway, three more years and Grace is over the hump. Maybe you can give me a hand and watch over her."

Joe's hand squeezed hers.

Mary jumped in her chair. "Joe!"

Her eyes locked on the EEG monitor. She willed the gray line to move, to assume its jackhammer pattern, but it remained flat. There was no spark of electrical activity in Joe's brain. His heart rate didn't budge, nor did any of the other vital signs register so much as a blip. Mary squeezed his hand, but it was limp to the touch. It had been a spasm. Some last reflexive and wholly unconscious response.

She gazed through the window into the corridor. Dr. Alexander and Don Bennett were deep in conversation. The resigned expressions on both their faces spoke volumes.

For another hour Mary held her husband's hand. She told him about the first time she saw him walking across Healy Lawn at Georgetown. He'd just completed his second summer of Officer Candidates School at Quantico. His hair was high and tight and his muscles were practically bursting out of his sleeves. He was one good-looking slab of All-American meat. *I want me some of that,* she'd told herself.

That fall they had shared a theology class called "Jesus in the Twentieth Century." Lots of essays by Karl Rahner and Martin Buber. And she saw that Mr. Joseph Grant wasn't some dumb jarhead. He was smart, and funny, too. And like her, he believed in some higher power. Not believed. *He knew.* Rahner called it love. She was good with that.

She told Joe that marrying him was the happiest moment in her life, and she asked if he remembered holding Jessie an hour after she was born, all of her fitting neatly on his forearm. He'd called her Peanut, because that's what she had looked like all swaddled, her face so red and wrinkled. And she said that they'd have to put off their anniversary celebration until another time. She wanted to say "until you are better," but Mary was a no-bullshit girl and Joe liked getting the truth straight, no chaser. Honesty was their bond. They did not lie to one another.

"I looked pretty good in that LBD," she said. "Don't know what you're missing."

Joe's hand remained slack.

The EEG didn't budge.

His chest rose and fell with the respirator.

"Goodbye, hon," she said. "Whenever you're ready."

Joe's body jumped as if he'd been given a jolt of electricity. An alarm sounded. Code blue. Mary stood. Her eyes locked on the heart-rate monitor as the numbers dived and nurses rushed into the room.

"Don't do anything," she said. "Let him go."

"Excuse me, ma'am," said one. "You'll have to leave."

Dr. Alexander was there a moment later. Mary looked at him, pleading, and he nodded.

Outside the ICU, she placed her palm against the glass and searched out her husband's face. A nurse wheeled the defib cart to the bed and took hold of the paddles, raising them above Joe's chest. Dr. Alexander stopped her, giving a firm shake of the head.

For a moment Mary caught a glimpse of her husband, the proud profile, the raised chin. She closed her eyes, wanting to see him as he was, as she remembered him when he was away.

It was in Samui. Joe walked ahead of her on the beach, Jessie and Grace to either side. He kicked water at them and they kicked it right back. She heard him call their names and laugh. A happy man.

Mary opened her eyes to say goodbye.

"Safe journey."

5

It was the third lap and Ian Prince was falling behind.

He curled the fingers of his left hand around the throttle of the P-51D Mustang and eased it forward, keeping one eye on the rpm's, the other on the panorama of earth and sky that wrapped itself around the Perspex canopy and the planes flying above and below him. His right hand gripped the stick lightly as he approached the third pylon, a red-striped oil can set atop a fifty-foot telephone pole. The plane whipped past the pylon, Ian pushed the stick over, and the plane banked sharply, wings tilting to ninety degrees, the Nevada desert an adobe blur. He clamped his mouth shut, holding his breath and tightening the muscles of his core. He was pulling five g's through the turn, shoulders digging into the seat, jaw burrowing into his neck. The engine whined magnificently, a buzz saw cutting hard lumber. He completed the turn and leveled the wings, the g's easing, shoulders freed from gravity's grip.

Ian focused on the tail of the bird in front of him. It was Gordon May's bird, the *Battleax*, a P-51D like his. Stalwart of the Second World War. Packard piston engine. Four-bladed propeller. May had painted the plane fire-engine red, his company's logo covering every inch of the fuselage: MAY MICROCHIPS.

By contrast, Ian's plane looked factory-new, silver steel skin without a blemish, the Stars and Stripes of the United States Army Air Corps decorating the wings. It had looked no different in May 1945, when George Westerman, a pilot with the 477th Fighter Group, had flown it above the fields of Bavaria and shot down fourteen German aircraft.

Ian had rescued the machine from a scrap-metal yard and, after extensive reconstruction, renamed it *Lara*, after his mother, which was a nicer name than she deserved. Like his mother, *Lara* the plane was a mean, hot-tempered bitch who'd kill you as soon as look at you.

Ian feathered the throttle and scanned the instrument panel. The temperature gauge was running high. He looked at the white needle tickling the red. To hell with the heat. He couldn't wait any longer or May's lead would be insurmountable.

Ian didn't like Gordon May.

He disliked losing more.

He pushed the speed back up to 400 knots. The plane shook, reverberations rattling his spine. He held the stick steady. He had thick wrists and large, strong hands. His grip surprised people. Executives in the information technology industry were not renowned for being fit. Somehow it had been ingrained in the public that there was an inverse relationship between IQ and strength. Ian confounded the perception. He was nothing like what people thought he should be.

A fat, slow Grumman Bearcat slipped below him to his left. A relic. A Commodore to his Cray. The comparison pleased him. A smile formed beneath Ian's goggles and helmet. The smile hardened when he saw May's tail flash in the sun, only a second or two ahead.

Ian was gaining.

Approaching the last pylon, he brought the plane down to fifty feet, low enough to see the faces of the crowd below. Twenty thousand people had gathered in the high desert north of Reno for the race. The course measured eight miles, an extended oval around ten pylons. Eight times around determined the winner. Pedal to the metal all the way. A sky full of screaming eagles.

Ian had won two and lost two, both losses to Gordon May.

"Not this time," he said aloud.

He executed a hairpin turn around the outermost pylon, the colorful oil drum threatening to tear off the canopy. Nearer he drew to May, and nearer still. If he could just reach out . . .

He zipped past the control tower.

Lap four was complete.

Ian held his position through the next two laps, content to hang on May's tail. The temperature needle had moved firmly into the red. There was nothing to be done. The engine would make it or it wouldn't. He would win or he wouldn't. It was a binary universe.

Yet even as he raced and part of his mind swore victory, another part was focused on business. Today was momentous for a number of reasons, of which the air race was the least important. On this day twenty years ago he'd sold his first venture, ONEscape, for $200 million to U.S. Online. And it was exactly a year ago that he'd begun his quest to acquire Merriweather Systems. The deal hadn't been without a hiccup, but he'd taken the necessary measures to emerge victorious. The acquisition had brought the value of ONE Technologies to a wafer over $200 billion.

Ian completed lap six. *Battleax*'s flaming red tail remained a plane's length out of reach, but May was played out. If he had any juice left, he'd have used it by now.

Ian pushed the throttle forward, *Lara*'s nose nipping at *Battleaxe*'s tail, twenty feet separating them. He eased himself closer, and closer still, his plane bucking in the slipstream.

Faster, he dared May, the taste of victory on his tongue, filling his mouth.

Ian pulled the stick right, going for the pass. May took his plane outside in an effort to block. Ian feinted right as if trying to go abreast; May kicked out again. It was a reckless move, inviting disaster. Ian saw it coming and ducked to the inside, pushing the engine as hard as it could go. His airspeed jumped to 450 knots. He cruised past May, buzzing his aircraft, essentially leapfrogging him. May's plane juked in the wake. To save himself, he pulled out of the loop and flew high and clear.

May was done.

Ian never looked back.

He won the race by ten seconds.

Ian Prince walked across the tarmac, helmet in hand. He was nearly six feet tall, forty years of age, narrow-beamed but sturdy, with Ray-Bans hiding his eyes, at ease in his flight suit.

"Hey there," shouted Gordon May, running to catch up. "Prince, you bastard. Hold up. You almost killed me." He was fifty, a fiery bantamweight with red hair and a complexion like mottled leather.

Ian didn't break stride. "I could say the same."

May laid a hand on Ian's shoulder. "You passed on the inside. That's against the rules. I'm going to file a complaint with the stewards."

Ian stopped. "I had no choice," he said calmly. "You kicked out twice. It was pass inside or collide. I think the stewards will see things my way."

"Is that right?" said May. "Or else what? Not all your rivals crash and burn."

"Excuse me?" Ian said.

"I'm talking about Titan. John Merriweather wouldn't sell you his company if it was the last thing he did. Those machines were like his children. Merriweather was a genius. Not some one-hit wonder who cashes in, then spends the rest of his life on a shopping spree, taking credit for everyone else's achievements. He was a visionary."

"Yes," said Ian. "He was. We'll honor his legacy."

"Now that you forced his heirs to sell."

"I made them an offer. They accepted. I completed the deal out of respect for John. The company isn't the same without him."

"Maybe they were afraid their plane might go down, too."

A crowd had gathered. Ian was careful with his words. "Be quiet, Gordon."

"Crash and burn," said May accusingly, enjoying his audience, the chance to make Ian squirm. "Without John there was no one left to oppose you."

Ian grabbed a fistful of the pilot's flight suit. He felt the rapt eyes on him, sensed their violent ardor. He could not walk away. Not after what May had said. "You're out of line."

"Is that what you said to John Merriweather when he refused to sell?"

A fit, ruddy-faced man wearing a tan suit broke through the bystanders and took hold of May's shoulder. "That's enough," said Peter Briggs, Ian's chief of security. "You have a problem, take it up with the stewards. Mr. Prince is otherwise occupied."

Still May held his ground. "The race is on tape," he said, jabbing a finger at Ian. "You can't buy your way out of this one. No one cares about your money here. No senators, no congressmen to smooth your way."

"Goodbye, Gordon."

"Last race is next week. I'll see you there. Crash and burn, buddy. Just you try something."

Ian didn't respond as May stalked off toward the control tower.

"Miserable prick," said Peter Briggs.

"I need to get cleaned up."

6

Mary Grant sat in her car, bathed in the gloom of the parking lot. She had signed all the paperwork and collected Joe's belongings: his wallet, watch, belt, and tie clip. His suit had been cut off him by the paramedics, and it was hinted that she might not wish to see the ruined garments. The phone was government property. She had thanked Don Bennett and all the other agents from the Austin residency who'd come to the hospital. She had looked for a Sid, but none of the agents present had that name. She had cried and was done crying. And when Bennett asked if she'd like an escort home, or to have someone stay with her, she had declined his offer, politely but firmly.

Everything was copacetic.

The married couple's code.

Mary took her phone from the dash tray and accessed her voice messages. She needed to hear Joe speak to her one last time. She needed to believe for one more minute that he was still alive. She recalled her daydreaming in the car earlier that afternoon. Dinner at Sullivan's. A night on the town to celebrate their seventeenth anniversary.

Stop, she ordered herself. It was too easy to fall into the abyss.

She glanced at the screen. The first voice message listed belonged to Jessie and came from that afternoon at 1:55.

"Mom, I'm waiting by the fountain. You're late. Where are you?"

Actually, she'd been on time. Jessie's summer school class in computer programming at UT ended at two. The second message was from Carrie Kramer, her next-door neighbor, confirming that she'd be over at 6:30 to babysit. Several more followed. From friends, from the new school, from the doctor's office.

But nothing from Joe.

Mary sat up straighter. Joe's had been the last message she had received. It should stand at the top of the list. She felt a pang of anger as she accessed the deleted voice messages. How could she have been so careless?

Again there was no record of Joe's message.

She popped back to the home screen and checked all recent calls. Joe's number popped up at the top of the list. Call received at 4:03. Duration: 27 seconds. There it was.

Back to voicemail.

Nothing.

The message was gone.

Mary shifted in her seat, assiduously reviewing her actions. She'd left the phone in the car the entire time she was in the hospital. She'd listened to the message twice before that: once as she'd left home and a second time prior to running into the hospital.

Again she checked the call log. Again she confirmed that Joe had called, before she jumped back to the screens showing current voicemails and deleted voicemails, then back to the home screen.

No message.

Mary lowered her head, fighting a raw, physical urge to scream. It was impossible. The message couldn't be gone. For it to be truly erased from her phone, she would have had to first delete it from the current messages, then delete all the previously deleted messages. She had done neither. So where was the message?

Dread took hold of her. Joe was gone. Forever. She'd never hear the last words he spoke to her again. Loss pooled inside her. Her breathing grew labored. The abyss beckoned. She dropped the phone onto the seat next to her and caught a glimpse of herself in the mirror. Red-eyed. Frantic. Losing control. Queen Mary the Lionheart was nowhere in sight.

Someone rapped on the window, and Mary jumped in her seat.

"I'm sorry," said Don Bennett, kneeling beside the car. "You okay?"

Mary wiped at her eyes before rolling down the window. "You surprised me."

"I know it's a tough time and I hate bothering you, but I was wondering if I might hear that message."

"I don't have it anymore," said Mary. "It was here—I mean, it was on my phone. I listened to it twice earlier and now it's gone."

"Did you delete it?"

"No."

"It might be in the deleted messages file. I do that all the time."

Liar, thought Mary. "I checked," she said. "It's not there."

Bennett pursed his lips, the handyman who just might have the right fix. "Do you think I could take a look at your phone? Maybe you missed it."

"No," said Mary. "I looked everywhere. It's not there anymore. It's not anywhere."

Bennett thrust his hand through the open window. "Please."

"No!" Mary recoiled and turned her body away from Bennett, clutching the phone against her body.

Bennett withdrew his hand. He remained on his haunches, face-to-face with her. "Mary, this is a serious matter. There're going to be a lot of questions about what happened to Joe out there. I'd be grateful for anything that might shed light on it."

"I'm not an idiot. I know how to use my phone. If I can't find it, you can't."

Bennett nodded, then smiled easily. It was his patronizing, "I'm in the FBI and know better than you" smile. Joe had one, too, and it drove her crazy when he flashed it. "Maybe if you let us take the phone to our lab," he said, "we can get a closer look. Often something you think is deleted isn't actually permanently erased."

"I already told you what Joe said. It was more a feeling than anything else."

"He didn't say anything specific about what was wrong?"

"He just said he didn't like being out there, he thought it was a bad idea, and that he loved us."

"He didn't tell you anything more—maybe something about who he was with or what exactly was troubling him?"

"Don't you know who he was with?"

"I'm just wondering if he might have given you any details."

"No."

"Even so, I'd like to take a look. There might be something you missed."

"I said no."

"I could subpoena that fuckin' thing," said Bennett, eyes pulsing, his face flushed, seemingly a size larger.

"What did you say?"

Bennett eased back from the car. "I didn't mean that. I'm upset about Joe's death, too. I just want to do everything I can to find out what really happened."

Mary jumped on the words. "Don't you know what really happened? You said the informant shot him. Who was Joe meeting?"

"I can't go into that. I'm sorry . . ." Bennett stood, shoulders slumped, hands upturned. "Sorry to trouble you. If there's anything we can do—me, the office—anything . . . let us know."

Mary watched Bennett walk away. He might have asked to see the phone tomorrow, or even in a few days. What kind of a man threatens a grieving woman with a subpoena?

It came to her that Bennett didn't know what had happened to Joe. Or for that matter who Joe had been meeting. For some reason Don Bennett was frightened.

As Mary started the car and eased it out of the garage, she could think of no other reason that he wanted the message so badly.

Joe, she asked silently, whose business were you looking into?

7

Ian Prince stepped inside his race headquarters, a sixty-foot RV out-fitted to his needs. Peter Briggs followed him inside, closing the door behind them.

"That Mick has it in for you." Briggs was a blunt-faced South African with heavy pouches beneath his eyes and blond hair shaved to a stubble. "Think he'll make trouble?"

"Gordon May is upset because his is the only company in Silicon Valley I never tried to buy." Ian unzipped his flight suit, opened the fridge, and grabbed a plastic bottle filled with amber liquid. His recovery drink: water, glucose, guarana, and ginseng. "You see my pass?" he said after guzzling half the bottle. "Only thing I could do."

"You were in the right, boss," said Briggs. "The stewards will see things your way. May's just a bad loser."

"Maybe." Ian never forgot a slight, and May's words had come perilously close to slander.

He finished the bottle and chucked it in the trash. An office occupied a compartment behind the driver's bay. Personal quarters were to the rear and included a bedroom, bathroom, and rejuvenation center. He hit a switch on the wall, activating the anti-eavesdropping measures. The RV was now a SCIF, a "sensitive compartmented information facility." Whatever he said in Reno stayed in Reno. "Any news?"

"Problem resolved."

"Too bad it had to end that way."

"It had to end. Period." Briggs had grown up deep in the veldt, and his English carried a thick Afrikaans accent.

"Agreed," said Ian. "So it's all tied off?"

"To the very top. Bank it."

"Banked," said Ian.

After his shower, Ian Prince sat naked in the salon chair as a tall, muscular woman clad in tight black pants and a T went about her business.

Her name was Dr. Katarina Fischer, and she was his private longevity consultant.

"Can't you hurry things, Kat?" Ian asked the Berlin-born physician. "Copter's coming in an hour. Back to home base. The big test's tomorrow. Titan. It's what's made me such a grump these last months."

"You are like an impatient little boy. First your vitamins." Katarina handed him a tray filled with thirty vitamins and other supplements. There were the usual: B12, D, E, Omega-3s, antioxidants. And there were more exotic ones: alpha-lipoic acid, chromium, selenium, CoQ10. Ian swallowed them five at a time.

"Now you will live forever," said Katarina. She was more handsome than beautiful, her thick white-blond hair cut above the ears, blue eyes couched behind rimless glasses, a broad jaw and broader shoulders.

Ian extended his arm. "Do your worst."

Katarina drew a vial of blood for analysis. He knew his good cholesterol and his bad, his lipids and his liver function. Recently he'd had his exome sequenced, the portion of his DNA that contained his protein coding. It showed markers for Parkinson's disease and diabetes, meaning that he was at greater risk than others of contracting them. He had a lesser chance of cancer. And still less of heart disease. The results of today's blood work would be uploaded to his mailbox in an hour.

"And now your magic potion," she said, capping the vial.

"Not magic," said Ian. "Science. Keeps the cells new. Key to aging is the telomere. My 'magic potion' stops the ends from chipping off. Like shoelaces. Keep the tips intact and you can live forever."

"*Quatsch*," said Katarina, who knew about these things. Nonsense.

Ian laughed. When Katarina was an eighty-year-old Hanseatic hag with boobs drooping to her buckled knees, he would be climbing mountains, flying his P-51D, and preparing for his next eighty years.

Katarina wheeled the IV stand closer. She swabbed rubbing alcohol on his arm, then slipped the needle into his forearm and slapped on surgical tape to keep it in place. "No moving," she said. "I'll be back in thirty minutes."

"*Zum Befehl.*"

Ian looked at the clear solution seeping into his system. His "magic potion" was a substance called phosphatidylcholine and it was a primary ingredient found in human cells, more specifically cell walls. It took the human body one year to regenerate all its cells. Ian wanted each and every one as healthy and robust as an adolescent male's. One liter of phosphatidylcholine twice a week did the trick. To that he added his daily regime of ninety supplements, four liters of alkaline water, and a Mediterranean diet high in fish oils, nuts, and fruit.

His thoughts turned to Gordon May and his public accusations of Ian's having a hand in John Merriweather's death. By all accounts Merriweather's plane had gone down in bad weather over the Owens Valley near Lone Pine, California, an area notorious for wind shear and turbulence. No evidence of foul play or tampering was ever uncovered. Ian reviewed his actions in the affair from inception to closure. He had nothing to worry about. Everything was tied off. "Banked," in Briggs's word.

Ian combated his anxiety by turning his attention to business. Work: the universal healer.

"Pending," he said, and a list of topics appeared in outline form superimposed on his vision: *1. Titan 2. Bluffdale 3. Clarus.*

In his right eye he wore a prototype of an augmented-reality contact lens integrated with newly invented optoelectronic components, including LEDs, microlasers, and the smallest antenna ever created.

He focused on *Titan*. The font darkened and grew larger. He blinked. The file opened. There, hovering in the middle distance in crisp three-dimensional form, stood the design of John Merriweather's creation: the Titan supercomputer.

Ian and his team had shrunk the machine as much as possible, yet it was still the size of a refrigerator. Size, however, wasn't the problem. Heat was. After an hour of operation, temperatures inside the machine surpassed 200° Fahrenheit, wreaking havoc on the circuitry. To solve the problem, Ian had written a software patch to reprogram the cooling system. The first test of the Titan supercomputer under maximum operating conditions was set for the next morning at ten o'clock. By this time tomorrow he would know if the cooling system worked.

Ian noticed that he was picking at his fingernails. He stopped immediately. Thirteen all over again. Well, not quite. The fat was gone, as were the overbite and the Coke-bottle eyeglasses. He had a bit more money in his wallet, too.

He blinked twice, closing the file.

The bag of his magic solution was only half depleted. Ian visualized the substance cleansing his cells, buffing his telomeres to a spit shine. He imagined himself in fifty years and he looked more or less the same as today, save a gray hair here and there. He didn't want to be a freak, after all.

He opened his eyes and stared at his figure in the mirror. Here is what he saw:

Hair: black, thick, combed back from his forehead. Eyes: one brown, one hazel. Ethnicity: Cosmopolitan. His father was British, an Oxonian by way of Newcastle, tall, square-jawed, blue-eyed, hair black as a raven, skin pale as a day-old corpse. His mother was a platinum-haired beauty from Kiev, her Mongol blood evident in her sloe eyes and razor-sharp cheekbones. Ian wasn't sure what that made him. His skin was the color of honey, his nose as aquiline as a Roman emperor's. Other parts had long since been replaced or improved, and as such were no help either.

Ian had given up a flag to claim as his own long ago. Born in London, he'd spent his childhood skipping across Europe as his father advanced rung by rung up the endless hierarchy that was the British Foreign Office. It was a tour of second-rate diplomatic backwaters, with Sofia, Tallinn, and Leipzig the shining lights among them. Still, until he was fifteen, he had considered himself the Queen's proudest subject, as loyal as John Bull himself.

And then, in an instant, everything changed.

It was a rain-soaked Monday morning in Bruges, no different from any of the dismal January days preceding it. A family breakfast of eggs, beans, and sausage, or as close to a "fry-up" as his Russian mother could manage. Looking back thirty-odd years later, Ian saw the scene as if he were living it. There was the usual banter about football matches the day before. And then it was time for goodbyes. Peter Prince left first, as work demanded. Father and son rose from the table. It was their daily ritual. A handshake and a kiss on the cheek. His father was dressed no differently than on any other day. Navy pinstripe suit. Maroon silk tie. Hair parted with a razor-straight slash. Satchel in his left hand.

"'Bye, son."

A last look over his shoulder. A door closed. And he was gone.

Never to be seen or heard from by any living being again.

Not dead. Not imprisoned. Not kidnapped. Not any one of a thousand explainable disappearances.

Peter St. John Prince simply vanished into thin air.

And so began the second half of Ian's life.

The unknowing.

All this Ian saw when he looked into his own eyes.

He'd never stopped searching for his father. And now—if the cooling system worked—he had the tool to help find him. *Titan.*

Ian snapped back to the present. He focused on the second topic. *Bluffdale.* He blinked and the file opened. He drew up the latest photographs of the massive facility. It was alternately called the Utah Data Center, and it belonged to the National Security Agency, the United States' most secretive intelligence organization.

Sitting on 240 acres of land above the Jordan River in the northernmost part of the state, the Utah Data Center had one goal and one goal only: to collect the combined traffic of everything that passed through the Internet: e-mails, cell-phone calls, web searches. Everything.

The NSA had chosen the world's most powerful supercomputer for the task.

In two days Ian was set to fly to the East Coast for a meeting with Titan's most important client. The meeting was at Fort Meade, Maryland. The client was the National Security Agency. The United States government would not be pleased to learn that it had purchased a supercomputer that had a tendency to melt when operating at full capacity.

Ian closed the file.

The bag of his magic potion was empty.

He pulled the needle from his arm and stood, making sure to place a wad of gauze over the puncture.

He looked at himself in the mirror.

So who was he, then?

In the end, Ian preferred to think of himself in terms of numbers. Height: Five feet ten inches. Weight: 175 pounds. Body fat: 16%. IQ: 156.

There was a last number he liked best: 58.

As of this unpleasantly hot day in July, Ian Prince was worth $58 billion.

8

It was a quiet night in Pedro's Especiale Bar and Grill in Austin, Texas.

Tank Potter sat atop his favorite stool, elbows on the bar, eyes glued to the envelope placed in front of him. Pedro kept the joint as dark as a Brownsville cathouse, and Tank had to squint to read the words typed across its face: *Henry Thaddeus Potter. Personal and Confidential.*

Only a few of the regulars were in. Dotty and Sam, the swinging septuagenarians, were swilling margaritas at one end. French and Bobby had taken claim of the TV and were cursing at ESPN at the other. Tank's stool was in the middle. He called it his "umpire's post," because from it he was able to adjudicate any disagreements that might break out. He was hard to miss no matter where he sat. At forty-two years of age, he went six-four, two-fifty, with forty-six-inch shoulders. There was also the matter of his hair, which was thick, brown, and unruly and defied the best efforts of his brush. To combat any impression of carelessness, he made a point to dress neatly. This evening his khakis were pressed, his Oxford button-down starched so that it could stand on its own. As always, he wore Nocona ropers to remind him that he was a Texas boy, born and bred.

"Pedrito," he called, raising a hand to give the place a little excitement. "*Uno más, por favor.*"

A chubby middle-aged man with slicked-back hair and a Pancho Villa mustache poured him a shot of Hornitos in a clean glass. "Good news or bad?"

"What do you mean?"

"You been staring at that envelope for the last hour. You going to open it or what?"

"Already did." Tank tapped the envelope on the bar, feeling the single sheet of paper slide from side to side. He was a journalist by profession, and he was hard put to come up with ninety-six words that more concisely conveyed the message on that page.

"And?"

"Buggy whip," said Tank.

Pedro opened a Tecate and placed the bottle next to the tequila. "What is a leather crop used to hit a horse to make it pull a carriage or one of them hansom cabs in Central Park? Buggy whip."

"Wrong," said Tank, with a polite tilt of the bottle before he took a swig. "And you don't have to repeat the word at the end. This isn't a spelling bee."

"What do you mean, wrong? What do you think a buggy whip is?"

"Technically, you're correct," Tank conceded. "But it wasn't a question."

"You trying to make some kind of point?"

"You asked about the envelope."

Pedro leaned against the bar. "Okay, then. Shoot."

And so Tank told Pedro the story.

At the turn of the twentieth century, everyone rode horses to get around. Wagons and carriages were the most popular means of transport for groups of people traveling any kind of distance. You couldn't have a carriage without a buggy whip. Buggy whips were everywhere, and so were the companies that made them.

Then one day automobiles appeared. They were regarded as marvels and quickly became objects of envy. But for many years they were too expensive for regular folk. Still, little by little the price of this newfangled invention fell. Each year more people bought automobiles and fewer people rode in horse-drawn carriages.

"What do you think happened to buggy whips?" asked Tank in conclusion.

Pedro drew a finger across his throat.

"Exactly. The second cars got cheap, demand for the buggy whip collapsed. The buggy-whip manufacturers tried everything to improve their products and make them less expensive, but it didn't matter. People couldn't care less whether a buggy whip looked sharper or lasted longer. They were driving Model T's, Chryslers, and Chevrolets. No one needed a buggy whip, no matter how nifty it was. Until finally one day no one was riding in a carriage at all." Tank downed his shot and banged the glass on the bar as a fitting endnote. "Goodbye, buggy whip."

"Why are you telling me this?" asked Pedro.

"Because you're looking at one," said Tank.

"A buggy whip? I thought you were a reporter."

"Same thing. You're looking at a living, breathing example of technical obsolescence. A walking anachronism. Like the abacus or the typewriter or the fax . . . and now the newspaper."

"How's a buggy whip like a newspaper?"

"It's like this: a reporter is to a newspaper as a buggy whip is to a horse-drawn carriage. Follow?"

Pedro's face lit up. "Now I know what's in the envelope."

"Well, you don't have to look so stinkin' happy about it."

Pedro frowned and retreated to the end of the bar as Tank finished his beer. He put down the empty and swiveled on his stool, looking at the piñatas hanging from the ceiling and the velvet black-light paintings of Selena and Jennifer Lopez.

Tank's real name was Henry Thaddeus Potter. He'd started life as Henry, then Hank, then Hank the Tank, by virtue of his playing fullback on a state championship team at Westlake High. After four years as a Texas Longhorn, he was just Tank. It made for good copy. He was stuck with it.

His phone rang and he checked the caller. "Yeah, Al."

"You at Pedro's?" demanded Al Soletano, managing editor of the *Austin American-Statesman*, Tank's employer for the past sixteen years. "Betty said she saw your car there. I need you to come in."

"I already got my envelope."

"You read it all the way through? The new management is itching for an excuse to fire you for cause. It would save them a lot of dough. You have thirty days until the deal clears. Keep your nose clean until then. In the meantime, we got a breaking story. An FBI agent got himself killed in Dripping Springs. Thought you might want to handle it. You know—a last hurrah."

"My beat is state politics."

"This one's in our backyard. I'm not giving it to a wire service. I've still got my pride."

"You mean you're short a crime reporter."

"Press conference is at nine at the Federal Building."

"In the morning?"

"Tonight. Don't be late. And Tank—no more cocktails."

Tank hung up and asked for his tab. Pedro put the bill on the counter, concerned. "Leaving already? The señoritas aren't here yet."

"Duty calls."

The bartender flashed his most optimistic smile. "So you're not fired?"

Tank slapped the envelope on the bar. "Buggy whip, Pedro. It's only a matter of time."

9

Tank crossed the street and climbed into his '98 Jeep Cherokee. The engine turned over after a few tries, no buggy whip needed. His first task was to roll down the windows. The air conditioning was DOA and the fan had as much power as a fruit fly's wings. This accomplished, he reached under his seat for a backstop and took a two-second swizzle of Cuervo. Soletano had said no more cocktails. He hadn't mentioned pick-me-ups.

The FBI residency was off Ben White in South Austin, no more than a fifteen-minute drive. Tank made a U-turn against traffic and headed north. To the west the sky was flaming red. A wavy black line rose from the river and climbed east into the purple dusk. A gust of warm, fetid air washed through the car and he grimaced.

The bats.

Each spring a million bats migrated north from Mexico to Austin to nest beneath the Congress Avenue Bridge. Every evening they left the damp, cool recesses of the bridge and flew east to scour the countryside for insects. The air was thick with their musty, throat-clawing odor.

Tank continued on Lamar, skirting the south shore of the Colorado River, the skyscrapers of downtown Austin to his left. He spotted Potter Tower, built by his grandfather in the late 1980s. To answer Pedro's question, yes, there was money in the envelope. Or at least the promise of money. More money than Tank was likely to see again in one lump sum.

The Potter family money was a thing of the past. Oil dried up. Real estate crashed. Besides, his mother wasn't the first Mrs. Potter and he wasn't the first male heir to carry on the family name.

Tank arrived at the FBI's office ten minutes later. The lot was half full and he parked in a far corner. He scoped out the place and took a quick snort from his backstop. It was just 8:30, and he chided himself for leaving Pedro's so quickly. A car pulled into the lot and he spotted a slim, eager-looking man in short sleeves and a black tie hustling inside.

It was the AP stringer out of Dallas. The enemy. No small-market paper could afford a full complement of reporters these days, not with circulation down 50 percent in the past ten years.

A minute later two dark sedans pulled into the lot, braked dramatically by the double glass doors, and disgorged several men in business suits. He recognized Don Bennett, the agent who headed up the Austin residency. Another ten minutes remained before the press conference was scheduled to begin. God knew they never started on time.

Hurry up and wait. It was a reporter's life.

Tank sipped from the Cuervo and turned up the music. Bob Wills and His Texas Playboys sang about lost loves and ruined lives. The night had cooled, and Tank leaned his head back and gazed out the window at the darkening sky. He remembered his own cheatin' wife, gone these past five years. There hadn't been anyone serious since, just the floozies from Pedro's . . . though he did enjoy their company. He thought he saw a shooting star. He relaxed a notch.

Damn if it wasn't a beautiful night.

Tank woke with a start.

He grabbed the steering wheel and pulled himself upright, then wiped away a lick of drool that had dried on his cheek. It was 10:45. He'd passed out for almost two hours. He looked around, still getting his bearings. The lot was empty. The press conference was over.

He bolted from the car, ran to the front doors, and banged furiously. A young hotshot came down the hall and opened the door a crack. "Yeah?"

"I need a summary from the press conference."

"And you are?"

"Tank Potter. *Statesman*."

"Press conference ended an hour ago." The hotshot was hardly old enough to have his first hangover, with a fresh high-and-tight and his sidearm high on the hip. A real greenhorn.

"Just give me your write-up, okay?" said Tank. "Don't be a dick about it."

The hotshot gave him a look, then smiled. "Sure. Wait here."

"Thanks, bro."

Tank retreated down the steps and lit a cigarette. He checked his phone and saw that Al Soletano had left ten messages. Tank swore under his breath. They couldn't dismiss him for missing a press conference.

The hotshot came outside and handed him the summary. "Headed out?"

"Yeah," said Tank. "Bedtime." In fact he was hoping to get back to the office, file his story, and make it to Pedro's by midnight.

"I'll walk you. That you in the corner?"

"The Jeep? That's it. Got two hundred thousand miles on the original engine. A real trooper. You with the Bureau?"

"APD. Detective Lance Burroughs. Liaison."

"Really? Detective? Didn't know they were promoting right out of college."

"I'm thirty-two."

Tank tried to read the release, but his eyes sucked and the light was too low anyway.

"Did I miss anything?"

"You'll find everything we have there. There'll be a follow-up conference sometime tomorrow."

"Sounds good." Tank reached his car and Burroughs opened the door for him. Tank looked at him for a second, then climbed in and closed the door. "Thanks again, detective. Appreciate it."

"Say, Tank, where do you live?"

"Tarrytown," he said as he started the engine. "Why do you ask?"

"You may not be making it home tonight."

"What do you mean? Car runs fine. Secret is to change the oil every two thousand miles."

The hotshot had stepped away from the car and stood with hands on his hips. "Sir, would you turn the car off?"

Tank dug his chin into his neck. "Why would I want to do that?"

"Just do as I say, sir. Turn off your engine and step out of the vehicle."

"But . . ." Tank looked down. It was then that he saw the fifth of Cuervo lying on the seat beside him.

"Now, Mr. Potter. You're under arrest for driving while intoxicated."

10

It was late when Mary returned home. She parked in the front drive and stayed behind the wheel after she cut the engine. Through the front window she could see the girls watching television. For the rest of their lives they would remember that they were watching *Survivor* when their mother came home and informed them of their father's death.

Mary got out of the car and managed a few steps toward the house before stopping. The front door was twenty feet and a mile away.

Mountains don't get smaller for looking at them.

Mary listened to the buzzing of the cicadas, the murmur of the television, the cycling of the air conditioning on and off. One more minute of innocence. One more minute of not knowing. One more minute of not feeling like she did.

Jessie spotted her car and jumped up from the couch. Grace rose, too. Both hurried to the front door, eager to learn why she was home so late. Their children's sense had warned them that something was wrong. They had no idea.

Jessie opened the door. "Mom, what were you doing just standing there?"

Mary started up the walk. "Coming, peanut."

Grace pushed her way in front of her older sister. "Where's Daddy?"

TUESDAY

11

The next morning Mary sat on the edge of her bed reading the newspaper. The headline read "FBI Agent Killed in Dripping Springs Shoot-Out."

"Veteran Special Agent Joseph T. Grant was killed yesterday in the line of duty. The shooting took place at approximately 3:15 p.m. outside of Dripping Springs on the grounds of the former Flying V Ranch. FBI spokesperson Donald G. Bennett stated that Grant was interviewing an informant deemed cooperative and unthreatening when the informant drew a weapon and shot Grant in the chest. The informant, whose name is being withheld due to the sensitive nature of the ongoing investigation, also died at the scene. Grant recently transferred to Austin from Sacramento, where he had been the assistant special agent in charge."

A color picture ran above the fold. It showed Joe's car with the windshield shattered, shot through. On the ground, visible between the milling law enforcement officers, lay a body draped by a sheet. The informant, identity unknown.

Mary stared at the photo, trying to imagine what had happened, how Joe had allowed an informant to get the drop on him. She looked closer. The informant lay several steps away from Joe's car. From the pool of blood on the ground near his head, it appeared that he had been shot there, not in the car. Questions formed in her mind. Discrepancies with Bennett's nervous and contradictory explanation.

She could hear Joe's voice, snippets of the message. "Everything's copacetic. Tell Sid. He's one of the good guys."

So there were *bad guys*?

The door to her bedroom opened. A curvy, attractive woman dressed in yoga tights and a lululemon jacket entered.

"All right," said Carrie Kramer. "That's enough of that. There's a bunch of gals downstairs who are waiting to give you a shoulder to cry on. They've brought enough carbs to fill two refrigerators. I hope you and the girls like chicken potpie and grits. That's what passes for comfort food around here."

Mary put down the paper. "I'll pass."

"How 'bout some coffee?"

"Maybe later."

Carrie sat down on the bed next to her. She was Mary's newest next-door neighbor and the best friend she'd made in God knew how long. Carrie was her age, a mother of two girls and wife to a husband who, like Joe, worked far too many hours. Mark Kramer taught electrical engineering at UT and had recently taken a consulting job at the new Apple campus. Joe had "the job." Carrie's husband, Mark, had "the lab." Like Mary, she was a de facto single mom.

Then there was the matter of their looks. Both were blondes a few pounds from being "athletic," with hair cut to their shoulders; they were more or less the same height, with blue eyes, ready smiles, and a little too much energy. They couldn't go out without someone asking if they were sisters. This led to spirited banter about who looked older. In fact Mary was older by a year, but in the name of détente and neighborhood peace, they decided to respond that they were the same. They called themselves the Texas Twins.

"You hanging in there?" asked Carrie.

"I can't stop from thinking," Mary began, "what might have happened if I'd just answered the phone."

"It wasn't your fault you missed Joe's call. These things happen."

"I wasn't there when he needed me. I knew it was a mistake to let Jessie play with my phone."

Carrie laid an arm around Mary's shoulder. "You can't go back, sweetheart. What's done is done. There's no saying you could have helped him anyway."

"He called me at 4:03. I didn't hear his message until after Don Bennett phoned two hours later. I sure as hell could have done something."

"You told me he didn't tell you where he was or what he needed. Who would you have called if you had gotten the message?"

Mary stood. "I don't know . . . someone—anyone. Two hours, Carrie. Why didn't I . . . ?"

"Because it slipped your mind. Because you couldn't have known what Joe was calling about. Because you're a human being like the rest of us."

"And then I went and erased the message. I don't know how, but I did."

"How do you know it was you? Machines screw up all the time. Mark's iPad just goes and shuts down sometimes. He's always yelling about losing this or that."

"They don't lose the last message your husband ever sent you."

Carrie studied her. "What are you getting at?"

Mary dropped her hands and paced the room, exasperated at her inability to recall her actions. "All I know is that one minute the message was there and the next it was gone."

"So someone else erased it?"

"I left the phone in the car when I went into the hospital. I guess someone could have broken into my car, erased the message, then locked the car back up. But even then there'd be a record of it on my message log." Mary knew her Sherlock Holmes. Eliminate the impossible and what remains, no matter how improbable, is the truth. "You're right. It was the phone. It had to be. Something just happened."

"Take it to Joe's office. Give it to what's-his-name . . . Dave—"

"Don Bennett. Joe's boss."

"Have him take a look at it."

"I don't like him. He practically tried to rip the phone out of my hands last night. He scares me."

"The FBI scares me, too, hon, but I trust 'em."

"I know them better than you." Mary tried her best to recall Joe's words. She closed her eyes and saw them hovering just out of reach. "It's just that I can't remember everything he said."

"Give it time. It'll come." Carrie nodded toward the door. "And the girls?"

"Jessie is in her room with her door locked. Gracie woke up and cried until she fell back asleep. They're in shock."

"Does Jess know about the message?"

"No," said Mary forcefully, surprising herself. "I won't tell her. It wasn't her fault I missed the call. She was just doing what she always does."

"She's really into that tech stuff," said Carrie. "Programming and creating apps."

"Her summer school teacher told me that some people just get it, and Jess is one of them. He said she has the gift."

"Mark was that way, too. Turned out good for him, even if he is still a geek." Carrie stood and came closer. "What're you going to do, hon?"

"I'm not sure. I can't imagine moving again. The schools are good. Grace likes her new doctor. Besides, where would we go?"

"I'd imagine you'd want to be nearer your folks."

"They're all gone. I've got a brother floating around on an aircraft carrier somewhere in the Pacific, and Joe's got two sisters in Boston. That's it. I don't have anyplace to go."

"Texas has done right by us. You could do worse."

"Do I have to become a Republican?"

"Mandatory after five years—otherwise they kick you out." Carrie went to the door. "Can't keep your fan club waiting forever."

"Five minutes."

"Take ten. I'll stall for you." Carrie winked and closed the door.

Mary picked up the newspaper again. She looked at the shattered windshield and the body on the ground. She contrasted the picture with Bennett's muddled explanation of what had occurred. Something didn't match. Or, as she'd heard some good ol' boy say, "That dog don't hunt."

Mary walked to the bathroom, washed her face, put on makeup, and brushed her hair. It wouldn't be right to show them how devastated she was. The admiral wouldn't stand for it.

She picked up her phone on the way out, pausing at the door to access the calls log. She spotted the number she wanted right away.

"Federal Bureau of Investigation. How may I direct your call?"

"Don Bennett, please."

12

It was not this hot in England.

Ian tried not to hurry as he crossed the broad expanse of lawn known as the Meadow. Christ Church, and the comfort of his air-conditioned office, were ten steps behind him and already he was sweating. He continued up Dead Man's Walk, then cut over to Merton Street, passing Oriel and University before reaching High Street.

Oracle had its "Emerald City." Google had its "Googleplex." Ian had his own private Oxford.

There was New College and Radcliffe Camera and the Bodleian Library. There was even the River Isis. The buildings were exact replicas of the originals, built from the same English limestone and mortar on a three-hundred-acre plot of land overlooking Lake Travis, five miles from the Austin city limits. A little bit of England in the Texas Hill Country.

He crossed the High and entered a warren of alleyways, heading toward Brasenose, the "college" that housed ONE's research-and-development labs. Each "college" contained offices, a cafeteria, and a quad where employees could get outside and recreate. New College housed the Server Division. Oriel housed Online Sales. And so on.

Great Tom sounded the quarter hour. Like the original hanging in Tom Tower, the bell weighed six tons and was cast from smelted iron. It tolled over a hundred times at nine each night, not in memory of the original students enrolled in Christ Church, but to celebrate each billion dollars of ONE's annual sales. In the year of our Lord 2015, Great Tom was programmed to toll 201 times each night.

"Ian!" It was Peter Briggs, coming out of the White Stag.

"Come on," Ian called. "They're waiting on me."

Briggs pulled up alongside him. "That bastard May's remarks made it into an article about the race in the Reno papers."

"The sports section." Ian had seen the piece while doing a little background on Gordon May. "Right before the part about the race stewards denying his objection."

"He sounds serious."

"Like I said, he's a sore loser. Now everyone knows it. Anything else about John Merriweather comes out of his mouth, we'll sue him for defamation. Shut him up once and for all."

"That's what I like to hear."

"To think," said Ian, dismissing May's monstrous accusations. "John Merriweather was a dear friend."

The men walked a ways farther, leaving the main campus and continuing along a paved road toward the R&D facility, a black glass rectangle the size of a city block surrounded by a twenty-foot-tall fence.

"This is it, then?" said Briggs as they passed through the security checkpoint. "You get the cooling system all squared away?"

"That's what we're going to find out."

"Better have," said Briggs. "Utah's ready to rock 'n' roll. They don't like delays in D.C."

Ian ignored the admonishing clip to his voice. "Let me worry about D.C."

"Whatever you say. You're the boss."

It was an object of beauty.

Ian ran a hand over the face of the machine. An undulating wave of black titanium as alluring as a centerfold's curves glimmered beneath the lab's soft lighting. Form married to function. The ONE logo had been painted across the panels in electric-blue ink that seemed to lift right off them. The apotheosis of design and intellect.

Titan. The world's most powerful supercomputer.

Half a dozen engineers were conducting last-minute checks of the equipment. All wore hoodies or fleece. One sported a down parka. Outside, the temperature was pushing 100°. Inside, it was a chill 58°.

"Ah, Ian, welcome," said Dev Patel, the chief programmer on the Titan project, hurrying toward him. "Can we get you a jumper?"

"I'm fine," said Ian. "Are we all hooked up?"

"All according to your instructions." Patel placed a hand on top of Titan. He was short and round, a native of Madras who'd come to ONE by way of IIT, Caltech, and the Oak Ridge National Laboratory. "We've connected two hundred machines for today's test. Our footprint is about four thousand square feet."

"Two hundred? That enough?"

"Good lord, yes." Patel tugged at the thatch of graying hair that fell across his forehead, looking like nothing so much as an aging school-boy. "And then some."

Ian patted him on the back. John Merriweather's coup was to marry graphics processing units (GPUs) with conventional central processing units (CPUs) to create a hybrid that was at once more energy-efficient than anything before it and capable of an order of magnitude increase in computational power. Titan used 25,000 AMD Opteron 16-core CPUs and 25,000 Nvidia Tesla GPUs. "Memory?"

"Seven hundred ten terabytes," said Patel, "with forty petabytes of hard drive storage."

Seven hundred ten terabytes was the equivalent of all the text found in a stack of books running from the earth to the moon. "And that gives us?"

"A theoretical peak performance approaching ten exaflops—about twenty thousand trillion calculations per second—give or take."

"That means we're tops, right?"

"No one else is even close."

Ian spoke over his shoulder. "Get PR. I want that information out to everyone on the Net a minute after the test is completed." He put a hand on Patel's shoulder and guided him to a private corner. "Is she ready?"

"I'll keep my end of the bargain if you keep yours."

Ian's end meant seeing to it that the new cooling system functioned as advertised. Patel's end meant pushing Titan to the max, getting all twenty thousand trillion operations per second from it. It was time to push the needle into the red once more. "All right, then. Let's light this baby up."

Patel's eyes radiated excitement. He turned toward the engineers and raised his arms. "Light this baby up."

The engineers retreated to their workstations behind a glass wall and placed noise-canceling headphones over their ears. The ambient buzz Ian had noted since entering the lab grew louder. A metallic clicking noise emanated from the machines, the cadence and volume increasing by the second, as if hundreds of steel dominoes were being shuffled and shuffled again.

"Would you prefer to watch the demonstration in a different man-ner?" asked Patel.

"Everest?" Ian struggled to keep from clapping his hands over his ears.

"Yes," shouted Patel.

The men walked down a corridor to a smaller, quieter room. The room was empty except for one wall made entirely of dark translucent glass. This was Everest, the "exploratory visualization environment for science and technology," a thirty-seven-megapixel stereoscopic wall made of eighteen individual display monitors.

Three vanguard codes had been selected to test Titan's maximum operating capabilities. S3D modeled the molecular physics of combustion in an effort to lessen the carbon footprint of fossil fuels. WL-LSMS simulated the interaction between electrons and atoms in magnetic materials. And CAM-SE simulated specific climate change scenarios and was designed to cycle through five years of weather in one day of computing time.

"We're running CAM-SE," said Patel. "We might as well find out whether or not the earth is going to be here fifty years from now."

"Might as well." Frankly, Ian was more interested in whether Titan would be in working order fifty minutes from now or a flaming pile of silicon. He crossed his arms and faced the wall of black glass. Six closely spaced horizontal lines ran the length of the wall: red, yellow, orange, green, blue, and purple.

The room lights dimmed.

Phase One Initiated flashed in the upper left-hand corner. Titan had begun its work.

Below it a reading displayed the supercomputer's internal temperature: 75° Fahrenheit.

The lines on the glass wall began wiggling, interweaving, dancing with one another as if bothered by a weak current. The temperature display jumped to 80°, then 85°. The lines' movements grew more frenzied, each assuming a life of its own, oscillating into sine and cosine waves. The lines were a visual manifestation of Titan's calculations as the machine worked its way into the complex code, analyzing billions of possible climate models. There were no longer just six lines but twenty, then thirty, and then too many to count, a rainbow of gyrating colors.

Meanwhile the temperature continued to rise.

A buzzer sounded.

Phase Two appeared.

Titan was working faster.

On command, the lines escaped their two-dimensional confines and leapt into the room. Ian and Patel were surrounded by a sea of multicolored, undulating wave functions, awash in an ocean of neon light.

120°

150°

The machine was heating too rapidly.

Ian said nothing. To speak was to scream. He glanced sidelong at Patel. The programmer no longer looked like an enthusiastic schoolboy. In the darkened room, his round, pleasant face illuminated by the wildly gyrating lights, he looked like a doomed prisoner awaiting a dreadful sentence.

170°

180°

Ian hummed to himself, blinking inadvertently each time the number rose. If Titan's internal temperature surpassed 200° for a period of thirty seconds, the supercomputer would shut itself down. There would be no meeting at Fort Meade. The giant array in Utah would be removed and shipped back for repair. Months would be needed to rework the cooling design.

Despite his anxiety, Ian felt outside himself, part of some bigger scheme: intelligence, the universe, he didn't know what to call it. Maybe progress. The first computers had used punch cards to tabulate election results. Then came transistors and silicon wafers and microchips. The latest was nanochips, chips as thin as a human hair, so small they needed to be viewed with an electron microscope. Today a smartphone retailing for $99 held the computing power necessary to launch *Apollo 11* and land two men on the surface of the moon.

Titan possessed one billion times that power.

Deus in machina.

God in the machine.

Everest glowed blue.

The buzzer sounded again. The terrific noise grew.

Phase Three appeared.

Titan had reached its maximum speed. In a single second it performed as many calculations as the first mainframe had been able to perform in an entire week.

200°

"Shut it down," shouted Patel. "We're going to burn."

"Wait," said Ian.

It was all or nothing. Time to push the needle into the red.

Ten seconds passed. Fifteen.

"Ian . . . please. Shut it down."

"Another second."

"You must!"

And then something wonderful happened.

190°

The temperature decreased.

180°

And decreased again.

Patel grabbed Ian's arm. Ian stood still, not protesting. The panel turned from blue to red. Patel began to laugh. "It works," he said, though his words were impossible to hear above the clatter.

Ian nodded, saying nothing. His anxiety vanished. His calm returned. And his confidence, perhaps even greater than before.

"Of course it works," he wanted to say. He had designed it.

13

In his short time in Austin, Joe had adopted Threadgill's on North Lamar as his home away from home. The restaurant was a local landmark built inside the shell of an old service station and dressed up in fancy paint and neon lights. Mary regretted suggesting meeting there as soon as the words left her mouth, but Don Bennett had agreed so quickly, she hadn't had the time to change her mind.

She found Bennett waiting inside, dressed in a three-piece suit, stiff as ever, seated at one of the booths and playing with the jukebox that decorated the table. "What are we listening to?" she asked as she slid onto the leather banquette.

"Elvis." Bennett dropped a quarter in the slot and thumbed a button. Elvis Presley began singing "Hound Dog." "Wanna eat?"

"You have time?" said Mary, surprised. "I thought you'd need to get out to the crime scene."

"That's shut down."

"So you figured out what happened?"

"I already told you."

"You didn't seem so sure last night."

Bennett stared at her but said nothing. He appeared to have cut himself shaving.

"The informant shot Joe, and Joe shot him before he died," she said. "You're sticking to that story?"

"Those are the facts."

Mary let it go for the moment. The waiter came and handed them menus. Mary put hers down. Threadgill's stock-in-trade was downhome cooking: fried chicken, catfish, collard greens. She and Joe always ordered the same thing: chicken fried steak. She grabbed a biscuit out of the basket and spread a dollop of honey butter across it. It no longer mattered if she fit into the LBD.

Bennett set down his menu. "How can I help?" he asked.

"I'd like you to take a look at my phone," said Mary. "If you're still interested, that is."

"That won't be necessary," answered Bennett.

"For you or for me? I'm asking a favor."

"I can't extend the Bureau's services to a civilian."

"I didn't leave the message. My husband did—minutes before he was killed in the line of duty. I'd think you'd be damned interested."

"I'm sorry, Mary, but the Bureau cannot assist you."

"Cannot or will not?"

Bennett leaned closer. "Mary, your husband died twenty hours ago. The Bureau extends its condolences. I'm happy to talk to you about his final pay package, insurance, and all benefits due to you and your family. But that's all. Now go home. Be with your daughters. Grieve."

"You're not telling me what happened," Mary said.

"The incident is closed."

Mary took the front page of the morning paper from her purse and unfolded it on the table, turning it so that it faced Bennett. "I looked at this for a long time. Right away I knew something was wrong, but it took me a while to figure out just what. You see, Don, you said the informant got in the car and neither of them got out. But look, there he is on the ground. Fine—I'll let that go. Maybe a question of semantics, you picking the wrong words. But tell me this: when exactly did the informant shoot Joe? Was it when he was already outside the car? Did his first shot miss and take out the windshield, or did he fire again after Joe shot him? See all that blood on the sheet by his head? I'd say the informant's first shot had to hit Joe, because he sure as shit didn't shoot him after Joe shot him in the head. I'm asking because yesterday at the hospital, the surgeon, Dr. Alexander, said that Joe was shot point-blank and that the bullet severed his spinal cord. The informant isn't anywhere near to point-blank, and Joe couldn't have pulled the trigger once he was shot. Joe would have called that 'a problem of chronology.' So tell me again, Don, what happened out there?"

Bennett said nothing.

"I'm waiting," Mary said.

"Please, Mary."

"Don't 'please' me." Mary pushed her phone across the table. "Are you afraid of what you might hear?"

Bennett blinked, his eyes holding hers, avoiding the phone. "Anything else I can help you with?"

"As a matter of fact, yes. Who exactly called 911? If Joe was all alone out there in Dripping Springs, it seems to me that no one would have found him for hours. No backup, right? That's what you said. But the EMTs got there twenty minutes after he was shot."

"The investigation is closed."

"Yours, maybe."

Bennett rose from the booth. "Are we done here?"

"No," said Mary. "Not by a long shot."

She's got true grit

14

Don Bennett, age forty-eight, twenty-three-year veteran of the Federal Bureau of Investigation, special agent in charge of the Austin residency, former navy corpsman, winner of the Bronze Star, veteran of the first Gulf War, rabid Cowboys fan, lover of Elvis Presley, and father of five, stood in the blazing sun, phone to his ear, asking himself what he was going to say.

It was a few minutes past one in the afternoon, and Bennett was drunk. He'd waited for Mary Grant to pull out of the lot, then marched back into the restaurant, ordered a Jack on the rocks, and drunk it down in a single draft. Then he did it again. The alcohol did little to quiet his mind. Mary Grant's questions were his own, if more crudely put. He possessed information she did not. He had answers to her questions. *Some . . . not all . . .* but enough to trouble his obedient self.

Bennett gazed up at the sky. It was white with heat, the sun a blinding abstraction. He asked himself the question again, the question he knew his master would ask, and he had his answer. Bennett considered himself a fine judge of character. He recognized a fighter when he saw one. A scrapper. Mary Grant was the kind of person who did something just because you told her she couldn't, the kind who'd continue even if it brought harm to herself. It was not the answer he desired, but it was the truth.

The phone rang a third time.

Bennett was a fighter, too, he reminded himself. A scrapper. He'd made it out of situations his brethren had not. Still, there were rules, and rules had to be followed. He believed in the chain of command and in obedience to your superiors. He'd built his life on doing as he was told. It was a successful life. A happy life. There was no reason to change now.

"Yes, Don," his master answered.

"She's asking questions."

"You couldn't convince her otherwise?"

"She doesn't buy the official version. He called her before the incident. Apparently he knew something was up."

"What did he say?"

"I'm not sure. He left her a message, but she deleted it. She asked for our help to retrieve it. I declined."

"Best we didn't know."

"Yes, sir."

"Did you keep your mouth shut?"

"I did."

"Of course you did," said his master. "You're a reliable man, Don. I appreciate that."

"Thank you, sir."

"One last question . . ."

"Sir?"

"Will she be a bother?"

There it was. The question he'd seen coming. It would be easy to lie. But Don Bennett followed orders. He believed in the chain of command.

"Will she continue to ask questions?" his master repeated.

"Yes, sir. I believe she won't stop until she finds out the truth."

A lengthy pause followed. Bennett could sense his master's anxiety, and it quickly became his own. "Sir?" said Bennett.

"That's all, Don. Take the rest of the day off. See the family. Consider it an order."

Bennett hung up.

There was truth and there was honor. He had never known them to war with each other.

15

It worked.

Ian stood in the center of his office, feeling the perspiration dry on his forehead. His nerves were gratifyingly becalmed. His heart had stopped doing the quickstep. Titan's cacophonous clatter was a distant memory.

"It worked."

He turned over the words in his mouth like a piece of candy. The maximum internal temperature recorded at the peak of Titan's frenzied, divinely ordered calculations—when each and every one of the machine's 50,000 CPUs and GPUs had been pressed to their limit, straining to solve one of the world's most complex equations, and in reaction generating their own "cybersweat" in the form of radiated heat—was 206° Fahrenheit, fifty degrees lower than previously measured.

Ian walked to his desk and sat down in his chair. He sat solemnly, aware of the occasion.

It worked.

Two words that unlocked the future . . . *and might unlock the past.*

His assistant's voice came over the speakerphone. "Mr. Briggs to see you. You have calls from Mr. Roarke in New York and from Ms. Taggart in Hollywood. You need to leave in fifteen minutes to make it to your meeting downtown."

"I'll roll the calls as soon as I'm on the road. Tell Briggs to give me five minutes."

Briggs could wait. First Ian needed to share the news of his triumph.

He turned the chair slowly and gazed at the satchel in the corner of his office.

It was a black satchel, old, worn, the leather creased and scarred, but still sturdy. A satchel built to last, but then, so was the British Empire. A strap and a lock secured the case. Above the lock, the initials *PSP* were embossed in gold leaf. They'd found the satchel in the parking garage next to his father's car.

After all these years, he thought, after the endless queries, the fruitless leads, after exploring shadowy path after shadowy path, all to no avail, just maybe there was a chance.

His eyes rose, catching a shadow. A man was standing next to the satchel. He was tall and upright, dressed in a navy chalk-stripe suit, a maroon necktie done with a perfect dimple, lace-up shoes polished to a regal shine. "Lobb of London. Only the best, right, son?"

Peter Prince's black hair was cut short, parted immaculately on the left and shining with brilliantine. He was a gentleman, to look at. A man of authority. He was not a man who walked out of his home one morning and vanished without a trace. He was not a man who left his satchel beside his car.

"It worked," said Ian proudly to his father. "I fixed it."

Peter Prince dipped his gaze. His eyes narrowed, searching the room.

Ian raised a hand in greeting. A smile pushed at the corners of his mouth. "Dad . . . over here . . ."

"Five minutes, my ass!"

Ian spun back toward the door as Peter Briggs stormed into the office.

"You going to keep me waiting all day, then?" Briggs said. "Think I came over just to gossip? I know how to use a phone, too. We're not all of us idiots who don't know what *Everest* stands for. Christ!"

"What is it?" Ian asked.

"Urgent." Briggs sat down in a guest's chair, snapping his fingers in the air. "You all there? This one requires your attention. Semaphore."

Ian glanced over his shoulder. His father was gone. There was only the black satchel by itself in the corner. "What about Semaphore? 'Tied off,' you said. 'Bank it.'"

"The wife. She's asking questions."

"Excuse me. 'The wife'? What do you mean?"

"The agent's wife. Mrs. Joseph Grant. She's got quite the bee in her bonnet."

The mention of the dead agent's wife was like a dash of cold water. "How so?" asked Ian, his attention squarely on Briggs.

"She doesn't believe her husband could have been killed by an informant. Claims there are discrepancies in the FBI's story. Wants to know what's what." Briggs helped himself to a fistful of almonds from a bowl on the desk, flicking them into his mouth one at a time. "You know the type. Nosy. Doesn't know when to let well enough alone."

"Are there?"

"Discrepancies?" Briggs shrugged. "Don't know. Doesn't matter. It's the call. He must have said something to her."

"Not that I recall." Ian had listened to Joseph Grant's message several times and was sure he hadn't mentioned anything about Semaphore or ONE. "Anyway, I erased it from her phone. No evidence there."

"She's a woman. She doesn't need evidence. She has intuition."

"And the rest of it . . . besides the woman?"

"Tied off."

Ian averted his gaze. He was beginning to despise the term. "We can't afford any problems. Nothing that might put things in jeopardy."

"I understand," said Peter Briggs.

"I know you do," said Ian. "So it's just the woman?"

Briggs nodded.

"What's her name?"

"Mary Grant."

"Her full name."

"Mary Margaret Olmstead Grant."

Ian wrote the name on his ledger. "Go ahead, then. But easy does it. Nothing heavy-handed. Level one and that's it. We don't want to stir things up." Ian stood, signaling that the meeting was over. "She can't find anything anyway. It's 'tied off,' right?" He looked hard at Peter Briggs.

"Bank it."

Ian stared at the name on the ledger.

Mary Margaret Olmstead Grant.

He knew what it was like to lose a loved one under mysterious circumstances. He knew about the power of unanswered questions. He knew about curiosity hardening to obsession. He also knew better than to take anyone for granted. Not even an ordinary housewife.

Ian called his assistant and asked her to push back his schedule fifteen minutes. He typed Mary Grant's name into the Search bar and got three hits: Facebook, Austin real estate registry, and a Shutterfly account.

The Facebook account was under the name Mary Olmstead Grant, the private information available to her friends. Still, as a beginning it was promising. There was a picture of a tropical beach, two children walking at water's edge. He guessed it was somewhere in southern Mexico, Costa Rica, the Philippines, or Thailand. A photograph of a woman he assumed to be Mary Grant was inset in the landscape. It was an odd photo, showing only half the woman's face, purposely cropped to disguise her identity. Still, he could see that she was blond, pretty, and vivacious. Her eyes held the camera.

She listed her work as "household engineer." She had studied at Georgetown. She lived in Austin. She liked Stevie Ray Vaughan, Coldplay, and Alfred Brendel. She also liked the American Cancer Society, Sacramento Children's Hospital, and the Susan G. Komen Race for the Cure. She had forty-three friends.

Again, not much, but a beginning.

A private woman proud of her upbringing, not wanting to lose her maiden name and all that it meant to her. An intelligent woman with an education. A woman who had traveled the world. A woman who had been touched sometime in her life by cancer, either her own or a family member's. A woman who valued her privacy and was not comfortable sharing personal information with strangers. A woman who chose her friends carefully.

Ian's concern grew. A formidable woman, he sensed.

He drew up yesterday's work log to locate the number Joseph Grant had called minutes before his death. He noted that Mary Grant was not currently a ONE Mobile customer. (This had not prevented him from using the competing carrier's equipment to gain access to her phone. Traffic between wireless carriers demanded cooperation on the most intimate technological levels. He had nearly unfettered access to his competitors' servers, routers, and relay stations.) ONE Mobile had strong market share in Sacramento. Perhaps she'd been a client and switched carriers upon her arrival in Austin.

He logged into ONE Mobile's Sacramento database and plugged in her name.

Bingo. In fact Mary Grant had been a customer of ONE Mobile during her residence in Sacramento.

He pulled up the customary information: date of birth, home address, banking details (Mary Grant was an autopay customer), and Social Security number. He smiled inwardly. This last piece of information was crucial. A person's Social Security number was a skeleton key that could unlock troves of personal, often confidential data.

He continued for a few minutes longer, downloading phone records for the prior two-year period. Digging deeper, he found a record of her voicemail password: 71700. He guessed it was either an anniversary or the birth date of a family member, most probably one of her children.

The Shutterfly hit yielded only two photos, but to Ian they were important. Both showed two girls seated together. One was dark-haired and olive-skinned, the other fair and sickly pale. Mary Grant's daughters.

The real estate registry showed that Mr. and Mrs. Joseph Grant had purchased a home on Pickfair Drive in northwest Austin ninety days earlier for the price of $425,000.

All of this was information to be stored away. Nothing useful now, but it might come in handy later. He saved the pages to a new folder in his ONE Platinum account before placing a call to Investigations.

"This is Ian. I have a Social Security number for you. Give me a full workup. And make it a priority."

16

"Mr. Briggs," called the guard. "Your badge."

Peter Briggs stormed past the porter's lodge of Brasenose and continued to the elevators. He was fed up. There was only so much you could take of hanging around a bunch of grown men who grew sexually aroused talking about petaflops and hard drives and GPUs. He was certain that Patel had been sporting some wood as he brushed up against Titan.

Briggs got off at the third floor and headed for the operations room. A dozen men sat at desks positioned along the perimeter of the office. Not one of them gave a flying fig about petaflops or hard drives or GPUs. Briggs was certain about that.

"Fire under control in K.L.?" he asked.

"Damage localized to a chip storage area."

"Plant back on line?"

"Yessir."

"Outstanding."

Running security for ONE was a twenty-four-hour-a-day job. Briggs had a thousand employees under his command, safeguarding the corporation's offices and manufacturing facilities in twenty countries around the globe. His responsibilities broke down into three areas: physical plant and manufacturing, cybersecurity, and personal protection.

Cybersecurity was giving him the biggest headache these days. ONE's servers were under attack from hackers day and night. Most came from China or eastern Europe. The Chinese attacks emanated from a military unit charged with gaining industrial espionage secrets from Western companies. The eastern European attacks came out of Bulgaria and Romania, the work of organized criminals contracted by smaller technology companies to steal ONE's R&D. Between the two, ONE defended itself against more than five thousand attacks a day.

As was his habit on entering the ops room, he checked an electronic world map that broadcast the location of the company's top executives. Today he noted that ten were in Austin, four in Palo Alto, two in Mumbai, two in Guangdong, one in Berlin, and one in Nepal.

"Get the plane ready for D.C.," he said to Travel. "Party of five plus crew. We fly at dawn. Boss wants the Kraut. Tell her to be at the airport at five a.m. and to make sure she has her bag of nostrums."

Travel looked up. "Bag of what?"

Briggs patted his shoulder, pleased to be in the company of a man with a vocabulary nearly as limited as his own. "Never mind, lad. Just call Katarina and get the plane arranged."

"Yessir."

There was a new symbol on the map that Briggs hadn't seen that morning. The symbol was a silhouette of a jet, and it appeared whenever company execs were en route or due to embark on a flight. He touched the jet and its flight information appeared on the screen.

ONE 7 / N415GB
JER—AUS 7.31.
0700MST—1900CST.

ONE 7 was a Boeing business jet with tail number N415GB, departing from Jerusalem at 0700 hours local time and arriving in Austin at 1900 hours tomorrow night.

The Israelis were coming.

Briggs couldn't help but feel his pulse quicken. Ian was right. They could not afford any more slipups. Not now, with Titan up and running. Not with the Israelis on the way.

Briggs continued to his office. First there was ONEscape, the browser, then came software, and after that hardware: servers, routers, switches—the machines that made up the Internet's backbone—then ONE Mobile, the wireless phone carrier, and now, just a few months back, Allied Artists, the country's biggest movie and television studio.

But all of it was but a prelude for the Israelis. Ian had called them his Praetorian Guard and talked about a "new Jerusalem." Briggs knew better than to ask about a new messiah.

He sat at his desk and pulled up the report from his contact at the FBI. *Semaphore.* It was the case that wouldn't die.

"Go easy," Ian had said. "Nothing heavy-handed."

But Briggs hadn't gotten where he was by going easy. He hit speed dial for Firemen.

"I need a team to do a little scouting work for me. A local job."

"Level?"

Level one, or L1, was a simple look-and-listen on a target's phone and Net usage.

L2 added wireless surveillance, plus eyes on the subject for defined daily intervals.

L3 amounted to a digital cavity search—all of the above plus twenty-four-hour surveillance and infiltration of the target's home or office with the goal of installing malware to take full operational control of all the target's digital systems: tablet, laptop, desktop, mainframe, and mobile communications devices.

"L2," he said.

"How soon do you want work to begin?"

"Immediately."

"Have anyone in mind?"

In the end there was really only one team he could trust with the job.

"Get me Shanks and the Mole."

17

Showtime.

Tank Potter parked at the back of the office lot and checked his appearance in the mirror. Hair freshly washed. Eyes marginally red. Shirt clean and pressed. All in all, not too bad after twelve hours in the clink.

He reached into the bag on the seat beside him for a box of Band-Aids. His hand shook as he freed one from the box and shook more as he struggled to peel off the wrapping.

Reinforcements needed.

He dropped the bandage and delved under his seat for his backstop, ducking his head below the dash to take a pull of tequila. His hand was rock-steady as he peeled off the wrapping and affixed the Band-Aid to his forehead.

"Thank you, JC." Jose Cuervo, not the other guy.

For a minute he looked at the *Statesman*'s headquarters. Thirty days and all this was history. It didn't come as a surprise. Every paper in the country was slashing its staff, and he was no Pulitzer winner. Even so, he'd thought it would be easier.

A last helper to calm the nerves and he was good to go.

He stashed the bottle, then rummaged in the glove compartment for his Altoids, counted out five, and popped them into his mouth. Fortified, he climbed out, feeling capable, calm, and only mildly hung-over.

"Potter!"

Al Soletano stood outside his glassed-in office in the center of the newsroom, hands on hips, his face flushed a shade past fire-engine red. Tank raised a hand in greeting as he made his way down the main aisle. The newsroom was a sea of vacant cubicles. A plague zone, he thought as he entered Soletano's office.

"Sit."

"I'm okay."

"I said sit."

Tank sat down in the visitor's chair.

"How you feeling?" Soletano was short, with a gut, a tonsure of black hair, and a voice that could be heard in all six neighboring counties.

"Not bad, all things considered."

"Your head?"

"It hurts, but I'll be all right." Tank had spoken to Soletano as soon as he was freed from the holding cell. He had a story ready. He'd been in a fender bender, banged his head, and spent the night in the emergency room.

"You don't have to be going fast to do some damage."

Tank touched his bandage gingerly. "You can say that again."

"Say, buddy, do me a favor. Hand me my glass of water, would you? I'm thirsty."

Tank looked to his right, where a glass of water sat on the desk's corner. The glass was full to the brim. He looked back at Soletano, leaning against the wall, not making the slightest effort. Tank clenched a fist, then picked up the glass. Water spilled onto Soletano's desk. He set the glass down.

"I'm waiting."

Tank stared at his hand, willing it to stop shaking. Standing, he picked up the glass and walked over to his editor. Halfway there, a spasm shook his hand and water sloshed onto the floor.

"And that's after the snort in the parking lot," said Soletano. "By the way, where'd you get hit? I didn't see any dents—or any new ones, at least."

Tank said nothing.

Soletano approached him and ripped the bandage off his forehead. "I hear you met one of my friends last night. Lance Burroughs. Young guy. Detective." He circled his desk and picked up a piece of paper. "Your arrest report," he said, by way of explanation. "You blew a point thirty-four. That's four times the legal limit. I have to be honest, Tank. God knows I love to tie one on as much as the next guy, but point thirty-four . . . that's enough booze to knock out Godzilla."

"It's been a stressful few days."

"And nights. A federal agent murdered in our backyard and I'm buying the story from a stringer out of Dallas. It's embarrassing."

"At least you'll have practice for when the suits finish the deal," said Tank.

The suits were the private equity guys from Wall Street who'd been running around the place for the past month figuring ways to cut costs.

Soletano didn't take the bait. He stood, arms crossed, shaking his head. "You used to be a decent journalist."

The tone hit Tank hard. He'd been a damned sight better than that.

"There's another conference later this afternoon," he said. "I'll be there. Did you read the release? Bennett is stonewalling us. Once we find out the informant's identity, we'll have a beeline to what the feds were looking into. I mean, Dripping Springs, for Chrissakes. That tell you something?"

"Maybe the CI's from Dripping Springs?"

"It tells me that it's a pretty big case if they're meeting their CIs twenty-five miles away to make sure they're not seen." Despite the air conditioning, he was beginning to sweat. "You know how many FBI agents have been killed in the line of duty in the past twenty years?"

"Four."

"Yeah, four. Not many. This one's got legs. I can feel that there's something here. Let me run with it." He smiled sheepishly. "Everyone gets a DUI. It's not a big deal."

"You're a day late and a dollar short, pal. I told you to read that letter."

"One DUI. Come on. It's a misdemeanor."

Soletano snapped a finger at the arrest report. "You forgot to mention that it's your second offense. Two DUIs in ten years. That makes it a Class A misdemeanor. Mandatory suspension of license for one year. Fine of up to ten grand. What you did is more than enough for rightful termination."

"You're firing me?"

"You fired yourself. You saw those suits in here. They get a chance to knock a hundred grand off their liabilities, they're going to jump on it."

Tank threw up his arms. His severance package gave him one month's salary for every year he'd worked at the paper. The total came out to a little over $100,000.

"Let me have this story, Al. I'll prove to you I'm the reporter I used to be."

"What story?" said Soletano. "Just because the Bureau isn't divulging the name of the informant doesn't mean there's a story. They're probably waiting a day or two to get their ducks in a row, inform the guy's family, and then they'll release it. This isn't Waco or Ruby Ridge. There's no Pulitzer at the end of the rainbow. It's just a case of an agent making a dumb mistake."

"I'm not so sure . . ."

"I am," said Soletano. "There is no story. You're done. You blew a point thirty-four. You're not some cute first-time drunk. You're a monster. Don't you get that? *A point thirty-four.* I'm surprised you didn't spontaneously combust. I can't have a reporter driving drunk all over town. The word *liability* mean anything to you?" Soletano opened the door and motioned for Tank to leave. "Get out of here. Go away. Get some help. You're a sick man."

Tank walked back to his car, hands in his pockets, arms stiff as ramrods to make sure he stood straight in case Soletano was watching. He opened the door and slid behind the wheel. All spirit went out of him and he laid his head against the steering wheel.

His hand dropped to his backstop and he took a healthy slug. Screw Soletano. He could watch all he wanted.

He dropped the bottle and grabbed the copy of the day's paper off the passenger seat. The headline read: "FBI Agent Dies in Dripping Springs Shoot-out." The story carried an AP byline, no name attached. The future of print journalism, he thought ruefully.

The lead paraphrased the Bureau's press release, and the body offered nothing that indicated any actual reporting. No suggestions about what case the agent was working or any background on him besides the boilerplate info, no quotes from the widow, and, most important to Tank's mind, not a whisper about the informant's identity. He could have filed it from the holding cell.

Tank banged his fist against the glove compartment and took out the envelope with his name on it. An hour ago the letter had held the promise of a new life. A hundred thousand dollars went a long way. After expenses, he'd figured he'd have enough to hit Pedro's five nights a week, go hunting in Nacogdoches in the fall, head down to South Padre Island at Christmas, maybe even get a haircut once in a while. It was a recipe for high living.

He started the car and gave it a little gas.

A decent journalist.

Soletano's words scratched at something buried deep. He wasn't sure if it was pique or pride. Whatever, they dug at something he'd suppressed for a long time. He suspected it was ambition, which he'd once possessed in abundance.

He kissed the envelope, then tore it in half and threw the pieces out the window. The future he'd dreamed of was gone. It was up to him to make another.

He unscrewed the cap of the bottle of tequila and brought the bottle to his lips.

Hell, he'd been a crackerjack journalist.

Tank took the bottle from his lips. For some unknown reason, he chucked it out the window, too. Al Soletano could clean up his mess.

Tank put the Jeep into gear and punched the accelerator. By the time he pulled out of the lot, he had his phone to his ear. Don Bennett was stonewalling about something, and that something was the informant. Tank still had one contact who might be of help.

"Austin Medical Examiner's Office."

"Give me Carlos Cantu," said Tank. "Tell him it's urgent."

18

Mary stood inside the foyer of her home, the blast of air conditioning doing nothing to cool her temper. Forty minutes after leaving Don Bennett, she remained incensed by his behavior. One moment he was ripping the phone out of her hand, the next he didn't want to glance at it. It didn't take a genius to figure out that something or someone had changed his mind.

Mary shook her head, vowing action, and walked into the kitchen. She dumped her purse on the counter and took a bottle of water from the fridge. Her eye stopped on the colorful cans of energy drinks neatly arranged in the back corner. Joe's drinks. She thought about throwing them out, then changed her mind. She needed him with her for a while longer.

Her phone buzzed. The number belonged to an old friend. Another condolence call. She let it roll to voicemail. She had more important items to attend to. There were the funeral arrangements to make, flights to book, hotel rooms to reserve. She couldn't mourn. She had too much to do. But before any of that, something else required her attention.

If Don Bennett wouldn't tell her what Joe was working on, she'd damn well find out herself.

Mary nudged open the door to Jessie's room. "Hi, sweets. Can I come in?"

Jessie lay facedown on her bed, arms splayed over the edges. "Go away."

Mary took a step closer. It was no time to argue. A truce had been declared between all mothers and their teenage daughters. "I need your help," she said. "I'm looking for my in-house IT squad."

A groan was the only response.

She entered the bedroom tentatively. Clothes covered the floor. A glass of root beer sat on Jessie's desk, and next to it an ice cream wrapper. The posters of horses and boy bands were long gone. On one wall, done up as a lithograph, was a quote from Julian Assange about "information wanting to be free," and on another a street advertisement for DEF CON, the hackers' convention in Las Vegas. The room was essentially a battlefield. The frontline between adolescents and parents.

Mary sat down on the bed. She waited for an outcry, a command to get off, or just a plaintive "Mom!" Jessie was silent. Progress, thought Mary. She ran a hand along her daughter's back. Fifteen years old. Already taller than her mom. Mary's firstborn was a young woman.

"It's about my phone," she went on. "I think I lost a message."

"So?"

Mary fought the reflex to pull her hand away. "It was from your dad."

"When?"

"Yesterday."

A moment passed. Still Jessie didn't move. Mary gathered a measure of the sheet in her fist. She gave Jessie until three to move or to show the smallest hint of civility.

One . . . two . . .

Jessie grunted, then pushed herself up to an elbow. "Give it."

Mary handed her the phone. "I thought maybe you could tell me how I lost it or if I can get it back."

"Maybe." Jessie sat up and put her feet on the floor. She cradled the phone in both hands, head hunched low over it like a priest blessing the sacred host.

"He called at four-oh-three," said Mary. "But I didn't check the message until around five-thirty."

"I see it."

Mary's heart skipped a beat. "The message?"

"No," said Jessie. "The call."

Mary tamped down her disappointment. She caught a glimpse of the screen. Lines of letters and numerals and symbols as alien as cuneiform or Sanskrit. Her daughter, Champollion.

"Not here," said Jessie.

"I thought maybe I deleted it by mistake."

"And then deleted the deleted messages? That would be lame."

"I didn't do it. You can check—"

"The older messages are still there," said Jessie. "I can read."

"I listened to it once at home and then before I went into the hospital to see your dad. I told Mr. Bennett that I'd gotten it and—"

"Why?" Jessie sat up straighter, a hand pushing the hair from her face, tucking strands behind her ear. For the first time she looked directly at her mother. Mary found her gaze oddly innocent, frightened.

"I thought he would be interested in what your father said."

"What did Dad say?"

"It doesn't matter. It was about his business." Mary took a breath. "And so when I came back for my phone, the message wasn't there anymore."

"Then why are you so hot on getting it back?"

Mary hesitated, suddenly slack-jawed. How had Jessie managed to take control of the conversation? "Dad said that he might be in trouble. He said that he loved us all very much."

"He was in trouble? Like how?"

"I don't know."

"What did he say?"

"I can't entirely remember. I was upset when I heard it." Mary gestured to the phone, anxious to get clear of dangerous waters. "Do you think you can—"

"So he called when I was unlocking your phone?"

Mary nodded.

"And it was before . . ." Jessie stopped. Her eyes flitted around the room, gathering pieces of the puzzle. "So you're saying it was my fault."

"No, sweetie, of course not. I'm just asking for your help to see if we can get the message back somehow."

Jessie tossed her the phone, stood, and brushed past her. "You're trying to tell me that if I hadn't been unlocking your phone, you would have gotten the call and maybe we could have done something to help Dad."

Mary rose. "Of course not. You have nothing to do with it."

"Really? Then why are you telling me about it?"

"Because the FBI won't help me. Because I don't know who else to ask."

"He's dead. What does it matter? Daddy's dead." Jessie threw herself back onto the bed. "Why did you tell me about the message?"

Mary sat down and placed a hand on her shoulder. "Jess, please."

Jessie knocked the hand away. "It wasn't my fault. Get out."

"Jessie."

"Did you hear me? Leave." Jessie dug her head into her pillow. A sob racked her chest.

Mary walked to the door. Grace was there, peering in, eyes wide. Mary returned to the bed and knelt by Jessie's side. "It wasn't your fault," she whispered. "Don't you ever believe that."

A cry escaped the pillow. A plea to break a mother's heart.

"Why did you tell me, Mommy? Why?"

19

The man named Shanks drove down Pickfair Drive. Late in the afternoon, the neighborhood was alive with children riding bicycles and mothers pushing strollers along sidewalks. No one looked twice at the work van belonging to the nation's largest phone and Internet provider.

Shanks parked at the corner of Pickfair and Lockerbie, across the street from the target's home. "We're here," he said.

No response came from the work bay. He looked over his shoulder at the Mole, seated at the surveillance console, eyes locked onto the monitor.

Shanks climbed out and walked around to the sliding door. He was big and muscular, his pecs straining against his technician's uniform. He rapped his hand on the door before sliding it open. "Let's get this done. Too many eyes on the street for my liking."

"Target is inside but not currently using her phone. Same goes for the girls." The Mole didn't avert his eyes from the monitor. He was small and wiry and pale. If Shanks's uniform was too tight, his was too loose. Tattoos of snakes and daggers and skulls covered every inch of his thin, gangly arms.

Shanks poked his head inside the van to get a glimpse of the monitor. A dozen nine-digit phone numbers filled the screens. It was a wireless capture protocol called Kingfisher and worked by transmitting signals that mimicked the nearest cell tower to pull all nearby mobile calls out of the air. "What girls are those?" he asked.

"She has two daughters. They have phones, too."

Shanks stepped outside. He didn't ask how the Mole knew about the girls. "Just concentrate on the woman. Mr. Briggs said level two. Don't get carried away."

The Mole shifted his gaze to Shanks. "You giving me orders?"

Shanks came out of Cabrini-Green on the Near North Side of Chicago. He'd served his time in the Corps, and then harder time in Florida State Prison. He'd seen his share of hard types. No one had eyes like the Mole. Black as day-old blood and set a mile deep in their sockets. "Just do what you got to do and let's motor."

The Mole left his seat and grabbed his work bag as he stepped out of the van. He walked to the junction box, a beige pillar standing three feet tall a few yards from the corner, and pried off the plastic cowling. Penlight in his mouth, he scanned the connections terminus, moving down the handwritten addresses posted next to each. He paused, teeth clenching metal, hands holding an ordinary laborer's tools. Once upon a time he'd been a star student at the MIT Media Lab. Negroponte's favorite acolyte. Now he was the Cable Guy.

The Mole stopped at "10602 / Grant" and unscrewed the fiber-optic cable that delivered telephone, television, and Internet service to the home. With his free hand he drew a Y-cable from his bag and screwed the tail onto the terminus. He attached the fiber-optic cable to one fork and his black box to the other, checked that the connections were firm, then replaced the hood.

"Keep going," said Shanks, who acted as lookout. "No eyes on you."

The Mole selected a sturdy oak tree nearby with a clear view to the target's home and affixed a micro hi-def camera to the bark. The camera was no larger than a shirt button and once camouflaged with a bit of putty would be invisible.

The camera and the black box were only superficial measures. The camera wirelessly transmitted high-definition images of the home in a five-mile radius. The box captured all digital traffic to and from the target's house and passed it on to Peter Briggs: landline, television, cable, Internet. It recorded what numbers the targets dialed, what phone conversations they had, what websites they visited, what articles they read, what shows they watched on streaming content services like Netflix, Hulu, and Amazon Prime, what books they ordered—you name it.

Neither provided a granular view of the target's activities or, more importantly, her intentions. E-mails could not be decrypted. Banking transactions likewise. Anything requiring a password was beyond their grasp.

There was a better way. The Mole's way.

He stared at the house, imagining its occupants. One adult. Two children. He'd done his research. It was so easy to find out all about them. Mary, Jessie, and Grace were their names. He could be at the front door in three seconds, and inside ten seconds after that. There would be at least one laptop, maybe a tablet, a phone for every member of the family. Each presented an entry point, a means to burrow into their lives.

The Mole thought about the girls. One was fifteen, the other eleven. How interesting it would be to know more about them. Whether they liked boys or girls, whether they drank or took drugs, whether they looked at pornography. The older girl was dark and tall. The younger was fair and delicate. He liked to imagine her fine wrists, her vulnerable neck.

"You done?" asked Shanks. "I don't want to have to answer questions about what movies are on special this month."

The Mole climbed into the van without answering. A moment later he was back in his seat, those deep dark eyes locked onto his machines as if he were some kind of droid powering up.

Shanks knew what he was thinking about.

Nothing good.

20

"It wasn't your fault."

Jessie sat on her bed, staring out the window. She had her Beats on, the music loud enough to crowd out any ugly thoughts. Her mom's words played like a loop over the dark electronic groove, louder than the bass, louder than the guitars, overpowering everything. Everything except Dad.

Dad understood. Dad knew about code and software and how cool tech was. He didn't think it was weird that she liked what she liked. He totally got the part of her that liked to disappear into the Net, the part that came alive when she held a phone in her hand. When she was connected.

Now he was gone. Dead. And dead meant forever. She tried to understand forever, but she couldn't. It was too scary.

Jessie picked up her own smartphone—a cheap Android platform—and opened the mail she'd sent herself containing the screenshot of the log from her mom's phone. Smartphones remembered everything. Somewhere there was a record of every call, every website visited, every keystroke the user ever made. You might erase texts or e-mails or voice messages, but you could never erase the traces they left behind. Not unless you destroyed the phone, and by that she meant grinding it up into a thousand pieces. Even then, there was a record at the ISP and maybe even the wireless carrier.

She brought the screen closer in order to read the blizzard of letters and numbers and backslashes. The notation showing all traffic to the number was clear enough: calls made, calls received, calls missed, voice messages, time, duration. She spotted the incoming call from her dad at 16:03:29 and ending at 16:04:05. (Phones used the twenty-four-hour clock.) She calculated that his message had lasted twenty-five seconds, because her mom's greeting took forever.

"Hi. This is Mary. Please leave a message and I promise to get back to you as soon as possible. Have a great day." Jessie mouthed the words.

So cheerful, so original . . . *so boring.* Hey, Mom, she thought, news flash: they know it's you. They dialed your number.

Jessie reviewed the lines of code that followed, noting that there were no further voice messages. It was 17:31 when her mom finally listened to her dad's message. And 18:30 when she listened to it a second time. But nowhere in the lines of code did Jessie spot any instructions to delete a message. At least her mom wasn't lying. With adults, you never knew.

"It wasn't my fault," Jessie admonished her mother. "It's yours for not listening to it earlier."

Jessie returned to a line of code that appeared different from the others. It was nothing but a jumble of letters and symbols. Meaningless. She was pretty sure she'd seen almost every kind of computer language, but she hadn't seen this.

She sent a text containing the mysterious code to Garrett, the only other high school student in her class at UT. He was no Rudeboy, but he was okay smart.

"G. WTF is this? Found it on my mom's phone. Help."

Jessie dropped the smartphone on the bed, then pulled off her headphones and stood up. She felt different, like herself again. She realized that she hadn't thought about her dad the entire time she was looking at her phone. That was enough to trigger another wave of tears. She cried for a minute, but that was all. She was too tired to cry anymore.

She got dressed. Jeans, Zeppelin concert T (the '74 Stairway to Heaven tour). She brushed her hair and looked in the mirror long enough to make sure she didn't have any zits and her face wasn't puffy and blotchy. She pulled her shirt tight across her chest. She hated how big her boobs were getting.

She left her room and crossed the hall. Grace's door was open. She lay on the bed reading.

"Hey," said Jessie, poking her head inside.

Grace looked up, then back at the book.

Jessie saw the cover. Another mermaid. Ugh. She sat down on the edge of the bed. "Good book?" She had no idea where the question came from. She hated mermaids and Grace knew it, but she didn't know what else to say. She was the big sister. She was supposed to console her little sister.

Grace put the book down. "You want to read it after me?"

"Not a chance," said Jessie, then softened her tone. "I mean, no thanks."

"You don't have to be nice to me."

"Yes, I do." Jessie forced herself not to leave. "How are you doing, mouse? Feeling better?"

"I'm okay, I guess." Grace rolled on her side. "I think I was just carsick."

"I should have cleaned up the mess."

"It's okay. Mom did it."

"I didn't mean that. I mean about Dad."

"I'm sad. I can't talk about him or I'll cry."

"Me, too."

"How's Mom?"

"Mom's mom. She'll be fine."

"She said you're going to have to wear a dress at the service."

"I know."

"Are you?"

"Yes. For Dad." Jessie glanced at the empty pet cage on Grace's dresser. "Gonna get another hamster?"

"Maybe. I still miss Lucky."

"Lucky didn't do very much except eat and sleep. Whenever you held him he pooped in your hand. Is there something better you want? An iguana, maybe?"

"No!"

"How about a snake? A boa constrictor?"

Grace's eyes widened in horror. Before she could answer, Jessie's phone trembled. It was a text from Garrett. "Gotta go."

"But—"

Jessie ran into her room and slammed the door behind her. The text read: "Wow. That's some serious shit. Think it's NITRON."

"No way," wrote Jessie. "NITRON's for WCs."

NITRON was a software language used exclusively by wireless carriers—WCs—namely phone companies like Sprint, AT&T, and ONE Mobile.

"You mess with the handset?" wrote Garrett. "Maybe you got 'em pissed."

Jessie had never considered that it might have been something she'd done that had erased her father's message. "Didn't touch it. Swear."

"No worries. We can ask Linus in class."

Linus was Linus Jankowski, the TA who taught Jessie's summer school computer class. The course was titled "Exercises in Extracurricular Programming," but everyone in class called it the Hack Shack.

"For sure," texted Jessie. "He'll know." The thought offered some relief. No one knew more about hacking than Linus. He'd almost won Capture the Flag at DEF CON last year.

"I'm really sorry about yr dad. That sux."

"I'm ok."

"No really. Feelin' for you."

"Tx."

"TTYL."

Jessie leaned against the door. She prayed that Garrett was wrong about the code being NITRON. She'd lied about not touching the handset. If the code had come from the mobile carrier, it meant they'd sent it because she'd unlocked the phone and that was against the rules. The code was probably an automated response she didn't know about that did something crazy to the phone.

Jessie slid to the floor and covered her head with her arms.

Maybe it *was* her fault that her father's last message had been erased.

21

Mary stood in the hall outside Joe's office. It was four. The house was too quiet. Jessie should be rummaging through the refrigerator, complaining that there was nothing good to eat. Grace should be in the living room, watching an episode of *Pretty Little Liars* for the umpteenth time. Instead of melancholy and loss, she felt anger. A will to act. The silence acted as a call to arms, as stirring as a bugler's tattoo. No one, she realized, was going to help her.

Mary flipped on the light. Joe's office was a small, wood-paneled room with venetian blinds and a rattan ceiling fan. She took a look around before sitting at his desk. There were magazines and folders and a few paperback books, as well as the latest tomes from Home Depot on a dozen do-it-yourself projects. She saw nothing of interest that might be from his work. No court orders, no case files, no subpoenas, no warrant requests.

Somewhere there was a clue to what he had been doing. Jessie said that anything you did on a phone left a mark. People left marks, too.

Mary opened the drawer. It contained a riot of pens and pencils, erasers and rubber bands, unused DVDs still in their wrapping, and plastic packs of Zantac. There was a box of his business cards and another containing cards he'd collected, mostly from fellow agents and colleagues in the law enforcement community. She ran a hand to the back. Her fingers touched another box, this one containing a variety of flash drives. Several were standard stick drives, but the others were more imaginative, designed to conceal the aluminum dock. She found a silver pendant shaped like a heart, a big fat car key, a box of matches, and her instant favorite, a pack of bubble gum.

Mary carried the flash drives into the kitchen. One after another she plugged them into the desktop. All were unused. She found no stored information anywhere. Another dead end.

She returned to Joe's office. A single personal decoration was on the desk: a small jolly brass Buddha, a souvenir of their time in Bangkok. They'd entertained Joe's Thai colleagues often, hosting barbecues on the terrace of their apartment overlooking the Chao Phraya River. It was Joe's practice to stage a charm offensive upon his arrival at a new posting. He'd invite the SAC, the agents he'd be working with, and any other noteworthy personalities. It was only now that Mary realized that Joe hadn't brought home any of his new colleagues from the Austin residency.

There was something else. It came to her that Joe had given up speaking about his work to her. The FBI didn't encourage its agents to divulge details of investigations to their spouses, but it wasn't the CIA either. The Bureau maintained nothing close to a code of absolute silence. There was no "bromerta" among agents. And yet she couldn't recall the last time he'd spoken to her about anything specific he was working on, other than the occasional trip to San Antonio for bureaucratic necessities.

She put down the Buddha and stood to leave. She paused at the entry and looked back. It took her a moment to spot what bothered her. The answer was nothing. The problem, she realized, was that the room was too clean.

Joe had the neatness habits of an eight-year-old. She'd spend an hour straightening up his office only for him to have it looking as if a hurricane had moved through ten minutes later. Her last effort to bring order from chaos had been five days ago. Since then, she knew, Joe had spent several late nights here, but there were no papers littering the floor, no empty cans of Red Bull in the trash.

And so? she asked herself. *What am I driving at?*

She didn't know. Something was just . . . *wrong.*

Everything . . . *and everyone* . . . left a trail.

Mary started at the door and walked the room's perimeter, tilting the bookcase, peering behind the easy chair, getting on her knees and looking under the desk. She found it lodged between the wall and the shredder. One crumpled-up ball of paper. She freed it gingerly and unfolded it on the desk, smoothing it with her palm.

Joe's nearly illegible scrawl covered the page. There were mostly numbers, an address, some names, and a whole lot of doodles. Hardly the treasure trove she'd hoped for.

A phone number was printed at the top of the page with the name Caruso below it, and then "Exp. Confirmed 7/25."

"Exp." meant what? Expired? July 25 was only a few days ago.

A few inches lower, printed diagonally across the page, was an address: "17990 Highway 290 East. 3PM." And then, a few inches further down: "FK. Nutty Brown Cafe. 1PM."

Mary shook her head. Only in Texas could there be a Nutty Brown Cafe.

Below this were doodles of sticks and triangles, a dozen of them at least.

Mary hurried to the bedroom for her iPad and returned. First she typed the address into the query window. A satellite photo of burned central Texas landscape appeared, with a white line denoting Highway 290 running through it. The X showing the location of the address appeared in the middle of a tract of scrub. She zoomed in and dotted property lines appeared. Closer still, and a name. "Flying V Ranch."

She zoomed out until the town of Dripping Springs appeared to the west.

The Flying V Ranch was where Joe had been killed.

Next Mary typed "Nutty Brown Cafe" into the query window. The café had its own website and advertised itself as a restaurant and outdoor music venue. Pictures showed a long, low-slung building set back off the highway, a white awning running its length bearing the café's name. A twenty-foot-tall neon cowboy slinging a lasso welcomed visitors. She plugged in the address and a map appeared showing the café to be located on Highway 290, fifteen miles east of Dripping Springs.

"FK. Nutty Brown Cafe. 1PM."

She assumed that Joe had met someone at the café at one p.m. yesterday. Was that someone "FK"?

She dredged through the names of Joe's colleagues, looking for one that started with an *F*. She didn't remember any, offhand. She asked ONELook to search "Boys' names beginning with F." A long list appeared, but she didn't remember any Farleys, Franks, or Fredericks.

Or was "FK" the informant's initials? Mary didn't think so. It didn't make sense to meet an informant in a public place, then drive out to a secluded ranch to meet him again a few hours later.

She returned to the phone number written at the top of the page. She picked up her phone and dialed. Four rings and then: "Angelo Caruso speaking."

"Hello, Mr. Caruso?"

"State your business." A crusty voice. Older. Tobacco-cured.

"I'm Mary Grant."

"Do I know you?"

"My husband was Joe Grant."

"Who's that?"

"Special Agent Joseph Grant of the FBI. He was killed yesterday."

A pause as Caruso cleared his throat. "I'm sorry for your loss, ma'am. But I don't think I can be of help."

"I saw your name and number on his pad and—"

"Then you know that I am a superior court judge for the state of Texas, Travis County. Any business I had with your husband must and shall remain confidential. May I ask why you are calling?"

"I had some questions about his work. I saw your name on his legal pad. I thought that maybe—"

"Your husband was a federal agent, Mrs. Grant. As such, his business did not concern his family. I suggest you halt your inquiries. Good day. And again, I am sorry for your loss."

Caruso hung up.

Mary lowered the phone, stunned by the man's bluntness. He might as well have slapped her across the face. Who was he to say that Joe's business did not concern her or that she should halt her inquiries?

"And F you too, Judge Asshole," she said aloud.

It was at that moment that Mary Margaret Olmstead Grant formally assumed the role of her husband's advocate, protector, and voice in this world.

I will find out what happened to you, Joe, she promised his spirit, though she had no idea what in the world she might be getting herself into. At that moment she didn't care. Something was being kept from her. She wanted to know what.

Mary studied the wrinkled paper, her eyes fixing on the doodles scrawled across its lower half. They were pairings of triangles colored solid blue with little sticks extending from one side. No, not that. She had it wrong. Twin sticks connected at one end like the hands on a wristwatch, each leading to a blue triangle. The triangles were positioned differently. The first at twelve and three. The second at four and eleven. The rest at odd variations thereof. Phone doodles made while Joe carried on a conversation.

Mary folded the paper in half and stood. The thought came to her that Don Bennett wasn't the only one hiding something.

And then she remembered that she still hadn't examined one thing.

Something that had come home from the hospital along with Joe's shoes, belt, wristwatch, Marine Corps tie clasp, and the beloved Saint Christopher medal he'd worn around his neck since the age of thirteen.

She ran upstairs.

22

Joe's belongings sat on her dresser where she'd left them the night before. A drawstring bag held his shoes and belt. A smaller zip-lock bag held his wristwatch, tie clasp, and Saint Christopher medal. Mary selected the remaining zip-lock bag, which contained his wallet. It was a standard leather billfold, scuffed and worn. A Christmas present from the girls to their dad three years before, to replace the horrid Velcro one he'd used for years. She removed it and looked inside. As usual, she was amused at how few credit cards Joe carried. There was a government-issued Visa for his work expenses and an American Express card for personal use.

Joe believed in paying off all his debts each month. It was a nice concept, but quaintly outdated in the era of a laptop for every student and prescription medications that cost $600 a month. Consequently Mary was in charge of family finances and merited an honorary degree in juggling balances between her four MasterCards and her bank custom credit line.

She slipped her fingers into the pouches beneath the cardholders. One side yielded several school portraits of the girls, an organ donor's card, and a business card for a roofer who'd visited the house a week ago to check on a leak Joe couldn't patch. At the bottom of the stack was a small, folded piece of paper, gossamer soft, fraying with age. Once it had been sky blue, but now it was white. She unfolded it carefully, her chest tightening as she realized what she held in her hands.

A younger woman's flowery, hopeful script read: "You have made me the happiest woman in the world. I love you. M."

Mary looked away quickly. It was the note she'd given Joe on their wedding day, hours before the ceremony. She hadn't thought about it since, yet here it was, soft and frayed, evidently unfolded and read hundreds of times over the years. The sky-blue paper, her youthful, innocent handwriting, the crazily optimistic words, were an indelible snapshot of one day in her life. It was something to cherish and to treasure. Something permanent. She looked at the words again, then folded the note and slipped it back into the wallet.

That was that.

Mary sighed. She was pleased to have discovered the wedding note but disappointed that Joe hadn't left her another clue. She wasn't sure what she'd expected to find . . . just something to add to the skein of information gleaned from the crumpled paper in Joe's office.

As an afterthought, she cracked open the wallet to count Joe's money. She thumbed through a ten, a five, and four ones. There was a receipt, too. It was from the Nutty Brown Cafe and dated yesterday. She stepped out of the closet to read it in the daylight.

The time listed was 2:05 p.m. Items included one cheeseburger, one French fries, one Coca-Cola, one egg-white omelet with green peppers. One coffee.

On the flip side Joe had penned, "SSA FK 7/29."

Mary forgot her disappointment. There was FK once again. If she was no closer to guessing his name, at least she knew more about him. "SSA" stood for Supervisory Special Agent. FK, whoever he might be, was not the informant. He worked for the FBI.

The walk-in closet was as big as Mary's childhood bedroom. Two cabinets hung from the ceiling, Mary's to the left. Joe's to the right. She opened her husband's. The smell of him wafted over her. Sandalwood and citrus. The scents were sharp and nearly provoked an onslaught of tears. Mary steeled herself and concentrated on the job at hand. Some spare change and a few golf tees were scattered across the top shelf. A box of matches from Chuy's, a fun Mexican place downtown.

She started on Joe's suits. He owned six or seven, usually buying two a year and retiring two. There weren't too many casual Fridays with the Bureau. She found a napkin from Whataburger in one pocket, a few dimes, a handkerchief, and a bonus card from the local car wash. Her movements grew sloppier in lockstep with her frustration. She stopped returning his slacks to the rack, instead dropping them onto the carpet. The pockets were empty. All of them.

When she'd finished, she put her hands on her hips and sighed. She'd succeeded only in messing up the closet. One by one she picked up the slacks and hung them. She fixed the jackets on their hangers just so, with a half-inch between them.

"Nothing good comes easy."

The admiral was having a last laugh.

A pile of dirty laundry lay in the corner. She scooped up the clothing, carried it to her bed, and dumped it there in a heap. Three shirts and a rumpled olive suit. She checked the pants first. A Kleenex. Two pennies. And a napkin from American Airlines with a tomato juice stain, which meant it came from a morning flight.

Memories of Joe flooded her mind.

He was seated next to her on a flight—she didn't know where from or where to. It was early in the morning and he'd just ordered a tomato juice from the attendant. She looked on as he emptied the can into the plastic cup, then raised his gaze to hers and stared into her eyes, saying nothing, saying everything, saying *I love you.*

Mary saw herself from a distance, shaking her head, smiling warily, thinking to herself, Don't spill that on your white shirt.

"Me?" said Joe. "Never."

Mary bolted at the sound of his voice. "Joe," she said aloud. "Are you here?"

He was there. He was with her in the bedroom.

The echo of her own words brought her back. The voice was in her head. Joe wasn't there. He'd never be there again.

Keep moving, she ordered herself. You haven't finished yet.

Mary ran a hand over the olive jacket. Her fingers delved into the pockets. She took hold of a piece of paper. She pulled and it snagged. She pulled again and came away with a boarding pass stub.

American Airlines. Grant, Mr. J. Flight 83. AUS—SJC. Seat 13D. Date: 6/1

On June 1, Mr. J. Grant had flown on American Airlines Flight 83 from Austin to San Jose.

Alarm bells sounded.

She checked the stub again. Yes . . . *San Jose.*

Mary ran downstairs to the kitchen and sat at the phone alcove. She opened the family agenda and flipped backward through the pages until she reached June 1.

"JG—San Antonio" read the entry in Joe's block-letter writing.

Mary looked at the boarding pass. Not San Antonio. *San Jose.* A difference of sixteen hundred miles.

They had a rule. No matter how sensitive the case, Joe must inform her when he was traveling long distance. In return, she promised never to ask why or what it was about. The rule was inviolate.

Honesty was their bond.

Mary closed the agenda as if slamming a door. She wiped at the tears running down her cheeks. Joe had lied.

No, she argued. Not Joe. It was the Bureau. They had forced him to lie.

But she couldn't accept that either. No one forced Joe to do anything. If he'd lied to her, it was his choice.

Mary slipped the boarding pass into her pocket.

Why, Joe? she demanded, some part of her still wondering if he just might be listening. What case could be so important as to warrant putting your wife's trust, your marriage, and even your family in jeopardy?

23

"Don't do it."

From her window, Jessie looked on as Grace jumped higher and higher on the Kramers' trampoline next door. On the fourth bounce she threw a front flip. Her feet landed well, but her forward momentum propelled her into the mesh siding. She appeared to strike the iron support bar and toppled to her side.

"Ouch," said Jessie. "Get up."

Her eye went to the Kramers' kitchen. Of course Mom was keeping an eye on Gracie, too. The sliding door rocketed open and her mom dashed to the trampoline. In their house it was all Grace, all the time.

Jessie pulled her e-cigarette from her pocket and sparked a hit. She wasn't jealous of the attention Grace got. It wasn't that. It was just annoying how everyone expected her always to be all right on her own. "Jess has her computers." Or "Jess doesn't like to be bothered." Or "She's happier by herself."

Yeah, right.

It didn't matter anyway.

In fact she was proud of her sister. All that time in the hospital. All the terrible stuff they did to her, the puking, losing her hair. And now she acted as if it had never happened. Saint Grace.

Jess looked on as her sister got to her feet, giggling, and her mom went back inside, white as a sheet.

"Again," Grace shouted, and started bouncing once more on the trampoline.

Jess shook her head. Her sister was pretty tough. She'd give her that.

She vaped again, then slipped her e-cig into her pocket and lay down on her bed with her laptop. Her wallpaper showed a picture of Def Leppard with all her favorite apps and icons of lots of her (supposed) favorite websites. She hit an encrypt key. Def Leppard disappeared and the Jolly Roger appeared, dotted from corner to corner with icons of her *real* favorite sites.

Jess double-clicked on an icon showing a large S. The Sugardaddies .com home page appeared and she felt the delicious tingle of excitement. It was her naughty feeling. She typed in her name, Lolita2000, and her password. Her profile page appeared. There was a picture of a tall, slim brunette in a bikini who was definitely not Jessie. Below it ran her description: "Good Girl Gone Bad. Naughty, but Oh So Nice." There followed a short tease. "Only the most discriminating gentlemen wanted. I'm a smart, young, motivated woman interested in being mentored by a successful gentleman. Located in northern California but willing to travel and dying to see the world. I love great cuisine, stimulating conversation, and long, deep kisses that make me feel like a woman."

She wasn't sure about that last part, but lots of other girls on the site said similar things.

Her mailbox showed that she'd received sixty-seven messages in the past two days. A sample of the headers included "Hey Classy Lady," from Nantucket Sailor; "Just How Naughty?" from Rich in NYC; and "You Are Smokin' Hot!" from Julio J. Studley. Jessie was pretty sure that wasn't his real name.

Halfway down the list she spotted a familiar handle: 40, Rich, and Bored.

Her heart quickened and she opened the message.

"Hi Lexie." Lexie was her Net name. "Still waiting on that special pic you promised to send. I sent you mine. Did you dig it? Hope you put the five hundred bucks to good use. Consider it a down payment on a good time when we hook up. Did I mention I just picked up a new Benz S Class? Be a good girl—or a bad one!!—and I'll buy you one, too. Gotta run. Send me that pic, pretty lady!"

She clicked on his handle, and several pictures of an okay-looking guy with dark hair and a tan standing next to a BMW came up. Forty was old, but not that old. Fifty was old. Forty was *almost* old, and this guy looked like he was younger. He even had a six-pack.

She opened another tab and typed in her bank's address, then logged in to her account. The balance stood at $3,575. 40, Rich, and Bored's payment of $500 had arrived the day before. At least she knew he wasn't lying about the rich part. He'd already sent $1,000 the month before. The thought made Jessie nervous and ashamed. She knew it wasn't right to steal money, but this wasn't exactly stealing. She asked for it and men sent it. Of course, she promised to send pictures of herself and also to do stuff to them when they met. Even so, they knew that they were taking a chance. They probably rubbed themselves off in the shower thinking about her. Pervs. If they were stupid enough to send money to any girl who asked, they deserved to lose it.

Jessie got up and glanced through the window, making sure that Grace and her mom were still next door. She walked to the mirror and tried out a few poses that she thought he might find sexy. She lifted up her shirt to expose her midriff. Polar bears were darker. She turned around and stuck her butt at the mirror. *God, no, Jess. Your ass is the size of a tractor.*

Maybe she should just send him a picture like the one he sent her. Totally naked. She picked up her phone and hit the camera app, feeling that naughty sensation, daring herself to go for it . . .

The front door slammed. Terrified, Jessie froze. Footsteps drummed up the stairs. Jessie threw herself onto the bed. A second later Grace opened her door and bounded into the room. "Jess, guess what?"

Jess hit the encrypt key. The Sugardaddies website disappeared and was replaced by her fake home screen. She looked up, bored beyond measure, even as her heart was exploding. "What now?"

"Mom said we might get a dog."

"Oh."

"Wouldn't that be incredible? I mean, we've wanted one for so long. A dog!"

Jessie looked back at her laptop. "Yeah," she said. "Awesome."

24

It was nine p.m. when Tank Potter arrived at the office of the Travis County medical examiner. The doors were locked. A single bulb burned at the end of the corridor. Tank rapped his knuckles against the glass and did his best to stand up straight. He'd kept himself on a tight leash all afternoon. One snort from his backstop an hour, strictly for medicinal purposes. By tomorrow the shakes would be a thing of the past.

A thin, dark-haired man in a lab coat rounded the corner and hurried down the corridor. Tank raised his hand in the Longhorn salute—pinkie and index finger extended, his other fingers curled into a fist. "Hook 'em, Horns."

"Hook 'em, Horns," replied Carlos Cantu, raising his own hand in salute as he opened the door. "Hey, buddy. We're closing up shop. I can give you five minutes."

"That ought to do." Tank stepped inside the building and followed Cantu down the hall to the "icebox," the room where the corpses were stored. The medical examiner shared space with the city morgue and handled autopsies for Travis and five surrounding counties, a geographic footprint that included Dripping Springs. Cantu wasn't the ME or even the forensic investigator. He was just a morgue assistant whom Tank had known since his playing days, when he'd been a star and Cantu a student trainer who'd wrapped his ankle, laundered his uniforms, and folded his towels. Tank had kept in touch over the years, if only for this purpose.

"Thought you were covering politics these days," said Cantu.

"I'm back in the saddle," said Tank, dodging the question. "Wouldn't miss this one for the world."

"Something's up with this guy. No question."

"Really?"

The morgue looked no different from when he'd last visited, three years ago. Low ceiling, fluorescent lights, white tile floor and walls,

and the inescapable, eye-watering scent of ammonia. Cantu pulled a
holding tray out of the wall. The informant lay inside a pale green body
bag. "We had the FBI in here all day, asking lots of questions."

"One of 'em Don Bennett?"

"Who's he?"

"SAC in the Austin office. Bald, mustache, looks like he has a rake
up his ass."

"He was here. But he wasn't the one in charge."

"Who was?"

"Short, gray-haired guy. New Yorker. All business."

"Name?"

Cantu shook his head. "Ted? Or Ed? All I know is that he was the
one ordering Doc Donat around and telling him what to do with the
bodies."

"What do you mean? The ME's required by law to do an autopsy."

"That's just it. They're sending the bodies to D.C. for the postmortems. I'm supposed to have them ready for transshipment by tomorrow at noon."

"Both?"

"The guy with half a head and the FBI dude."

Tank took this in. He was fairly certain that sending a body out of
state for autopsy was not standard operating procedure. Postmortems
of homicide victims were conducted by the nearest medical examiner.
It was a question of cost, convenience, and timeliness. Decomposition
began the moment a heart stopped beating and accelerated as time
went on.

Carlos Cantu had one hand on the zipper. "Didn't have a bean-and-
cheese burrito for dinner, did you?"

Tank said he had not.

"Fair warning." Cantu unzipped the body bag. Tank looked, then
looked away, sucking down a gulp of air to steady himself. Timidly he
returned his gaze to "the guy with half a head." One eye remained, the
lower half of a nose, lips, and a chin. The rest of the skull and brain was
gone as cleanly as if a shovel had sheared it away.

The FBI's press release stated that Special Agent Joseph Grant had
been mortally wounded in the course of debriefing an informant but
had managed to kill said informant prior to expiring himself. Tank had
seen plenty of dead bodies. His time on the murder beat had given

him a lesson in the fine art of gunshot wounds, from .22s that looked like little more than cigarette burns to .44 Magnums that went in big and came out bigger. No handgun was capable of this kind of damage. Tank's childhood of hunting deer and javelinas told him that only a high-caliber rifle was capable of shearing off that much of a man's head with a single shot.

"Can I look at the other guy? The Fibbie?"

Cantu dug his hands into his lab coat. "I'm pushing it as it is, Tank. I have to be out of here by nine-fifteen."

Tank peeled off a twenty and put it in Cantu's hand. "Would have bought us a case of Heini's back in the day."

"I'm good with a sixer of Shiner Bock." Cantu pocketed the bill, marched down the row, and pulled out the tray bearing Joseph Grant's corpse. He unzipped the bag and pulled it over the corpse's shoulders, revealing the mortal wound. It was apparent that the body had come straight from the hospital. There was still tape around the mouth and dried blood all over the chest and torso. Grant had been shot a single time in the chest. The entry wound was the size of Tank's middle finger, a round black hole.

"Can you lift him up?"

Cantu hoisted the corpse, exposing an exit wound the size and appearance of a crushed grapefruit. Tank had two impressions. First, no handgun did that kind of damage. Second, the diameter of the entry wound was too big to come from a pistol. They added up to a single, undeniable fact: Don Bennett was lying.

It was evident why the FBI wanted to get the bodies into friendly hands and away from prying eyes. Away from reporters like Tank.

"Can I put him down now?" grunted Cantu.

"Sure thing." Tank walked back to the informant. He was already growing accustomed to the gruesome corpse—getting his sea legs back, so to speak. "No name on this guy?"

"John Doe."

"Where's his wallet?"

"All his valuables had been removed."

"You lift his prints, dental records?"

"What for? The feds knew who he was."

"Let me see his papers."

"In the ME's office with the valuables. Locked."

Tank looked closely at the body. He tagged him early forties, five-nine or so, arms and legs like pins, soft belly, no tats, nice fingernails. He lifted one of the hands. Not a callus, scratch, or scar. A man who'd never done a day's labor in his life. White-collar all the way. He noted that the ring finger on the left hand was creased but was not paler than the rest of the finger. He inferred that the informant had separated from his wife or divorced in the past ninety days. Someone would be missing him soon.

Tank used his phone to take photographs of the bodies.

"No pictures," said Carlos Cantu. "You know the rules."

"I'm not putting it on YouTube."

"Erase them. Please."

"I can't do that. Not this time."

Cantu blocked the door, arms crossed. Tank freed two more twenties from his money clip and extended them, something between a bribe and a peace offering. Cantu took the bills.

"Burning your bridges, Tank."

"This may be the last one I'm crossing."

25

Carlos Cantu returned to the icebox to put away the bodies. Forty years old and taking bribes to make ends meet. Not quite the way he'd expected things to turn out.

He slid the trays into their lockers and cleaned up the room, remembering the sunny afternoons at Royal Stadium, the burnt-orange jerseys running up and down the field, eighty thousand wildly cheering fans filling the stands, the old siege cannon firing after every touchdown.

The good ol' days.

Cantu laughed dispiritedly. He'd been too much of a runt to play, but he'd enjoyed being a trainer. It had been his dream to become a doctor, but he'd dropped out senior year to look after his mother, who was ill. Time passed. His mother died. He'd never stopped wanting to be a doctor, or even a physical therapist. Somehow he never managed to get a degree.

Finished cleaning up, Carlos turned off the lights and locked the door. He checked that all the offices were empty and that he was the last to leave. On his way out he stopped at his desk. Unlocking his file drawer, he took out a zip-lock bag containing a wallet, a gold bracelet, and a wristwatch. He'd lied to Tank. It had been his job to bag the informant's valuables. Dutifully he placed the man's wallet and bracelet into an evidence bag and sealed it. He kept the watch for himself. It was a Patek Philippe. Swiss. Perpetual calendar. Eighteen-karat gold. Crocodile strap. Retail price $126,000, according to a site on the Net. He hoped to auction it off for no less than half that amount.

He turned it over in his hand. There were initials engraved on the back of the case.

"To H.S. Thanks, I."

26

Mary Grant was coming to life before his eyes. Image by image. Pixel by pixel.

Not a picture of her. Ian Prince had no practical interest in her physical appearance. Standing in the center of his office at a few minutes before ten p.m., he was looking into her true self, her life as defined by her activity online.

Ian was having Mary Margaret Olmstead Grant *indexed*.

The office was large and airy, the size of a tennis court, with wooden floors and a vaulted ceiling. Windows offered a vista across the Meadow toward Great Tom. Ian's gaze was not on the illuminated belfry, however, but on the holographic images that rose from knee level and formed a circular tower around him—a patchwork quilt of the web pages Mary Grant visited on a regular basis.

There was her home page at Amazon and her log-on page at Chase. There was her Facebook page and her Shutterfly account. Mapquest and Google. WebMD and Pandora. Citicards and Wells Fargo. There was the *Austin American-Statesman* and the *New York Times. Huffington Post* and *Drudge Report*. Yet another showed the portal to her health insurance company. Some of the pages were recent, as reported by the tap put on the Grant family's online access earlier in the day. But more had come from her browsing history.

Another panel showed pages linked to her Social Security number. These included her credit report, mortgage information, home equity line of credit (from Sacramento), and federal tax information as reported to the IRS.

It was simplicity itself to retrieve the information. All ONE servers were powered by software containing a collection filter that Ian alone was able to access. The filter looked for all manner of personal data, everything from phone numbers to credit card numbers to Social Security numbers, and once found, stored it permanently. Ninety-one percent of all traffic on the Internet passed through a server, router, or switch manufactured by ONE.

He touched a screen hovering in front of his nose. The portal to the *Austin American-Statesman* opened. He noted that she'd been reading the article about her husband. Nothing strange there. He touched the screen and it shrank to its original size.

Next he looked at Mary Grant's account at Chase Bank. Until he had a password, he could not go deeper. Likewise, he could not access her detailed credit card records or her insurance accounts.

Ian touched the screen and the page shrank to its original size.

For now, Mary Grant's index was a precaution. If and when she became a threat, he would obtain her passwords. It would not be difficult. He would dig deeper. The circular tower would grow to contain hundreds of web pages. He would know everything Mary Grant had done in the past and everything she was doing in the present.

Most important, he would know everything she would do in the future.

27

It was late. The girls were asleep. Or at least Grace was. Jessie no doubt was on her laptop, doing whatever she did until all hours. Mary padded downstairs to Joe's office. She had on her sweats and one of Joe's Georgetown T-shirts. He was in her thoughts constantly, so much so that she felt almost as if he were still alive, only in a different form. Every doubt, he extinguished. Every fear, he allayed. She had only to say "I can't," for him to counter, "Of course you can."

Mary set down her mug of tea and her iPad. Seated at his desk, she dug the boarding card out of her pocket. Her eye found the seven-digit code below his name. 7XC5111. Joe's frequent-flyer membership number.

She called up the American Airlines web page, then selected "Rewards Program" and entered Joe's number. A box asked for his password. She typed it in and was directed to Joe's page.

Hon, she said to him, you're so easy.

Mary had warned herself to be ready. Where there was smoke, there was fire. If Joe hadn't told her about one trip to San Jose, there would be others, to either San Jose or elsewhere.

The page listed Joe's recent trips. She began counting at the top of the page and continued through two more. Twenty-seven flights in all. She had her agenda open and ticked off each trip against her record. Many flights matched perfectly. She recalled Joe's comments about the cases he was covering at the time. She had no qualms with those.

But many did not. There were two in November. One in December. Three in January. And so on through July.

Not just fire; a five-alarm blaze.

The phone rang. The call was from the funeral home. "Mrs. Grant, this is Horace Feely. I'm sorry to disturb you so late, but there seems to be a problem."

Mary turned her chair away from the desk. "I'm listening."

"To be brief, we're unable to take possession of your husband. Usually the medical examiner releases the body after the autopsy has been performed. However, there seems to have been a delay."

"What kind of delay?"

"In performing the postmortem. At the FBI's request, the medical examiner has exercised his right to keep your husband's body until such further time as decided. I would count on a week minimum."

"A week. But—" Mary bit back her words. Anger wouldn't change anything. She thanked the funeral director and hung up.

She put down the phone. No one had informed her that an autopsy was to be performed on her husband. What could a medical examiner find that the surgeons hadn't? It was all part of the scheme, she realized. First Don Bennett refusing to help her retrieve Joe's message, then Judge Caruso telling her to halt her inquiries, and now a delay of at least a week in performing the postmortem.

Not a scheme.

A conspiracy.

But for what? she asked, only to laugh derisively at her naïveté. Weren't conspiracies always about the same thing?

Mary turned back to the desk and tallied her findings. Beginning in November of the past year, Joe had made sixteen trips to San Jose without her knowledge. Twelve while the family was in Sacramento and four since the move to Texas. For these most recent trips, the notations in the agenda read "Bastrop," "San Antonio," "fieldwork," and so on. Never once was there a mention of San Jose.

Sixteen trips were enough.

Mary put down her pen. The conclusion was there to see plain as day. Joe had not come to Austin to work on municipal corruption cases. He'd come to follow a case that had begun in Sacramento, a case that required him to fly to San Jose, California, on a frequent basis and that had ended with him being shot by an informant while sitting in his car on an abandoned ranch in the middle of nowhere.

Mary powered down the iPad. For an hour she sat drinking her tea, contemplating her new reality. There were lies and there was deception, and then there was this: a secret life.

An idea came to her. Joe hadn't called just to say he was in trouble. He knew she wouldn't be able to help. He'd called to tell her the truth.

Joe knew about the conspiracy, too.

28

Darkness.

A penlight illuminates a patch of wall. Trophies on a shelf. A basketball. The pale light stops on a poster of a football player, #52 of the San Francisco '49ers. Then closer. An autograph: "To Billy Merriweather, Your friend, Patrick Willis."

The light moves again. Now it is on the boy's face. He lies asleep on his bed, sheets pulled to his chin. He is nine or ten. Blond. We are closer now, close enough to see the fuzz on his cheek. A hand approaches the boy's face. The hand holds a knife. It is a stiletto, the blade long, slim, razor-sharp. The blade traces the chin, the nose, and stops a breath from the boy's closed eye. As frightening is the tattoo visible on the man's hand. It is a skull with vipers squirming to escape the empty sockets.

A man whispers, "Die."

End.

All this in six seconds.

Repeat.

Darkness.

A penlight illuminates a patch of wall. Trophies . . .

"How many times are you going to watch that?" asked Shanks.

"You don't like it?" asked the Mole.

"I liked it fine the first twenty times."

The two men had exchanged the white work van for a custom-built Mercedes Airstream and were parked in a commercial lot a mile from Mary Grant's house.

The Mole put away his phone. He'd made several more Vines, six-second clips that he uploaded to the Net. All were similar in content. Only the actors differed.

He'd filmed the first inside John Merriweather's brother's home. It showed a sleeping couple and his straight-edge razor. A second came from inside the home of Merriweather Systems' cofounder and second largest stockholder. The last was his favorite. It came from the home of John Merriweather's daughter. Like the Vine he'd just watched, it featured a child—in this case, a six-year-old girl with black hair and a delicious birthmark on her cheek. It had been a warm night and the girl had been sleeping on top of her covers. At the very last moment he'd touched the birthmark with the tip of the blade.

"They worked," he said. "The Merriweather deal went through, didn't it?"

"Is that what they were for?"

"Don't fuck with me," said the Mole. "You know good and well. Briggs loved 'em. Said they even scared the hell out of him."

Shanks moved to the rear of the van and lay down.

The Mole watched the Vine again. He was thinking of the girls inside the house. He wanted to film a Vine with them.

WEDNESDAY

29

At seven a.m. the sun bore down on the tarmac of Ben Gurion Airport on the outskirts of Tel Aviv. It had been a hot summer in the eastern Mediterranean. The last rain had fallen one hundred days earlier. In the north, the olive groves of Judea were withering. The River Jordan had dwindled to a trickle. The forecast for the days ahead offered no relief. Once again in its tortured history, the state of Israel was under siege.

Inside the private air terminal, a group of ten men milled freely in the air-conditioned lounge. Most were in their forties and fifties. All were slim, tanned, and fit. They dressed similarly in dark blazers, open-collared shirts, and pressed slacks. The habit of wearing a uniform was too deeply ingrained to discard altogether. They spoke in hushed tones, never raising their voices. This, too, was a habit. In the secret world, even a whisper could be too loud. The men knew a thing or two about listening.

The transit bus arrived. The men filed out of the building and climbed aboard. None availed himself of a seat as the bus drove across the airfield, darting in between Lufthansa jumbo jets and El Al 787s taxiing for takeoff. All stared intently out the windows, as if memorizing the surroundings.

The bus continued to the southern edge of the field. Its destination was a gleaming white Boeing 737 parked at the far corner. The plane bore no insignia apart from a stylized Roman numeral I painted on its tail. A blond flight attendant welcomed the men aboard with a broad smile and a personal greeting. "Good morning, General Gold . . . Colonel Wolkowicz . . . Major Aaron . . ."

The men were impressed, even if no one commented. It had been years since they'd been addressed by their rank, and never by a buxom blonde with a pleasing Texan drawl.

Once aboard, all were free to sit where they chose. The plane offered thirty seats, two to a row. Each seat was its own private sleep station, with a recumbent lounger, desk, and entertainment center.

Aft was a lounge with couches, desks, a kitchen with gourmet food, and a fully stocked bar.

The flight attendant passed through the cabin taking orders for pre-flight libations. Nine of the men ordered orange juice—again the habit of lifelong soldiers. Only David Gold ordered a beer, but he was the group's leader and not subject to group norms. The beer was a Lone Star. Of course it was.

Gold looked around him. At Aaron and Wolkowicz. At Stern and Silverman. The past seemed to well up around him. He saw them as they'd been in their newly issued khaki uniforms, hair shorn, standing at attention inside the barracks at Glilot. How long ago was it? Twenty years? Thirty?

Even then they had been brilliant. Top graduates of his country's university's electrical engineering and computer science programs. He had not been able to spare them the rigors and indignities of basic train-ing. Nor had he wished to. Though they would never lift a weapon in their country's defense, they required toughness nonetheless. The task of listening demanded unimagined stamina.

"You are now members of Unit 8200," he had announced all those years ago, "the most important unit inside the Israel Defense Forces. It is your job to keep our country safe."

Started in 1952 with a roomful of surplus American radio equip-ment, Unit 8200—also known as the Central Collection Unit of the Intelligence Corps—was responsible for every aspect of the nation's signals intelligence operations. It was the unit's job to monitor all security-related intelligence from television, radio, newspapers, and, more recently, the Internet. In the United States, the National Security Agency performed a similar function. In Great Britain, the surveillance corps went by the name GCHQ, the Government Com-munications Headquarters.

No one, however, could spy like the Israelis. In terms of engineer-ing skill, operational creativity, and sheer audacity, they had allies and enemies beat by a mile.

For years Gold had led the unit, turning raw recruits into the sav-viest band of surveillance artists the world had ever known. But that was then. A man had to make a living. He had to support a family. A life on a government salary held little appeal.

So when David Gold left the army, he took his recruits and their skills with him and founded a company to sell those skills to the highest bidder. He named the company Clarus. And it flourished.

The flight attendant closed the forward door. Minutes later she requested that they all take their seats and attach their safety belts. The plane trembled as it began its transit to Runway 29er. The captain welcomed his esteemed cargo aboard and announced that flying time to Austin, Texas, would be seventeen hours, including a refueling stop in Tenerife, Canary Islands.

The plane was lightly loaded and took off steeply into a royal-blue sky. The men gazed out the windows and took a last look at their home, the land of Isaac and Abraham. The plane banked to the west and in minutes was cruising at an altitude of 41,000 feet over the Mediterranean Sea.

The executives from the Clarus Corporation relaxed and retreated deep into their thoughts. They would not be coming home for a long while. Yet not one regretted his choice.

They were all about to become enormously wealthy.

30

Up at first light.

Mary was a sailor's daughter, trained to rise without lingering. By the time her feet hit the floor she had a dozen tasks lined up and ranked in order of importance. She brushed her teeth, washed her face, and combed her hair. She avoided her eyes. It was not a day for soul-searching and self-pity. Joe wouldn't have it. It was a day for action.

Finished in the bathroom, she padded down the hall and checked on the girls. Jessie lay on top of her sheet, legs splayed, phone within reach of her hand. She was like a secret agent who never slept without her gun hidden beneath her pillow.

Mary left the room and continued down the hall. Grace lay solemnly beneath her sheet, her breathing measured, her position unchanged from when Mary had tucked her in.

Squirm. Struggle. Knock off the sheets.

If she wanted Jessie calmer, she prayed that Grace be more forceful. One child fought too much, the other not nearly enough.

Gently she pulled back the sheet. She saw it and her breath caught. There on Grace's thigh, where she'd hit the side of the trampoline enclosure, was a bruise the size of a tennis ball. Or was it something else? Something that had weakened Gracie's system so that she had vomited when she'd taken her new medicine?

The disease was known as acute lymphoblastic leukemia, or ALL. In its most basic form it was a cancer of the white blood cells. Some mutation in Grace's DNA caused her body's bone marrow continually to produce malignant immature white blood cells, which crowded out the normal blood cells in the marrow before spreading to other organs. The overall cure rate in children was 80 percent, but the doctors worried that Grace might have a more aggressive variety of the disease, one that had the potential to go crazy really fast and be fatal in weeks or even days. Though the illness had been under control, Mary could never stop worrying. Every bruise was a cause for concern. The perpetual uncertainty was a mother's worst nightmare.

Mary rearranged the sheet as it had been. Grace didn't move a muscle.

Mary kissed her fingers and touched her daughter's forehead. "Love you, mouse."

In the kitchen Mary brewed a pot of coffee, then powered up the desktop and entered the address for the local paper. She was anxious to learn what new information the FBI had revealed about Joe's death and in particular whether they'd released the name of the informant. To her bewilderment, there was no mention of the shooting on the front page. She had to go all the way to page nine to find an article about Joe, and even then it was unsatisfying. There was no news about the informant's identity. The only new material discussed Joe's career at the FBI. One line in particular gnawed at her. "Grant was passed over for promotion to headquarters earlier in the year and transferred from Sacramento to aid in the Austin residency's criminal investigations."

Mary fumed. Who were they to say Joe was passed over? Again she felt Don Bennett's hand at work. She shifted in her seat, recalling his pat explanation: "The investigation is closed. I told you what happened."

Liar.

Mary checked the *New York Times* and *Washington Post* websites. Neither offered further insight into her husband's death. Worse, both carried the same line about Joe's being passed over for promotion. It was a smear, pure and simple, a purposeful effort to besmirch his reputation and shift blame for the shooting away from the Bureau and onto him.

Mary opened her drawer and took out the boarding pass stub for the flight from Austin to San Jose. In the past Joe had traveled frequently with a fellow agent named Randy Bell. Randy had been over to the house dozens of times. He was a kind, avuncular man ten years Joe's senior. It was only then that she realized that Randy hadn't called to offer his condolences.

She still had his number programmed into her phone. Six a.m. in Austin meant four a.m. in Sacramento. She made a mental note to call him in a few hours.

She spent a few minutes reading e-mails, checking her bank balance.

Thoughts of the future elbowed their way to the front of her mind. Worries about money, about Grace, about . . . well, everything.

A knock on the sliding glass door made her jump. Carrie Kramer stood in her running gear, pointing at her watch. Six a.m. Mondays, Wednesdays, and Fridays was their designated run time. Once the sun rose above the treetops, it grew too warm for anything but a brisk walk.

"Not today," said Mary as she unlocked the sliding door.

"What do you mean? It's six. Let's motor."

Mary thought of Grace and the blasts and the boarding pass and the call she needed to make to Randy Bell. "I can't. There's too much—"

"Three miles before it gets hot. Come on. You need to do this."

Mary put aside the iPad. Carrie was right. Running cleared her mind and kept her sane. Today she needed that respite more than ever. "Give me a second."

She returned in five minutes. She looked at Carrie and laughed. Both were wearing blue shorts, white T's, and white caps, ponytails pulled through the hole. "Twins," she said.

"And the girls—still sleeping?"

"No one opens an eye until eight," said Mary lightly, refusing to worry about Grace until she got back. "You're right. I need to do this. Let's go out the front."

"Twenty-nine minutes," said Carrie.

"You're on."

31

"We've got some action," said the Mole.

He and Shanks sat in the work area of the Mercedes Airstream. The interior was a hive of high-definition monitors and state-of-the-art surveillance equipment. The van was engineered for use by law enforcement and built by Guardian TSE ("technical surveillance equipment"), one of hundreds of companies owned by ONE Technologies. Images from the camera the Mole had installed the day before lit up the screen. The men watched the women leave the house and start their run.

"Which one you want?" asked Shanks. "Me, I like the one with the yellow shoes and the nice ass. You can have the one with the big rack."

"Not my type," said the Mole.

"Ah, yeah. I forgot. You don't like 'em that way."

"What way is that?"

"Ripe."

Another screen listed all online activity performed by the computers inside the house on Pickfair Drive, each device identified by its specific fifteen-digit IP number. The Mole checked the recent sites visited. *Austin American-Statesman. New York Times. Washington Post.* He clicked on each and was rewarded with links to the articles Mary Grant had read, the time spent on each site. It appeared that she was checking on her husband. Nothing mysterious about that.

Afterward she'd accessed her e-mail account, but the site was encrypted and he was unable to see whose mail she read or to whom she'd sent messages.

So far this morning, Mary Grant was being a good girl.

The Mole stood and moved into the driver's seat.

"What are you doing?" asked Shanks.

"We're taking a ride. I'm not going to sit inside this van forever."

The Mole left the parking lot and drove past the Grants' house, stopping a half block farther on. Shanks put a hand on his shoulder. "Don't."

"Move your hand before I cut it off."

"If Briggs finds out—"

"If?" said the Mole. "That's the point of this exercise."

Shanks looked at the Mole. Little guy. Five-eight, tops. One hundred and fifty pounds dripping wet. He could tear a runt like that apart limb by limb. Yet the Mole sent a shiver down his spine as surely as if it were the Reaper staring him in the eye. He pulled his hand away. "All you, man."

The Mole chuckled, his tongue dashing over his lips.

The sliding door at the rear of the house was unlocked. The kitchen appeared empty. The Mole slid the door on its track and stepped inside. Head cocked, he listened. He loved this moment most: the thrill of trespass. He crossed the room and peered around the corner. He saw no one. He turned and made a circuit of the kitchen, an eye open for Mary Grant's cell phone. He picked up a tablet, but it was locked and would take far too long to break into.

Another scan of the countertops. No phone.

He returned to the hall. A bowl by the front door held car keys, chewing gum, mints, but nothing of interest. He climbed the stairs. A door on either side of the hall. The nearest was ajar. He nudged it open. A blond head peeked from beneath the covers. Golden hair. Flushed cheeks. His breath hitched. It was the younger girl, Grace.

Half against his will, he stepped inside, forgetting all about Mary Grant's phone. He wanted a trophy. He held his phone in front of him, slipped his knife free, the stiletto. He moved his hand into the frame, making sure the tattoo was visible, and began filming.

The hand moved the blade toward the girl's cheek, her ruby lips, her fluttering eyelids. He smelled her breath.

Across the hall, a footfall. The floor groaned beneath a person's weight.

The Mole hurried out of the room. A look toward the master bedroom. He saw a phone on the nightstand. Inches away, a shadow passed beneath the door. It was the other daughter.

Still, the Mole did not flee. He clutched the stiletto tightly, asking himself if the moment had come. If, finally, he would act on his desires. His fingers tingled with anticipation.

All she had to do was open the door.

The shadow moved and he walked down the stairs and left the house.

32

"You won."

Mary bent over, hands on her knees, breathing hard. Sweat dripped from her brow onto the ground.

"Today doesn't count," said Carrie, bent over double right next to her.

"Thanks."

"Was I right?"

Mary stood up, finally catching her breath. They'd done three miles in twenty-eight minutes. Not their best, but far from their worst. "Yes," she said. "You were right. I needed that."

"What time do you leave tomorrow?"

"We're not. They're keeping Joe longer to do an autopsy."

"Oh?" said Carrie. "Is that normal?"

"The funeral home director says it is. There's nothing I can do about it. To tell you the truth, I'm relieved. The girls don't love Boston."

Mary walked up the front path and entered the house. In the kitchen she poured them both a glass of water. Carrie drank hers down and set the glass in the sink. "Have you started thinking about what's next for you and the girls?"

"Not yet."

"Did Joe leave much?"

"There's his pension and life insurance." *$6,000 a month and a check for $00,000*

"What about savings?"

"With two kids, on a government salary? At least we'll still get his health coverage. Either way, I'm going to have to go back to work."

"What about med school? You told me you wanted to be a doctor. This could be your chance."

"Four years before internship and residency. Yeah, right."

"So you've thought about it?"

"Long enough to know it's not going to happen." Mary looked at Carrie, then looked away. She would consider her options at a future date. After she figured out what had happened to her husband.

"If you need something in the meantime . . . you know, something to tide you over. Mark's making bank these days. Maybe he can get Jess something at Apple next summer. You know, an internship."

"That's sweet, but we're okay." Mary gave Carrie a hug and squeezed her tight for a long time. "Thanks."

Carrie checked her watch. "Gotta run. You okay?"

Mary nodded and gave her bestie another hug. Carrie left through the sliding door.

Mary went upstairs and showered, reminding herself to call Randy Bell as soon as she got out. She remembered he liked his scotch. Maybe she'd catch him hungover and in a mood to spill about his and Joe's trips to San Jose.

Finished, she towel-dried her hair. Once or twice she heard a faint noise and stopped to listen, but then it was gone. She brushed her hair and got dressed for day two of widowhood. No black for her. She chose tan shorts and a navy T. Joe would have liked it this way. She went into the bedroom and heard the noise again. Someone was moaning.

Grace.

She ran down the hall and opened the door to her daughter's room. The girls lay on top of the bed, Jessie pointing at the bruise on Grace's thigh and laughing. "She looks like a Minion, Mom. All yellow with a big black dot in the middle."

Grace knocked her sister's hand away. "Tell her to stop teasing me."

Jess kept pointing. "No, not like a Minion. It's like grackle poo. Even worse."

Grackles were loud, obnoxious birds the size of crows that clustered in the hundreds at shopping malls and parking lots around the city.

"Jess, please," said Mary. "Be nice."

"Grace has grackle poo on her leg."

"Mom."

"Jessie, stop bothering your sister."

"She called me fat."

"I did not. I was just watching a video when Jess came in and started bothering me."

Mary sat on the bed beside Grace. "Does it hurt?"

"No," said Grace. "It's nothing."

Mary fetched an ice pack from the freezer. When she returned the girls were friends again, shoulder to shoulder, watching a video on the laptop. Gingerly she placed the ice pack on Grace's leg, but Grace paid no attention.

"What are you guys doing up so early?" asked Mary.

"You woke me up," said Jessie without looking at her. "I heard you walking around Grace's room."

"You did?"

"Then I heard you shut the sliding door."

"But Carrie and I went out the front."

"Whatever." Jessie turned her attention back to the video playing.

Mary dismissed Jessie's comment as . . . well, just Jessie. She craned her neck to look at the computer. The girls were watching some kind of animal in a crib. It had its paws on the railing and seemed to have a silly expression on its face. "What in the world is that?"

"A sloth," said Jessie.

"A what?"

"A two-toed South American tree sloth," said Grace between giggles. "Isn't he cute?"

Mary turned away to wipe at a tear, drawing a breath and telling herself to relax. When she looked back at the laptop, she was smiling. "Yes, he is cute," she said, trying to get in the spirit of things. "You just want to cuddle him, don't you?"

Jessie sprang up onto an elbow. "Can we get one? Please!"

33

After Mom and Jess left, Grace looked up sloths on Wikipedia. She was fascinated to learn that they slept twenty-three hours a day and that it took them an hour to walk one hundred yards. They really were as slow as everyone said. She decided that she loved sloths, even if her mom had said that there was no way on God's green earth they were ever getting one.

Grace closed the laptop and sat up. The sudden movement made her wince. Her leg felt as if it were glued to her hip. It didn't want to move. She looked toward the door to make sure it was closed and no one was watching, then she stood up. It took her a while, and it hurt a lot. She was glad no one could see.

She went into the bathroom and pulled up her nightgown. She prodded her thigh and gasped. Bruises didn't usually hurt so badly. Maybe it was the other thing. The thought frightened her so much she wanted to cry. She bit on her finger to stop. It wouldn't be fair to Mommy to tell her. Not now, with Daddy gone. Mommy had enough problems.

Grace limped back to her bed. She spent a minute talking to her father, asking if he was all right. He didn't answer. She thought that was because he wasn't in heaven yet. She didn't really believe in heaven. At least, not like in the Bible. She believed in something else. Something just as good. It was warm and welcoming and somewhere up in the night sky. She knew her dad was there and he'd talk to her when he could.

Grace needed to ask him about the bruise. The doctor said she was all better, but Grace had read lots about the disease that had tried to kill her. She knew that not all girls got cured. Someone had to be one of the two out of ten who didn't make it.

She took another look at the bruise. She told herself it was from the trampoline. It wasn't cancer. God wouldn't do that to their family. Not after taking Dad.

She decided not to tell Mommy about her leg. She didn't think she could take it right now.

34

"Mine."

Fort George C. Meade sat on five thousand acres of rolling Maryland countryside twenty-six miles northeast of Washington, D.C. First opened in 1917, it was chosen as the home of the National Security Agency in the 1950s because of its proximity to the nation's capital. With the Cold War at its peak and the Cuban missile crisis fresh in American minds, Fort Meade was deemed close enough to Washington for easy commuting and far enough away to survive a nuclear attack. Now Fort Meade was home to more than forty thousand employees, many of whom held a top-secret security clearance.

The fort had its own post office, fire department, and police force. Electrified fences ran the length of the installation's perimeter. Security cameras and motion detectors covered every square foot. To block any electromagnetic signals from escaping, protective copper shielding wrapped every one of the more than 1,300 buildings inside the compound.

Waiting at the checkpoint as his identification was examined, Ian Prince looked through the rows of fences at the rectangular black glass office building a half mile away that housed the headquarters of the nation's most secretive intelligence organization.

"Mine," he repeated to himself.

It was the NSA's mandate to collect and analyze all signals communication and data relating to foreign intelligence, by overt and clandestine means. Thirty years ago that meant intercepting suspicious radio, telephone, and satellite traffic. Today it meant all that plus policing the Internet, not just monitoring all forms of online traffic for clues to evil intent but protecting all United States government communications and information systems from foreign interference and disruption. On this sunny, humid day, Ian and his colleagues had come to offer ONE's assistance with both objectives.

"Here you are, sir," said the guard, returning Ian's ID and those of his passengers, Peter Briggs and Dev Patel. "Welcome to Fort Meade."

Ian noticed the guard's quizzical gaze. "Anything wrong?"

It was not his first trip to Fort Meade, or his second, or even his tenth. Since October 2001 he'd been secretly visiting three or four times a year. Each time he got the same dumbfounded look.

"I wasn't expecting you to be driving," said the guard. "I thought you'd have a chauffeur."

"I always drive," said Ian, giving a salute.

"Yessir. Have a good day."

The gate rose. Simultaneously the steel Delta barrier sank into the ground. Ian headed down a long winding lane toward the black building, officially known as OPS2A. He remembered the feeling of awe he'd experienced on his first visits, the visceral thrill of being so close to the most powerful data-collection apparatus in the world. It was then that the idea had first come to him.

Over time his awe had tempered as he and ONE became the NSA's partner, albeit a silent and secret one. Today, as he closed in on his dream, as the changing of the guard grew near, he felt only pride. A father's pride. One day soon this would all be his.

The Emperor was waiting inside the conference room when Ian arrived.

"Good to see you, Ian," said General Terry Wolfe of the United States Air Force, director of the National Security Agency, chief of the Central Security Service, and commander of the U.S. Cyber Command. He was known throughout the intelligence community as the Emperor. "Has it been six months?"

"Seven," said Ian. "December, I believe."

Wolfe greeted Patel warmly, addressing him as Dr. Patel. Briggs waited outside.

"Time flies," said Wolfe, leading them to the table. "Must have been before all that Merriweather nonsense."

"It was," said Ian. "That's all behind us, I take it."

The "nonsense" was the lengthy investigation conducted by the FBI into allegations of bribery and extortion surrounding ONE's acquisition of Merriweather Systems. The same allegations Gordon May had made two days before on the airstrip in Reno, though there had never been any mention of complicity in the plane crash that took John Merriweather's life.

It was in response to these charges that Ian had deemed it necessary to hack into the FBI's central computer system. He'd been able to gather enough information to put a stop to the FBI's queries. But the price had been high. His work had not gone unnoticed by the Bureau's Cyber Investigations Division and Special Agent Joseph Grant.

"The FBI says it is. Who am I to argue?" Wolfe took his place at the head of the conference table and motioned for Ian to sit at his right.

The director of the NSA was of medium height and medium build, with thinning hair, a puffy, pleasant face, and timid blue eyes that blinked often behind rimless eyeglasses. Not so much an emperor as a middle-aged father who'd been up late the night before helping a child with his homework. In his tenure at the helm of the NSA, he had turned a once sleepy, unheralded intelligence agency into the nation's most vaunted fighter of terrorism. When General Terry Wolfe wanted something, both Congress and the military came running, checkbooks at the ready.

Ian opened the bottle of mineral water placed before him, waiting for any mention of Semaphore. The word was not spoken.

With Wolfe was Bob Goldfarb, director of the Oak Ridge National Laboratory, the nation's foremost computer research hub. Goldfarb was old and gnomish, with as much hair sprouting from his ears as on top of his mottled head.

"Hello, Bob," said Ian. "Long time."

"Exaflops," whispered Goldfarb. "Can it be?"

Ian answered with a cryptic smile. All good things to those who wait.

"Shall we get down to brass tacks?" said Wolfe. "Are we to understand that you've solved the heating problem?"

"That's correct," said Ian.

"And none too soon," said Goldfarb. "Cutting it close, are we?"

"We can't risk another incident," said Wolfe diplomatically. "Bluffdale is our number-one priority these days. We have a lot invested in the demonstration."

Bluffdale, Utah, was home to the Utah Data Center, soon to be the world's largest intelligence collection and storage site, where six months earlier the NSA had installed two hundred Titan supercomputers. It was billed as "a state-of-the-art facility designed to support the intelligence community in its mission to enable and protect national cybersecurity." In reality the Utah Data Center was a vacuum cleaner designed to suck up as much of the world's communications traffic as technologically possible. It collected traffic from undersea cables and underground fiber-optic cables, from satellites high in the sky and dishes on firm ground. Its servers were so large that they measured contents not in gigabytes or terabytes or even petabytes. They measured their take in yottabytes, where one yottabyte equaled 500 quintillion (500,000,000,000,000,000,000) pages of text.

It was the Utah Data Center's primary mission to gather and store all communications traffic generated by the entire world for the next ten years.

"And ours, too," said Ian. "But that was six months ago, immediately after we took over the project from John Merriweather. As you'll see, we've made some improvements."

"Frankly, the boys at Oak Ridge are skeptical," said Goldfarb. "A few of us are more than that."

"Until yesterday I was doubtful, too. I can promise you that the specs are accurate."

"Exaflops," said Goldfarb. "Really?"

Patel chimed in. "It was our team's primary consideration when we took over management of the project. Speed's the primary factor when executing algorithmic strategies."

The strategies Patel referred to involved decrypting encoded messages, or, in the vernacular, "breaking a code." There was only one reason the NSA wanted the world's most powerful supercomputer. It was during an initial test that Titan had overheated. A second demonstration was scheduled for the following morning, with many high-ranking government officials set to attend, including the vice president. It would be Titan's second and final chance.

"I'm sure we'll be able to judge for ourselves," said General Wolfe, playing the peacemaker. "So? The test?"

Ian nodded at Patel, who distributed a set of bound notebooks to the NSA men. No one spoke as the government officials studied the detailed results of the prior day's test. The men finished reading. Their eyes met each other's, then Ian's. Ian imagined that Franklin Roosevelt and his advisers must have looked much the same way after Robert Oppenheimer informed them of the successful test of the atomic bomb in May 1945.

"Exaflops," said Goldfarb.

"Exaflops," said Ian.

"Exaflops," said General Wolfe, taking ownership of the word.

"Two hundred degrees Fahrenheit," said Goldfarb. "Sounds low."

"Two hundred six, actually," said Ian. "Then the cooling system kicked in."

"At which point Titan's internal temperature decreased to one hundred eighty degrees," added Patel.

"How?" said Wolfe. "It's a gosh-darned miracle."

"Just a little tinkering," said Ian. "An extra fan here and there."

"Whatever you did," said Wolfe, "we want Titan on-site at Fort Meade."

"I believe that's another contract," said Ian.

"Soon you'll have a monopoly," said Wolfe. "There won't be a network in D.C. that doesn't come from ONE."

"Maybe one day," said Ian.

Bob Goldfarb's skepticism had vanished. His dark eyes sparkled greedily as he placed his elbows on the table and leaned forward. "How soon can we install it?"

"Dev can work with your people to install the software patch today. If all goes as it should, we can keep to our plan for the demonstration tomorrow morning."

"That's cutting it close," said Wolfe. "You're sure?"

"I don't think you'll be disappointed."

"Tomorrow morning it is." Wolfe moved to a table at the end of the conference room and poured glasses of sparkling apple cider. Beltway bubbly, he called it as he offered round the glasses.

"To Titan," said Wolfe.

"To Titan," the others chimed in.

Ian touched glasses with each man in turn and drank his cider.

Afterward Peter Briggs took Ian aside and offered a handshake. "The king is dead," he whispered. "Long live the king."

"You mean the Emperor," said Ian.

35

Mary called Randy Bell at eight on the dot. He answered on the first ring, sounding chipper and alert. So much for her plan of catching him hungover and with his defenses down. Her career as an investigator was not off to a promising start.

"Randy," she said. "It's Mary Grant."

"Gee, Mary, I'm so sorry about Joe. Did you get my message?" Bell had a high, youthful voice. He was in his midfifties, with hair white as snow, but on the phone he sounded like a twenty-year-old.

"E-mail? I haven't had time to look through them all, but thanks all the same. Sorry if I woke you."

"It's nine o'clock," said Bell. "I've been up two hours."

"In Sacramento?"

"I'm in D.C." Bell paused, then added, "Just visiting the old crew. Gosh, Mary, I don't know what to say. I'm crushed. I can't believe what happened. None of us can. How you holding up?"

She told him that she was fine and that the kids were going to make it through. She took a breath, suddenly nervous, not sure how to begin. "Randy, I know you and Joe were buddies," she said. "When was the last time you talked?"

"June. Right after the playoffs."

"How'd he sound?"

"Like Joe. A little crazy 'cause the Celtics lost. But he sounded good."

"And work? You guys talk shop?"

"I'm retired six months now," said Bell. "I'm out of the loop."

"Still, Joe thought a lot of you."

"He was a good kid."

That's twice he's avoided the question, thought Mary. She walked into Joe's office. The yellow legal pad was on the desk where she'd left it. She stared at her husband's writing, at the funny little flags all over the page, wondering how she was supposed to lead Randy Bell subtly to the question of Joe's trips to San Jose.

word said to a widow?

"What was that case you two were working—the one he was always going on about, about the Asian syndicate pirating those jet designs?"

"Pricks were hacking into Boeing's mainframe, downloading designs for the new wing it's building, and selling them to China."

"And the other case," she went on. "You know, the one where you guys were always flying down to San Jose. I forget who Joe said you were seeing."

Randy Bell didn't answer.

"Randy . . . you there?"

"Why are you asking about this?"

"Just trying to tie up some loose ends."

"What kind of loose ends?"

The cat was officially out of the bag. Mary gave up all effort at pretense. She was no investigator. She was just a wife who wanted to know the true circumstances surrounding her husband's murder. "Sixteen trips. That's how many times Joe went to San Jose without telling me. You guys were partners for at least eight of those. He kept flying out there even after we moved. I'm guessing that's why we came to Austin, so he could continue to work that case, only from out here. I'm guessing that's what got him killed."

"I can't talk about this, Mary."

"There's something fishy about the explanation of Joe's death. It isn't right."

"Did you hear me? I can't discuss this."

"Come on, Randy. We're talking about Joe. You were like an older brother. Can you see him getting into a car with an armed informant? Can you?"

"Mary, please—"

"They're painting it like it was his fault. But it wasn't. Joe knew he was in trouble. He was scared. A scared man doesn't get into a car with someone whom he believes might want to hurt him."

"Mary, stop. How do you know he was scared?"

"He called me before he was killed. I didn't speak with him, but he left me a message. He knew something was wrong. He told me to find someone named Sid. Do you know who that is?"

"No. Can't say I do."

"What about a Judge Angelo Caruso? Travis County Superior Court?"

"Where are you getting this stuff? Last I looked, Joe's casework was confidential."

Mary shook her head, staring at the notepad, running a pen over the silly blue flags. One more stonewall. She wondered if Don Bennett had gotten to Randy, too. "Sure you don't know someone named Sid?" she asked again. "Joe said he was one of the good guys."

"Please, Mary. Stop asking these questions."

Mary stared at the little flags that Joe had drawn all over the page. It dawned on her what they were. Of course. It was obvious.

"Semaphore," she blurted.

"What did you say?"

"Semaphore. Why?"

"Shut up, Mary."

"Excuse me? Did you tell me to shut up? Randy . . . are you there?"

"I'm here. Whatever you do, don't say that word again."

"What word?"

"Never. Do you hear me? Goodbye now."

"Randy?" she said, but the connection had ended.

She called back and the phone went to message. "Randy. What did you mean about not saying that word? What word? *Semaphore?*"

36

"She's in danger," said Randy Bell. "We need to pull her in."

"And do what with her?" said Dylan Walsh, chief of the FBI's Cyber Investigations Division. "Shall I put her up at my place? And the girls, too?"

"Maybe Keefe can help."

"He's on the bricks for three days. Can't come near the office until he visits the company shrink."

"We've got to do something," Bell argued. "Between Mason and Prince, she won't last a minute."

"Calm down," said Walsh sternly. He was tall and handsome and sturdy, forty-two years of age, a graduate of Carnegie Mellon with an advanced degree in computer science. Dressed in a dapper blue suit, his brown hair combed perfectly, he was an exemplar of the new FBI. "I understand your concern, and I appreciate your loyalty to Joe's family. I don't want anything to happen to Mary any more than you do. But we need to look at all the pieces here."

Bell nodded a grudging agreement. "You're the boss."

Walsh patted Bell on the shoulder. "All right, then. Run this by me one more time."

"She said it: 'Semaphore.' Just like that—out of the blue. It's not exactly a word used in everyday conversation."

"You have a point there."

Dylan Walsh ran a hand across the back of his neck as he paced his office on the fifth floor of FBI Headquarters in Washington, D.C. Semaphore had been a small operation to begin with. Just four full-time agents, including himself. The number was limited by necessity. You didn't raise a red flag when you wanted to investigate the man who had hacked into the Bureau's mainframe. Not when that man was Ian Prince. That went double when your biggest rival in the organization was in Prince's back pocket.

The Cyber Investigations Division had been formed five years earlier to help combat threats to national security through computer strikes, namely illegal attempts at intrusions—hacks—into mainframes belonging to the government and private enterprise. To that end, Walsh oversaw his team's cooperation with all members of the U.S. intelligence community (CIA, NSA, Homeland Security, and so on), as well as state and local law enforcement agencies. In those five years, a ten-man "fire team" had grown into one hundred dedicated agents, nearly all with master's degrees in computer science, tasked with stopping computer and network intrusions, identity theft, and Internet crime.

Inside the Bureau, the Cyber Investigations Division went by the moniker CID, pronounced "Sid," to differentiate it from the standard CID, the Criminal Investigative Division.

"Still," Walsh went on. "Her saying it doesn't mean anything of itself."

"She knows Don Bennett is covering something up. That's enough. I know her, Dylan. She won't give up until she finds out the truth about her husband's death."

"I wouldn't either."

Bell sipped from a mug of coffee. "Any word from Mason?"

"Flew down there yesterday to oversee matters. A show of the Bureau's concern for one of our own."

"As if."

"Ed Mason keeps peddling the same moonshine. He believes that if anything bad happens to ONE, or to Ian Prince and that supercomputer of his, it'll jeopardize the NSA's ability to do their job. Our job isn't to stop the bad guys from snooping on our computers only to let Mason and the Emperor do it at their will."

"Don't know about that," said Bell. "I do know that if we believe Mary Grant's going to keep looking, then so does Ian Prince."

"Exactly," said Walsh, walking to the window and looking out across the Mall at the Washington Monument and the Smithsonian Building. "That's what I'm counting on."

37

"I can't just stay here," said Jessie, standing with her mother in the kitchen. "It's depressing. I missed class yesterday. I can't miss again today."

"You need to be here with your sister."

"Grace is fine. She can go over to the Kramers' and play."

"Jess, please." Her mother's face hardened, her lips tightening over her teeth. "Not today."

"But . . ." Jessie tried to act like Grace. She held her arms at her side and didn't slouch. It was harder keeping her voice all upbeat and chirpy. "It's okay, Mom. I'll stay if you need me."

"Thanks, sweetie. That's nice of you. I appreciate it." Mary tilted her head. Her mouth softened, and a weight seemed to lift from her shoulders. "Come to think of it, Grace will be fine."

"Sure? I don't have to go."

Mary smiled and checked her watch. "Class starts at eleven, right?"

"Eleven to one. But I can hang around afterward." Jessie winced at her choice of words. Parents thought "hanging around" meant looking to score weed or commit a jailable offense. "I mean, I can stay and talk to the teacher. He's wicked smart."

"Professor Gritsch?"

"No, the TA, Linus. He teaches the class."

"Linus? Don't hear that one much. Like Linus and Charlie Brown."

"Yeah," said Jessie agreeably, all singsongy like Grace. "Like that." Her mom looked at her, and she thought she'd gone too far. But then her mom picked up her car keys.

"You ready?"

Jessie nodded, trying hard not to appear too excited. "Good to go," she said. It was one of her dad's expressions from when he was in the army or Marine Corps or whatever.

"I'll tell Grace." Mary stopped when she was nearly out of the kitchen. "Jess?"

"Yeah, Mom?" Here it comes, thought Jessie, her heart sinking. She's going to change her mind.

"Do you think you could stay at school until two? It's pretty far for me to drive there and back, and I have some errands."

Jessie forced herself to count to three before answering. "I guess that might work."

"Good. I won't be a minute later than that."

The classroom was full when Jessie arrived. She slid her pack off her shoulder and scooted through the aisle to her seat. She felt all eyes on her. She wasn't just the youngest student in the class, but also the only girl. Most of the others were a bunch of rejects or kissy-ups headed straight for Redmond. Except for Garrett. She saw him out of the corner of her eye. He was almost cute, if you liked the Abercrombie type—straight blond hair hanging in his eyes, tall, always smiling and talking to everyone. She noted that he was wearing a Mumford & Sons shirt. Dork.

Linus, the TA, walked into the room, carrying a coffee. Technically he was Dr. Jankowski, but he told everyone to call him by his first name. He was short and had a beard and wasn't cool at all. Still, the class shut up the second he walked in.

"So, you guys," said Linus, dumping his satchel onto the table. "Before we get started, Mr. Clark wanted to say something. Go ahead, Garrett."

Jessie kept her eyes on her desk, only partially seeing him stand out of the corner of her eye.

"Umm . . . yeah," said Garrett. "Jessie, we know this is a hard time for you. We all wanted to say we're really sorry about your dad. We think you're pretty awesome just for being in here in the first place. You're, like, fourteen. It's amazing. And you're really brave to come back to school so fast. So, anyway, um . . . hang in there. It'll get better."

Jessie tried to say thanks, and that actually she was fifteen, but the words caught in her throat. She didn't dare look at the others. She couldn't or she'd cry. A few people offered condolences. She nodded and kept her eyes on the desk. Mostly she could feel Garrett staring at her. He probably hated her Zeppelin T-shirt as much as she hated his Mumford & Sons. No Winger T-shirts?

Linus announced that the topic for today was breaking encryption algorithms. He lectured for ninety minutes, filling up all the whiteboards with code. At 12:45 he dropped his marker on the desk. "For the last fifteen minutes we're going to have a test. No, not a test—let's call it a race. We're going to see who can figure out a cool hack the fastest. Or, I should probably say, whether anyone can figure it out at all."

Linus explained the rules as he wrote the challenge on the whiteboard. "Root the box with admin privileges and capture the flag. Simple enough. Winner gets a Heineken. You guys have fifteen minutes. Go."

Jessie looked around the room. Everyone was already hard at it, heads down, tapping away at their keyboards like mad. Garrett glanced up from under his brow and saw her looking at him. He raised his eyebrows and made a horrified face, as if this were the hardest problem in the world. Jessie looked away. She thought about the chunk of code she'd found on her mother's phone. No one in the chat room had had any idea what it was or what it was supposed to do. They did say, however, that it wasn't NITRON. Whatever it was, it was unique.

After a minute Jessie turned her attention to the problem. She was good at rooting the box. She decided to give it a shot. What did she have to lose?

"Time's up."

Linus Jankowski surveyed the room, chuckling to himself as if he knew no one had gotten it right. "Who's got my answer?"

Five students raised their hands, mostly the buttoned-up guys headed to Microsoft or Oracle. Linus called on them one at a time, displayed their answers on the whiteboard, and one at a time shot them down, sprinkling in comments like "Thanks, propeller-head, but no," "Couldn't be more wrong," and "Seriously, that's as good as you got?" When he'd finished tearing them apart, he took up position in the center of the classroom. "Anyone else?" he asked. "Don't be shy. Abject humiliation and embarrassment await."

Jessie kept her head down, her hands covering her answer.

"Garrett? Got something for me?"

"I could only crack five of the six hashes."

"There are a dozen websites that could have gotten you the last one."

"Sorry, Linus, maybe next time."

Linus moved down the aisle. "Jessie? Anything? Anything at all?"

Jessie winced at the sound of her name. She felt Linus's eyes on her and shifted in her seat.

"Nothing?" Linus prodded. "No one?" He chuckled some more, looking way too pleased with himself. "Okay, then."

"Umm," said Jessie.

"Miss Grant."

Jessie raised her head. All the other students were staring at her.

"We're waiting . . ."

Jessie met their eyes, accepting the challenge from each, something inside her growing strong.

"You've got our attention," said Linus.

"It's easy." Jessie flashed her answer onto the whiteboard and went to the front of the class to set forth her solution. "There," she said when she'd finished. "Captured the flag."

Linus examined her work. "You've never seen this problem before, have you?" he whispered, his beard close enough to scratch her cheek.

Jessie shook her head.

"Swear?"

"Swear."

"Okay, then. We're done here."

Jessie returned to her seat, dejected. She'd been sure she had the right answer.

Linus opened his satchel and took out a bottle of Heineken. He popped the cap with his teeth and guzzled the beer. He belched, then walked down the aisle and set the empty bottle on her desk. "Congratulations, Miss Grant. You nailed it."

The class broke into applause. Garrett hollered her name.

Jessie kept her eyes straight ahead as her chest swelled with pride and her cheeks suddenly felt as hot as the sun.

Linus leaned down and whispered, "I didn't say the beer would be full."

38

"I hereby declare this closed hearing of the Senate Subcommittee on Intelligence in session."

Ian took his seat at the witness table and adjusted his necktie. His attorney sat beside him and patted his arm as if Ian were the accused and needed reassurance. Ian figured the arm patting was included in the attorney's $700-an-hour fee. Peter Briggs sat behind him, along with three of the attorney's assistants. The assistants billed at $400 an hour. Maybe for that much, they'd hold Briggs's hand.

"We are here to conduct our semiannual review of our cooperative assistance program with ONE Technologies," said Senator Bailey Fisk of Tennessee, subcommittee chairman. He was old and vigorous and unrepentant about the steel-wool toupee he'd worn for the past twenty years. "Representing ONE Technologies is Ian Prince, founder and chairman. For the record, may I express our profound thanks for your presence here today and our recognition of your long-standing cooperation with the United States government. Welcome, Mr. Prince."

"It's my pleasure," said Ian. "Had to do something to earn my passport, didn't I?"

Ian gazed at the four men and two women facing him on the elevated dais. He knew each of them personally—in fact, far better than any of them realized. Both Senator Fisk and Senator Bowden were ONE Mobile customers. As a matter of course, he recorded their every conversation and catalogued all photographs and texts made from their phones.

He knew, for example, that Senator Fisk was carrying on an affair with a twenty-one-year-old male staffer (sexts, photos) and that Senator Bowden had refused to seek treatment for alcohol and prescription drug addiction. He'd recently been privy to a conversation between the senator and her husband in which she'd drunkenly informed him that enjoying two bottles of cabernet a night was her right and that the "American people could screw themselves" if they thought she was a drunk.

Ian had no plans to use any of the material . . . for the moment. He considered it money put aside for a rainy day. It paid to be a saver.

"Our agenda today is composed of four items," said Fisk. "Obelisk, Lynchpin, Rosetta, and Prime. We'll start with Obelisk."

Ian smiled benignly. There was public Washington and private Washington. The first acted for the benefit of the media and the unknowing citizenry. The second did what it deemed necessary, critics be damned.

Public Washington chastised the intelligence community for its overzealous nature and the infringements it made on the individual's right to privacy in the name of policing international terrorism and transnational crime. At the same time it accused corporate America (Ian and his counterparts at the country's largest technology companies) of acquiescing to the intelligence community's demands too quickly and too willingly.

All the while, private Washington contrived greater and more sophisticated means to continue collecting any and all intelligence that might serve to protect its citizens, and got down on its bruised and bleeding knees to beg the private sector's cooperation.

"If I may," said Ian, "I would like to once again refuse the government's generous offer to repay us for services rendered. As a global citizen, ONE is happy to absorb all legal and compliance costs stemming from our in-house attorneys and support staff who oversee Obelisk." It was his turn to pat his attorney's arm. "Thank goodness they're not as pricey as my private counsel seated with me today."

Senator Fisk barked out a laugh and threw a hand on the table. He and Ian were two good ol' boys who understood each other just fine. The only thing missing was a bottle of sourmash from his home state (though of course Ian didn't drink).

"Obelisk," said Senator Fisk. "Where do we stand?"

Obelisk, formerly known as Prism, was a program permitting the government access to ONE's central servers, and those of every other major Internet provider. The government placed filters on all Internet traffic, both domestic and foreign, to search for keywords that might indicate pending acts of terrorism or individuals and/or organizations unfriendly to the cause—"the cause" being anything remotely related to the national security of the United States of America.

Once a keyword was spotted, the government presented ONE with a warrant requesting copies of all e-mails and/or other communications linked to the offending account holder, including but not limited to Skype, Internet queries, wireless communications, and so on. A single red flag often triggered an avalanche of private information.

"Which brings us to Lynchpin," said Fisk.

Lynchpin involved ONE's software division. Ian's engineers inserted a back door into all software for overseas sales and export—word processing, spreadsheet, presentation, database—allowing any party with a "skeleton key," or password, full and unfettered access.

A recent example of Lynchpin dealt with ONEWord, a word-processing program licensed to the German Ministry of Defense. Upon signature of the contract, Ian had dutifully informed the Pentagon of the transaction, and the Pentagon in turn had requested that Ian insert code into the software that automatically copied every document written and saved by the German military establishment and sent it to Washington.

In the past twelve months, this type of custom tailoring had been done on software sold to institutions in India, Pakistan, Poland, the Netherlands, Indonesia, Singapore, France, and Japan. Only Ian Prince held the password to all.

"Rosetta," said Fisk.

Rosetta trafficked in a similar concept, but for hardware: ONE's servers, routers, switches, laptops, tablets, and the like. Every device—no matter its intent or end user—was manufactured with a back door somewhere in its DNA. When it was sold to a customer designated "of interest" to the government, Ian shared how to exploit it.

". . . which brings us to the last item on our agenda," said Fisk. "Prime."

Ian sat up straighter. The last two hours had been strictly warmup. This was the main event.

Fisk looked at his colleagues on the dais. "Is the subcommittee prepared to offer its recommendation regarding the purchase of ONE hardware and software for the new intranet being developed for the Central Intelligence Agency?"

Prime was the name of the top-secret communications network (an intranet) being developed for the CIA to enable the agency to bypass the open-format Internet. Coupled with the NSA's use of Titan in Utah, Prime would give Ian access to the entirety of the United States' intelligence networks.

Peter Briggs placed a hand on Ian's shoulder. "Wrap this up, boss. We have a problem."

Ian raised a concerned finger. "One minute, Senator Fisk."

"Of course, Mr. Prince."

"What is it?" Ian whispered through a clenched smile. "Not Gordon May, I hope."

"No," said Briggs. "The woman."

There was no need to ask which woman. These days there was only one. "What now?"

"She's asking about Semaphore."

"How's that?"

"It is. That's all that matters."

Ian turned back toward the dais. "Please go on, Senator."

He answered the remaining questions as succinctly as he knew how. It was the longest hour of his life.

39

Tank Potter checked the address painted on the curb and killed the engine. Without thinking, he reached beneath the seat for his backstop. An exposed coil stabbed his finger. "Ouch!"

Old habits died hard.

Chastened, Tank walked to the door. A steady hand rang the bell. Though he had the Grants' number, he hadn't called in advance. The first rule of journalism: never let them see you coming.

A pallid girl dressed in leggings and a T-shirt opened the door. "Hello."

"Hello," said Tank. "Is your mom around?"

"Who's asking?"

"Tank Potter. I'm a reporter. You guys get the *Statesman*?"

"What's that?"

"A newspaper. Ever seen one?"

"My mom reads the *New York Times*. Online. We subscribe to *People*." The girl extended her hand. "My name's Grace. Nice to meet you."

Tank's hand swallowed hers. "Nice to meet you."

"You're big."

"My mom wanted to make sure nobody missed me."

"It worked. My mom's not here right now. She's taking my sister to summer school. Did you come to ask about my dad?"

"I did. I'm sorry about what happened."

"We can't understand how someone so smart could let a bad guy get close enough to shoot him."

"Did your mom say that?"

"No. I did. She's still upset about losing Dad's voicemail. She's blaming my sister, but Jessie swears she was only unlocking the phone and didn't erase it."

"I see." Tank smiled as if he knew what she was talking about. "Do you know when your mom will be—" The squeal of an automobile turning tightly into the driveway cut short his words. He turned to see a late-model Nissan come to a halt at the head of the walkway.

"There's Mommy," said Grace.

Tank waved shyly. He didn't want to appear menacing, but there was only so much you could do when you were his size.

A trim, attractive woman got out of the car and rushed up the walk. "Can I help you?"

"Mrs. Grant? Tank Potter. I'm with the *Statesman*."

"It's a newspaper," said Grace.

Mary Grant stopped a foot away, checking over his shoulder that her daughter was fine before fixing him with a decidedly unhelpful look. "Why wasn't there anything new in the paper today about Joe?"

"I came here to talk to you about that. First, may I offer my condolences?"

"Thank you." She pointed a finger at him. "Potter? You didn't write the article yesterday."

"I was on another story."

Mary stepped around him to address her daughter. "Grace, go inside. Give me and Mr. Potter a minute."

"His name is Tank," said Grace, rolling her eyes.

"Shut the door, sweetheart," said Mary.

"Bye, Tank," said Grace as she closed the door.

"And so," asked Mary, "what took you so long?"

"Excuse me?"

"To figure out the FBI is lying. That's why you're here, right?"

Tank nodded tentatively. It was his job to assume the FBI was lying. He wondered what had convinced Mary Grant of the fact. "Is there anything you'd like to tell me?"

"Is there anything you want to tell *me*?" She stepped forward. "Are you feeling all right, Mr. Potter?"

"I'm fine." Tank cleared his throat and stood taller. He could feel sweat beading on his forehead, his tongue dry as felt. "Can we talk inside?"

"After I see your press credential."

Tank flashed his *Statesman* ID. Mary Grant clutched his hand to bring the pass closer. "Henry Thaddeus Potter."

"Are you a football fan?" he asked as she compared his face to the picture on the pass. "I played at UT."

"I went to Georgetown. We prefer basketball. Come in."

———

"She's got a visitor," said the Mole.

Shanks kicked his feet off the control console and sat up to study the monitor. "Big fella, ain't he?"

"What do you think?" asked the Mole. "Family? Friend?"

"Friend. Doesn't look like any of them, that's for sure. You get a read on his license plate?"

"Forget the license. We have his face." The Mole duplicated the last sixty seconds of images transmitted from the hidden camera and replayed the loop on a second monitor. He and Shanks watched as the Jeep pulled to the curb and the tall, florid man climbed out of the car. For an instant the visitor stared directly at the hidden camera. "Gotcha."

The Mole froze the image and uploaded it to PittPatt. "All right, baby," he said. "Go to work."

Short for Pittsburgh Pattern Recognition, PittPatt was an advanced facial recognition software program developed at Carnegie Mellon University to help hunt terrorists in the days following 9/11. ONE had purchased PittPatt a year earlier and tweaked the technology for a different purpose. It planned on licensing the technology to merchants of every stripe, who would use it to identify their customers and, based on past purchases and publicly available personal information—age, sex, zip code, credit history—send news of sales, discount coupons, or the like directly to their smartphones. The only terrorists it was interested in finding were those with a credit score of 700 and an American Express Gold Card.

"Image captured," said an officious female voice. "Mapping completed."

Shanks and the Mole waited as PittPatt conducted a search of every public database on the Net for images that matched the visitor. It searched Facebook and Instagram and Google Images. It searched Tumblr, YouTube, Match.com, Picasa, and a thousand more like them.

It also searched private databases. These included the National Crime Information Center; the Department of Public Safety and its equivalent in all fifty states; the National Missing and Unidentified Persons System; and Interpol.

Images filled the screen, six to a line, the lines rapidly scrolling down the page. The first picture to appear was of a football player running down the field.

"Tank Potter," said the Mole, reading the caption. "Never heard of him."

"He was almost famous."

"Let's go deeper." The Mole requested that PittPatt search for more detailed and personal information. The name Henry Thaddeus Potter led to property records showing him to be the owner of a home in Tarrytown and the former owner of homes on Blanchard Drive and Red River Street. Mention of a Potter family trust was found in a bankruptcy filing for a Mrs. Josephine Willis Potter which listed a sole son, Henry Thaddeus, and gave his date and place of birth.

PittPatt did all this in .0005 second.

"Still waiting on the jackpot," said the Mole. "Got it!"

Potter's name coupled with his place and date of birth helped the program find batches of Social Security numbers issued in Houston on or around his birthday. Time and again an algorithm paired Potter's name with a probable Social Security number. Though the algorithm had a tiny chance of success on each try, it continued to run through all possible numbers until it found a match, in this case a credit report that listed the last four digits of his Social Security number.

The Mole read to the bottom of the list. In ten seconds he had learned more about Henry Thaddeus "Tank" Potter—impoverished heir to a once-great fortune, All-State football star, washed-up college athlete, divorced father of two children who lived with their mother in Arkansas, and journalist—than Mr. Potter's closest friends ever would.

"Not a friend of the family after all," said Shanks. "A reporter."

A final picture appeared on the monitor. It was Tank Potter's mug shot from two nights before.

The Mole smirked. "And a drunk."

40

Class was over.

Jessie took her time putting away her laptop, keeping an eye on the front of the room, where the older students were talking to Linus. Normally she liked to be first out, but today she had a reason to wait.

"That was amaze-balls," said Garrett, taking the seat next to her, swiping his blond hair out of his face. "We haven't even talked about that stuff. How did you do it?"

"Just figured it out, I guess."

"Maybe you can explain it to me. You want to get a hamburger or something for lunch?"

"I ate earlier," said Jessie.

"How about a coffee? I can give you a ride home, too, if you want. I'm eighteen. It's okay."

"My mom's getting me."

"Well, um . . . ," Garrett stammered, and Jessie almost felt sorry for him.

"Miss Grant." Linus Jankowski stood in front of her desk. Garrett stood, giving a wave and a "See ya" before shuffling out of the classroom.

"Hi, there," said Jessie.

Linus sat down. "So, young lady. Mind telling me how you did it?"

"I already explained it."

"I mean how you came to possess that kind of knowledge."

"It just seemed kind of obvious."

"Really? That's not usually a word I've heard attached to advanced encryption algorithms, but okay. So why didn't you speak up when I asked the first time?"

"I don't like attention," said Jessie. "It creeps me out."

"Humility. What a concept." Linus trained his eyes on Jessie. "Do you know the last person to solve that hack? It was Rudeboy at DEF CON last summer. He did it to win Capture the Flag."

"Rudeboy solved it?"

"He wasn't the only one, but he was the quickest. Five minutes flat. I came in third. Three minutes behind. You, Miss Grant, needed thirteen minutes and seventeen seconds."

"But . . . how did you know that I'd—"

"I was watching you. None of the other propeller-heads in class stood a chance." Linus stood and picked up his satchel and his endless cup of coffee. "I'm gone tomorrow. See you after that."

"Yeah, sure. See you." Jessie watched helplessly as he walked out of the classroom. "Linus," she called, rising from her chair and running into the hall. "I need your help with something."

"Homework?"

"Not exactly. It's kind of private."

"Not now."

"But—"

"Tonight. Crown and Anchor. Nine o'clock."

The Crown & Anchor was a pub on San Jacinto Boulevard. "No—ten."

"Even better. Ten."

Jessie left the classroom and headed downstairs. Outside she sat by the fountain. She put her hand in the cold water, asking herself what she'd done. Meet Linus at a pub at ten? Was she crazy? She wasn't allowed to leave the house on her own at night. Even if she managed to sneak out, how was she supposed to get all the way downtown . . . and then back again? And what about going into a pub? Could she even do that?

She took a fruit roll-up from her pack and ate it. How could someone smart enough to solve the hack that won Capture the Flag be so stupid?

"There you are."

Jessie looked up as a flash of blond hair sat down next to her. "Hi, Garrett."

"Lucky I ran into you."

And then it came to her. The solution was in front of her all the time.

"Yeah, lucky coincidence." Jessie smiled. "Did you say something about having a car?"

41

Ian ran up the stairs of ONE 1 and entered the cabin of his jet without looking back.

"Christ, I hate that place," he said. "Like the Inquisition without the party favors."

A flight attendant took his jacket and handed him a bottle of Penta water.

Peter Briggs followed him into the aircraft, pulled the door closed, and locked it. "Activate the ECMs," he said.

The flight attendant moved to a control panel and turned on the plane's electronic countermeasures.

Ian collapsed into a chair. "What the hell is she doing now?"

Briggs sat in the chair opposite. "She's asking about Semaphore. Said it by name in a conversation with her husband's former partner, Special Agent Randall A. Bell."

"How is that possible?"

"How do I know?" Briggs's face was redder than usual, his pale blue eyes brooking no challenge. "Maybe her husband left the case file open on his desk. Maybe she reads his e-mails. Maybe he whispered it to her while he was banging her the night before he died. Does it matter *how*? She said it. Listen for yourself."

Briggs set his phone on the table and played the recording of Mary Grant speaking to Randy Bell.

"Sounds like it was a shot in the dark," said Ian.

"No such thing."

"But she called Bell back to ask which word she wasn't supposed to repeat. If she was certain it was Semaphore, she wouldn't have needed a confirmation."

"Well, thanks to Randy Bell she has it. He might as well have attached a homing beacon to the word. After the call she performed searches for the word *semaphore* alone and in combination with *FBI, CIA, cybercrime, pirating,* you name it." Briggs banged a fist on the armrest, index finger extended for good measure. "Mason told us she was a pain in the ass. He said she wouldn't quit."

"Ed Mason thinks that everyone who doesn't work for him is either a pain in the ass or a risk to national security."

Deputy director of the FBI Edward G. Mason III was either his best friend or his worst enemy. Ian walked to the front of the cabin to make sure that none of the attendants were listening. "What else has our intrepid widow been up to?"

"See for yourself."

Briggs handed Ian a printout of the surveillance data collected from the Grant home. Ian looked over a list of online activity. Someone in the house liked to watch videos of cute animals on YouTube. Kittens, puppies, and sloths. *Sloths.* Despite his ill temper, he smiled. His own sons spent hours watching cute animals on YouTube. Ian didn't mind. It beat spending hours watching less cute videos of men and women that were as easily available. Twelve-year-old boys didn't watch kittens playing the piano forever.

"We'll deal with this when we get back. Till then—"

Briggs raised a hand. He had his phone to his ear and his face had gone from red to redder. "What did you say? . . . A who? . . . What? . . . Oh, Christ. Fuck me."

"What is it?" asked Ian.

Briggs dropped the phone onto the table. "She's got a visitor. A newspaper reporter. Still want to wait till we get back?"

42

Tank sat with Mary Grant at her kitchen table. He was grateful to be out of the heat. And more grateful for the iced tea she'd offered. He knew she wasn't from the South because the tea didn't have enough lemon or sugar. But it was cold and wet and he drank down half the glass before he knew it.

"Well, then," he said, setting down the glass. "Why do you think the FBI is lying to you?"

Mary Grant sat on the edge of her chair, anxiety radiating from every pore. "According to them, it's an open-and-shut case. Joe let an armed informant get into a car with him and the informant shot him."

Tank set his phone on the table and asked permission to record their conversation. Mary nodded and went on. She described a voice message she'd received from her husband (Tank assumed that this was the voicemail Grace had referred to) and her fractious interactions with Don Bennett. "First he wanted to take my phone, then he didn't want anything to do with it. He point-blank refused to help me find the message. Why?"

"Maybe he knew what was on it."

"The whole thing didn't make sense," she continued, more calmly. "The doctor said that the bullet that killed Joe struck his spinal cord. He would have been paralyzed instantly from the chest down. He couldn't have shot anyone after that. I just don't get it." She sighed and looked Tank in the eye. "Mostly, Mr. Potter, I just know they're lying. I know Joe and I know he wouldn't get himself into that situation. Your turn. Why are you here?"

Tank finished his iced tea. He wasn't sure how much to tell her. She didn't need to know that he too had questions about who shot whom. It was a cardinal rule of reporting to keep your ideas close to your vest.

"I share your opinion that the FBI has been less than forthcoming about the case," he said. "If we could just find out who the informant was, we'd be a lot closer to figuring things out. Can you tell me anything about what your husband had been working on lately?"

"Supposedly we came to Austin so that Joe could work a municipal corruption case, but it was a lie. There was no corruption case."

"How do you know?"

"I just do." She hesitated, then said, "He was working on something else. A case that had begun in Sacramento."

"Really? And how long ago was that?"

"Nine months. Maybe ten. Last October or November."

Gold. He could sense it. Tank knew better than to push. It was a matter of letting her air her own suspicions. She poured him more iced tea, then turned back to get a glass for herself. Tank's heart jumped a beat. She was going to spill.

"This is what I know," she said, sitting down and fixing him with determined blue eyes. She described in detail her actions since her husband's death: searching his clothing; finding the boarding pass; discovering his secret trips to San Jose, which had begun all the way back in November and continued through the past week; finding out about her husband's contact with Judge Caruso; and finally hearing the bizarre reaction evinced by her husband's former partner, Randy Bell, when she said the word *semaphore*.

"Does any of this make sense?" she said in closing.

"I don't think it's uncommon for an FBI agent to work a confidential case. Still, if you think there's something wrong, there probably is."

Tank looked away, not wanting to be a party to her hopes. He glanced at his hands, noticing how lousy his nails looked. Probably like the rest of him. He glanced up to find Mary Grant still staring at him. His problem had always been that he was a sucker for honesty. Straight talk was the chink in his armor.

"I visited the medical examiner's office last night," he said. "I was trying to get the lowdown on the informant. I didn't, but I saw something that convinced me in no uncertain terms that the FBI is being untruthful. It's not a pleasant matter."

"Go ahead, Mr. Potter. I consider myself forewarned."

As gently as he knew how, Tank gave his opinion that the wounds suffered by Joe Grant and his informant, identity unknown, could not have been inflicted with a handgun, and as such did not jibe with the FBI's official explanation.

"What are you trying to say?" asked Mary.

"That doctor in the hospital was telling you the truth. Your husband couldn't have shot the informant. I don't think the informant shot him, either. It's my opinion that your husband and his informant were murdered by a third party, and that they were shot with a rifle, not a handgun."

Mary Grant sat back. He could see her working through what he'd said, coming to the conclusion, almost against her will, that her suspicions were accurate. The FBI was lying. Her husband had been murdered. Someone was orchestrating a cover-up. Her eyes watered, and for a moment he thought she was going to break down. She looked away and drew a tremendous breath. He thought it was as if she'd swallowed a kind of stone, as her features hardened into a grim mask.

"Have you shared this with the paper?" she asked.

"Not exactly."

"Why not?"

"It's important for me to have corroborating evidence first. My opinion isn't enough."

"But you saw the bodies . . ."

"Even so. I need proof."

"Did you take pictures?"

Tank lied without blinking. "Not allowed."

"Won't the autopsy reveal what kind of bullet killed my husband?"

"In principle, yes."

"I spoke with Mr. Feely at the funeral home last night. He said the FBI is keeping my husband's body a few days longer. The results should prove that what you said is true."

"Actually, the postmortem isn't going to be performed here. Your husband is being sent to the FBI's forensic lab at Quantico. The autopsy will be performed there."

"Is that normal?"

"Not to my knowledge. Postmortems are performed in the county where the death took place."

"So they're stealing his body to cover up what happened."

"Slow down," said Tank, though he shared the same conviction. "We have no idea why they want to send the body to Quantico. There could be a dozen other reasons to perform the autopsy there."

"When are they transporting my husband's body?"

"Sometime after twelve p.m."

"Today?"

"Yes, ma'am."

Mary bolted to her feet and threw her purse over her shoulder.

"Grace," she shouted upstairs, "I'm taking you to Carrie's house. We need to go. Now."

Tank stood as Mary scooped up her car keys and shepherded her daughter outside. "Where are you going?" he asked.

"Downtown. To the medical examiner's office. I'm not letting them take Joe without a fight."

43

Mary paused before climbing into her car. "Aren't you coming?"

Tank Potter stood watching her, hands in his pockets, tousled head cocked at an angle. "It's not my job to confront the FBI," he said.

Mary placed her foot inside the car. She realized she'd gone too far. He was after a story. She was after much more. "I don't expect your help, Mr. Potter, but I wouldn't mind a witness."

Potter made no move to join her.

Mary got in the car and started the engine. With dismay, she noted that the gas was on reserve. "Don't go yet," she called as Tank was climbing into his Jeep. Elbowing the door open, she jumped out and ran up the street. "Tell me you've got enough gas to get me downtown."

Five minutes later the Jeep was barreling down Mopac, the speedometer pushing 75. Mary sat with one hand locked on the armrest, her feet positioned on either side of a gaping hole in the floorboard, praying that they wouldn't run over a loose rock or stray branch.

"Are you all right, Mr. Potter? You were looking a little pale before."

"I'm good." Potter offered an anemic smile. If she hadn't thought he was hungover before, she did now.

Midday traffic was light. In ten minutes they were zipping past the Arboretum. Potter swung the Jeep east onto 183, skirting the gargantuan new Apple campus, National Semiconductor, IBM, and, finally, ONE Technologies. Mary thought of Jess, her own little Bill Gates . . . No, who did she say was the greatest programmer? Her own little Rudeboy.

"We're making good time," said Tank. "Hopefully they won't have moved your husband yet."

"Hopefully," said Mary. "Anyway, thanks."

"For what?"

"For asking questions."

"It's my job."

"Even so. It means something to me."

"I'm a reporter. I'm not doing you any favors."

"You didn't have to drive me."

Tank looked at her, narrowing his eyes. "Do you really think you can stop them from sending your husband to Virginia?"

"No. But at least they'll know we're keeping an eye on them."

"Lady, I'm not sure that's a good thing."

Mary noted the warning in Potter's voice. It reminded her of Randy Bell's admonition never to say *semaphore* again. It came to her that she was putting her nose where it was not wanted and that her inquiries might not be taken lightly. Still, it was the FBI. Joe's FBI. They might be angry with her, but nothing more. She was a citizen. She had a right to ask questions.

"I have to make a call to my buddy," said Tank. "This whole thing may be a wild-goose chase."

One half mile behind the battered Jeep, the Mercedes Airstream rolled down the highway, maintaining a similar speed.

Shanks drove while the Mole sat in the work bay, monitoring surveillance. Though the Jeep was out of sight, there was no chance of losing it. Along with the dozens of pictures of Tank Potter, PittPatt had turned up his phone number, found easily enough on the employee profile page of the *Statesman*'s website. A cross-check of the number showed that Henry Thaddeus Potter was a ONE Mobile customer.

"You're mine," whispered the Mole as he ordered a real-time tap on the number. A live feed was beamed to the communications console. Potter's position as defined by the GPS transponder in his phone was denoted by a pulsing blue dot on a mixed terrain/traffic map.

Next the Mole uploaded a blanket surveillance app onto Potter's phone. The process was similar to updating the phone's operating system, only he didn't need Potter's consent. The app essentially cloned Potter's phone, copying all his e-mails, his call log, his voicemails, his browsing history, and everything else stored inside its forty-seven apps. For all intents and purposes, the phone belonged to the Mole. Potter was only borrowing it.

The Mole had a final trick up his sleeve. Worming his way into the captive phone's settings, he activated the built-in microphone so that it would pick up everything being said inside the car. In effect, he'd turned the phone into a bug.

The Mole played the audio over the speaker. The quality was spotty. He guessed that Potter had the phone in his pocket. Even so, with only minor digital enhancement, he could hear Rascal Flatts singing "Fast Cars and Freedom" loud and clear.

"Looks like he's headed downtown," said Shanks.

"Isn't the paper there?"

"South side of the river."

"Quiet," blurted the Mole. "He's making a call."

The phone number Tank Potter dialed appeared on the screen. Then, a moment later, the name of the account holder. "Cantu, Carlos. 78 Sagebrush Road, Buda, TX." A picture of Cantu flashed onto the screen, and on an adjacent monitor a map showed the address and coordinates of the phone's location: 1213 Sabine Street, Austin, TX. Travis County medical examiner.

The Mole hit the Record button.

"Carlos, it's Tank."

"What's up?"

"I'm calling about those bodies. You know—the Fibbie and the informant."

"What about 'em?"

"They still there?"

"Yep. We've got 'em packed up and loaded. Bennett and his boss are completing the paperwork. Only thing left to do is box up the blood and fluid samples."

"How long till they take off?"

"An hour, maybe longer. They don't appear to be in any hurry."

"All right, thanks, Carlos. Appreciate it."

The call ended.

"What was that all about?" asked Shanks.

"Don't know," said the Mole. "But I can tell you where they're headed. Twelfth and Sabine."

Thirty-five thousand feet above the earth and eight hundred miles away, Ian Prince and Peter Briggs were also listening to Tank Potter's conversation with Carlos Cantu.

"Stand by for instructions," Briggs said to the Mole after Potter had hung up.

Ian crossed the cabin and sat down at his work console. A live map of Austin pinpointed the location of Potter's vehicle traveling south along Interstate 35. He slipped on a pair of earphones and opened a channel to Briggs's men on the ground.

"Why the morgue?"

"Don't know," said the Mole.

Ian had his own ideas, and they centered on the probability that Potter had discovered that Bennett's version of the events in Dripping Springs differed significantly from the actual record. "Bring up Potter's call history."

A list of phone numbers appeared on the monitor. Ian scrolled through and noted that Tank Potter had spoken to Carlos Cantu, the man he'd phoned minutes earlier, the night before.

"Potter send any texts?"

"One," said the Mole. "Transmitting now."

The text appeared on the screen in a pop-up window. It read: "Here. Waiting out front." The timestamp showed 21:07.

"Dig down and get me a GPS fix on that text."

"Sent from 1213 Sabine. Travis County Medical Examiner's Office."

Peter Briggs stood beside Ian. "Potter must have visited the morgue last night. According to the after-action report, Grant and Stark were each killed with a single shot from a sniper's rifle. If Potter examined the bodies, he knows that Bennett's version of events is incorrect. No wonder he visited Mary Grant. He thinks he has a story."

Ian took off the headphones and moved to a quiet corner of the cabin to place a private call.

"Mason."

"Hello, Ed. You're about to have some visitors."

"What's going on?" asked Edward Mason.

"Mary Grant and a reporter from the *Statesman* are headed your way. She's not too keen on your moving her husband to Quantico."

"How the hell does she know anything about that? For that matter, how do you?"

"Give us some credit. We're the ones that hacked into your mainframe. Just get used to the idea that we know everything."

"Limey prick."

"What was that, Ed? I didn't quite catch it."

"Nothing."

"I suggest you hurry up your business. Mrs. Grant is currently moving into the right lane of I-35 to take the Twelfth Street exit. I estimate that you have six minutes."

44

Tank parked across the street from the Travis County Medical Examiner's Office, a large white two-story building running the length of the block. "Go in," he said. "Tell them that you're the next of kin. You have a right to view your husband's body."

Mary got out and walked around the front of the Jeep. As she crossed the street, a dark Ford sedan pulled out of an alley and accelerated sharply, forcing her to jump back a step. A van belonging to the Medical Examiner followed closely behind. Before she could cross, another Ford sped past. The driver looked hard at her. She recognized the gleaming dome, the accusing eyes. The Ford braked, tires screeching, and backed up. Don Bennett rolled down the window.

"What are you doing here, Mary?"

"Why are you taking Joe to Virginia?"

"It's not your concern."

"He's my husband. Of course it's my concern."

Another man sat in the passenger seat. He was older, well groomed, bristling with authority. She'd seen his face in one FBI publication or another, but his name escaped her.

"Go home," said Bennett. "We've got everything under control."

"You said that two days ago. I still don't believe you. What are you hiding, Don?"

Bennett rolled up the window and drove down the street. Mary ran alongside for a few steps, banging her fist on the glass. "What is it, Don? What's Semaphore?"

The Ford accelerated, leaving Mary behind as it barreled past a stop sign and disappeared from sight. Mary ran back to the Jeep and jumped into the passenger seat as a third Ford left the medical examiner's parking lot.

"I asked him about Semaphore."

"It rattled him. He took off like a bat out of hell."

Tank made a U-turn and set off after the FBI convoy.

"Where are you going?" asked Mary. "We can't keep up with them in this wreck."

"We don't need to," said Tank.

Edward Mason smoothed his necktie and settled into the passenger seat for the drive to Bergstrom International Airport. "Mrs. Joseph Grant, I take it."

"Yes," said Don Bennett.

"You didn't mention that she was so attractive."

"Does it matter?"

"Or so forceful," Mason added. He thought Bennett looked anxious, ill-at-ease.

"You asked if she'd give up. I said no. Does that qualify as forceful enough?"

Edward Mason registered his subordinate's anger. He was beginning to wonder if Bennett was entirely with the program.

"Damn," said Bennett. "The Jeep just got onto the freeway a quarter mile back."

Mason swiveled to look out the rear window. He caught a flash of blue paint six or seven cars behind them. "I don't want any record of our transferring Grant's body to Quantico. If the public is made aware that we're taking anything other than absolutely standard measures with regard to this case, they'll demand to know why. Are we clear, Don?"

Bennett nodded. "Yessir."

"Impress me."

The Jeep was doing seventy on the interstate, the engine whining, the steering wheel shaking as if it had dropsy. Don Bennett and the medical examiner's van were somewhere far ahead.

"Your husband never mentioned having to head out to Dripping Springs?" asked Tank.

"I would've remembered Dripping Springs, and I certainly would have remembered the Nutty Brown Cafe. We would have had a laugh."

"And Semaphore? You never heard him mention it?"

"I told you already. I was looking at these doodles my husband had made on his legal pad and the word just popped out."

"Out of the blue? Boom . . . *semaphore*? Just like that?"

"Yes—all those signal flags. When I figured out what he was draw-ing, the word flew out."

"So all we have is Semaphore, secret trips to San Jose, and a receipt from the Nutty Brown Cafe," said Tank.

"Don't forget Judge Caruso," said Mary. "And the fact that you think Joe wasn't killed by a handgun, which means the informant didn't kill him."

"I don't 'think' it," said Tank. "I know it."

He guided the car off I-35 onto 290 east. Mary looked out the win-dow. A sign read, AUSTIN-BERGSTROM INTERNATIONAL AIRPORT 8 MILES. The city had vanished. Untended fields spread to either side of them, dotted with corrugated-tin warehouses, broken fences, rundown farm equipment. She caught a flash of black out of the corner of her eye. "Watch out!" she shouted as a Chevy Tahoe cut in front of them.

Tank hit the brakes and Mary lurched forward, the seat belt pre-venting her from striking the dash. Tank honked. "Watch it, asshole!" Then, to Mary: "Excuse me, ma'am."

"Watch it, fucker!" shouted Mary. She looked at Tank's wide eyes and the two shared a nervous laugh. "Excuse *me*, sir," she said.

Tank moved into the left lane and the Tahoe mirrored him, block-ing his progress. "Okay, funny guy, we get the picture. Now get out of the way."

"Pass him," said Mary.

"I can't. There's someone in the next lane."

Mary looked to her right. Another SUV filled the lane beside them, maintaining the same speed as the Tahoe, effectively boxing them in. "Slow down," she said. "Go around him."

Tank slowed to fifty. The Tahoe blocking them slowed too, as did the SUV to their right. "There's someone behind us, too."

Mary looked over her shoulder. A third dark SUV sat behind them. The driver wore a suit and sunglasses. She looked at the car to their right. Also a white male in a dark suit with sunglasses. The car looked familiar, too. Joe drove the same model from the FBI's motor pool.

"Bennett has his men surrounding us," she said. "I recognize one of them from the hospital. Forget it, Mr. Potter. We've made our point. Let's go home."

"It's our chance to get pictures of Bennett moving your husband to Quantico."

"I'm not sure what good they'll do."

"Leave that to me."

Mary glanced at her watch. It was two o'clock. *Jess.* "I've got to get my daughter from school," she said. "I'm late already."

"She can wait."

"But . . ." Mary stifled her worries. Jess was fine. The fact of the matter was, she was used to waiting.

Tank continued to drive below the speed limit. Traffic was stacked behind them. He slowed and put on his turn signal. His intention was clear. He was giving up the chase. After a few seconds the SUV to their right accelerated, granting them room to scoot over. Tank changed lanes as they passed beneath a sign that read: AIRPORT FREIGHT ½ MILE.

The lead Tahoe accelerated. The SUV behind them broke off as well. In seconds the FBI's vehicles disappeared from view. The pent-up traffic rushed ahead, passing them as if they were a rock in a stream.

"Seat belt on?" asked Tank.

"Yes. Why?"

"Hold on." Tank yanked the car to the left as he downshifted into third gear and rammed the accelerator. Behind them, tires squealed. Horns blared. The Jeep bounded across two lanes of traffic and hit the dirt shoulder, its front tires leaving the ground before landing with a spine-jarring thud. Tank steered down the embankment and up the other side. Both oncoming lanes were empty. He cut across the highway and down the on-ramp.

"Look out!" shouted Mary.

Fifty yards ahead, a big rig was barreling straight at them. All Mary could see was its enormous chrome grille and the headlights, which she swore were staring right at her. The air horn sounded. Mary gripped the armrest and braced for impact. Tank slotted the Jeep left, his door striking the safety barrier, sparks flying. The rig passed within an inch, close enough that the change in air pressure made her ears pop.

Mary covered her head and screamed.

And then the rig had passed. They were down the ramp, turning right and shooting across the underpass and onto the frontage road.

"What was that?" asked Mary, pinned to her door.

"Highway chicken. Old college game."

"You're serious? You mean you've done that before?"

"I saw it all the way. We weren't in danger for a second."

"And the truck?"

"You got me there. Kind of came out of nowhere."

Mary let go of the armrest as anger replaced fear. "Why did you do it? We're too far behind to catch them anyway. They're probably already aboard the plane."

But Tank appeared unfazed. For the first time that day he didn't appear as if he were about to throw up. "Trust me, Mrs. Grant. We'll beat them there."

45

The FBI's convoy idled at the entry to the private aircraft concourse at Bergstrom International Airport as the gate rolled slowly open.

"We're too late," said Mary.

Two hundred yards separated them. Tank Potter had chosen to use the old construction road running across the back of the airport complex. The route was longer, but there were no traffic signals and few vehicles. She watched nervously as the gate continued on its track. The Tahoe and the other SUVs that had hemmed them in on the freeway pulled up behind the sedans. The last vehicle backed up and turned in order to block both lanes of traffic. They'd been spotted.

Driving much too fast, Tank rounded a last curve and turned into the private aircraft entry. Instead of stopping at the improvised roadblock, he swung the Jeep left, mounted the curb, and accelerated across an expanse of grass before swinging back onto the road.

The gate was three-quarters open. The first sedan nosed forward.

"Slow down," said Mary.

Tank kept the Jeep on a collision course with the Ford.

"Stop," said Mary. "You're going too fast."

"This may get ugly. Hold on." Tank braked hard. The Jeep skidded before colliding with the front left wheel well of the Ford.

FBI agents swarmed from their vehicles and surrounded the Jeep, weapons drawn and aimed at Tank and Mary. Don Bennett strode toward them. "Out of the car."

Tank climbed out, hands high. "It was an accident."

"Shut up, Mr. Potter," said Don Bennett. "Consider yourself under arrest."

"You know me?" said Tank.

A younger agent approached from his rear and slugged him in the kidney. Tank dropped to a knee. The agent yanked his hands behind his back and cuffed him.

Mary confronted Bennett. "I'm not letting you take him."

"Back off, Mary, or I'll cuff you, too."

"Everyone, let's calm down." The slim, authoritative man approached, buttoning his jacket. "Holster your firearms, gentlemen," he said, turning in a circle, waving his agents' guns down. "Mrs. Grant, I'm Edward Mason, deputy director. May I offer my sincerest condolences, both personally and on behalf of the Bureau?"

"I know your name."

"I have to admit that I'm not used to having my car rammed."

"And I'm not used to being blocked in on the freeway."

Mason's lips tightened in something between a grimace and a smile.

"I'm sure Don Bennett explained everything to you on the ride over," said Mary. "Why are you taking Joe to Quantico?"

"The law requires us to perform a postmortem on your husband, and it's our policy to carry out the procedure in Virginia with our own trusted team of physicians."

"That's not true," said Tank.

Mason continued, unruffled. "I understand it's your wish that Joe be buried in Boston. Naturally we'll make sure that he's sent to you as quickly as possible."

"How soon might that be?"

"I can't promise, but a week should be sufficient. Ten days at the outside."

"To perform an autopsy?" Tank stated. "It should have been done already. Joe Grant and the informant he was meeting with were each killed by a single shot from a high-caliber rifle. Why are you trying to keep that fact a secret?"

Mason put a hand on Mary's arm, gently turning her away from Potter and Bennett. "Mrs. Grant—*Mary*—can we speak privately?"

Mary looked over her shoulder at Tank Potter, arms bound behind his back, forced to his knees. "Yes," she said.

Mason led her to his car. The two climbed into the rear seat. The engine was running, and the interior was cool and comfortable. "So," he said with an emphatic sigh. "How in the world did we get here?"

"Don Bennett lied to me about the circumstances surrounding Joe's death. Now you're moving Joe's body out of Austin so that you can lie about the results of the autopsy. It's my intention to find out how and why my husband was killed. I'd say that summarizes things."

"Well put," said Mason. "Clear. Succinct. None of the bullshit I usually get."

"Don't patronize me."

"I didn't mean to. I guess I'd want to know the same thing. Don told me you'd received a call from Joe indicating that he was in some kind of trouble."

"That's correct."

"Can you give me details about what he said?"

"Are you admitting that you lied to me and the press about Joe's death?"

"I'm suggesting that you and I might be working toward a common goal."

Mary considered this. If she wanted to hear his side of the story, she owed him hers. "I can't remember all of Joe's words. He called to tell me that he was in danger. He feared for his life."

"He said that?"

"In so many words."

"But nothing specific about the case he was working on?"

"No."

"Or the man he was meeting?"

"Don't you know who he was meeting?"

"We know, but it's important that neither you nor anyone else does . . . at least for the time being. Let me be honest with you—and please, what I say remains between us."

"You mean I shouldn't say anything to Mr. Potter."

"I'd appreciate it."

"All right."

Mason drew a breath. "Joe was working a sensitive case. *Confidential* doesn't begin to describe it. I can't go into details, but I will tell you that his work involved the highest levels of national security. Joe delayed taking his promotion to D.C. to continue working it. One day soon you'll read about it in the papers. You'll learn everything. But for now we need to keep it locked down. That includes guarding the identity of the informant. Should his name be revealed, it would adversely impact the investigation. I'd go so far as to say it would shut it down. I know you wouldn't want to jeopardize something that Joe gave his life for."

Mary looked closely at Edward Mason, the grave, officious face of the government. She noted the neat gray hair cut an inch above his collar, the steady blue eyes, the crisp button-down shirt and dark necktie. Mason was the Bureau's number-two man, and he carried the power of office easily. He exuded the steady, reassuring demeanor associated with airline pilots or astronauts, or movie stars charged with carrying out desperate missions in the face of daunting odds. One of Joe's fellow Marines, judging by his tie clasp. A man's man. Joe would gladly have followed him into battle.

And Mary? What about her? She was a good citizen. Loyal. Patriotic. Daughter of a family with a proud naval tradition. Who was she to question the actions of the FBI? Who was she to doubt Edward Mason's word? To refuse his earnest request?

And yet . . .

"What about what Tank Potter said?" she asked.

"About the gunshot wounds?"

Mary nodded.

"I wouldn't put much stock in Mr. Potter's words."

"He's a reporter. It's his job to get the truth."

"Not exactly," said Mason. "He used to be a reporter."

"Excuse me?"

"Mr. Potter was arrested two nights ago for driving while intoxicated. He no longer works at the *Statesman*. From what I understand, he's a very sick man. You might consider the possibility that Mr. Potter manipulated you to drum up a story so he could get his job back. It's a reporter's job to lean on their sources until they spill, so to speak."

"But he has pictures."

"Pictures? Of your husband—"

"And the informant. A pistol doesn't do that. At least, that's what Mr. Potter said."

"Maybe it would be wise to have an expert look at them."

"Maybe," said Mary.

Mason fixed her with his steady eyes. "For now, all you need to know is that Joe died heroically in the service of his country. The United States will be a safer place because of his work. I'll see to it that his pension is based on the salary he was to receive after his promotion to the Senior Executive Service. When this is all over, you and your family can expect a commendation from the president."

"The president?" said Mary, but all she was thinking about was the enormous impact on the family's finances that a promotion to the Senior Executive Service would bring.

"The highest levels of national security, Mary."

Still, her curiosity demanded one thing. "So what is Semaphore, then?"

Mason cocked his head. "What was that, Mary?"

The hint was plain enough. She heard Randy Bell ordering her never to say that word again. "Nothing," she said. "I must have misheard something."

Mason placed his hand on her arm. "Mary, you're a civilian. Our work can be dangerous. May I have your word that we won't be running into you again . . . *for your sake?*"

"Yes," said Mary.

"Promise?"

Mason extended his hand and she shook it, looking directly into his eyes. "Promise."

"Thank you for your cooperation. I can see that Joe was a lucky man."

Mary reached for the door handle.

"And Mary," Edward Mason said, in an entirely different voice. Her kind uncle had been replaced by the admiral in one of his black moods. "Vehicular battery is a serious offense. A felony. Add to that interfering with a federal investigation. You and Mr. Potter nearly got into a lot of trouble. I don't think your children need to see their mother in a federal penitentiary on top of losing their father."

"Thank you, Mr. Mason."

"Ed—*please.*"

Mary stepped out of the car. During their tête-à-tête, someone had extricated the Jeep from the Ford. Despite the impact and the deafening noise of the collision, there appeared to be little damage to Tank Potter's car. The Ford wasn't as fortunate but looked drivable.

Mason came around the front of the sedan. "Cut Potter loose," he said.

"But . . . ," Don Bennett protested, hurrying toward his superior.

"Do it," said Mason.

Tank Potter got to his feet and stood patiently as an agent cut the plastic cuffs. Mason approached him and whispered a few words that Mary couldn't hear, but the effect was to make Potter wince repeatedly. She imagined he'd gotten the same warning as she had, but without the sugar coating. Keep your nose out of the FBI's business or your ass is getting thrown in jail.

"You're free to go, Mr. Potter," said Edward Mason. "I'd get those brakes checked if I were you."

"Thank you, Mr. Mason. I'll be sure to have my car looked at imme-diately."

Tank watched Mason head back to his car, then walked over to Mary. "What did he tell you?"

"Is it true?" She was surprised at the anger she felt toward him. More than Bennett or Mason, he had manipulated her. Their actions, however mercenary, were on behalf of their country. Potter's were strictly for personal gain.

"The DUI? Yeah, it's true. But that doesn't—"

"And you no longer work at the *Statesman*?"

"Technically . . ."

"Do you or don't you?"

"No, ma'am. I'm no longer an employee."

"So you visited me to drum up a story to get your job back. You came to my house to lean on me and see if I spilled?"

"To 'lean on you'? Where'd you get that? I'm a reporter. We inter-view people. We ask questions. It's our job. I wasn't leaning on you."

"You used to be a reporter," said Mary, her voice, her body, trem-bling with rage. "Now you're just an unemployed drunk who pressures widows into divulging private information."

"It's not like that. I'm not making any of that stuff up. Ask Mason. He knows it's true. Why do you think they're moving the bodies?"

Mary pinned her shoulders back and raised her chin. "I don't have anything more to say to you, Mr. Potter. I'd appreciate it if you left my family and me alone."

"What kind of Kool-Aid did he give you, lady?"

"Just the truth. Next time you'd be well advised to do the same. Goodbye."

Mary walked to Edward Mason's car and tapped on the window. "Would it be possible for one of your agents to give me a ride home?"

"Our pleasure."

"I apologize for any inconvenience. It won't happen again."

46

As ONE 1 began its initial descent into the Austin area, Ian stood in his personal quarters, humming a song from a favorite musical. ONE 1 was essentially a bespoke 737-900ER designed to his requirements. There was a screening room and a fitness room, an office, and a bedroom. His quarters took up the rear of the plane. The office was identical to his offices in Austin, Palo Alto, Guangzhou, and Bangalore, if on a smaller scale: dark carpets, birch furnishings, minimal, spare, efficient.

"You wanted me?" asked Briggs.

"Come in," said Ian. "Shut the door."

"Did you ask to see me so we could sing show tunes?"

"Do you know any?"

Briggs regarded Ian as if he were mad. "What are you so damned happy for? We have a problem and we need to tie it off."

"I thought you already told me it was 'banked.' Once—or was it twice?"

"Call me a gentleman. I have a soft spot for women."

"And your suggestion?"

"You don't need to know."

"Didn't you hear what Mason said? Mary Grant apologized for damaging the investigation. She promised not to disturb things further."

"You believe her?"

There was no point in answering the question. Belief was subjective. Ian trafficked in certainties. "Show a carpenter a nail and he hits it with a hammer."

"Excuse me?"

"You're the carpenter," said Ian. "An excellent carpenter, to be sure, but a carpenter nonetheless. Sometimes a more elegant solution is called for."

"The woman has to go. How's that for elegant?"

Ian walked to his desk and sat. He'd spent the past half hour sorting through the angles. Eliminating an FBI agent was one thing: a single, orchestrated act with all pieces in place to control any possible damage. Eliminating the agent's wife was something else entirely. Her death only days after his would not go unnoticed. Questions would be asked. The story had all the makings of a tabloid sensation. Edward Mason was a powerful official, but he had no means of controlling the investigation into the murder of a private citizen, or the press coverage it would garner.

There was more. Ian refused to orphan two young girls. He knew about growing up without a father. He hadn't wanted to get rid of Joseph Grant, but in the end there had been no other choice. Grant was too tenacious, and Hal Stark had far too much information. In the end it was Ed Mason's decision as much as his.

"About the reporter," said Ian. "The one with the pictures. What's his name again?"

"Potter. Tank Potter."

"Yes, about Mr. Potter and his indiscreet friend at the medical examiner's office . . ."

"Cantu."

"Yes, Mr. Cantu." Ian drummed his fingers on the desk. "Those two are nails. Feel free to use your hammer."

Briggs appeared happier: a horse given his reins. "And the pictures?"

"Tell the Mole to make them disappear. I believe that's well within his skill set. Let me take care of the woman."

"You're sure about this elegant solution?"

Ian spun in his chair and gazed out the window.

"All right, then," said Briggs. "We'll do it your way." He paused at the door. "What's that song, anyway? I think I've heard it."

Ian kicked his feet onto the desk and sang aloud. *"How do you solve a problem like Maria?"*

Briggs looked away, sickened, and hurried fore.

Ian shook his head. Of course Briggs hated *The Sound of Music.* No one was killed in it.

He continued singing, his voice growing louder, his hands moving theatrically. *"How do you catch a moonbeam in your hand?"*

He had the answer.

Sloths.

47

Tank Potter made a beeline across the newsroom to Al Soletano's office. "I've got proof," he said, holding his phone above his head. "I told you I had a story. Here it is. Proof."

The few reporters at work popped their heads above their cubicles to see what the commotion was all about. A few called his name. Tank paid them no heed. His wrists burned from the flex cuffs. His back ached from the kidney punch. But worst was the injury to his professional integrity.

"Al!" he shouted. "You there? Come out of your hobbit hole."

Soletano emerged from his office, a sheaf of paper in one hand, a cup of coffee in the other. "What are you doing here, Potter?" he asked wearily.

"I was right about the story—about Joe Grant."

"I don't want to hear."

"Proof," said Tank, brandishing his smartphone.

"Take it somewhere else. You no longer work for this newspaper."

"The FBI was stonewalling. I knew it all along."

"Did you hear me?

"I have pictures showing that Grant and the informant weren't killed by a handgun. They directly refute Bennett's official account."

"Sorry, Tank. Can't help you."

"Did you hear me? Pictures. Evidence."

"Did you hear me? Get lost."

"Fine. I'll take them over to AP. I'm sure the Associated Press will be happy to look at them. And when they do, it'll be their story."

Soletano stared at him a second, then inclined his head in the direction of his office. "In. Sit. Talk."

Tank entered the office and sat down. "By the way, do you have a glass of water? I'm dying of thirst."

"Look who's the smartass," said Soletano, following him in and closing the door. "One day without a drink and you think you deserve a medal." He perched on the edge of his desk, arms crossed over his belly. "I'm listening."

Tank struggled to fit his bulk into the chair. With painstaking detail, he described his visit to the medical examiner's office the night before and his certainty that both Joseph Grant and the informant had been killed not with a handgun but with a high-powered rifle. Before showing Soletano the photographs of the corpses, he recounted his interview with Mary Grant that morning, beginning with the troubled voice message left by her husband (then mysteriously erased) and ending with her call to Randy Bell, Joseph Grant's former partner. "She thinks the case her husband and Bell were working on was called Semaphore."

Finally he gave Soletano a blow-by-blow narrative of his visit to the medical examiner's office three hours earlier and the race to reach the airport before the FBI in order to chronicle its shipment of the corpses to Quantico.

"You rammed your Jeep into the FBI?" said Soletano.

Tank nodded.

"And they didn't arrest you?"

"I'm here."

"You got balls, Potter. I'll give you that. It's a wonder you're not in jail." Soletano pushed himself off the desk. "Let me see your proof."

"You can show the photos to a forensic pathologist. No way a handgun did this. Wounds this size come from a rifle."

Tank opened the photo roll. The pictures of Joseph Grant and the informant were the last he'd taken, and as such should have been the first he saw. Oddly, the pictures weren't there. "Just a sec," he said. "I'm getting them."

Soletano looked unimpressed.

Tank closed the photo app, then reopened it. The last picture taken was always visible in a frame placed in the lower left-hand corner of the screen. He double-tapped the image and got a topless picture of Jeannette, a buxom blond favorite from Pedro's.

"Any time now," said Soletano.

Tank went back to the photo roll.

Nix. Nada. Zip.

The pictures he'd taken at the medical examiner's office were no longer there. Tank was a master at jumping to conclusions. First Joseph

Grant's voice message had been erased from his wife's phone. Now it was Tank's turn. In the time it had taken him to drive from the airport to the *Statesman*, someone had hacked into his phone and deleted the photographs.

But who?

No one knew about the pictures except himself, Mary, and of course Carlos Cantu. The FBI might infer that he had pictures from the fact that he had admitted to seeing the corpses, but they had no proof. Unless Mary Grant had told Mason. Either way, they didn't have his phone number or the unit's IP address.

Or did they?

Tank recalled Mary Grant asking him if he'd "leaned on her to spill." If the words sounded familiar, it was because he'd e-mailed a buddy from the paper earlier that he was heading over to her house to do exactly that. And why had the FBI been tearing out of the ME's building when Carlos Cantu had told him barely fifteen minutes earlier that they didn't appear to be in any hurry? Somehow they'd known he was coming. Even before Tank and Mary reached the airport, they'd been listening in.

All this came to him in a second.

"Well," said Soletano, "are you going to show me or not?"

Tank put down the phone. "Actually . . . *not*."

"What do you mean? Let me see 'em."

Tank shook his head. "You know what, Al? You're right. I'm not sure I do have a story."

"You bullshittin' me? You get me all hot and bothered, and now you're giving me nothing?"

"Sorry, Al. My bad. I'll be back when I'm sure."

"Don't bother. You've wasted enough of my time as it is. Now get out."

On the ground floor, Tank stopped in the break room and bought a can of Coke. The loss of the photographs didn't discourage him. On the contrary. The fact that the FBI—or another interested party— was hacking into his phone and listening in on his conversations was a tonic. You didn't destroy evidence unless there was a crime. Tank was on the right track.

He looked at his phone.

Traitor.

There was only one punishment for treason.

Outside the building, Tank walked briskly back to the Jeep. Crouching, he placed the phone beneath the rear tire, wedging it between asphalt and rubber. Once behind the wheel, he put the Jeep into reverse. He heard a crunch, and then another as the tire passed over the handset. Still he wasn't satisfied. Phones were tough little bastards these days. He'd dropped his a dozen times, and though the screen was cracked and the case was chipped, it still worked.

Sliding the transmission into park, he stepped out of the car and examined the handset. The phone was crushed but looked more or less intact. He imagined that somewhere inside it a battery was still connected to a transmitter that still emitted a signal that someone somewhere with the proper technology could track.

Tank dug his heel into the metal and glass and ground it into the asphalt. Finished, he picked up the phone. He had to marvel at its design. It just didn't look dead.

He had an idea.

Tank threw the phone onto the passenger seat and drove around to the front of the building. Twenty yards away flowed the green, fast-moving waters of the Colorado River. He got out of the car, strode to the riverbank, and threw the phone as far as he could. He watched the handset tumble end over end, sparkling in the sun, before dropping silently into the water.

Let 'em track that, he thought.

Satisfied that he was alone—really and truly alone—and that no unseen witness was tagging along beside him, keeping a record of his every word and movement and reporting them to his master, he returned to his car and accelerated out of the lot.

It was almost five.

Happy hour.

There was only one place he wanted to be.

48

"Do you know who Odysseus is?" Ian asked Katarina as he entered the spa. ONE 1 had landed a while ago, but he needed to stay at the airport to greet the Israelis.

"A Greek," said Katarina. "Was he a god or a man?"

Ian closed the door and disrobed. "Man. A warrior. The chap who led all the others inside the Trojan Horse."

Katarina was wearing shorts and a tank top, her admirable biceps on display. She handed him his third batch of supplements. No magic drip today. After taking his pills, Ian lay down on the massage table. Katarina disrobed and when she was naked began to massage him, concentrating on the shoulders and neck, kneading his muscles with her strong fingers.

"Why do you ask about Odysseus?"

"Just curious."

Katarina found a knot deep down and applied pressure to it for a full minute. Ian sucked in air through clenched teeth. The pleasure was excruciating.

"You are never curious," she said. "Why are you thinking about the Trojan Horse?"

"Ah, Katarina, you're too smart by half."

The German moved her hands lower, working each arm, then his chest, then lower still. Ian gasped. The hands moved expertly, clinically, one professional working with another. He closed his eyes and let the pleasure engulf him. He was not thinking about a woman or a man or anything remotely physical. He was thinking about Odysseus. Not the warrior, but the software of his own creation, and it was far, far sexier.

Odysseus was malware, a piece of software designed to take control of a computer independent of its user. He'd written it to perform three tasks—to surveil and transmit every keystroke of its host; to copy and transmit the contents of the host's hard drive and any attached flash drive, backup drive, or auxiliary memory device; and to grant Ian complete control of the platform so that he might roam around it at will and edit, amend, copy, steal, or otherwise corrupt things as he saw fit.

Upon landing, he'd shut himself inside his private quarters and spent much too long surfing the Net in an effort to find the most amusing video of an animal he could. He looked at Zen kittens, talking puppies, dancing fish, laughing giraffes, and a dozen other cute, cuddly, and altogether adorable creatures.

Of course he also looked at the clip of the sloth. The sloth wasn't the cutest by a long shot, but according to their browser log, the Grant girls must have thoroughly enjoyed it.

Ian quickly found three additional clips of sloths that he found particularly irresistible. *Irresistible* was the key word in this endeavor. Finally he chose the one he thought the girls would like best.

The trap was simple enough. E-mails would arrive in the mailboxes addressed to Grace and Jessie Grant carrying the header "Cutest Sloth Ever!" Opening the mail, the girls would be presented with a link to the video Ian had selected. The success of Ian's ploy rested on one of the girls clicking on the link. Once they did, the video of the sloth would begin playing. Attached to it, ready to crawl into the deepest, darkest crevasses of the Grants' computer, was Odysseus, as stealthy and cunning as the Greek warrior of ancient lore.

Katarina's fingers stroked him expertly, dispassionately. His back arched and she put her mouth on him. Ian allowed himself release, lips pressed together to stifle any escaping sound.

Katarina cleaned him quickly and neatly. "Ian, may I ask you a question?"

"Yes."

"What happened to Odysseus?"

"No one knows. He died, I suppose. Everyone must."

Katarina laughed, fixing him with her cold blue eyes. "Yes, Ian, everyone must. Even you."

Ian slapped her. "Don't ever say that again."

49

"He went dark," said the Mole.

"How's that?"

"Signal vanished."

"But you just had it." Shanks glanced over his shoulder. The Mole sat at his console, headphones draped around his neck, eyes glaring at the monitor. Shanks returned his attention to the road. Rush hour, and traffic on I-35 was slow. "Find it?"

"There's no 'it' to find," said the Mole. "One second he's blasting in the clear. The next he's dark. A ghost."

The Mole recommenced the search protocol by entering Tank Potter's mobile phone number. The handset's corresponding eleven-digit alphanumeric identification appeared on the screen. Potter was a ONE Mobile customer and theoretically easy to locate. The Mole requested that the number be pinged. A signal was broadcast to the handset in order to establish its real-time location as measured by the internal GPS chip standard in all cell phones. Two minutes earlier the phone, and presumably Tank Potter, had been inside the premises of the *Austin American-Statesman* at 305 South Congress Avenue. Now the pulsing red dot denoting his location had vanished.

"He knows," said the Mole.

"About time. You wiped his photos an hour ago. His story just went up in smoke."

"Continue to his last known location. Let's hope for a visual."

Shanks pulled into the *Statesman*'s parking lot five minutes later. "A rusted-out Jeep Cherokee shouldn't be hard to spot."

The Mole slid into the front seat beside him and scanned the parked cars.

"No joy," said Shanks after he finished a circuit of the lot. "You sure he was here?"

"GPS doesn't lie."

"He's gone now."

"I give him a ten-minute head start."

"What do you suggest?" asked Shanks. "We lick our finger, stick it into the wind, and guess where he's headed?"

"Pull over and be quiet."

Shanks slid the Airstream into a spot at the back corner of the lot. "Better be quick. Briggs wants this guy taken care of."

The Mole began feverishly typing commands into the console. It wasn't a matter of guessing where Potter was headed but of analyzing his past actions to predict where, statistically, he was most likely to go, the pertinent question being, where could Tank Potter usually be found at five p.m.?

First the Mole asked ONE Mobile's servers to provide a history of Potter's movements between the hours of four and six p.m., based on GPS readings transmitted from his phone. For a data range the Mole chose the past fifty-two weeks, with data points chosen randomly four times each hour. A jumble of nearly three thousand dots clogged the screen. It was immediately evident that he spent the preponderance of his time at or close to the *Statesman* headquarters.

The Mole narrowed the search parameter to Thursdays while keeping the time period constant. Approximately four hundred dots remained and only confirmed that Potter rarely left a two-square-mile area surrounding his office. The problem was that many of the coordinates had been taken while Potter was driving and failed to offer an establishment where he might be found. Still, there were four smaller but statistically significant clusters of dots at defined locations other than the *Statesman*.

The Mole accessed a record of all text messages sent from Potter's phone on Thursdays between four and six p.m., winnowing the time frame to the past six months. He was not interested in the messages themselves but again in Potter's geographic location when he sent them. A sample set of two hundred dots appeared. The four clusters were now just two, not counting the *Statesman*.

The Mole activated the map's tagging feature. The names of all nearby banks, restaurants, boutiques, and gas stations appeared. Potter had sent 107 texts from inside a single 50-square-meter perimeter.

The Mole sampled several texts randomly, the messages appearing on an adjacent monitor.

At P's. You coming?
Billy boy, get down here. The joint is jumping!
Hi darlin! Hanging at P's. When can I expect you?

All three had originated from 16415 Barton Springs Road. Pedro's Especiale Bar and Grill.

The Mole brought up the website on his monitor. The screen filled with a picture of a black velvet painting of Salma Hayek in a bikini. "Throwback Thursdays. Happy Hour 4–8."

"Good news," said the Mole. "We got him."

50

"Well," said Jessie. "What was that all about?"

Mary waved as the Ford pulled out of the driveway. "I needed to talk with some of Dad's colleagues."

"Why didn't you drive?"

"Someone else gave me a ride."

The front door opened. Grace stepped outside. "Where's Tank?"

Mary hesitated and Jessie pounced. "Who's Tank?" she asked, dark eyes instantly suspicious, darting between Mary and Grace for any sign of treachery.

Mary smiled. "Let's go inside, Jess. It's hot out here."

Jessie had been too awed at seeing her mother being chauffeured by a young, handsome FBI agent to ask any questions on the ride home from UT. She'd been in surprisingly polite form the entire way and spent the trip talking about how she'd been the only one in her class who'd solved some kind of challenging problem. "A hack," she'd called it.

"Rudeboy did it in five minutes," Jessie had explained. "Okay, I'm not him. I needed thirteen minutes, but at least I did it, Mom. I did the Capture the Flag hack. I'm as good as Rudeboy, and he's the best."

Mary shut the front door and walked into the kitchen, her daughters following like a lynch mob.

"Who was driving that car, Mom?" asked Grace.

"The FBI," said Jessie. "Now be quiet. Mom didn't answer my question yet. Who's Tank?"

"He's a reporter," said Grace.

"For the *Statesman*," said Mary, adding inadvertently, "kind of."

"Kind of? What's that supposed to mean?"

Grace giggled. "He's really tall and he has messy hair."

"Shh," said Jess, her eyes never leaving Mary.

"He had some questions about your father. That's all."

"Was it about Dad's voice message?"

There it was: the reason for Jess's worry. Mary had been foolish to think her soothing words would allay Jessie's fears that she'd been the one responsible for erasing Joe's voice message.

"No," she said, trying to sound light, breezy. "Just about his work. Nothing that concerns you two guys." She took a bottle of orange juice from the fridge and poured two glasses. "Here you are. Why don't you find something for all of us to watch on TV?"

Jessie didn't budge. "Mom, something's wrong. We can tell. You're not acting normal."

"Yeah," said Grace. "I heard you talking to Tank before."

"He was here?" demanded Jessie. "In the kitchen?"

Grace said, "What really happened to Daddy? What did he mean when he said that they were lying about what kind of gun shot him?"

"Who was lying?" Jessie looked from Mary to her sister. "Grace, what did the reporter say?"

"I'm not sure," said Grace. "But he didn't want them to take Dad to Virginia. That's why Mom went with him downtown."

"Mom, you need to tell us what's going on. We're old enough to know."

Mary looked at her daughters. Chalk and cheese. She was at a loss for words. How much should she explain? Were they old enough to share her concerns? She felt cornered. She wished Joe were there to help.

"Tell us the truth," said Jessie. "This is about Dad. We have a right to know."

"What's Semaphore?" asked Grace.

Mary snapped, "Shut up, Gracie."

At once Grace's eyes welled up.

"Mom!" shouted Jess. "You shut up."

"Don't talk to your mother that way," Mary retorted.

"Both of you, stop." Grace looked between them, crying. "Don't argue with each other. I hate it."

Mary wrapped her arms around Grace. "Come now, mouse. It's all right. I didn't mean it. Mommy's just upset. I'm sorry." She kissed Grace's blond head and saw a shadow of resentment cross Jessie's face. Mary opened her arm and motioned Jessie closer. "Come here, peanut."

Jessie shook her head, arms crossed.

"Please," said Mary.

Jessie remained rooted to the spot, glaring at her mother. Mary sat down with Grace at the table and held her until she stopped crying. She noted that Grace had winced a few times since she'd come home. "What is it, mouse?" she asked. "What's the matter?"

"Nothing," said Grace.

"You're sure?"

"Don't change the subject," said Jessie. "She said she's fine. Stop doting on her. She's not some fragile piece of china."

"I'm fine, Mommy," said Grace with a smile, wiping her eyes.

"Really?"

"Promise."

Jessie shrugged her shoulders and sighed dramatically. The only thing missing was a roll of the eyes. "Tell us about Dad."

"First of all," began Mary, "you have nothing to worry about."

"Who said we were worried?"

"That's enough, young lady," Mary snapped, fire in her eyes. Jessie swallowed and appeared to shrink an inch. Mary drew a breath and spoke calmly. "After your father was killed, I had some questions about exactly what happened. Mr. Potter had some questions, too, but he and I aren't going to be talking about it anymore. This is something only I can figure out."

Jessie pulled out a chair and sat. "What do you think happened?" she asked, no longer the antagonist.

"I'm not sure. Just—"

"Did they take Dad to Virginia?"

"Yes." Mary related her conversation with Edward Mason, making sure to pass along his words about their father's heroism. She had no doubt that Joe had acted heroically, no matter the exact circumstances of his death. Still, she felt disingenuous.

"Sounds like bullshit," said Jessie.

"No curse words, young lady."

"Or what?"

Mary leaned forward and patted her leg. "Or I'll wash out your mouth with soap."

"Gross," said Grace. "Soap tastes like poop."

Mary smiled. Even Jessie laughed.

"So what are you going to do?" asked Grace.

"Mr. Mason told me that your father was working on an important case to help keep our country safe. He said we'd find out all the details soon. Your father is going to receive a commendation from the president."

"Wow," said Grace, beaming. "That's amazing."

But Jessie pursed her lips as if she'd chewed on a lemon rind. "You believed him?"

Mary looked at her older daughter, hair hanging in her face, eyes staring like lasers right through her. The problem was that Jessie was too smart. She never accepted a word as the truth until she could prove it herself. Her cynicism had come at a price. She'd heard too many doctor's promises, seen too many medicines that didn't work, sat by her sister's bed too many days. Life had taught her to believe in deeds, not words.

"Maybe," Mary answered finally. It was as close to a declaration of her own feelings as she was willing to make in front of the kids.

The answer satisfied Jessie. She nodded and her frown relaxed. Distrust was a safer place from which to view the world, and Mary realized that for now, anyway, she shared that same dark promontory.

"I'll make dinner," she said, standing, rubbing her hands together. "I'm starving."

"Chicken fingers," said Grace. "With French fries and mustard."

"Barf," said Jessie. "I want a hamburger."

"Dog barf," said Grace.

Mary smiled, happy for even that small measure of relief.

Order was restored.

For now.

51

Shanks slowed the van as it passed Pedro's Especiale Bar and Grill on Barton Springs Road.

"Is he there?" The Mole poked his head from behind his work console.

"Like clockwork." Shanks stared at the blue Jeep Cherokee parked in front. The lot appeared full. He turned at the corner and continued down the street. To his dismay, cars occupied every inch of curb space.

"Must be a popular place," said the Mole. "Looks like half of Austin's here."

Shanks continued to the end of the street and turned around. The alley behind the restaurant was likewise packed. He stopped behind the bar's back entrance. "Any cameras?"

"None outside. We're good."

"Take the wheel. I'm going to go in. Make sure our man is there."

"Don't make a scene."

"If the opportunity presents itself, I'm not going to let him get away. The matter is time-sensitive. That stiletto of yours goes in real easy. A little poke through the ribs, nick his heart. The man will be dead before he knows what got him."

The Mole slipped his knife from its sheath on his calf. "Make it quick."

Shanks slid the blade up his sleeve. "Lightning."

Tank sat on his favorite stool and raised a hand. "Long day, Pedrito," he called. "*Una cerveza, por favor.*"

He'd made it through a day without a drink. Or almost a day—not that anyone was counting. If Mary Grant didn't want him investigating, that was fine by him. He could take his time, dig up more evidence about what Edward Mason and Don Bennett were covering up. Good stories required patience. How long had Woodward and Bernstein needed for Watergate? A year? Two?

Pedro set a bottle of Tecate on the bar and poured a generous shot of tequila, the amber liquid overflowing the edges. "Throwback Thursday, man. You forget to bring your jersey?"

"Left it at home."

"No one's going to know who you are without it."

"Thanks," said Tank, wrapping his fingers around the beer. "Appreciate the vote of confidence."

"Got you something," said Pedro.

"A bottle of La Familia?"

"Nah. Something we were talking about." Pedro reached beneath the bar and came out with a braided leather quirt. "Not exactly a buggy whip, but pretty close. It's yours. Help you figure out what to do now that you're not a journalist anymore."

Before Tank could respond, Pedro left to help another customer. Tank set the riding crop on the counter and lifted the beer to his lips. Who said he wasn't a journalist anymore? Al Soletano? Mary Grant? Edward Mason?

If you're a journalist, what are you doing in Pedro's?

Tank looked at the crop. A journalist tracks down sources and gathers evidence. He digs out the truth, no matter how cleverly it's hidden. He doesn't give up until he has his story. A journalist has a sacred obligation to the truth.

Once he'd believed all that garbage.

And now?

He ran his fingers along the crop, waiting for an answer.

Shanks slipped into Pedro's through the back entrance. The dining room was dimly lit and he needed a few moments for his eyes to adjust. The first thing he noticed was the colorful plastic fish hanging from the ceiling. Then the velvet paintings of Hispanic stars. Real class. Only a few tables were occupied. None of the diners matched Potter's description.

A din was coming from the bar area. He crossed the room and ducked his head around the corner. The place was a madhouse. Students, young professionals, even a few oldsters. Many wore dated clothing and sported old-school hairstyles. He noticed a sign advertising THROWBACK THURSDAY and BEERS $1.

Shanks edged his way through the crowd, keeping low, eyes scanning the faces. He was intent on finding Potter. This was his chance. He didn't have the gift like the Mole. He wasn't an electrical engineer or a code pounder, or in any way technically gifted. He hadn't gone to Harvard or MIT. But he wasn't dumb.

William Henry McNair—Shanks to his friends—was a proud graduate of King College Prep on Drexel Boulevard in Chicago. And not just a graduate, an honors graduate. His diploma had the words *cum laude* printed right below his name. *With distinction.* That didn't matter much when your mother was loaded all day and your father was doing time in Joliet. No one in his family had even thought about college.

Shanks didn't want to follow his brothers onto the street. He was a good kid, with only two smears on his rap sheet. The day after graduation he was on a bus to Parris Island, South Carolina. The Marine Corps Recruit Depot. He saw action in Iraq, made sergeant in three years, and was offered a slot in Officer Candidate School. By then, though, the headaches had begun, and he decided he'd had enough of the Corps. While he liked the idea of getting his butterbars just fine, the prospect of earning $100K a year was more appealing, and that was what his brother had promised.

His brother had lied. Instead of $100K, he got a ten-year sentence for armed robbery. He served six, but six was more than enough. Shanks was done working with thieves. He liked having a real job with a real company with a real salary and real benefits. As of this fine day he was pulling down ninety-four grand a year, with health, dental, and a 10 percent kicker to his 401(k). He aimed to keep it that way.

It was lighter in the bar area and he had a good view of everyone's face. He made a circuit of the room, keeping his eyes peeled for a tall, shaggy guy with drooping cheeks and sad eyes. He saw no one, and after double-checking the dining room, he made a second tour of the bar. There was a single unoccupied stool. A $10 bill was tucked beneath a full bottle of beer on the counter. Whoever had left the money had left a shot of tequila, too.

And something else. A fancy braided leather riding crop.

Where in the world was Tank Potter?

Shanks hurried out the front entrance.

The Jeep was gone.

———

"Get out of my seat."

Shanks slammed the door and handed back the stiletto.

"You missed him."

"He left."

The Mole moved to the work bay and took his place at the console. "Briggs is going to be pissed when he finds out you let him get away."

"I told you, he left," said Shanks. "Anyway, we have another nail to take care of. You know how to get to Buda?"

52

Time to make money.

Carlos Cantu hurried in from his car and ran upstairs to his bedroom. He couldn't believe it was already six and he was only now getting home. Buda was a good thirty miles south of Austin, and this evening traffic had been snarled owing to an overturned fertilizer truck.

Carlos threw off his sweat-stained scrubs and jumped under the shower, keeping the water on full cold, which at this time of year was no better than 80°. As he washed, he thought of only one thing. Money. He wanted $35,000 for the watch. Not a penny less.

Finished showering, he dressed in shorts and a Longhorns T-shirt, then opened his nightstand and picked up the evidence bag containing the Patek Philippe watch he'd lifted yesterday. Now that he was clean, he tried it on. The gold sparkled dully. The second hand swept smoothly across an ivory guilloche face. The crocodile strap complemented his skin.

Carlos returned the watch to the evidence bag for safekeeping. If it weren't worth so much, he'd be tempted to keep it for himself. But $35,000 would go a long way. It would pay off his mother's medical bills, help his sister with college, and, hopefully, leave enough to buy himself a new car.

He didn't like stealing from the dead. He preferred to look at his action more as "purposeful misplacement." Things got lost all the time between the crime scene, the hospital, and the morgue. If they happened to find a way into his pocket, all the better.

Downstairs, he set up camp in the dining room. A coffee and a frozen Snickers bar counted as dinner. He logged onto eBay. At the moment he had a single auction running. A photograph of the Patek Philippe watch filled the screen. He'd received three bids so far, all for well below his asking price. He checked the bidders' identifications. Two were watch dealers in Florida. The third was a private individual in Seattle. All of them seemed legit. He frowned. He wouldn't accept less than thirty. Thirty was the magic number.

His phone chimed. He saw it was a text from Tank Potter asking to come over.

"Not again." Carlos picked up the phone, unsure whether to respond. He'd already done Tank enough favors. The problem with reporters was that they always wanted more. Then he remembered how Edward Mason had screamed at him to hurry up and load the bodies into the van when they weren't even ready. The man had a serious attitude problem. Carlos decided he'd be happy to help his buddy, if only to screw the officious little turd.

He texted Tank to come over when he wanted and added that he should enter through the back door.

"See you soon," Tank texted back.

Carlos put away the phone and returned his attention to the auction. There was a new bidder.

Twenty-five thousand or nothing.

It was his final price.

53

"Do you believe him?"

Mary stood inside her walk-in closet, eyeing the racks of clothing.

Blue blazer.

Navy slacks.

White shirt.

She selected the garments with care, setting them on the bedspread like she used to lay out her Sunday best for church. At the moment, however, she did not entertain any angelic thoughts. The Lord's Prayer, "Onward, Christian Soldiers," and the Twenty-third Psalm were the furthest things from her mind.

Mary Grant was angry. She was sick of being pushed around, and sick of being lied to and manipulated. Mostly, though, she was sick of not knowing the truth.

Joe had not called her to say goodbye. He'd called to tell her that something was profoundly wrong with his current situation. He'd called to give a shout for help, even if he knew she could not render the assistance he needed.

He did not call Randy Bell.

He did not call Don Bennett or Edward Mason.

He didn't call anyone from the FBI.

He called his wife, a civilian twenty-five miles away driving on a crowded freeway with her two daughters, doing nothing more hazardous than navigating the ordinary, mundane vicissitudes of everyday life.

Joe had called his wife because she was the only person he could trust.

Mary put on her slacks and shirt, tucking in the tails so the fabric pressed across her chest. She slipped on a pair of sensible brown loafers she'd worn exactly twice. Finally she put on her blazer. In the bathroom she brushed her hair and drew it into a ponytail. With a warm washcloth she wiped away a bit of her mascara, scrubbed the foundation off her cheeks, and removed her lipstick.

She appraised herself in the mirror.

Stand straight.

Shoulders back.

Don't smile.

Still, something was missing.

She opened Joe's drawer and rummaged through his things. She raised her chin as she pinned the American flag to her lapel. She looked the part but didn't feel it. She lacked a certain gravitas, an air of authority. She was a mother heading out to address the PTA or the secretary of the neighborhood homeowners' association. She was not a seasoned law enforcement officer.

Mary returned to the closet. Kneeling, she slid aside Joe's trousers to reveal a squat black safe a little bigger than a minifridge and ten times as heavy. Joe's gun locker. She knew the combination, and within seconds she'd opened the door and removed a Glock 17, a box of shells, and a holster.

Mary took the gun into the bedroom. Like any good military brat, she knew her way around weapons. She knew you always chambered a round and kept the safety on, and that when you drew, you fired. She hadn't taken a shot in years, but that didn't matter. She had no intention of using the pistol. Joe's gun gave her the swagger she needed to pull off her masquerade.

She returned to the bathroom and took up her position in front of the mirror.

She looked the same but felt entirely different.

Forty-eight hours ago she was a grieving widow a breath away from becoming a basket case. As of this moment she was an FBI agent investigating the murder of Joseph Grant.

"Do you believe him?"

No, Mary admitted to herself. She did not believe Edward Mason. Not for one second.

54

Tank made the turn off the highway, grumbling as the Jeep bucked and groaned down the dirt road. He'd bent the axle ramming the Ford, and the steering was pulling to the left. There was a hatchet-sized dent in the front fender, too, but it blended in with several others. It was the axle that needed fixing.

A gray clapboard house appeared around a curve, half hidden beneath a perilously sagging willow tree. Two dingy windows bracketed a door with paint so chipped and flaking that the door looked like a hedgehog. Weeds had overtaken the lawn years ago. The house looked all but abandoned. The only sign of an occupant was Carlos Cantu's ancient Honda parked out front.

Tank honked and pulled to a halt. Grimacing, he climbed out of the car, his back aching from the kidney punch he'd taken. "Anybody home?" he called. "Carlos—it's me."

He made a trail through the waist-high weeds toward the door. The drive to Buda was a crapshoot. As of two hours earlier, he had officially adopted radio silence. That's what you did when someone hacked into your phone. In fact, more than hacked into it, took over the entire device. *Bodysnatched it.*

No more efficient spying device had ever been invented by mankind than a smartphone. It allowed you to speak with one friend or a dozen, and to see their faces. It could access any piece of information in any public database in the world within seconds. It took pictures and movies so clearly they appeared lifelike. It informed you of your location within ten feet anywhere on God's green earth and then told you every kind of store and business that was around you. The problem, Tank had learned firsthand that afternoon, was that it could be used to spy on you, too.

Tank rapped on the door. "Surprise visit. It's me, Tank. Open up."

He listened for the floorboards to creak as Carlos came to the door. The place had been built in 1920, and he was sure it still had every last original plank and nail. He knocked again, and when no one answered, he took a step to his right and yelled through the open window. "Carlos, you in there?"

No sound at all came from the house. The silence made him nervous.

As a reporter, Tank had done plenty of things to piss people off. It was practically a requirement of the job. Either the cops, the DA, or the perp objected to something you wrote. Over the years he'd received his share of threats, bodily and otherwise. This was the first time, however, that someone had actively interfered with his investigation by destroying evidence.

"Carlos?"

Tank scooted closer to the window. It was then that he saw it and his stomach turned.

He retreated to his car. A search beneath the front seat turned up no liquid courage. Breathing hard, he leaned against the Jeep, looking at Carlos's house, seeing the overturned chair, the unmoving feet, wondering what to do.

It was on him. There was no way around it.

Steadying himself, he began a slow walk back to the house. The front door was locked, so he walked past the horseshoe pit and around to the back. He stepped onto the porch, the planks groaning beneath his weight. The kitchen door was ajar. He saw something dark in the passage leading to the dining room, something dark and viscous and alive. Against his better instincts, he stepped inside. The smell of cordite stopped him in his tracks. He stared at the pooled blood and the flies busily gorging themselves.

A coward runs, but who stays? An idiot? Certainly not a hero. A hero didn't get his friend in trouble in the first place.

A journalist stays.

Tank passed through the kitchen and entered the dining room. Carlos Cantu lay on the floor facedown, a bullet hole at his temple. Tank knelt to check for a pulse. His friend was dead.

For a minute Tank remained crouched, doing his best to piece together what had happened. A cup of coffee and a half-eaten candy bar sat on the table next to an open laptop. The mug was still lukewarm. Coffee and a Snickers bar were not his idea of a last meal. A phone lay on the floor a few feet away.

When the ache in his arthritic knees became too great, he stood, his joints cracking like a couple of brass doorknockers. From all appearances, Carlos had been working when someone sneaked up behind him and shot him in the head. The gunshot had toppled him from his chair. His eyes were open. He had died unawares, or at least without putting up a fight. But who could walk across this rickety floor without making a noise?

It was Tank's fault. He knew this at once. It was Tank who'd called Cantu en route to the medical examiner's office and, later, Tank who'd voiced his brash and all-too-public accusations that neither Joe Grant nor his informant had been killed by a handgun. There were texts. E-mails. And, of course, the pictures. All of it pointing to his coconspirator's identity.

It was suddenly very important to know who had done this.

Tank picked up Carlos's phone and checked the call log. He recognized the prefix of the last call Carlos had received, approximately an hour earlier. He thumbed the screen and the phone connected him to the number.

A harried man answered on the fourth ring. "Don Bennett. How you doin', Mr. Cantu? I hope you're not calling to weasel out of your interview Monday morning."

"No," said Tank. "I'll be there. Just wanted to confirm the time."

"Nine a.m. Everything okay?"

"Just fine, sir. I forgot to write down the time."

Tank hung up. Hearing Bennett's voice provided a measure of relief. In his rattled state, he was not beyond believing that the FBI had had a hand in killing Cantu. The good news was that you didn't schedule an appointment with someone you were going to kill. The bad news was that if the FBI hadn't slain Carlos, the party or parties responsible for killing Joe Grant and his informant had.

Tank rubbed his forehead. Was it more dangerous to stay or to leave? He pulled up Carlos's texts. The last exchange had taken place at 6:15. It read: "Hey, Carlos, you at home? I'd like to come by. It's about the pics."

Cantu: "At home. Come whenever. In for the night."

"See you in a few."

Cantu: "Come around back. Front door broken."

Tank stared at the texts, feeling something close to vertigo. What he saw didn't make sense. According to Carlos's phone, it was he, Tank

Potter, who had sent the texts. The screen showed his name and his number. The problem was that Tank had thrown his phone into the river two hours earlier.

Radio silence.

His first reaction was anger, then incredulity, then fear. Hacking into a phone to destroy some pictures was one thing. Sending texts from his number—after he himself had destroyed his phone—was a whole different level of magnitude.

Yet despite his fear, he couldn't help but rejoice just a little. "Oh yeah, Al," he whispered to himself. "We got ourselves a story."

He turned his attention to the laptop. He hit the Return key, and a listing on eBay appeared, showing an eighteen-karat gold wristwatch with a crocodile strap. The starting bid was $35,000. The seller was CC Austin Timepieces. "CC" for Carlos Cantu.

Tank spotted the watch in an evidence bag placed on the sideboard, with an identification tag attached to the strap. He removed the timepiece from the bag. The ID tag showed the initials of the owner and the date taken: "H.S. 7/30."

Carlos had stolen the watch from the morgue the day before. The day after Joseph Grant and his informant were killed.

Tank thought of the body he'd seen lying on the tray. Ample belly, soft hands, manicured fingernails. It was a rich man's body.

He picked up the watch. A Patek Philippe. Real gold, judging by its weight. A chronograph with day and date. It was a rich man's watch.

He flipped it over and noted that the case was inscribed "To H.S. Thanks, I."

Tank replaced the watch in the bag. Who was H.S.? And why had I. given him a wristwatch worth $35,000? More importantly, was H.S. the informant?

Tank didn't know, and he didn't think it wise to do his thinking while standing next to a guy with his brains oozing out of his head.

He gave a last look around. The journalist had completed his work. It was time to leave.

He saw the shotgun on his way out. It sat on top of a cupboard in the kitchen, the long steel barrels extending over one edge. He took it down and held it in his hands admiringly. Heavy. Weighted to the front to counteract the kick. A double-barrel twelve-gauge as old as the house itself. He broke the chamber and saw that it was loaded. Fresh shells.

Outside, Tank tossed the gun onto the backseat of his Jeep. He owned three shotguns and a variety of handguns and kept them locked up safely. But he wasn't going anywhere near his home.

On the highway he kept his foot to the floor, urging the Jeep to pick up some speed. The world looked different to him somehow. Clearer, maybe. Less confused. Certainly more dangerous.

He sneaked a look toward the backseat. The sight of the shotgun reassured him, but not for long. Over and over his mind came back to the same fact: whoever killed Carlos Cantu wanted Tank Potter dead, too.

55

ONE 7 touched down on American soil at 7:01 p.m., sixteen hours and forty-seven minutes after departing Israel.

Ian Prince paced back and forth at the foot of the mobile stairwell, watching the plane approach. Until now all had been planning. The acquisition of Merriweather Systems, the upgrading of the Titan supercomputer, the agreement with the National Security Agency, the purchase of Clarus and the wooing of its senior leadership—each action constituted one iteration within a larger plan, no different from a line of software code within an application.

The arrival of the Israelis marked the turning point. Planning was over. The program had been written. The machinery was in place. It was time to hit Return and execute.

Founded in 2002, Clarus was a developer and manufacturer of surveillance systems designed to collect all types of electronic data from the Internet. Its primary product, Clarus Insight, was a supercomputer capable of intercepting voiceover IP (VoIP) calls through services such as Skype, phone and mobile communications that passed through the Internet. Clarus's proprietary software utilized deep packet inspection to sift through the vast quantities of information traveling over the Internet and permit IP providers and network managers to inspect, track, and target content from users of the Internet and mobile phones as it passed through routers. A company press release stated that the Clarus Insight Intercept Suite was "the industry's only network traffic intelligence system that supports real-time precision targeting, capturing, and reconstruction of webmail traffic . . . including Google Gmail, Hotmail, Yahoo!, and AOL mail."

And now it belonged to Ian.

The plane reached its parking spot and stopped. The stairwell docked with the fuselage. The door opened inward. The executives of the Clarus Corporation descended the stairs eagerly, faces turned toward the sun, taking deep breaths of the fresh Texas air.

Ian greeted each warmly as he set foot on solid ground. "David," he said, gripping the hand and arm of David Gold, the firm's founder and CEO. "Welcome to the new world."

"Ian, we are pleased to be part of your team."

"Not team," said Ian. "Family. Are you ready to make history?"

Gold nodded, but there was no mistaking the fervor in his eyes. Like Ian, he was a true believer.

"You're sure about the decision?"

"To the core."

Next came Menachem Wolkowicz, the company's chief technology officer, a man considered by many to be the world's leading cryptologist. "Menachem, so good to see you again. I'm honored by your presence."

"The honor is mine."

"Are you sure about your decision? There's no going back."

"I wouldn't have it any other way."

And so on, until all ten men had deplaned and climbed into a fleet of luxury SUVs.

The vehicles transported the group to the customs hall. Formalities were handled briskly. Passports were examined, stamped, and returned to their owners. Bags passed directly to their owners without search.

Ian wished the men a pleasant ride and informed them that he would join them for a welcoming dinner that evening. He waited until the last man had stowed his luggage and the final SUV had left the airport grounds before walking back into the terminal and continuing to his own mode of transport: a Bell Jet Ranger helicopter.

The Visitors' Lodge at ONE headquarters was a four-story building modeled on London's famed Connaught Hotel. Inside his suite, each man found a chilled bottle of Cristal champagne, a tin of Beluga caviar, toast points with chopped egg and onion, as well as a platter of cold meats, sweets, and a selection of mineral waters.

An engraved invitation reminded the Israelis that dinner was at nine p.m. Formal dress requested.

The last instruction caused great consternation. None had brought a dinner jacket. Several had forsworn business suits altogether. What did Ian Prince mean by "formal dress requested"?

The men went to hang up their jackets and pants. Each one gasped as he opened the closet and beheld what was inside.

Years ago they had been soldiers.

Tonight they would be soldiers once again.

56

"One nail hammered," said Peter Briggs.

Ian Prince entered his office, trying to conceal his anger at finding Briggs perched on the corner of his desk. "Which one?"

Briggs shook his head. "Doesn't matter."

"And the other?"

"Don't worry about that for the moment. We've got something else."

Ian glanced up. The tone said everything. Her again. The woman.

"You'll want to take a look," said Briggs.

Ian stood alongside his chief of security and watched the twenty-second video clip taken outside the Grant home. In it, Mary Grant left the front door dressed in business attire and climbed into her car. Briggs froze the picture as she unbuttoned her jacket and slid behind the wheel. "See anything?"

Ian took the phone in his own hand to study the freeze frame. "She has a gun on her belt."

"Does that look like a mother staying at home to care for her little ones? Or like a woman setting out to get into trouble?"

"Have her followed."

"I already know where she's going. Someplace called the Nutty Brown Cafe, on the way to Dripping Springs. She looked up driving instructions ten minutes ago."

Ian put down the phone. His eye wandered across the office to the black satchel resting in its place in the far corner. For a moment he saw his father staring back at him. Peter Prince shook his head. The message was loud and clear.

"Follow her," said Ian. "And that's it. Send your man . . ."

"Shanks."

"Yes, Shanks, the one who did such a fine job the other day. Have him follow her, but that's all. I'll take care of her later."

"You're playing with fire."

"Don't you trust me?"

"Tell you the truth," said Peter Briggs, "no."

"Anything else to report?"

"About the Israelis?" Briggs shrugged. "They liked the grub. No one opened the bubbly."

"Anything I should worry about? Doubters? Anyone looking to jump ship?"

"They're with us lock, stock, and barrel. Bloody well should be, all the dough you're paying them. Just don't tell me I have to call them General Gold and Colonel Wolkowicz."

"Only if I do, *Sergeant* Briggs. Coming to dinner?"

"Need a shower first. Maybe a short kip."

"Don't forget we leave at six in the morning."

"You never give up, do you?"

"It keeps me sharp."

"How many years in a row is it now?"

"Seven," said Ian.

"Lucky number."

After Briggs left, Ian walked to the window and gazed across the Meadow. The sun rested in the lower quadrant of the western sky, its rays warming the stone ramparts of Magdalene and Brasenose. Normally this was his favorite time of day. The hard work was behind him. He could catalogue progress made and chart progress to come. By rights he should be ecstatic. The NSA had signed off on the demonstration of Titan early next morning. *(It worked!)* The Senate was in his pocket. The deal to build out the CIA's new intranet was a formality. And the Israelis had arrived.

He could report progress on all fronts.

Instead he felt unsettled. And not just that, but something more troubling. An emotion he had not experienced in a long time. He felt powerless.

All because of one woman.

He poured himself a glass of acai juice, then moved to his desk, where he checked his agenda, confirming that he had scheduled a call with his sons, Trevor and Tristan.

He placed the call, and after a few seconds a floor-to-ceiling monitor blossomed, showing the kitchen of his new home in Bel-Air. His wife had seized on the acquisition of Allied Artists as reason to move the kids to California for the summer and, Ian suspected, longer.

"Your stock price is in toilet. Earnings are down six percent since April. Ten hedge funds have dropped ONE from their core portfolio holdings in last year. What fuck is going on?"

Wendy Wong Prince sat on a high stool at the kitchen counter, Bluetooth in her ear, lululemon tights and T showing off the best body that Bikram yoga and the good doctors of Austin, Manhattan, and Beverly Hills could sculpt. She was a tall, striking Asian, Cantonese by birth, a Harvard MBA by way of Hong Kong and Vancouver, with a PhD in computer science from Carnegie Mellon in her back pocket for good measure.

Ian sighed. All that education and she still dropped the definite article. "And good evening to you."

"So?" Wendy continued. "Did you close Titan deal?"

"On a conditional basis," said Ian.

"Conditional? Ian Prince doesn't do conditional."

Ian smiled. Sometimes it was hard to remember that she was on his side. "This is a little different from our usual work with the government."

"I know, I know," said Wendy. "It's confidential."

"Above top-secret, actually. One day, sweetheart, I'll fill you in. I don't want to jinx anything."

Wendy's face darkened. "Is that what I am now, jinx? Your wife, jinx?" She let fly a stream of Cantonese vitriol. Ian fired back his own, if anything more insulting.

"Now I know why I married you," she said. "You're only man who swear better than me."

"You married me, darling, because I was worth ten billion dollars, you received a prenup guaranteeing you a hundred million once the boys are out of the house, and you agreed that we never have to fuck."

Wendy's smile evaporated faster than a Hong Kong rain shower. There was a stirring at the far end of the kitchen. The boys ran into the kitchen, followed by their nannies.

"Hi, Dad," they said.

Trevor was fourteen and Tristan eleven. Trevor was tall for his age, strapping, and a gifted athlete. Tristan was short for his, chubby, and preferred playing his ONEBox to any real-world activity.

"Boys. How was your day?"

"Mom's not letting us miss any Chinese lessons," said Trevor. "I'm sick of it. I want to go to the studio. They're shooting the new James Cameron movie."

"Can't you go after your Chinese?"

"I have golf lessons at Bel-Air Country Club. Afterwards I get a massage."

"What about you, Tristan?"

"I like Chinese. Mom taught me how to say *dew neh loh moh*. Do you know what that means?"

"That sounds like Mom." Ian kept his smile in place. *Dew neh loh moh* meant "Go fuck your mother." "Hey, Premier League starts next week. We're flying over to catch the opening match. Arsenal's playing West Ham."

"Arsenal will destroy them," said Trevor. "Are we sitting with the coaches?"

"We own the team, don't we?"

Ian had purchased Arsenal Football Club, one of England's oldest and most prestigious, three years earlier and thrown in a sponsorship deal that put the ONE logo on the football players' jerseys.

"I don't want to go all the way to London for a stupid soccer game," said Tristan. "Can't I stay here and look after the animals?"

Since moving to Los Angeles, the boys had assembled a veritable menagerie. There was a chinchilla, two hamsters, a cat, a boa constrictor, and a three-legged rescue mutt named Howie.

"We'll see, Tristan. I'd love to have you in the cockpit with me. I'll even let you land the plane. What do you say?"

Tristan shrugged, uninterested. "Maybe."

"I'll land it," said Trevor. "Just as well as you, Dad!"

Ian laughed. "Gotta run, fellas. Take care of Mom. And Tristan, no more animals."

He hung up, feeling lonely. He loved the boys dearly, and he didn't see them nearly enough. He walked to the rear of his office and entered a large dressing area accessed through a revolving bookcase. He showered and changed for dinner, dressing in black slacks and a form-fitting black dress shirt. He gave himself a final check in the mirror and froze in horror. It couldn't be. Not already. He brought his face closer to the glass. And yet . . . there it was.

A gray hair.

Not gray, white. As bleached as a snowflake.

He found a pair of tweezers, plucked out the offending hair, and dropped it into the sink, where it disappeared, blending with the porcelain.

Mortality was the one concept he could not grasp.

57

Peter Briggs walked down the High toward his own quarters. *Sergeant Briggs.* Ian had some cheek. Of course, he was the boss and was allowed. Still . . .

He lit a cigarette and exhaled the smoke bitterly. Always the NCO, never the officer. So be it, then. He walked around the corner of the building and looked out across the Meadow toward the River Isis, or whatever name Ian had given to the dried-up excuse for a stream. Oxford in Texas. What nonsense. And yet Ian had done it. He had commissioned an architect. He had imported the stone. He had spent two years and more than $1 billion building a damn-near-perfect replica of one of the world's oldest universities. And Peter Briggs had been at his side the entire time.

A batman.

That was the term they'd used in the Boer War for an officer's noncommissioned adjutant. The batman took care of all his officer's affairs. He arranged his clothing, shined his boots, prepared his meals when necessary, looked after his mount, tucked him in at night, and gave him a bloody kiss on the cheek. And after all that, he fought at his side.

Like it or not, Briggs was Ian's batman. It was his job to look after his officer's welfare, and that meant undertaking actions the officer might not realize were in his own best interest. The actions Briggs was considering regarded Mary Grant.

He called Shanks. "The woman. She's on the move."

"The Mole told me. I'm on my way."

"I'm impressed. Now let's see if you can impress me some more. This is what you're going to do. Listen closely."

It took him less than a minute to describe the actions he wanted Shanks to take in regard to Mary Grant. "Everything clear?"

"Crystal," said Shanks.

Peter Briggs hung up. Satisfied that he had taken the necessary steps to protect his officer, he set off to shower and dress for the gala dinner.

A loyal batman would do no less.

58

DRIPPING SPRINGS 20 MILES.

Mary pressed the accelerator, keeping the speed a hair under 80 miles per hour. Joe had a rule. No cop ever gave a speeding ticket if you kept the needle below 80. Eighty to 84, you were taking your chances. Above 85 you were toast.

It was 8:15. The sun hung directly in front of her, dirty dancing with the horizon. The sky was ablaze, the burnt orange of the Zane Grey westerns the admiral had so dearly loved. The road rose and dipped over and over again as it cut through the Texas scrub. Ten minutes outside the Austin city limits she felt isolated and apprehensive, a pioneer in strange, endless land. Any confidence she'd had looking in the mirror, safe in the confines of her home, was gone. Joe's pistol had lost its ability to inspire. It hung like a dead weight on her belt, reminding her of her folly.

And Joe? What would he do?

He'd do what she was doing. He'd pound the pavement and burn some shoe leather. He'd get out there and ask some questions. He'd shake the tree and see what fell to the ground.

The thought consoled her, but not as much as she would have liked.

She picked up her phone and called home. "Hey, Jess, just checking in. How's it going?"

"Fine."

"Whatcha doin'?"

"Same thing we were doing half an hour ago."

Mary had left the girls at home, with Jessie in charge. One look at their mom in a suit was enough to stifle any objections. "I'm going out," she'd said. "I'll be back by eleven, and you'd both better be in bed."

For once Jessie hadn't protested, and Mary had stood there dumbstruck, wondering if Jess was finally growing up—if maybe, as her daughter might put it, she was ready to "do floors and windows."

"And your little sister?"

"She's right here. Want to talk to her?"

"Just tell her Mom says hello."

"'Kay. Bye."

Mary hung up and tossed the phone onto the seat. Optimism might be premature. She should just be happy that Jess had accepted her assignment without mouthing off.

She entered the city limits of Cedar Valley, a small farm community. She passed the local Sonic and a gas station before spotting the twenty-foot neon cowboy tossing his lasso in the air and welcoming her to the Nutty Brown Cafe.

A signboard advertised that Gary Clark Jr. was playing that evening. The dirt lot was packed with cars snaking up and down the alleys. Parking spilled into two adjacent fields. She circled twice, settling for a spot at the far corner between an oak tree and an old VW van.

She locked the car and started toward the restaurant. Around her the last arrivals were making their way to the outdoor amphitheater behind the restaurant. Music from a blues band filled the air. She felt stiff and overdressed, wildly out of place. She had no idea what she was thinking, carrying a sidearm. She slowed, then stopped altogether. She looked at the entrance to the restaurant a hundred feet ahead and tried to work out what she was going to say. Nothing came to her. She turned and looked back at her car as the band kicked into an up-tempo number. The music gave her a little 'tude. She continued toward the café. She'd think of something when she got inside.

The black Ford F-250 pickup rumbled into the parking lot a minute after Mary had arrived. The driver was a big man with broad shoulders, skin the color of milk coffee, and a weathered USMC garrison cap on his head. He put his foot on the brake and scanned the lot, his eyes quickly locating the blond woman in business attire, staying with her as she picked up her gait and entered the café.

"Hello, Miss Mary."

Shanks put the truck into gear and cruised the lot until he found a spot with a clear line of sight to the entrance. He raised a hand in the shape of a gun and took aim at the door. Give him his old Remington sniper's rifle and one round. From this distance it would be like shooting fish in a barrel.

He put down his imaginary rifle and placed a call. "She's here."

"Of course she is," said Peter Briggs. "Do this and you can count on a promotion."

Shanks opened the center console and removed a brass cigarette case. He had some time to kill and didn't know a better way. A flick of his thumb opened the case. He selected a slim, tightly rolled spliff and lit it. Shanks didn't touch alcohol or most drugs, but he did allow himself a taste of some fine kush now and then. He took a drag and flicked the cherry out the window. He held the smoke in his lungs, feeling his eyes water, his chest expand, his head grow warm and fuzzy. This particular strain was called Triple A, for "awake, alert, and aware." It got you mellow, took the edge off things, but gave you a little kick in the ass so you could remain sharp, on point.

He exhaled.

"Oh yeah," he said, seeing a rainbow arc across his vision. He blinked and the colors vanished. "That's the ticket."

Shanks considered taking another hit, then thought better of it. One was more than enough. He didn't know what Joseph Grant had wanted with Mr. Prince. He imagined it had had something to do with the Merriweather deal last winter. It had been a stressful time for everyone at the company. Mr. Prince had ridden the troops hard to make sure ONE completed the acquisition. And Briggs had ridden his boys in security harder. There was lots of B&E work, strong-arming, that type of thing. It was around then that the Mole had started making his creepy Vines.

Since then Shanks had moved steadily up the ladder. Briggs made it clear that it was his job to protect Mr. Prince and his company. He talked about ONE as if it were a country, not a corporation. Shanks liked that just fine. He was a man who gave his allegiance wholly, and ONE represented everything he admired. It was powerful, influential, admired, and, best of all, color-blind. ONE was a meritocracy. It was all about ability.

If his job called for him to shoot a federal agent, fine. He looked at it as killing the enemy, a task no different from taking out an insurgent in Iraq. You were either with ONE or against it. Besides, Shanks had suffered at the hands of the FBI. To him, the job was a chance for some payback—to balance the scales of justice, so to speak. And if his job called for him to take care of another kind of problem, he was fine with that, too.

He checked the time and noted that the Grant woman had been inside the café for an hour. This was not a positive development. He had an educated idea of what she was doing in there, and he was certain Mr. Briggs would not be happy when he learned of it.

Shanks opened his glove box to check for his real gun, a Beretta 9mm, ten-shot clip plus one in the barrel, modified Python ammo. He didn't need a rifle tonight. This job would be up close and personal.

He closed the glove box and settled down to wait.

He was already rehearsing what he was going to say to Mary Grant before he killed her.

59

"My name is Mary Grant. FBI. I'd like to speak with the manager."

The hostess glanced at Mary's badge. "Yes, ma'am. Please wait right here while I find him."

"Thank you."

The hostess disappeared into the back of the café. Mary kept her hands at her sides, her posture its best, as she waited. If this was the kind of response a badge got, she planned on carrying it more often.

A minute later a tall, thickset African-American man of about fifty wearing a denim shirt approached. "Cal Miller."

Mary introduced herself and presented Joe's badge. "Is there somewhere quiet we can speak?"

"Can I ask what this is about?"

"Two days ago an agent was shot and killed at the Flying V Ranch up the road. The agent ate here just before. I'd like your help in finding out who he may have been with."

"My office is in the back."

Miller led the way to the rear of the restaurant, through a door marked *Private* and into a cluttered office the size of a broom closet. Posters of past acts covered the wall: Vince Gill, Bruce Hornsby, and Willie Nelson. Miller wedged himself behind his desk while Mary moved a stuffed armadillo off an armchair. As she sat, she unbuttoned her jacket just enough to allow him a glimpse of Joe's Glock. It was only then that she noticed he was wearing a sidearm beneath his shirt, too, something very big and very shiny.

She handed him the receipt she'd found in Joe's wallet. "Is the server here? I'd like to ask her a few questions."

"That's Mindy. She pulls a double Mondays and Thursdays. Let me get her."

Miller left the office. Mary took a breath and tried to relax. She'd passed the bullshit test. All she had to do now was keep calm and authoritative and act like Joe.

Miller returned, trailed by Mindy, the waitress. She was a short, curvy redhead approaching middle age, with too much makeup and boobs spilling out of a tight black tank top.

"How do you do?" Mindy said, offering a hand. "Cal told me why you're here. I'm real sorry 'bout what happened to your friend. Do you have a picture of him? It might help."

"Yes," said Mary. "Of course."

Mistake one. She didn't have a picture ready at all.

She fumbled for her phone and embarked on a search for a picture of Joe to show the waitress. In every one Joe was either with the girls or with Mary. There wasn't a single snap of him alone. Finally, she selected a picture of Joe with the girls taken at Christmas last year. At least he was wearing a suit, and with a wrenching start, she realized it was the one he'd been wearing two days ago.

"Here he is."

"Those his daughters? Poor girls. They're real pretty."

"Yes, they are," said Mary, too quickly.

"Burger, fries, and a Coke. I remember him." She looked up and smirked. "The other guy—he was a piece of work."

"Go on."

"He'd just had an operation, something with his heart. He couldn't eat anything with too much fat or cholesterol. He was worried about how we cook our food. No vegetable oil. No trans fats. You know, all that New York City nonsense. *Hello* . . . we ain't the Four fuckin' Seasons."

"How do you know he was from New York?"

"He had an accent, that's all. He sure as heck wasn't from around here."

"Do you recall what he looked like?"

"Fat, red face. Kinda piggy, I guess. Hair combed over. Not someone you'd find on the cover of GQ. But the other one, the one in the picture, he was a dish."

"He's married," said Mary.

"I noticed," said Mindy, as if the fact didn't mean a thing to her or her lusty ambitions. "Is there anything else? I've got five tables that are probably having a conniption fit about now."

"That should cover it."

"I'm sorry about your friend. I can see you're real torn up." Mindy stepped closer and put a hand on Mary's arm. "Guess you didn't care he was married either."

"I was his—" Mary cut herself off. She had no reason to say anything more.

"Boots," said Mindy, halfway out the door.

"Excuse me?" said Mary.

"The good-looking guy called the fat one Boots. They looked like they were friends. Just sayin'."

Mindy closed the door behind her.

"Anything else I can help you with?" asked Cal Miller.

"There is." But Mary didn't know what. There had to be something. She hadn't driven twenty-five miles just to find out that Joe had eaten his last lunch with a fat FBI agent nicknamed "Boots" with a heart condition and a New York accent. Unfortunately, she didn't have a clue who Boots might be, and she didn't think Don Bennett, Randy Bell, or anyone else at the FBI would appreciate her asking. Certainly not Edward Mason. Not after her promise to keep her nose out of Joe's business and his none-too-subtle threat to jail her if she didn't. Besides, she didn't want to jeopardize the nation's security.

National security. The twenty-four-carat unimpeachable excuse for any and all government actions. Question at your peril.

"Ma'am?"

Mary sighed and stood up, knowing that she was forgetting something but not knowing what. "Thank you," she said finally as she squeezed past the stuffed armadillo and the desk.

Cal Miller opened the door. "If you're hungry, I'll be happy to get you whatever you'd like. On the house. We're famous for our chicken fried steak."

National security. And then it came to her. What about the Nutty Brown Cafe's security?

"Cameras," she blurted. "You have security cameras, don't you?"

Miller nodded. "Like everybody else, but I'm not sure they'll be any help."

"How many do you deploy?"

"*Deploy?*" said Miller. "We've got twenty-five cameras on the premises. The insurance company demands that we keep every square foot of the place covered."

"So there's a camera inside the restaurant?"

"Two. On the front door and the cash register. And of course there are several on the parking lot. That's where the trouble usually takes place. Fistfights, altercations, the like. The rest of the cameras are over in the outdoor pavilion. But it might be too late. The disk records over itself every two days."

"I'd like to take a look anyway."

"All yours."

"Let's start inside."

60

Jessie spotted the headlights pulling into the driveway. Hurriedly she took a last vape from her e-cigarette. "B rt thr," she texted.

Backpack. Laptop. Pepper spray. Jessie made sure she had everything she needed, then ran downstairs. Grace sat on the sofa, waving the remote. "Can we start now?"

Jessie left her backpack by the front door and plopped down next to her sister. The TV was tuned to *Survivor*. "I've got to go out, mouse."

"But it's the finale. We have to see who won."

"I know, but this is more important."

"You're supposed to look after me. Mom left you in charge."

"Sorry, but I have to. It's for Dad."

"Out where?"

"Out *out*. That's all you need to know."

"When will you be back?"

"I'm not sure."

"More than an hour?"

"Who are you, Mom?"

"I don't like being here alone. It's creepy."

Jessie shifted on the couch. She'd tried to be patient and understanding, but it wasn't working. Little kids only thought about themselves. "Lock the door and watch TV. Pretend I'm in my room like I always am anyway. Either way, you need to be in bed asleep by the time Mom comes home. You'll be okay. I promise."

"But you're not in your room."

Jessie stood. "Grace, you're almost twelve. You're going into seventh grade in a few weeks. Grow up."

"You have to at least tell me what you're doing."

"I want to figure out how Mom lost Dad's message. I think someone hacked into her phone. I'm going to talk to my TA to see if he can help."

Grace considered this. "You going with Garrett?"

Jessie looked out the window. She could see the blond head, the spiky, carelessly combed hair, at the wheel of the old VW bug. Maddeningly, her heart skipped a beat. "Maybe."

"You're wearing makeup."

"Am not."

"And perfume. You smell like Mom."

"Stop being a pest. I have to go."

Grace followed her sister to the front door. "What if I get scared?"

"You won't. And besides, Mom will be home before you know it."

"She'll know you're not here."

"How? She'll look in my room and think I'm asleep."

"Sometimes she comes in and sits on my bed. What if she does that to you?"

"I'm fifteen. Mom doesn't come into my room anymore."

Grace grabbed her sleeve. "If they hacked into Mom's phone, they might be watching us."

"Don't be ridiculous. Why would anyone watch us? Dad's dead."

"Why would anyone hack into Mom's phone?"

Jessie crossed her arms and blew out a frustrated breath. She'd asked herself the same question a dozen times and hadn't been able to come up with an answer. Which made it all the more important for her to figure out who'd done it. You couldn't know *why* without first knowing *who*. "I'm going. If you tell Mom, I'll kill you."

"I won't."

"Don't!" Jessie leaned down and gave Grace a peck on the cheek. "Wish me luck, mouse."

"Good luck, peanut." Grace watched her sister run down the walk and climb into the car. "For what?" she shouted after her. "The phone or Garrett?"

61

A child's bedroom.

Morning. Sunlight streaming through a crack in the curtains.

A girl sleeping in her bed. Blond hair fanned across the pillow. Pink cheeks. An angel.

A tattooed hand brings a razor-sharp blade near the child's face.

The blade passes over the girl's chin, her nose, her eyes.

As vipers writhe from the skull tattoo.

One mile away, in the parking lot of a minimall that housed a Papa John's, a 7-Eleven, and a Green Mesquite BBQ, the Mole sat alone inside the command van, watching the Vine he'd made earlier that morning of Grace Grant.

His angel.

A movement on the primary monitor drew his attention and he put down his phone. It was a VW Beetle pulling into the Grants' driveway. The Mole sat up straighter, watching the older girl run down the walk and jump into the car. Behind them, framed by the foyer's light, a thin blond girl stood in the doorway.

The Mole zoomed in on the girl. He saw a rustle of blue nightgown, a sheaf of blond hair, and then the door closed.

He leaned back in the chair, his heart pounding, his eyes unable to leave the monitor.

His angel was alone in the house.

62

"Gentlemen, welcome. I congratulate you on the momentous step you've taken. I'm grateful for the faith you've shown in me personally, and for your belief in my vision for the future. Thank you."

Ian Prince allowed his words to sink in as he looked out over the executives from Israel sitting among his own lieutenants at dining tables running the width of the room. Graves Hall was a cavernous space with heavy wood paneling and stained glass windows set high on the walls. Candles burned from wrought iron chandeliers. Life-sized portraits of Cerf, Jobs, Berners-Lee, and, of course, himself, stared down from the walls. To Ian's eye it was a cathedral, a sacred place for worshipping the great minds who had launched the digital revolution.

"We live in a bold new world," Ian continued. "A world of opportunity. A world where a beggar in Mozambique has access to the same knowledge, the same expertise, the same compendium of information as a billionaire in Manhattan. We live in the era of the superempowered individual, in which each of us is capable of unimaginable feats. A doctor in Atlanta can 'print' human tissue from a single cell. A scientist in São Paolo can alter DNA to eliminate faulty genes. A husband in Tokyo can speak to his wife in Quebec and not only hear her voice but see her picture . . . *on his watch*. It is the stuff of comic books and science fiction novels and old-time radio serials. Every day we reach into the future and harness it to the present. And none of it would be possible without the means to instantaneously access, respond to, and transmit information. All of which are the pylons on which ONE is built."

Ian paused. The room was so quiet he could hear a microchip drop. Faces looked up at him, eyes lit with ambition.

"Twenty years ago," he continued, "I had an idea about how to gather information from a nifty new creation called the World Wide Web. That idea turned into something called ONEscape. Back in that medieval time, we called it a web crawler. Today ONEscape is the world's most popular search engine."

He smiled, enjoying his colleagues' laughter.

"I didn't stop with ONEscape. I moved on to create a company that wrote software, and another that manufactured the hardware that made up the Internet's backbone. I built a company that designed smartphones and tablets to use that backbone, and most recently I purchased a company that produces content that passes through our hardware to be enjoyed on those smartphones and tablets. Still, that isn't enough. I have a greater responsibility, and that is to oversee this magnificent organism called the Internet—to guard it on behalf of the beggar in Mozambique and the billionaire in Manhattan. And then one day I discovered Clarus. And I knew at once that Clarus would give me this ability.

"I first took note of Clarus when I learned that it was your equipment that my friends at Fort Meade had chosen to collect all signals traffic coming into this country. I looked closer at Clarus when I was told that a certain country had used your equipment to shut down an enemy's entire air defense system. But it wasn't until I learned that a virus you engineered brought an unnamed country's nuclear development program to an abrupt and nearly catastrophic halt that I decided we must work together. Can anyone remind me of the name of that virus?"

Heads shook. Fingers waved, indicating that this was not a suitable topic of conversation. Ian expected as much from men who made their living from trafficking secrets.

He left his place at the table and walked down the aisle. "As all of you know, my purchase of Clarus was not an ordinary transaction. I did not just buy assets, orders books, and technical know-how. I wanted more. I requested that you gentlemen present here tonight come to my side and act as my Praetorian Guard. It will be your task to protect everything we have built to date and to protect the rest of the world against those who seek to do us harm. Only by having access to every facet of this magnificent organism can we maintain its health. Only by seeing the entirety of information coursing through its veins can we identify the viruses and parasites that threaten our existence and ruthlessly eliminate them. It is truly all or nothing."

Ian raised a glass. The assembled guests stood, crystal held high.

"And so tonight I formally welcome you to the ONE family, as together we transform ONE from a corporation into something more—something the world has yet to see."

63

Mary knew him.

She knew Boots.

She stepped outside the café as Cal Miller wished her good night and locked the door behind her. It was past ten and the parking lot was deserted. The show had ended thirty minutes earlier, and the establishment had a strict policy of rapidly vacating the premises. It was dark, and the lot looked different with so few cars. Several times she stopped to orient herself before finally spotting her car at the far corner of the adjacent lot, a few hundred yards away.

She walked briskly, thrilled at her good luck. Cal Miller had gone back fifty-eight hours to Monday at 12:30 (with only ten minutes to spare before the DVR taped over the pictures), but he'd found them. The security cameras filming the parking lot and front entrance both showed Joe entering the café, followed a minute later by a stocky man with a ruddy complexion and a comb-over. "Boots," according to Mindy's colorful description. More accurately, "SSA FK," according to the name on the receipt.

The security cameras were ten years old, their grainy images a far cry from HD. Still, Mary had no doubt that she'd met him. She just couldn't recall where or when. She suspected he'd been to their house, because that was the only place she ever met any of Joe's colleagues. But which house? And dammit, what was his name?

She placed her hand on her pocket, feeling the DVD that Miller had burned with the sequence showing Joe and Boots. She'd have plenty of time to review it at home. Meanwhile she dredged up memories of parties, searching for a glimpse of the pear-shaped man with the red face and wiry brown hair. Sooner or later it would come to her.

"Hey there."

Mary looked up, startled. An imposing man stood a few feet away, hands in his pockets, a garrison cap drawn over his eyes. "Hello," she said, keeping her pace, steering a path around him.

The man stepped in front of her. "You have something for me?"

Mary stopped. "Excuse me?"

"The disk sticking out of your pocket. Please hand it to me."

Mary took a step back, and the man advanced a step toward her. He was broad and muscular and bristling with aggression. Scream and he could be on her in a second. She looked around. There was no one nearby. The café was fifty yards behind her. A black truck was parked to her left, but the cab was empty. She checked over her shoulder. Cal Miller was nowhere to be seen. Her decision to park at the farthest point from the café suddenly seemed ill-considered.

"Who are you?"

"Never you mind. The disk. Now."

"Why do you want it?"

"Same reason you do."

Mary took another step back and the man took a longer step forward, narrowing the distance between them. She felt the Glock pressing against her waist.

"Stop right there," he said, his voice quiet and authoritative. "Or I'll have to quit being so polite."

The man lifted his head, and she saw his eyes in the moonlight. Pale, determined, ruthless. A chill shook her spine, and she had the certainty that he was going to kill her.

"Fine. I'll give you the disk."

"Slowly, now. Don't think I can't tell you're packing. Remember who you are, Miss Mary. You're just a mom."

He knew her name. Which meant he knew Joe.

Mary handed him the disk. "What was he investigating?"

"Something he shouldn't have been."

"I imagine someone always thinks that's the case."

"I imagine so."

"Who do you work for?"

"You'd be surprised."

"Try me."

"You know what they say—'I could tell you, but then I'd have to kill you.'"

"So you're not going to kill me?"

The man slipped the disk behind his belt. When his hand came back up, it was holding a pistol. "I didn't say that."

Mary ran. She made it two steps before he had her, an arm wrapped around her waist, lifting her off her feet, the other clapping a hand over her mouth. He spun and carried her toward her car as if she were no heavier than a sack of groceries.

"Mary, Mary, Mary," he whispered. "Always looking where you're not supposed to. Didn't they tell you to give it up?" A squeeze for emphasis. "*Didn't they?* But no, you had to keep on digging. You had to be a snoop like your husband. Don't you know we're the ones who do the snooping?"

Mary squirmed and struggled. She felt like an infant in a giant's arms. Every effort to free herself was countered by one twice as forceful. The man continued past her car, climbing a berm bordering the lot and carting her into the wide-open scrub beyond. In moments they were surrounded by clumps of mesquite and tangled brush, a wilderness of vegetation as tall as she. A hundred yards along, he set her down. When he stepped away, she saw that he had Joe's Glock, too.

"They'll know it was you," she said. "I saw the security camera feeds. They'll have your truck coming in, pictures of you leaving."

"Put on a suit, stick a gun in your belt, and you think you're a real Fibbie, eh? How's this, Miss Mary? The images won't even exist."

"Of course they'll exist. The cameras record everything."

"They could have infrared cameras filming me picking you up, carrying you out here, and shooting you dead, and it wouldn't matter. We'll just erase it. Cedar Valley's our territory."

"What do you mean, your territory?"

"The security system's hooked up to the Net. That means it all goes through our pipes. We own it." He tucked the Glock into his belt while his own pistol hung loosely in his hand. "Besides, no one asks any questions about suicides."

Mary held her ground. "I'd never kill myself."

"What about the note you left?"

"I didn't leave any note."

"But we will," he said. "Mommy's goodbye, sent from her own e-mail."

"You can't do that. You don't even know my e-mail."

"Really? Then how did we know you'd be out here tonight, or that you were rushing to the morgue this afternoon, or that you had a visit from that reporter who got himself a DUI two nights back?"

"Who are you?"

"We're the future." Carefully he affixed a fat cylindrical tube to the pistol's snout. A noise suppressor. She'd seen Joe toy with one at home.

"Please," Mary pleaded. "I'll stop looking. You have the disk. What else do you want?"

"I'm sorry," he said. "Really, I am. Now come on over here. I'll make it fast. You won't feel a thing."

"This isn't necessary. Like you said, I'm a mother. I know that now. I'll stop looking. I'll stop snooping."

"Promise?"

"Yes, yes. I promise."

"No, *I promise*." The man stepped toward her, his arm rising, the pistol aimed at her face. Mary stood tall, defiant, eyes wide.

Out in the darkness was a rustle in the bushes, a footfall, a grunt. She saw a shadow behind him. The man angled his head toward the noise. There was a splash of color in the moonlight, a mountainous figure crashing through the brush. The man spun and fired his pistol—once, twice—and then there was a mighty roar, a blinding flash of light, and the man was not standing beside Mary anymore.

Mary stumbled backward, tripping over her feet, landing on her behind. The gunshots rang in her ears. The man lay a few feet away, arms sprawled, eyes open, unblinking.

"You all right?" asked a familiar voice.

She propped herself on an elbow and gazed up as the shadow took form. "You?"

64

The Crown & Anchor Pub was located on San Jacinto Boulevard across from the university. It was long and narrow and dark and smelled of stale beer and burned hamburgers. A wooden bar ran the length of the room. Taps for a dozen beers protruded from fake barrels in the wall behind it.

Jessie made her way down the row of tables, searching for Linus Jankowski. If the smell was bad, the music nearly made her puke. Old English sea shanties blared from the sound system. She was six all over again, seated on the admiral's knees as he sang "The Wreck of the Edmund Fitzgerald" to her.

She found Linus seated at a round table in the back, just past the dartboards. Six or seven men were with him. Jessie recognized two propeller-heads from class. The others were TAs she'd seen around school, PhD candidates, or postdocs like Linus.

"You made it," said Linus. "Take a seat."

Jessie scooted around the table to the last open chair.

"Um, I'll just stand here," said Garrett, hands dug into his pockets.

Jessie nodded, wishing he weren't there. It had been an awkward ride downtown. Garrett had talked the entire time as if they were on some kind of date, asking what they should do after meeting up with Linus. All the while Jess was growing more and more concerned about Grace. What if she was right about the people who'd hacked into their mom's phone and they really were watching? Jessie had never been given responsibility for someone before. Not real responsibility concerning their safety and all that. The thoughts weighed heavily on her, and Garrett's incessant yapping made it worse. Finally she'd had to tell him to "just shut up and drive." Things were better after that. She'd come to the conclusion that boys liked being told what to do.

"Am I even allowed in here?" she asked, taking her seat.

"Technically, no," said Linus. "But who's checking?" He smiled, but she could tell from the way he made no effort to introduce her around that he wasn't too excited to see her.

"I found something on my phone," she said nervously. "Actually it was on my mom's phone. But I copied it, so now it's on mine. I've never seen anything like it."

"Slow down, Miss Grant," said Linus. "Start over."

Jessie scooted her chair closer, aware of the stares coming her way. She stared right back, reminding herself that none of these guys had solved the Capture the Flag hack in thirteen minutes.

"Okay," she said, looking Linus in the eye. "It's about my dad."

"Your dad? FBI, right?"

"Yeah," said Jessie. "Before he died, he called my mom and left her a voice message. I don't know what he said. I think it was important, but she didn't tell me, because she thought I'd get all depressed and upset. Anyway, what matters is that someone deleted the message from my mom's phone."

"Someone who wasn't your mom?"

"Yeah."

"Really?" asked Linus, with the same dismissive tone she'd used with her mom.

"That's what I said. My mom's nice, but she's a prole. I thought for sure she'd deleted it. But she didn't. Someone hacked into her phone and wiped the message. Only that message. Everything else was still there."

"And you want me to find it?"

"No," said Jessie. "I mean, *yes, for sure,* if you could . . . if that's even possible. Right now I just want you to look at the tracks I found."

"And figure out who hacked into your mom's phone?"

Jessie nodded. "Whoever did it killed my dad," she said. "I mean, right?"

By now conversation at the table had all but died. Linus's friends were paying close attention.

"Show me," said Linus. "Not here. Outside. Away from these propeller-heads."

Jessie pushed back her chair and stood. For some reason she grabbed Garrett's hand and led him outside. The pub was on the main drag that ran adjacent to UT, a neighborhood of bars, bookstores, and clothing boutiques. At ten-fifteen, it was packed with pedestrians.

Linus directed them around a corner to a quieter spot. Jessie brought up the screenshot of the code she'd found on her mom's phone. "Here it is. Tell me what you think."

Linus took the phone and studied the snippet of code. "See this?" he said immediately, pointing to a section near the end. "This comes from way up the food chain. You and me, we're minnows. This shit's from a great white shark. Someone who gained access to your mom's wireless carrier. And I mean deep access."

"So it's not from the carrier?"

"Not a chance. They don't need a skeleton key. That's what we're looking at. Whoever broke in was from outside the loop."

"So the message might still be somewhere?"

"Possibly. Carriers keep voice messages for a couple weeks on their main servers."

"Can you trace it?"

"Trace what? I mean, *look*. There's nothing here. All he left behind was a single line of code. Whoever did this is a pro. We're talking rocket scientist. I kid you not."

"Smarter than you?"

"Much."

"Maybe your friends can have a look," suggested Garrett.

Linus frowned. "I don't think they'd be too keen on getting into the middle of an FBI investigation."

"At least you can show them," said Garrett.

"Please," said Jessie.

"Look, Jessie. I'll be honest. I have a bad feeling about this. Those fingerprints have me spooked. Why don't you just let it go? What's done is done." Linus checked his watch. "I'm sorry about your dad, but I can't help you. It's late. Garrett, you should take Jessie home."

With that, Linus started up the block. Garrett put a hand on Jessie's shoulder. "He's right. We should go. But it's not that late. How 'bout we grab a Coney Island dog and a limeade slush at Sonic?"

Jessie knocked Garrett's hand away and ran. She caught up to Linus as he turned the corner. "Stop," she said, grabbing his sleeve, yanking him to a halt.

"Hey," protested Linus. "What the—?"

"You don't understand," she said. "He was telling my mom something important and I screwed it up. It's on me."

Linus stopped. "How did you screw up?"

Jessie dropped her eyes to the ground, then forced herself to look up, to look at Linus and own up to what she'd done. "I was unlocking my mom's phone when my dad called. It was because of me she missed his message."

"So?"

"Don't you get it? I killed him. My dad was calling to ask for help, and my mom missed the call because I was trying to show off how smart I am. I killed my father."

Linus stepped closer, his face knotted with indecision. "Give it to me," he said, grabbing the phone out of Jessie's hand before she could answer. "Wait here. This may take a while."

Jessie watched him stalk up the street and turn the corner. She lowered her head, embarrassed at her outburst. Garrett took her hand. "You okay?"

"Yes. I mean, no. Actually, I'm not okay. In fact, I'm pretty much the opposite. Is that all right?"

"Sure. That's all right."

She looked at Garrett—tall, blond, way too handsome. He'd changed the Mumford & Sons T-shirt for a vintage Aerosmith jersey. At least that was a step in the right direction. She saw his blue eyes staring at her in a way she knew her mom would call "adoringly," and she wondered for about the hundred thousandth time what he could possibly see in her. "You can hug me if you want," she said, pulling him closer. "But don't even think of kissing me."

Twenty minutes later, Linus Jankowski came around the corner. One look at his face and Jessie knew he'd failed.

"You're in trouble," said Linus.

"You couldn't do it," said Jessie. "None of you?"

Linus shook his head. "There's only one person who can do this . . . and that's still a maybe."

"Who is it?" said Jessie. "Where is he? Do you know him?"

"Not personally, but I know where he is."

"Where?"

"DEF CON. This is the week of the conference."

Jessie shook her head. "Him?"

"Rudeboy."

65

Tank Potter stood over the body. He held a shotgun in his hands, smoke curling from both barrels. His face was flushed, and in the dark it shone like the devil's. "You okay?"

Nodding, Mary pushed herself to her feet. "Is he dead?"

"Oh, yeah," said Potter. "I've seen dead before. That's it. You know him?"

"No. But he knew me. He wanted the disk."

"What disk is that?"

Mary found the transparent sleeve a few feet away. "This one," she said, picking it up. "I had it burned in the manager's office. It shows Joe meeting his contact at the café. I've met him. The waitress said Joe called him Boots. I can't remember his real name, but if I look at him long enough, I'm sure it'll come to me."

"Good news."

Mary brushed the dust from her palms. She felt faint and queasy, and her breath was coming too fast. She stepped toward Potter and her knees buckled. The reporter moved swiftly and caught her. "He was going to kill me," she said.

"Yes, ma'am. I believe that's what he does."

"Thanks for catching me," said Mary. "And also for . . . well, you know."

"Don't mention it."

"What are you doing here?"

"Same thing as you. When Mason let me go after ramming his car, he couldn't have hoisted the red flag any higher."

"Didn't he threaten you with prison if you continued to interfere?"

"So? I've lost my job, my pension, and my reputation. Going to jail can't be any worse. You have more to lose than I do."

"You asked me what kind of Kool-Aid Mason gave me. It was the kind about endangering national security and damaging all the hard work Joe had put in."

"That's their standard line. And here I was thinking you were a true believer."

"I am," said Mary. "Or else I wouldn't be here."

She looked down at the body, then swiveled her shoulders left and right, checking the landscape around them. Everywhere lurked silhouettes and shadows. It was difficult to see more than forty feet. A steady wind blew, bringing sounds of passing traffic from the highway and the eerie stillness of the plains.

"I ought to call the police."

"That's the right thing to do."

Mary punched in 911 but stopped before hitting Send. "He said he knew everything about me. He said that he knew I'd be here and that we were going to the morgue earlier and that you had visited me to ask about Joe."

"They were listening to us."

"How?"

"My phone, for one. When I called my buddy at the ME's office—the guy who let me take the pictures of your husband and the informant—he told me that Mason and Bennett were getting your husband ready to go. He didn't expect them to roll out of there until two or so. Do you remember how fast they were hauling ass when we arrived? The first sedan almost ran you over."

"What's your point?"

"Someone told Mason we were coming."

"Him?" Mary looked at the dead man.

"Or the people he works for."

"Then it means . . ." Mary didn't want to finish the sentence. It didn't seem possible that there could be a connection between the killer lying at their feet and Edward Mason.

"You still want to call the police?"

"We have to."

"Your husband didn't call the police when he was in trouble." He paused. "Or the FBI."

Mary considered this. She wondered what you called it when everything you'd spent your entire life believing was true and inviolate turned out to be false and manipulative. And you knew that you were alone. Absolutely alone.

After a moment she knelt beside the corpse and searched him for identification, grimacing as her fingers touched flesh and viscera and other things she didn't care to imagine. "Just what did you shoot him with?"

"Twelve-gauge. It does the trick."

"You've done this before?"

"Javelina. Wild boar. This is my first man. I felt worse for the animals."

Mary handed Potter the dead man's phone and returned Joe's Glock to her holster. She felt something hard and angular in the man's pocket. Car keys.

"Phone's locked," said Potter. "You get anything else?"

"No wallet. Just the keys."

Tank handed Mary his shotgun and crouched, his ruined knees sounding like millstones colliding. He pulled off the man's cap and used the phone's flashlight to read the name inscribed in Marks-A-Lot on the sweatband. "McNair," he said. "It's a start."

Mary gave him a hand to get to his feet. The knees cracked again, and she winced. "Sounds bad."

"I'm asking Santa for a knee replacement. I'm still waiting to see when the concussions kick in. My head took as many hits as my body."

"Drinking isn't going to help."

"No, it isn't. By the way, I was already fired. Laid off, actually. The DUI just hurried up the process."

The hour had gotten to 10:40. The moon was a sliver high in the sky. Stars punched through the canopy like machine-gun bullets. She looked back at the corpse. A man had been killed. The incident needed to be reported. She was the admiral's daughter, and the admiral did everything by the book. "We have to call the police."

"Mason will have us in jail by midnight," said Potter. "National security."

"They'll find us anyway."

"Maybe. Maybe not. In the meantime we'll figure this thing out. Maybe it's them who'll be running."

"Big words."

"I'm a journalist. I like 'em big."

The dead man's phone made a pinging noise. "Incoming text from someone named Briggs. Take a look."

Mary glanced at the phone. The text read: *"Done?"* "That big enough for you?"

"We need to go," said Tank.

Mary gave Potter back his shotgun and tossed him McNair's car keys. The two jogged across the flat landscape, winding their way around clumps of mesquite. They mounted the berm and ran down the other side to Mary's car. The Jeep was parked next to it. Halfway across the lot was McNair's pickup.

No lights burned from the café. Even the neon cowboy had gone dark.

"Fifty bucks says the truck's registered to him."

"Don't even think about it. Whoever sent that text is probably waiting a mile up the road. I don't want to be here when he comes to check why McNair didn't answer him."

"I'll take my chances."

"Be quick."

"Lady, *quick* is not an adjective that belongs anywhere near my name. But I promise to be thorough and I'll try to be swift."

Potter half ran, half hobbled to the truck. A minute passed, and another. She tapped her foot, wishing he would come back, her eyes on the highway and the access road feeding into the lot. She thought of calling the girls to reassure them. It was late. She was sure they were asleep by now—Grace at least. Instead she texted Jessie: "Home in forty minutes. Turn off the computer now and go to sleep. Love U."

Finally Potter left the truck and jogged back to her.

"Well?" she asked.

"Found some weed," said Potter, tossing a clear pouch to the ground. "Also found his automobile registration and insurance cards. His name is William James McNair."

"Anything else?"

"Wallet. Driver's license."

"Does he have a business card?"

"Didn't see one. We can check the rest later."

"That truck was here three days ago. I saw it on one of the surveillance feeds. It was parked close to the entrance when Joe left the café."

"He must have been watching Joe," said Tank.

"You think that's all he did?"

Just then Mary's phone vibrated in her hand. Text from Jessie: "Night, Mom. Love you." Mary breathed easier. "Love you too, sweetie," she replied. "On my way."

"Everything okay?" asked Potter.

"It's Jessie, saying good night."

"She's at home, right?"

"Looking after Grace."

"Good."

Only then did Mary register Potter's worried expression. "Why?"

"I didn't come out here only to see Cal. I came to find you. I drove by your place earlier, and when I didn't see your car, I figured you probably had the same idea as me."

"And?"

Tank drew a breath and related the details of his visit to Carlos Cantu's house. Mary felt cold and alone.

"This isn't over," he said. "They want you, me, and Carlos dead, and they're not going to stop until they succeed."

"I need to get home."

66

Thump!

Grace heard the noise coming from upstairs and muted the television. She sat frozen, breath locked inside her chest. The noise sounded heavy and hollow. Like a footstep.

The hackers had come. It was the people who had broken into Mom's phone. Now they were here. They were upstairs.

Thump!

Grace jumped in her skin. It *was* a footstep, and it came from the room directly above her. Jessie's room. She called her sister, but Jess didn't answer. "Come home," she texted. "Someone's in the house."

She clicked on her mom's number but didn't call. Not yet. Jess would kill her.

Grace rose from the couch and as quietly as possible walked to the base of the stairs. She stood there looking up, heart pounding. The hall lights were on. She thought she saw a shadow up there. She called Jess again. Again there was no answer.

The hackers were blocking her calls.

Grace began to tremble. She reasoned that she had three choices. Call Mom. Run to the Kramers'. Or go upstairs and confront whoever was there.

She couldn't call Mom. Going to the Kramers' was also out. Carrie would call her mom in a second, and Jess's secret would be out of the bag. She remembered Mom saying that problems don't get any smaller if you just stare at them. If Dad were here, he'd already be upstairs checking out what was making the sound. He wasn't afraid of hackers or anyone else.

"I'm coming up," she shouted. "If anyone's there, go away. I'm warning you!"

She started up the stairs, pausing at each one to listen. It was quiet. The hackers were hiding, waiting. She didn't know how anyone could get inside, let alone all the way upstairs without her hearing them. Still, everyone knew that thieves and murderers were clever and athletic, and it was hackers who had killed her dad. If they wanted to get in and kill her, they could.

Her phone made that whistling noise. Jessie texted back: "No one's there, scaredy-cat. Go to bed. Mom will be home soon."

Grace didn't bother answering. She swallowed and climbed another stair.

Thump! Thump! Thump!

Grace took off up the stairs. The noises weren't footsteps. Something was buzzing around, hitting the wall over and over. Hackers wouldn't do that. They were sneaky and bad, but they didn't buzz.

She reached Jessie's room and opened the door. Something big and green shot through the air at her. She ducked, barely able to keep from screaming.

Thump!

The big green glob bounced off the wall and kept flying. She retreated into the hall and watched the cicada going crazy. Stupid Jess had left her window open and the bug had flown inside. She watched it zigging and zagging around the room. It wasn't one cicada but two, one on top of the other as if they were glued together.

Yuck, thought Grace, they're doing it.

She hurried across the room and opened a second window and ran around waving her arms. Finally the mating cicadas flew outside. She closed the windows and ran downstairs. She was too creeped out to stay upstairs.

In the kitchen she poured herself a glass of milk and took two Oreos out of the bag. She sat at Mom's alcove and went on the computer. As always, she checked her e-mails first. She had four new messages. Her eye caught the third one down. "Cutest Sloth in the World! Watch this!"

Grace opened the message. The text read, "Watch this and die laughing. He is sooooo adorable!" A hyperlink was printed below it.

Grace positioned the cursor over the hyperlink but didn't click right away. Jess was always warning her and Mom about getting dangerous stuff in their e-mails. Never open an attachment, she told them, if you don't know who sent it to you. Something inside it could mess up your computer.

But a video about sloths? They watched tons of videos on YouTube about sloths.

Grace double-clicked on the hyperlink and was taken to the video. She watched, giggling as a baby sloth did its best to crawl out of a child's crib, gripping the slick wooden slats, climbing up a little, then sliding back down to the mattress and lolling on its back. The camera zoomed in as the sloth yawned, and Grace burst out laughing. A teenage girl reached into the crib, picked up the sloth, and cradled it to her chest. The sloth laid its head on her shoulder, eyes staring at the camera, wet nose sniffing contentedly.

Grace thought about Fluffy, her hamster. He'd been a climber, too, though he didn't yawn. Still, her heart ached for him. Jessie said Fluffy was only a furry rodent and he didn't have a personality, but Grace had loved him all the same.

She watched the video again and then once more after that. She decided she wanted a sloth. A three-toed South American tree sloth.

Before logging off, she forwarded the video to Jessie. Smiling, she went upstairs and crawled into bed.

Even Jessie would love the sloth.

If she ever got home . . .

67

"Do you know him?" Jessie asked.

"Rudeboy"? Linus scratched his beard. "Why should I?"

"I mean, do you at least know who he is? Like his name?"

"He's Rudeboy. That's all. No one knows his name. I imagine his parents do, and his close friends, but to us . . . no clue. That's how he's able to do what he does. You know, making service attacks on Amazon, shutting down the navy's mainframe for two hours, wiping half the hard drives of the biggest oil company in Saudi Arabia."

"Then how do you know he's at DEF CON?"

"He's won Capture the Flag seven years running. He has to defend his title. Of course he's there."

Jessie pulled up the DEF CON website. It showed a skull-and-crossbones pennant and gave the place and dates. "Crap," she said. "It ends tomorrow." She looked at Linus. "When do they play?"

"Play what?" asked Garrett.

"The last day," said Linus. "Capture the Flag begins at eight in the morning. They want to make sure everyone's still hungover."

"How long does it take?"

"As long as it takes. Eight hours. Ten. Depends on who has the strongest team."

"But you said that Rudeboy solved the hack in five minutes," Jessie retorted.

"Yeah, the hardest one, but there's a bunch more."

"Why didn't you go this year?"

"I'm teaching. I can't just cop out and fly to Vegas."

Jessie pulled up the website for Bergstrom International Airport and checked the flight schedule. "The last flight to Las Vegas leaves at eleven. It's already ten-thirty."

"Wait, wait, wait," said Linus, waving a concerned hand. "You're not going to Vegas."

"Who says?"

"Yeah," said Garrett. "Your mom isn't going to let you just go there alone."

Jessie shot him a venomous look.

"It's not that," said Linus. "You're not signed up for DEF CON. You have to register for the conference, and then you have to qualify to play the game. They don't let just anyone into the competition. You have to be part of a team."

"How much is it?" asked Jessie.

"I don't know," said Linus. "I think I paid eight hundred bucks last year. But that's beside the point. Didn't you hear what I said? You don't have a team."

"What about yours?"

"I told you, I'm not playing."

"Don't you know anyone who is?"

"Sure. But—"

"Call them. Tell them to let me play with them."

"I can't do that."

"Why not?" Jessie double-clicked on the flight number to bring up all the details. Her heart jumped. "It's delayed!"

"What's delayed?" asked Linus.

"The flight." Jessie realized she was shouting and told herself to get a grip. It was hard to be calm. For a second she believed that it all might just work. She would go to Vegas. She would play on the team with Linus's friends. She'd help them win it and afterward meet Rudeboy, who would solve the mystery of the unknown code in the drop of a hat and tell her who had hacked into her mother's phone. Jessie would figure out who had killed her father. "I'll pay the fee," she said. "I'll pay for your ticket. All you have to do is come with me and introduce me to your friends."

"I can't go, Jess. I'm sorry."

Jessie held out her phone. "Call them. Please. I won't embarrass you."

"Jess, your mom will kill you," said Garrett.

"Fine," said Jessie. "As long as it's after we win."

Linus continued to shake his head. "How long is the flight delayed?"

Jessie swallowed. He was considering it. Linus was actually considering it. "It doesn't say."

"Jess, you're not serious," said Garrett.

"Shh." Jessie called the airline and navigated as quickly as possible through the automated directory. It took two minutes before a human being picked up. "I'm calling about Flight 2998 to Las Vegas. I see it's delayed."

"That flight is closed. Boarding is about to begin."

Jessie turned away from the others, bowing her head. She began to cry. "My father just died. His name is Joseph Grant. He's in Las Vegas and the police need me to help them answer some questions. They think he was murdered. Please, ma'am. It's a family emergency. I have to get there. I don't know what else to do."

"Hold one moment."

Jessie lifted her head and stared at Linus, her cheeks dry. "Half of being a good hacker is social engineering, right?"

Linus nodded.

The airline representative returned to the line. "Hello, miss. There are two seats remaining. Will you be traveling alone or with any family members?"

Jessie covered the phone. "If I beat him, he'll have to meet me."

"You can't beat him," said Linus.

"Why not?"

"No one beats Rudeboy. That's why. Besides, you don't even have a hacker name."

"I do, too."

"Oh yeah? What?"

"Tuffgurl. Two f's and two u's."

Linus walked in a circle, talking to himself. Finally he threw up his hands. "She's crazy," he said. "Two f's and two u's. Crazy."

"Linus, please."

Linus Jankowski sighed. "I'm not going, but I'll make the call. I can't promise anything."

"I'll go with you," said Garrett. "I mean, if you want me to."

"Yes," said Jessie. "I'd like that." She put the phone to her ear. "Two seats," and she rattled off her debit card number, committed to memory long ago.

"The flight is scheduled to leave in forty-five minutes. If you can get to the airport by eleven, we'll do our best to get you aboard. We're very sorry for your loss."

"We'll be there." Jessie hung up, her eyes imploring Linus. "On you now."

Linus walked up the street and Jessie heard his raised voice over the thrum of the passing automobiles. He returned five minutes later, shaking his head dispiritedly.

"Well?" asked Jessie, sensing bad news, already working on another way to get to Rudeboy.

"It's your lucky day," said Linus. "They have a spot open. One of their team members drank too much and is too sick to play."

"And they'll let me take his place?" Jessie had known too much disappointment to believe him right off.

"But you have to pay the entrance fee."

"Done."

"Okay, then. You better get going."

Jessie rose on her tiptoes, allowing herself a moment's joy, a few seconds of triumph. "I don't know what to say."

"Thanks is fine."

"Thanks." Jessie rushed forward and kissed him on the cheek. His beard was softer than she'd expected. She turned to Garrett. "Don't just stand there. Move your butt."

Garrett took off at a jog. Jessie hesitated for a moment before following.

"You won't win," said Linus.

68

The malware entered the Grants' desktop computer like a virus entering a host's blood. Freed from its confines inside the video clip, it spread through the machine's silicon arteries at the speed of light. Its primary target was the operating system, where it branched out to all applications, probing each for weaknesses, vulnerabilities, flaws in the code that would allow it to gain entry.

Like any parasitic virus, the malware attacked multiple spots at once. It found the machine's permanent memory and set about copying every keystroke ever made. In batches of 100,000, it transferred the data to Ian Prince's computer, where it was plugged into an algorithm designed to identify usernames and passwords. Though nothing to match Titan, the computer employed next-generation microchips capable of performing a trillion operations a second. In the time it takes to blink an eye, the algorithm had ferreted out the ten most commonly used pairs of names and passwords.

Simultaneously the malware identified the most frequently visited websites requiring usernames and passwords and began plugging in the pairs. It was a simple process of trial and error. The malware was tireless and continued until it had successfully logged on to over sixty sites and gained access to the Grants' most confidential information.

Another arm of the virus took control of the computer's camera and microphone. The Grants' desktop was now a hot microphone and a secret surveillance camera.

Yet another arm allowed Ian to control its keyboard remotely.

In less than ten seconds, the computer and everything on it belonged to Ian Prince.

69

Dinner was over. Ian had finished his speech. The assembled executives had moved from the dining hall to the salon, a smaller, cozier room, for after-dinner digestifs. Instead of a butler in tails pouring snifters of brandy and cognac, there was a buffet offering coffee, tea, and Fernet Branca. The atmosphere was one of carefully contained excitement, all buzz and chatter about the imminent, possibly dangerous, and undoubtedly groundbreaking events to come.

Nearby stood a half-dozen engineers clad in navy jumpsuits, the word *Orca* embroidered in yellow stitching on their breasts. On the wall behind them was a photograph measuring four feet by six, taken from high over an elliptical island. The island was one mile long and half as wide, and its symmetry was astounding. Orca, the island's name, was printed in block letters at the bottom of the photograph.

"We've located the office campus at the southwest corner of the island," said Ian, pointing to a grouping of more detailed photos showing sleek low-rise buildings set amid fields of grass and lush vegetation. "We dispose of five million square feet of office space, more than enough to enable us to consolidate global management functions across business sectors in a single location. I know you'll appreciate the design. Koolhaas, Foster, Gehry are just a few of the architects we enlisted . . . oh, and I can't forget Calatrava. Moreover, between solar arrays and our own on-site nuclear plant, we're energy independent."

Ian moved to another group of photographs. "Here on the north side of the island is the residential sector. We offer both apartments and townhouses. For those of you hoping to spend your earnings building an estate to rival Mr. Gates's or Mr. Ellison's, I've just saved you three years of headaches, countless arguments with your general contractor, and a hundred million dollars. You can thank me later. The quarters can comfortably house up to six thousand men, women, and children. And best of all, they're free.

"Adjacent to the residences is our recreational sector." Ian pointed out the numerous sports fields, swimming pools, tennis courts, and the fitness center. "At the lee side of the island we've put in a beach that will rival anything in Thailand, Hawaii, or the Caribbean. Palm trees, hammocks, a nice clubhouse, and without any annoying natives trying to sell you a puka-shell necklace."

Ian returned to the overhead shot of the island. "To make sure work doesn't come home, you'll note that a rather large hill runs across the center of the island. I'd like to call it a mountain, but even my ego isn't that big." He smiled to let everyone know he was just one of the boys and that rumors of his self-seriousness were overblown. "Ideally, everyone will walk to work, but for the lazy ones among us there's a high-speed rail that will take you the entire thousand meters in about thirty seconds.

"Now here at the far southwest corner is where we've built our industrial sector—manufacturing facilities, warehouses, shipping, docks, the like. With a runway of just under four thousand feet, we can accommodate pretty much any aircraft except a fully loaded jumbo jet."

From across the room, Peter Briggs watched all this with a mixture of awe, admiration, and disdain. He'd forgone wine in favor of Wild Turkey, neat. He sipped from his glass, watching Ian work the room. He was too anxious to hear back from Shanks to pay close attention. For the tenth time in ten minutes, he checked his watch. Still not a word.

Ian had traded his salesman's spiel about the virtues of Orca for his "no boundaries" talk. "The world no longer has boundaries . . . old ways obsolete . . . our identity once defined by our tribe . . ."

Briggs could practically parrot the words of Ian's impassioned argument.

"We had no choice who we were . . . later it was a shelter, a castle, or a fortress . . . after that a piece of land bordered by a river or mountain range or an ocean and guarded by soldiers living within those geographic borders. We went from clans to cities to principalities to countries. But what is a country today?"

Briggs's phone vibrated. Thank God. It was time Shanks checked in. He slipped the phone from his pocket, only to discover that it wasn't Shanks but the duty officer. "Yes."

"I'm sorry to disturb you, but we have a code black."

"Code black" referred to an employee fatality.

"Give me a minute." Briggs left the salon, took the stairs to the ground floor, and proceeded outdoors to the esplanade. The last employee to die had been an SVP who'd dropped dead of a heart attack in Mumbai, brought on by eating the world's hottest chili peppers. "Who's the poor devil?"

"It's Bill McNair."

"Shanks? You're sure?"

"Yessir. We're all pretty shaken up."

Briggs walked to the balustrade overlooking the Meadow, wanting to be certain that he was alone. "What happened?"

"He was off-duty, so it's all pretty sketchy, but it looks like he was shot after going to a concert out in Cedar Valley."

Briggs ran a hand over his scalp, trying to make sense of the news. "Go on."

"His RFID coordinates put him at a place called the Nutty Brown Cafe. He was stationary for ninety-three minutes, then thirty minutes ago he moved a short distance. Five minutes later his data cut out. No heart rate. No blood pressure readings. It was so sudden we thought for sure it was a glitch. We called him immediately. There was no response."

"I'll be right there."

Briggs jogged across the Meadow, entered Brasenose, and took the stairs two at a time. A four-man skeleton crew was on duty. "Did you send a team?"

"Yessir. They located him in a field behind the venue."

"Only McNair? There was no one with him?"

"No, sir."

"Is the team still on-site?"

"Yessir."

"Put them onscreen and bring up McNair's bio data on monitor two."

A concerned Caucasian male appeared on the screen. Briggs asked for a complete rundown.

"We arrived and found his vehicle parked in the lot. The doors were unlocked and the keys were in the ignition. We had to call HQ to get a read on his physical coordinates. We found him three hundred yards away, lying in the middle of some scrub. There's no indication what he was doing out here, but he had his weapon drawn."

Briggs knew precisely what Shanks was doing out in the middle of the scrub. "Go on."

"The cause of death was a shotgun blast to the chest and neck. He still has his phone on him, but we can't find his wallet. Tell you the truth, I'm confused."

"Show me the body."

The security officer trained his camera on the prone, inert body of William "Shanks" McNair.

"All right," said Briggs. "Any sign of law enforcement?"

"Nothing."

"Good. Clean up the scene. Get him out of there. Bring his vehicle here. Do not contact the sheriff, understand? This is an internal matter."

"Excuse me, sir," said the duty officer. "But McNair was off-duty at the time. His wallet was missing. It may be a case of rob—"

"Do as I say. That is all. And get his vehicle out of there." Briggs directed his attention to a smaller screen displaying McNair's vital data as recorded by his bio bracelet. McNair's heart rate appeared to have been steady at sixty beats per minute, accelerating slightly in the last minutes of his life. His blood pressure increased similarly over the same period. Both readings were consistent with an elevated level of adrenaline in the system. Excitement, not fear.

And then . . . nothing. All readings plummeted to zero. No last-second spike in heart rate. No surge in diastolic pressure. Shanks died instantly and without foreknowledge. Death as brought on by a shotgun blast delivered at close range. He was bushwhacked.

"Let me know when everything's cleaned up."

"Yessir."

Briggs left the Ops Center. By the time he reached his car, he had a good idea what had transpired. His phone rang again as he left ONE's campus. It was the Mole, and he sounded as perplexed as Briggs was angry.

"Mary Grant just came home."

"Shanks encountered some difficulties."

"He let her get away?"

"Have some respect for the dead."

"Dead? Shanks? But how?"

"Just keep an eye on the home," said Briggs. "Let me know if you see any movement in or out."

"What are you going to do?"

"What I should have done a while ago. Take care of this matter once and for all."

THURSDAY

70

Mary parked in the garage as instructed, staying in her car until the door lowered behind her. She climbed out quietly, not wanting to wake the girls or to alert anyone else who might be waiting for her inside. It was a futile gesture. Anyone watching had seen her come home. If they had someone inside, they'd have passed along the word, though the thump of the garage door was warning enough.

She entered through the laundry room and crossed the foyer. The lights were dim, and all was quiet. She paused to take a look around, Joe's gun heavy in her hand. Her heart was pounding loudly enough to drown out a police siren.

Act like nothing's happened, Tank had cautioned her. *No calls. No texts. Assume they're listening to everything. Don't give them a reason to act. They'll find out about McNair soon enough.*

She checked that all the doors were locked and breathed easier. A light burned in the family room, which scared her all over again, but it was the television, sound muted. She turned it off, then returned to the stairs.

She paused to take off her sensible brown loafers, which were killing her more than her four-inch mules ever did. She held the pistol in front of her, one hand gripping the stock, the other supporting the barrel. If she saw anyone who was not her daughter—anyone at all—she was pulling the trigger until the gun was empty.

The door to Grace's room stood open a crack. Her baby girl's hair fairly shone on the pillow. Mary slid into the room and perched on the edge of the bed, listening to her daughter's measured breathing, thinking it was the most beautiful sound in the world.

One present and accounted for, she reported to the admiral.

Mary crossed the hall to Jessie's room. The curtains were drawn and she saw a lump beneath the covers. "Jess? You awake?" She stepped over a pile of clothes, her eyes getting used to the dark. "Jess?"

There came a ping from downstairs. A knock on the glass door. Tank Potter had arrived.

Mary left the room, picking up the dirty clothing on her way. Potter stood by the sliding door, hunched close like a teenager sneaking into his girlfriend's house. Mary flipped the lock and slid the door open. "Come in."

"Doing laundry *now?*"

Mary dropped the clothes onto the floor. "Never mind."

Tank pointed at the gun. "You might want to put that away."

"Sorry." Mary slipped the pistol into her belt holster.

"Everything okay?"

"They're both upstairs sleeping."

"We should go. They're going to discover McNair sooner rather than later."

"*Mommy.*"

Mary turned to see Grace standing at the foot of the stairs, clutching Pink Pony to her chest. "Hi, mouse. Did we wake you?"

Grace's eyes went from Mary to Tank and back again. She began to cry. Mary went to her and took her in her arms. "Are you still upset from earlier?" she whispered.

Grace shook her head violently.

"Then what is it?"

"I'm sorry," came the muffled response.

"What for?" Mary held her daughter at arm's length, wiping away a tear with her thumb.

Grace swallowed heavily. "I should have told you, but she said she'd be back. She promised."

"Honey, who are you talking about?"

"Jessie." Grace tried to speak but was overcome by another gust of tears.

"What about Jessie, dear?"

"She's gone. She went to go look for the hackers."

"No answer."

Phone in hand, Mary stood next to Jessie's bed, her stomach crawling with the thousand worries of every mother.

"Text her," said Tank.

Mary typed: "Jess. Call me immediately. You are not in trouble. I need to know you are all right. I love you. Mom." She added "Please," then erased it and sent the message.

"Don't worry," said Tank. "She's just with a boy. What's his name . . . Gary."

"Garrett," said Mary, then to Grace: "Do you remember his last name?"

Grace shook her head.

Mary admired the cleverly arranged pillows, the dark Red Sox cap set atop them to simulate her daughter's hair. "Jess doesn't like boys," she explained, as much to herself as to Potter. "I mean, she likes them, but they don't like her, so she doesn't . . . you know the drill. She likes computers and hacking and watching old episodes of *The X-Files*." Mary willed the phone in her hand to buzz, indicating her daughter's incoming text. "What if they . . . ," she said, looking at Tank.

"Don't jump to conclusions. There's no reason to think that—"

"No reason?" Mary whispered venomously. "Joe's dead. Your friend was murdered six hours ago. And I was almost—" She bit her tongue, aware of Grace standing in the doorway behind them.

"Is it the hackers, Mommy?"

This was the second time her daughter had mentioned hackers. "Excuse me, sweetie—what do you mean by 'the hackers'?"

"The people who erased Daddy's message—the people Jess is looking for. Did they get her?"

The hackers. Latest in a long line of imaginary nightmarish adversaries, following "Injuns" and "Nazis" and "alien abductors."

"It's not the hackers. Mr. Potter is right. Jess must be with Garrett."

"And her TA," added Grace. "So she's safe."

This was the first Grace had mentioned anything about a teaching assistant. "Pardon me? Do you mean Linus?"

"She said she was seeing her TA, too. He was going to help her figure out the clue."

Mary turned on the reading lamp above Jessie's desk and looked around for a notebook or a handout from school that might contain the TA's number. There was a *PC Magazine* and a copy of *Wired*. But nothing from the university about Jess's classes. What had happened to spiral notebooks and black speckled composition books?

She opened the drawer. Complete pandemonium. Pens and pencils and erasers and receipts. She freed a photograph. Jess and Joe at a symposium on the future of the Net that they'd attended last year. Mary replaced the photo and continued to rummage through the mess.

Her fingers touched something cool and round pushed against the back corner. "What's this thing?"

In her hand she held a slim green metallic tube.

"An e-cigarette," said Tank.

"A what?"

"You put some kind of oil inside and an electric spark vaporizes it. It's the latest thing."

"My daughter doesn't smoke."

"She doesn't like boys either."

Mary dropped the e-cigarette into the drawer. She knew she should feel shocked or disappointed, but all she could muster was a vague sense of surprise. At the moment e-cigarettes ranked low on her list of punishable offenses. She closed the drawer and made a search of the floor and closet. "No backpack," she said. "She has her laptop."

Tank stood in the doorway, biting his lip. "We should really go."

"Not yet."

Mary pushed past him and went downstairs. She took a seat at her work alcove and double-clicked on the search bar. "Don't," said Tank. "They see everything."

"I don't care," said Mary as she logged onto the UT website. "I've got to find Jess. I don't have time to play their games."

In a few seconds she'd pulled up a course description and syllabus of Jessie's summer school class. The professor's name stood at the top, along with his office address and phone numbers. Below was similar information for his teaching assistant, Linus Jankowski, PhD from MIT, with a concentration in artificial intelligence and game theory.

The call to his mobile number went to voicemail. "Mr. Jankowski, this is Mary Grant. I understand that my daughter may have visited you earlier this evening. It's almost one a.m. and she isn't home yet. If you've seen her or have any idea where she might be, please call me at this number. Don't worry about the time. I'll be up. Please consider this an emergency."

"Mom, where are we going?" asked Grace. "Do I need to get dressed?"

"Where are we going, Mr. Potter?" Mary asked.

"Not sure yet. First let's get to my car."

"Just a sec." Mary pulled up Netflix and selected *The Conversation*, the movie starring Gene Hackman.

"What's that for?" asked Grace, mystified by the old movie.

"It's about someone who secretly listens to people." Mary looked over her shoulder at Tank. "They should like it."

"Oh? What happens?"

"The people start secretly listening to him. It drives him crazy."

71

It was past midnight.

Alone in his office, Ian stood transfixed as Mary Grant came to magnificent three-dimensional holographic life before him. It was not a likeness in the ordinary sense but a rendering of her everyday life as reflected by her online activity, and as such, a far more penetrating portrait of her entire self. In a way it was a new form of art. Da Vinci had mastered perspective. Monet had given them impressionism. Picasso, cubism. Yet no matter the style, the artist was perpetually seeking a glimpse of the subject's innermost soul. Now Ian had penetrated those secret confines.

He turned in a circle, his face bathed in the eerie glow. He had programmed the malware to log on to each site the Grants visited, in order of frequency. As it did, the tower grew ever taller, while screens appeared behind screens—two, three, four deep—until he stood encircled by a stack of translucent images as tall as himself, extending outward to all corners of the room. It wasn't science. It was art. He would call it "Cyberrealism." Accurate to within a digital brushstroke.

Ian sipped from his tea as his eyes ran up and down the screens. He was looking for ways in, seeking his victim's most vulnerable spot. It was a question not of too few but of too many. Where to start?

Banking? He had unfettered access to her accounts and could do with her money as he pleased. Credit cards? It would take only a few purchases to push her over the limit. Social media? An unsavory message, a wildly offensive post, could destroy her reputation in an hour. His eyes flitted from one screen to the next, but when they stopped, it was not at a website for a bank, a credit card company, or a social media site but on an icon for a photo app.

He raised a hand toward the image, only to lower it a moment later, his fingertips tingling as if shocked. Not yet. Pictures were for dessert.

A turn of the head and he landed on Mary's e-mail account. He touched the screen and brought up all new mail. Most messages were from friends expressing condolences. He read a few, moved to older messages, skipping back in time, unsure what he was looking for.

He continued scanning past messages from family, friends, banks, schools, until his attention came to a halt at the word *Hazelden*. The mail was addressed to JS Grant and cc'd to Mary. Ian opened it immediately. It was a personal communication from the world-famous hospital informing its former patient, Joseph S. Grant, that he was delinquent on his payments and asking when he would settle the balance due for his stay three years earlier.

Ian turned, accessed the Grants' insurance site, and navigated to a history of past payments. Almost all were for the child's treatments, and they totaled hundreds of thousands of dollars. He scrolled back three years earlier and found a claim for $74,000 for a ninety-day stay in Hazelden's alcohol and substance abuse rehabilitation unit. The insurance company had paid $60,000, leaving the family with the balance of $14,000.

Ian turned and found the blue icon he had passed over earlier. He touched it with a fingertip and the screen filled with photographs of the Grant family. Most were of the girls, both alone and together, the younger, blond child irrepressibly sunny, the older, dark-haired child willful, challenging, even spiteful. The photos showed the family at the beach, rafting down a river. Then came the obligatory first-day-of-school pictures. The older girl, Jessie (he knew now), was dressed in baggy dark jeans and a T-shirt advertising a rock band. The younger girl wore a pleated skirt and a pink button-down shirt. At Halloween the older girl wore no costume, while her sister dressed as a strange yellow creature with a single eye. Ian believed it was called a Minion and was a mischievous character from a popular film. Further along he arrived at Thanksgiving. A photo of father and daughters. He tapped the photo and it filled the screen. So here was Joseph Grant. *Finally we meet.* He was tall, robust, and good-humored. No sign of the impetuous meddler. The man who would sacrifice his life for his career.

Ian tapped the photo again and returned to the library. Christmas. A photo of the family standing in front of a modest tree. Really, Mr. Grant, thought Ian uncharitably, can't you do better than that? The four Grants were dressed in their Christmas best: dark suit for the father (poor-fitting and of questionable quality), red cowl-neck sweater and pearls for the mother. The younger girl in a white dress, the older in her jeans and shabby T-shirt.

Ian continued examining the photos, awed by the sheer number. Was there an occasion that didn't warrant a few snaps? Grilling burgers at a community barbecue? Making Valentine's Day cards from construction paper? Getting a good report card? Watching television on the family couch?

His eye came to rest upon a close-up of Joseph Grant and his daughters. The FBI agent had an arm around each and was hugging them close. Ian looked away, ashamed, as if caught intruding on an intimate scene. After a moment he looked back. It was the father's gaze directed at his older daughter that provoked his response and filled him with a familiar emotion.

Ian ducked his head, peering through the canyon of screens to the far corner of his office. He found the scuffed black briefcase and fought to summon up an image of his own father, Peter Prince. He didn't care if it was one of such beaming paternal pride. Any image would do. Scowling, laughing, sleeping . . . *anything*.

As always, his memory betrayed him. For a man of prodigious intellect, he was able to dredge up but a single image. It came from the morning of his father's departure. Ian saw the pinstriped suit, then the shoes, then the dimpled tie, and finally the perfectly combed hair. It took a few seconds longer for his father's face to come into focus, and when it did, Ian still could not conjure the expression. No matter how hard he tried, he could not make Peter Prince look at him with anything but a neutral regard. Nowhere did he see the kind of pride and unconditional love with which Joseph Grant looked at his daughters.

It required a herculean effort to return his attention to the photo of Joseph Grant and his daughters. Instead of love, Ian now read hubris in Joseph Grant's features. In place of pride, selfishness. It was the FBI agent's fault. He'd been warned. Edward Mason had made it clear that he should cease and desist in his investigations. Grant had known what was coming.

Properly enraged, Ian closed the photo app. Sympathy ill-served a man in his position. He straightened his shoulders. With an invisible shudder, he focused his priority on the task at hand: gaining absolute and inviolable control over another human being.

Ian spun until he found the Grants' banking website.

There was no better place to begin.

72

Mary rapped her knuckles like a machine gun against Carrie Kramer's sliding glass door. Beginner's Morse code for *help*. A minute passed before a light went on and Carrie peered around a corner, her husband hiding behind her.

"What are you doing here?" she asked, sliding the door open.

"I need your help," said Mary.

"It's one in the morning. Why didn't you call?"

"Tell you in a sec." Mary looked over her shoulder. "Come on, guys." Tank and Grace emerged from the shadows and bustled into the kitchen. "Lock it," said Mary.

Carrie closed the door and flicked the lock. "Where's Jess?"

Fifteen minutes, two cups of coffee, and a judicious explanation later, Mary sat with Tank in the Kramers' study, chairs pulled up to the iMac. Grace was in bed, clutching her phone to her chest in case her big sister called.

Mary slipped in the disk containing the images from the Nutty Brown Cafe's surveillance cameras. "Think they found McNair by now?"

"You can count on it."

"Will they come to my house?"

"They'll come."

Mary took stock of her surroundings, telling herself that she and Grace were safe here, not quite believing it. For the tenth time she used Carrie's phone to call Jessie. For the tenth time the call went to message and she hung up. "Why isn't she answering?"

"She doesn't want to tell you what she's doing."

"Where in the world could she be?"

"Trying to help her dad. At least that's what she thinks."

"When I get a hand on that young lady, I'm going to . . ." Mary imagined the dressing-down she was going to give her daughter. No matter how hard she tried, her anger wouldn't last. "It's my fault. I should have been here. Who do I think I am? McNair said it himself. He said, 'Remember, Mary, you're a mom.' That's all I am. I'm not Joe."

"And you think Jessie wouldn't have gone off if you hadn't left?"

"Maybe . . . I don't know."

"Yes, you do."

Mary nodded. She'd set Jess on her path the moment she'd asked her about retrieving Joe's voice message. She didn't know what she'd expected Jess to do, but deep down, she knew she'd expected her to do something—to come up with some solution from her laptop of tricks. "And you? You all right?"

"Hanging in there." Tank smiled weakly, but his eyes were red, fatigued. His once starched shirt was terribly wrinkled, decorated with coffee stains and flecks of blood. She wasn't in this alone. Tank's name was on the same list as hers.

"Let's take a look at that disk."

Mary double-clicked on the first clip. The segment lasted fifteen seconds and showed Joe entering the café, followed by the man the waitress called Boots. Mary hit the Pause bar as Boots, or Supervisory Special Agent FK, stared into the camera.

"I know you," she said, pointing a finger at the screen. She studied the man's face: the sagging cheeks, the wiry comb-over, the sad, pouchy eyes. He had a loud voice, she remembered. He was a storyteller. A laugher. A "good-time Charlie," the admiral might say, referring to someone who liked to drink other people's liquor a little too freely.

"Fred . . . Frank . . . Floyd," suggested Tank with renewed verve. "Felix . . ."

"Stop," said Mary. "Let me think."

"Fulton . . . Phillip . . ."

"Phillip starts with a *p*," she said sharply, still glued to the image.

"Sorry. Forget I said that."

"Pardon me?"

"I said, 'Forget I—'"

"That's it. His name is Fergus."

"Fergus? You're sure?"

"I met him once. It was in Sacramento last year. In the fall. Sometime before Joe started going to San Jose. I remember his name because he's the only Fergus I ever met."

"Supervisory Special Agent Fergus . . ."

"We can look him up."

"Where?"

"The *FBI Law Enforcement Bulletin*. It's a monthly online review. It lists promotions, convictions, any big cases they make. If he's done anything important in the past ten years, he'll be in there."

Mary logged onto the *FBI Law Enforcement Bulletin's* website and typed "Supervisory Special Agent Fergus" into the search bar.

"I hope your memory is more accurate than mine," said Tank.

"I didn't have the concussions."

Two links appeared. The first read: "Supervisory Special Agent Fergus Keefe assumes post of Assistant Special Agent in Charge, San Jose regional office." And the second: "Deputy Assistant Director Dylan Walsh and Special Agent Fergus Keefe stand up Bureau's new Cyber Investigations Division."

"Fergus Keefe," said Tank. "Nailed him."

Mary felt a jolt of excitement. She double-clicked on the first link, bringing up a short article—hardly more than a press release—stating that Keefe had taken over as assistant SAC of the San Jose office in July of last year after working with Dylan Walsh at the Cyber Investigations Division since 2007. His past assignments included stints in Baltimore and New York. Keefe had graduated from the FBI Academy in Quantico in 2002.

Mary double-clicked on the second article, which discussed the founding or "standing up" of the Cyber Investigations Division. "Sid. That's what it means."

"I thought his name was Fergus."

"No, CID—it means Cyber Investigations Division. It's not someone's name. Joe said they were the good guys. I thought he was referring to an agent he worked with, but it's really the team Joe was part of."

"If Fergus Keefe was still attached to that division, it explains why he was stationed in San Jose."

"And why Joe was always traveling down to Silicon Valley. The question is, what brought Joe and Keefe all the way out here?"

"Semaphore?"

Mary typed "Keefe" and "FBI" into the Google search bar and hit Return. A dozen hits appeared. The first was from the *New York Times* and was titled "FBI Terminates Investigation into Claims of Extortion in Merriweather Systems Takeover."

Dated the past December 10, the article began:

The FBI has terminated an investigation into charges of extortion levied against ONE Technologies and its founder and CEO, Ian Prince, in relation to its recent purchase of Merriweather Systems, a San Jose–based manufacturer of supercomputers and Internet hardware, according to *The Smoking Gun*, an online investigative site. No charges will be filed.

In November, a lawyer representing William Merriweather, son of Merriweather Systems founder and CEO John Merriweather, informed the FBI that his client had been threatened by unknown parties if he failed to vote his shares in favor of the company's sale to the Austin, Texas–based tech giant. William Merriweather holds 6 percent of Merriweather Systems' stock.

Fergus Keefe, a special agent with the FBI's San Jose office, visited Merriweather Systems' offices in Sunnyvale, California, as well as other locations. The investigation was led by the FBI office in San Jose, according to a non-public document obtained by *The Smoking Gun*. A spokesman for the FBI said that, following policy, he could neither confirm nor deny the existence of an investigation.

Ian Prince, chairman and founder of ONE Technologies, did not immediately respond to a message seeking comment. A ONE Technologies spokeswoman referred all questions to the FBI.

"John Merriweather's dead," said Tank.

"The father? To tell you the truth, I've never heard of him."

"His death was a big story. He disappeared after leaving his winter home in northern California to fly to San Jose. They didn't find him for weeks."

"What happened?"

"Plane crash. He flew straight into the side of a mountain in bad weather."

"Do you think Joe might have been working with Fergus Keefe on the extortion investigation?"

"Could be. ONE's headquarters is here in Austin. They have offices in Silicon Valley, but so does everybody."

Mary remembered McNair's words. "Does ONE control the pipe in Cedar Valley?"

"Type in 'DSL' and 'Cedar Valley.'"

Mary typed in the keywords and hit Return. Three companies offered DSL service in Cedar Valley: AT&T, Gessler Cable Systems, and ONE Technologies.

"Gessler is a local firm," said Tank. "They don't have ops in Silicon Valley. Scratch them off our list."

"We're down to two, then. Should we flip a coin?"

"I have something better." Tank removed a gold wristwatch from his pocket. "Picked this up at my friend Carlos's house."

Mary examined the watch. "This is his?"

"Turns out Carlos was a thief. He took stuff from work and sold it. The evidence tag shows that Carlos stole the watch from the morgue two days ago. The day after your husband was killed."

"You mean he stole personal effects from the deceased?"

"Pretty much."

"Nice friend."

Tank pointed at the watch. "Turn it over."

Mary flipped the watch in her palm and read the inscription. "'To H.S. Thanks, I.'"

"My guess is that H.S. is your husband's informant."

"And I?"

"I is Ian Prince."

"*The* Ian Prince?"

"Only one, as far as I know."

"So Joe was investigating ONE Technologies?"

"It fits. ONE was the target of Keefe's investigation last year. He and your husband were investigating wrongdoing in the tech industry, dealing with a company that has offices in Silicon Valley and Austin. ONE controls at least part of the cable systems in Cedar Valley."

"Then who is H.S?"

"Move over," said Tank. "You're not the only one who knows how to find someone."

Mary scooted her chair to the side as Tank accessed the ONE Technologies website and pulled down the page listing the names and bios of the managers, beginning with Ian Prince. Tank scrolled down the page, past photographs of the executive chairman, the chief business officer, the senior vice president corporate development, and the chief legal counsel. None of the executives' names bore the initials H.S.

Mary pointed out a secondary tab. "What about 'Senior Leadership'?"

Tank double-clicked on the tab. More pictures of executives. Senior vice president knowledge, senior vice president advertising and commerce . . .

"Stop." She was looking at a head-and-shoulders portrait of a middle-aged man with horn-rimmed glasses and crazed salt-and-pepper hair that stood from his scalp as if he'd just stuck his finger in a socket. "'Harold J. Stark. Senior vice president special projects and infrastructure.'"

"H.S.," said Tank. "Who works for I. Has a ring to it."

"Is there a bio?"

Tank double-clicked on the photograph and read the condensed biography aloud. "'Harold Stark is senior vice president of special projects and technical infrastructure and a ONE fellow at ONE Technologies. Before joining ONE, he was an associate professor of computer science at the University of Texas at Austin. He received a PhD in computer science from Stanford University, where his research focused on large-scale, energy-efficient data collection networks.'"

"Is that it?"

"About Stark?" Tank typed Stark's name into the search bar. "Are twenty-five thousand hits enough?"

Among the links to Stark were articles titled "How We're Making the Web Faster," "The Ability to Store Unlimited Amounts of Data," "Open Networking Summit." And then something that really caught her eye: "'Hal Stark,'" she said aloud. "'The Genius Behind Ian Prince.'"

"Your husband had himself a heck of an informant," said Tank. "Stark was Prince's right-hand man, like Nathan Myrhvold was to Bill Gates."

"Nathan who?"

"Never mind. Just think of it like getting Judas to snitch on his boss back in the day." He opened Stark's Wikipedia page and read aloud. "'As ONE's twenty-first employee and its first VP engineering, Stark has shaped much of ONE's infrastructure. For the past four years he has worked closely with Ian Prince to map out the company's foray into supercomputing, and he was instrumental in the company's acquisition of Merriweather Systems."

"There's that company again," said Mary. "What do they do?"

"John Merriweather created really fast computers. Supercomputers. The most powerful in the world."

"We're still just guessing that Joe was looking into ONE."

"You really believe that?"

At the bottom of the first page was a link to Stark's ONE X page, a compendium of pictures and events that Stark found interesting. Halfway down was a photograph of Stark standing in front of a red sports car. A caption read, "Me and my million-dollar baby."

"Stark drove that car to the meet with my husband."

"A LaFerrari? How do you know?"

"You could see it in the photograph of the crime scene on the front page of your paper."

"Satisfied now?"

Mary nodded. "But why did they have to meet so far out of town? Why didn't Stark just e-mail him whatever he was giving him?"

Tank smiled ruefully. "All tech corporations spy on their own execs. As director of special projects, Stark would know about all the products being developed—what worked, what didn't, what was going to be the next big thing. Ian Prince is legendary for his paranoia. I heard that he makes employees go through a metal detector and empty their pockets each time they exit the building. Whatever evidence of wrongdoing Stark was giving your husband, he couldn't e-mail it to him. He had to deliver it in person. Joe needed hard evidence. That's the key."

"But we'll never—" Mary bit her tongue. *The key*. Joe had used those words in his message to her, hadn't he? She was no longer sure of exactly what he'd said, only that the word brought to mind something she'd seen much too recently, something that reminded her of Hal Stark's "million-dollar baby." "Bring up the picture of the car again."

Tank double-clicked on the photo, and there was Stark standing in front of his new sports car, staring right back at them with his best shit-eating grin.

"What is it . . . something about the car?" asked Tank.

"Not the car. The horse."

"There's no horse in the picture."

"On the hood. The Ferrari insignia." Mary zoomed in on the black stallion rampant on a yellow field. "I've seen it before."

"So has everyone."

"I mean, I've seen it at my house." Mary stood. "Stay here. I have to go get something."

73

Peter Briggs parked his BMW in the shadows of a willow tree a hundred yards past the Grants' house. Surveying the street, he slipped a pistol from his holster and affixed a noise suppressor. According to the Mole, Mary Grant and her younger daughter remained in the home while the older girl was out with a boyfriend. Briggs's plan was to enter, gain access to the bedrooms, and execute both targets, leaving the weapon behind to create the appearance of a murder-suicide. Distraught widow takes her daughter's life before taking her own. It happened every day. The older girl's absence would only add to the mystery.

Briggs chambered a round, then thumbed the safety on. He did not like disobeying Ian, but he had little choice. Men like Ian were divorced from the everyday nuts and bolts of a problem. They had forgotten that it takes a mower and a man pushing it to cut the grass. They only saw the result: an immaculately manicured lawn. It came down to a question of fundamental beliefs. Ian believed that technology could solve all his problems. Briggs knew better. Some things a man had to do with his own two hands.

Briggs left the car and disappeared into the shadows. He advanced at a jog, keeping close to the homes. It had been a while since he'd been in the field, and the adrenaline was pumping. Once it had been for his country. Tonight it was for his company, but his allegiance was no less fierce. Maybe all that rot that Ian spilled about the source of a man's loyalties wasn't wrong after all. Maybe countries were obsolete.

Two minutes.

Mary let go of the fence, landing awkwardly. She limped to the sliding door, let herself in, and collapsed on the first chair she saw. Her phone sat on the table, a decoy left behind on the chance their pursuers were tracking its location. A check of the screen showed that Jess had not called.

"Two minutes," Tank had said. "Get in, find what you have to find, and come back."

With an effort, she made it to Joe's study. She sat at his desk, retrieved his gadget box, and upended it, sending the flash drives clattering everywhere. In the dark she spotted the phony pack of bubblegum, the heart-shaped pendant, and the car key. Not any car key, she knew now, but the key to a LaFerrari owned by Mr. Harold J. Stark, senior vice president special products of ONE Technologies. Or a replica thereof.

She turned on the reading lamp. The key was fat and black, with the Ferrari insignia printed beneath a translucent orb in its center. She pressed her thumb against the stallion and out popped the flash drive.

Joe's plan came to her as if it were her own. She saw Harold Stark entering his office, inserting the flash drive into his computer, downloading the evidence Joe had asked him to procure. She saw him again at the end of the day, dumping the key into the plastic tray along with the rest of his personal effects and passing through the security checkpoint, no one the wiser.

A noise interrupted her thoughts. The sound of one of her wooden chairs scooting an inch. Her eyes went to the desk lamp.

The light . . .

The kitchen door was open an inch.

Briggs stepped inside. His pistol was drawn, held low, finger brushing the trigger guard. Inadvertently he knocked one of the chairs. It squeaked like hell, and hurriedly he lifted it off the ground. He froze, listening, thinking that it had been too long since he'd been operational. He waited until he was satisfied that the house was still and everyone asleep, then set the chair down. He crossed the kitchen and went through the foyer into the garage, wanting to confirm that the car was there. He retraced his steps, noting that a television was on in the family room, muted, no one watching.

Antennas bristling, Briggs raised his pistol and climbed the stairs. The doors to the girls' rooms were closed, as was the door to the master bedroom at the end of the hall. He stopped by the first door to the right. According to the Mole, it belonged to the younger girl. He steeled himself. It would be fast. He didn't want things getting out of hand.

He opened the door and stepped inside, activating the pistol's laser sight, pointing the beam of red light at the pillow. He fired twice, advancing toward his target. The bed was empty, sheets and covers pulled back.

Briggs turned on a heel, wary. He decided that it made sense that the girl wasn't in her bed. She was a frightened lamb. She needed her mother. He moved rapidly to the end of the hall. A check of the knob confirmed that the door was unlocked. He drew a breath, pushed it open, and walked toward the bed, arm outstretched. This time he did not fire. The room was empty.

He pushed his commo mike to his mouth and spoke to the Mole. "No one's here."

"I saw her drive home. I'm still showing her phone on the premises."

"She's smarter than we thought."

Briggs lowered the weapon. Mary Grant had done a runner on them. If she was really smart, she'd get as far away as possible. Not likely. Not her.

Back downstairs, he noted a light burning in a room off the front entry. Had it been on before, or had he missed it?

"Just checking one more thing," he said, starting down the hall. "Keep the channel open."

Tank stood at the curtain inside the Kramers' living room, keeping an eye on Mary's driveway. Five minutes had passed since she'd left— three more than he would have liked. He didn't see a reason to worry. No cars had driven past. He hadn't spotted any figures in the shadows, no silhouettes slipping toward the Grants' front door. Still, he was unable to dispel his butterflies. It wasn't Mary's delayed return that worried him so much as the larger, hopeless predicament they found themselves in. They were in over their heads, and they had no one to turn to. Not the paper. Not the police. Certainly not the FBI. It was down to him and Mary. Alamo odds.

"Tank?"

The timid voice made him jump. "Can't sleep?" he asked.

Grace stood in the doorway, clutching her stuffed animal. "Where's my mom?"

"She'll be right back. She had to get something from your house."

"I already have Pink Pony."

"Something else."

Grace remained where she was, pale and fragile as Meissen china.

"You okay?" he asked.

Grace shook her head.

"Don't worry about your sister. Jessie's going to be just fine."

"It isn't that."

"Oh? Would you like to tell me, or do you want to sit down and wait for your mom?"

"My leg hurts."

"Your leg? Did you sleep on it funny?"

Grace shook her head again. Tank took another look at the Grants' driveway. Nothing had changed. He had the window cracked a few inches. The neighborhood was silent as a grave.

"Show me."

Carefully she peeled back the hem of her nightgown to reveal a bruise covering her lower thigh.

"Where did you get this?"

"I fell on the trampoline."

"Looks like you were hit by a Mack truck." Tank saw her eyes well up. "I'm sorry, sweetie, I was just joshing. I mean, it looks kind of bad."

"Jessie said it looked like grackle poo."

"One mighty big grackle."

For a moment a smile broke through the pain. "I'm scared."

"It's just a bruise."

"You don't understand. I might be getting sick again."

"The flu?"

"ALL. It's when your body doesn't make enough white blood cells. The doctors are pretty sure I'll be okay. Eight out of ten children under the age of fifteen who have it survive."

"That's good." Tank nodded understandingly, hoping that a smile would hide his shock. He knew what ALL was. "I'm sure you're okay. Let's go get some ice for that."

Tank took the child's hand and together they walked into the kitchen. On the way he checked his watch.

Eight minutes.

Something was wrong.

Mary huddled at the rear of the desk's kneehole, pasting her body to the wall as the man pounded down the stairs. Footsteps crossed the foyer. She'd had no choice but to leave the lamp burning. Anyone watching the house would surely catch the study going dark.

A pair of boots appeared in the doorway, stopped for exactly three heartbeats, then came toward the desk.

"What's this, then?" the intruder said in a hushed voice.

In her hurry, she'd left the flash drives on the desktop.

The man sat down in Joe's chair. His boot shot forward, cleaving the gap between her knees and her head. She sucked in a breath, her face inches from the man's trousers.

Something thudded onto the desk. For the second time that night she smelled gunpowder, and she knew that it came from the intruder's pistol and that yes, those were shots she'd heard. He had come to kill her and the girls.

"You check Stark for cached thumb drives?" This time the voice was stronger, and she waited for someone to respond, horrified that a second person might be in her home.

"He must have had something," the man continued after a pause. "He didn't drive all the way out to Dripping Springs just to talk to Grant."

The accent was South African, and she knew he was speaking to someone over a phone or, more likely, a closed-circuit communications net.

"Keefe didn't know how Stark was bringing out the evidence. That bugger Grant didn't tell anyone. He knew that Mason was with us. He was a cagey one."

At the mention of Fergus Keefe's name, Mary nearly gasped. Now it made sense why she hadn't seen him at the hospital. Keefe had betrayed Joe.

"You'd better have checked the bodies."

The South African began swinging his boot like a pendulum, the laces brushing against Mary's cheeks.

"If any evidence does surface, your name is at the top of the list . . . I wouldn't be surprised if Ian thought you sold him out. I might think it, too . . . I'm glad you're sure. Then you have nothing to worry about. Because here's what I'm sure about: Stark had the evidence on him and you rank amateurs missed it."

Just then Mary's phone began to ring in the kitchen.

The chair slid back. The boot swung past her nose one last time. "Hold on."

The South African hurried out of the room as the phone continued to ring.

Jessie.

Mary looked at her watch. It was two-thirty. Suppose Jessie was on her way home. Suppose she was coming down Pickfair right this instant. Even if she wasn't, suppose the intruder managed to learn her location. He was a killer. Mary wouldn't allow her daughter to fall into harm's way.

She scrambled out from beneath the desk. She didn't try to move quietly. There wasn't time. She felt for Joe's pistol, but it was at Carrie's with her jacket and her purse.

"Hello," said the South African into the phone. He'd flattened his accent and sounded like the admiral. Annapolis aristocracy.

Mary picked up the bowl on the entry table. It was an iron cooking bowl from Thailand, heavy, with sloped sides and sharp edges, employed since their return to hold the family's keys. She entered the kitchen. The intruder was tall and lean, dressed in black, his back to her. One hand held her phone, the other a pistol. If he turned, he could shoot her dead. By all rights he should have heard her approaching, but she knew he was more intent on listening to Jessie, and anyway, he didn't think anyone else was in the house.

Using both hands, she lifted the bowl high and brought it down on the crown of his skull. She grunted as it struck his cranium, like she grunted when she hit a double in softball, her wrists and forearms aching with the contact. The man buckled at the knee as she lost hold of the bowl and it clattered to the floor. He turned and she saw camouflage on his face, pale blue eyes that shone even in the dark. He blinked rapidly, raising the gun as he collapsed. It was a reflex. He was not trying to shoot but reaching for a handhold even as he lost consciousness. Mary jumped back. He landed hard, leading with his cheek, and lay still.

Mary pried the phone from his hand. "Jessie?" she said. "It's Mom. Where are you?"

A man answered. "Mrs. Grant? This is Linus Jankowski. I'm returning your message. Calm down, okay? Everything's just fine."

"Linus? Is she with you? Can I talk to her?"

"No, ma'am. She isn't. I thought she might have called to tell you."

"Where is she? Is she all right?"

"She's fine, Mrs. Grant. At least, she was when she left. I told her to call you."

"What do you mean she left? Where is she?"

"Right about now, I imagine, she should be landing in Vegas."

"Las Vegas?"

"Yes, ma'am. She's going to DEF CON."

74

Ian set down his cup of tea, eyes watering from the strain of staring at so many screens for so long a time. His job was done. In the morning Mary Grant would discover the vastly altered landscape of her living situation. She was prideful and obdurate, to a fault. But she was not stupid. She would choose the carrot, not the stick.

Yawning, Ian crossed the office and sat on the corner of a credenza. You'd be proud, Father, he said silently, eyes on the black satchel. I'm not a bloody savage. You didn't raise me to do harm. I'm a diplomat like you. Or at least as you had us all believe. I know better, don't I? That's why you left your satchel behind. You wanted me to know.

Ian kneeled and with care unfastened the satchel's brass locks. He opened the case as a scholar might open an ancient text. Inside were files. Day-to-day circulars from the Prague consulate, circa 1988. Upcoming holidays. Office hours. A strictly worded communiqué stating that only the head of station and his assistant were to use the newly installed telefax machine. There was also a checkbook. The balance stood at £750. A study of the register showed regular checks written to one Off-Track Betting. The amounts came to £400 in the register alone. Further investigations had showed the sum total of all Peter Prince's wagers to be significantly higher: £137,000 over a fifteen-year period, to be exact. Nearly $250,000. Chump change today, but to a diplomat earning £38,000 a year, a tidy sum indeed.

Ian dropped the checkbook. There was one last item inside the case. He picked it up and laid it in his palm. Exhibit A: one Walther PPK nine-millimeter semiautomatic pistol. Government issue. Serial number 9987C.

Peter Prince wasn't a second-rate diplomat or a lousy gambler. He had not simply walked out on his family after squandering their savings, leaving them destitute. Rumors of his suicide were just that. It was all cover. Part of a carefully woven tapestry to obscure the facts of his true position. Ian's father was a spy. He'd died on duty for Her Majesty's government. Ian was certain of it.

Tomorrow he would finally gain the means to learn if he was correct.

He smiled in anticipation, replacing the pistol and closing the satchel.

That was when he heard the voice.

"Briggs?" he said. "That you?" Ian looked around, sure that no one else was in the office.

Briggs's voice was emanating from a screen inside the tower. Ian retook his position inside the curtain of websites. He scanned the tower top to bottom, side to side. Briggs spoke again and he pinpointed the source.

It was a screen displaying the surveillance feed courtesy of the Grants' desktop.

Ian stood straighter, his fatigue banished to a later time. He was not surprised, only disappointed. For now he paid close attention and watched until there was no longer need.

75

"What is it? What's wrong?"

Mary entered the kitchen to find Carrie Kramer pressing a bag of ice to Grace's leg and Tank hovering nearby like a concerned uncle.

"Just a bruise, Mom," said Carrie. "We're all going to be fine."

Tank broke away and walked to her, using his bulk to provide them with a moment's privacy. "What took so long?"

Mary stepped closer. "They tried again," she whispered. "I had to knock him out."

"To kill you? He's there now?"

Mary swallowed and her throat ached. "I'll tell you everything in a sec." She continued past him and sat down next to her daughter. "What is it, mouse?"

"My leg hurts," said Grace. "I tried not to let it bother me. I'm sorry."

"Don't be sorry." Mary gave her daughter a hug. "If something bothers you, tell me right away. Promise?"

"Promise."

"Now let me take a look."

Grace lifted the ice bag off her leg. "It got bigger."

Somehow Mary managed a smile. "You know what I think? I think it's just a big bad bruise from falling on the trampoline." She was lying. She'd never seen a bruise like that from a simple tumble. She prayed it was a reaction to the new medicine Grace was taking.

Grace poked at her leg. "It isn't coming back, is it, Momma?"

"Doctor Rogers said you're doing just fine. But tell you what—we should probably go to the hospital to have them check it out."

"Now?"

"I think that's best."

"Can they give me something to make it stop hurting? Carrie gave me an Advil, but it's not doing anything."

"I'm sure they can. Now can you wait here with Carrie for a few minutes while I talk to Tank?"

Grace replaced the ice bag. "Did you find Jessie?"

"She went on a little trip, but she's just fine."

"Where?"

"I'll tell you in a second."

"Did you talk to her?"

"Not yet."

Grace considered this with genuine concern. "Then how do you know she's fine?"

Mary laughed off the question as if it were part of some larger, amusing misunderstanding, then led Tank into the dining room. Once inside, her smile dimmed and she collapsed onto a chair.

"What happened?" asked Tank, taking the chair opposite her. "You look like hell."

"Jessie's in Las Vegas. She went with her friend Garrett to compete in some kind of hacking game. Apparently someone's there who might help her figure out who hacked into my phone originally."

"Slow down. Catch your breath."

Mary cradled her head in her hands until her breathing returned to normal. She felt the color coming back into her cheeks. Even better, her forearm stopped throbbing from the collision of bowl and bone.

It took her ten minutes to relate all that had transpired inside her home—finding the Ferrari key, hearing the intruder enter and the shots being fired upstairs, hiding beneath Joe's desk while the intruder sat inches away telling an associate that no evidence had been located on Stark's body, and finally hearing the call she'd thought was from Jessie but was from Linus Jankowski and her rash decision to attack the man.

"It was Keefe," she said. "He's the one who betrayed Joe. He told them that Stark was the informant. The South African said that Keefe didn't know how Joe's informant was bringing out the evidence and that Joe was on to Edward Mason. You were right. They won't stop until we're all dead."

Tank sighed. "I hate it when that happens."

Mary stood, feeling stronger, if only because she knew what was required of her. "I may be able to reach her. Linus gave me Garrett's number."

"Tell her to get somewhere safe. The sheriff or the police. Even the fire department."

"But the South African didn't speak to Linus. They don't know where Jessie is."

Tank stood and stepped closer to her, suddenly angry. "Be real. If you know she's in Vegas, so do they."

Mary left the room to borrow Carrie Kramer's phone and took it into the bathroom. Despite her prayers, Garrett Clark didn't answer his phone. She left a message. "Garrett, this is Mary Grant. Listen to me. I don't care that you and Jess are in Las Vegas. But you need to get away from that convention and go someplace safe. The people that hurt my husband—the men that killed Jessie's dad—know where you are. Go to the police station now. I'll be on the first flight out this morning to get you guys. Just go to the police station and stay there. Oh . . . and don't use your phones. Either of you."

Mary put down the phone and stared at her reflection. She was a mess. Her eyeliner was smeared. The circles beneath her eyes were dark enough to tar a driveway. She splashed water on her face and washed off the remaining makeup, then found a comb and tried to make sense of her hair. Standing straighter, she looked into her own eyes, trying to access some untapped reservoir of courage, to drum up some last measure of strength, or maybe just a little hope. After a moment she dropped her eyes. She had none. Still, what was she supposed to do? Give up? Throw in the towel? She couldn't. She was a mom.

She found Tank lying on the couch, drifting off. She roused him and told him her plan.

"You're sure?" Tank asked her when they'd finished hashing it all out.

"Can you think of anything better?"

"And your friend will help?"

"I think so. For Grace."

"Okay, then. Let's get moving."

"You still haven't told me where the car is."

"The Ferrari? Don't worry. I know exactly where it is."

"How's that?"

"I saw it yesterday."

76

The knot on his skull was the size of a grenade.

Staggering to his feet, Peter Briggs drew his fingers away from his scalp. There was no blood, only a feral and incessant hammering. All in all, he decided, it might be wiser to sit for a minute. He landed in the nearest chair and after a good deal of reckoning concluded that he'd been out for five minutes.

Briggs knew that he'd sustained a concussion. By rights he should be inside an ambulance, rushing to the hospital to undergo an MRI. The idea had as much appeal as a case of the clap. Ian Prince would not appreciate learning that his chief of security had been brained by the woman he'd been forbidden to interfere with, let alone murder.

The hospital was out.

Briggs arranged his commo headset, bringing the mike to his mouth. "You there?"

"What happened? You sound like you're dead. Must be some woman. Killed Shanks and got the best of you, too."

"Forget about the woman. Just tell me you captured the incoming call."

"I got the whole thing."

"Who was it?"

"You don't remember?"

Briggs's last memory was of being in Joe Grant's study looking at the flash drives. "Just tell me who it was."

"Someone named Linus Jankowski. He's a postdoc at UT."

"What did they talk about?"

"She wanted to know where her older daughter was."

"And he knew?"

"According to Jankowski, she flew to Las Vegas. I checked the flights. A Southwest Airlines jet out of Austin is due in at two-fifteen."

"Do we have any confirmation she's on it?"

"I'm working on the passenger list."

Briggs struggled to take this in. It was his belief that the older daughter had merely sneaked out of the house with a boyfriend. "Why Vegas? Why now?"

"She's going to DEF CON."

"You're kidding. Why?"

"I have an idea. Something I picked up off her texts yesterday."

Briggs forced himself to stand and get moving as the Mole revealed what he'd learned about Jessie Grant's interest in hacking and her questions about a particular line of code. "Why didn't you say anything about this before?"

"Didn't know we had any interest in the kid."

"Well, you should have."

"And that line of code she was interested in . . ."

"Don't worry about that," said Briggs. "We can continue this later. I've got to get out of here."

Briggs picked up his pistol and made his way outside. On the street he struggled to regain a measure of clarity, but his short-term memory was undergoing a denial-of-service attack. Too much input. Too little processing power. He stumbled repeatedly, and before long gave up tramping through flowerbeds and the protection of the shadows for the safety of the sidewalk.

He spotted his car and crossed the street, still weaving drunkenly. A vehicle approached, headlights on bright, traveling at high speed.

"Slow down," he called as a battered Jeep Cherokee whipped past him. He turned in time to see a large shaggy head at the wheel and a woman in the passenger seat.

Tank Potter and Mary Grant.

Briggs slid behind the wheel, tossing his pistol onto the passenger seat. His head no longer bothered him. His vision was back to twenty/twenty. His sense of purpose returned with a vengeance. He pulled the car into the street and accelerated, making sure to keep his lights extinguished. He rounded the first turn and saw their taillights mounting a gentle incline a hundred yards ahead. He closed the gap rapidly.

Ahead, the Jeep barreled past a stop sign.

For Chrissakes, thought Briggs, reinvigorated by the chase. Aren't we in a hurry?

He downshifted and ran the stop sign, too. He knew why they were driving so recklessly. They had the evidence. Mary Grant had risked returning home in order to retrieve the information that Hal Stark had smuggled out of his office.

Briggs gripped the wheel furiously. This was his chance. Were he to recapture the evidence, Ian would be in the clear. Fail and Ian was finished, and Briggs close behind him. It came down to one thing: stop Potter and the Grant woman at all costs.

The Jeep passed an elementary school and made a right onto Anderson Mill Road, wheels screeching so loudly Briggs could hear them a hundred yards back. Traffic was light, but there was enough to prevent him from taking active measures to disable the Jeep. Besides, there were electronic witnesses all around in the form of cameras posted on all traffic lights.

He followed Potter and the woman onto the four-lane thoroughfare, turning on his headlights. He knew the road. There was a blind section ahead, a long, bending curve cutting through a patch of undeveloped scrub. No stoplights. No cameras. He would have one chance to take them.

He punched the gas and came up on the Jeep's tail. The road began its curve. He noted with satisfaction that no cars were approaching. No lights were visible in the rearview mirror. He swung to the left and accelerated, catching the Jeep. Briggs lowered the passenger window, pistol gripped loosely in his right hand. The gap between the vehicles was a foot, maybe less. He aimed at Tank Potter. He expected the Jeep to veer away, but it did nothing to evade him. A last look ahead confirmed that no cars were oncoming. Briggs could shoot with impunity.

A burst of gas. He pulled even with the Jeep. He caught the driver's profile. Strong jaw. Tanned skin. It was him, all right. He straightened his arm. A three-shot burst would do the trick. Aim low to compensate for the kick. He felt a spurt of optimism as his finger brushed the trigger.

To be done with them . . . *finally*.

The driver leaned to the side and poked her head out the window. She was a pretty woman in her late thirties, and she appeared angry and resolute. Next to her sat a pale, wide-eyed girl with flaxen hair.

Not Tank Potter at all. And where was Mary Grant?

The woman extended her arm out the window and gave him the finger.

Briggs braked and watched as the Jeep pulled away and disappeared into the night.

"You flipped that man the bird!" shrieked Grace, slumping in her seat with embarrassment.

Carrie Kramer kept her eyes on the rearview mirror as the BMW receded from view. "I sure did, sweetie. He deserved it."

"What did he do?"

"It's what he wanted to do that scared me."

"Are we safe?"

"We are now."

Grace sighed and sat up a little straighter in her seat. "You can call me 'Mouse.' My mom does."

Carrie ran a hand across Grace's head. "Okay, mouse."

She turned south on Research. Even so late, traffic flowed steadily in both directions. The sight of so many headlights was a relief like no other. Mary's plan had worked, but only just. She wasn't sure she'd tell her about the man with the pistol. She looked over at her passenger. "How are you doing?"

"I'm okay, I guess."

"We'll be at the hospital in five minutes. Can you hold on that long?"

"I think so."

"Thatta girl."

Grace nodded, her eyes keen. "When you drive fast," she said, "it makes me forget all about my leg."

Carrie hit the accelerator. "You got it, mouse."

"You're sure it's here?" asked Mary.

Tank stared out the window. "I'm sure."

It was 3:30. They sat in Carrie Kramer's Lexus SUV, parked on the shoulder across the street from Bulldog Wrecker on South Congress, five miles south of the river, more out of town than in it. A sheet-metal fence surrounded the impound yard. Vacant lots bookended the property. Every few minutes a tow truck arrived, dragging its prey. The driver rang a buzzer, looked into a camera, and waited for the gate to rattle open.

"I picked up my car here Tuesday morning," Tank went on. "The cops had it towed after I was busted for my DUI. Cost me four hundred bucks to get it out."

Mary surveyed the lot. The neighborhood was a step below seedy and hovering just above dangerous.

"So what do I do?"

"Same thing you did at the Nutty Brown Cafe. Drive in. Flash your badge. Say you want to look at the car."

"It's the middle of the night."

"You're a federal agent working the homicide of a fellow law enforcement officer. You don't care what time it is. Own it and they won't blink an eye."

"What about you?"

"I'll be in the car if you need me."

Mary checked that no traffic was coming, then made a U-turn and pulled up to the gate. She rang the buzzer and held Joe's badge up for the camera. A moment later the gate groaned and rattled open on its track. Mary drove across dirt and gravel toward the office. Two drivers rested on the fenders of their trucks, smoking cigarettes and sharing a flask. Mariachi music blared from a stereo. She saw the Ferrari parked on the opposite side of the yard, next to a Toyota and a Ford pickup. "Guess you were right," she said.

"I know my cars."

"Wish me luck."

"You don't need luck," said Tank. "You're the law."

Mary climbed out of the car, adjusting her jacket to cover Joe's gun. A bell above the door tinkled as she entered the office. A Hispanic woman stood behind the counter. She had a pistol on her belt, too, and wanted everyone to see it. "We're closed. Open again tomorrow at eight."

"Emergency. I'd appreciate your cooperation." Mary badged her. "I'm here to take a look at the vehicle we brought in two days ago. I see you have it out front."

"Sorry. Keys are all locked up. Can't get to them till morning."

"What about the keys of the cars those fellas just brought in? What do you do with them?"

The woman eyed the two key chains on the desk, then shrugged, beaten at her own game. "Do you have the paperwork?"

Mary leaned in. "You have *two* Ferraris here?"

The woman stepped to her computer and tapped the keys for much too long. "Vehicle is registered to?"

"Harold Stark."

"And you are?"

"Special Agent Mary Grant."

The woman ducked her head around the computer. "Same name as that agent who was killed."

"No relation."

The woman considered this. She was short and solid, with tattoos covering both arms. The largest showed an eagle wrapped in a Mexican flag. She smiled, revealing a gold-capped tooth. "I want to be a police officer myself. I have my app in at APD, Department of Highway Safety."

"Good luck."

"I shoot competitively. Shouldn't have a problem there. What's that you're carrying?"

"Excuse me?"

"Your weapon . . . pistol . . . sidearm. Whatever you feds call it."

"It's a Glock."

"Nice. Nine, eleven, or sixteen?"

"Pardon me?"

"Rounds."

Mary looked at her watch. "If you don't get me the keys to that car, the only number you'll have to worry about is one, 'cause that's how many bullets I'm going to fire to get you moving."

The attendant bucked to attention. "Yes, ma'am."

"Thank you, Miss . . ."

"Garza. Yolanda Garza."

"Thank you, Miss Garza. If I have the chance, I'll be sure to put in a good word."

Yolanda Garza unlocked a cabinet on the wall behind her. When she turned back, she held a fat rubber car key like the one Mary had seen in Joe's study earlier. "Here you are, Special Agent Grant," she said, placing the key on the counter. "I'll need to see your government identification as well as your driver's license."

Mary patted her jacket and frowned. Earlier she'd forgotten to bring Joe's picture. This was a more serious offense. "In my purse. Be right back."

"Leave the key."

Mary set the key to the LaFerrari on the counter. "There you are. I'll just be a minute."

Garza was already back at the computer, eyes squinting as she scrolled down a page. "Take your time. I've got to call your boss first."

Mary paused at the door. "Pardon me?"

"This isn't the first time you guys have left a vehicle with us. I can't release nothing until I speak with the SAC. Company policy. Your company."

"You're taking your life into your hands," said Mary, doing a bad job of trying to sound funny. "Don Bennett doesn't like being woken up in the middle of the night."

"Then you shouldn't show up so late."

Mary shrugged. "Suit yourself."

The tow-truck drivers were still perched on their fenders, smoking cigarettes. Seeing Mary, they made a halfhearted attempt to hide their flask. Mary gave them a stern look, all the while forcing herself to walk, not run.

"We need to leave," she said, sliding behind the wheel. "She's calling Don Bennett. She needs his permission to release the vehicle."

"Did you get it?"

Mary opened her fist. "I switched keys when she wasn't looking."

"I'm beginning to think you missed your calling."

"Let's go before she talks to Bennett. The woman's packing a piece the size of a bazooka."

She put the car in gear and drove toward the exit, rolling over the pressure sensors that activated the gate. With a shudder, it began to roll on its track. Faster, she thought.

"Let's see if we were right."

Mary gave him the key. He pressed his thumb against the translucent dome in the key's center. Nothing happened.

"Try it again."

He thumbed the dome, harder this time. Still nothing. "You got any other ideas?"

"Give it to me." Mary grabbed the key and rammed her thumb against the dome. She felt something give. The flash drive shot out of the bottom of the key. "Woman's touch."

"Jesus. You were right."

"You didn't believe me?"

"Honestly? No." Tank twisted in his seat, an eye on the office door. "Ah, shit."

"What?"

"You weren't kidding about that gun."

A siren wailed. The gate stopped dead in its tracks. In the rearview mirror, Mary saw Yolanda Garza burst out of the office door, gun drawn. The woman was shouting something to the truck drivers, who launched themselves off the fenders and ran to their cabs. Both emerged holding handguns. There was a ping of metal and simultaneously a gunshot. Then more.

The side window shattered. A tire exploded. The car listed to port. Mary ducked. "We're at the fucking O.K. Corral."

"Get out of the car," shouted Garza. "Open your doors."

Mary complied.

Tank reached across and yanked it shut. "I am not going to be captured by Evelyn Ness over there."

"What are you going to do, shoot her? Get out of the car, Tank. It's over. We're done."

Tank stripped the gun from her holster. "The hell you say. It's not even close to over."

"Tank!"

"Listen to me. Do as she says. Get out of the car. Look nice and peaceful. Remember you're a mom, not an FBI agent. And on the count of three hit the ground."

"You aren't going to shoot anyone. I won't allow it."

"Eagle Scout's word of honor."

"But we can't go anywhere. The front tire is flat. The car is ruined."

"*This* car is ruined." Tank snatched the Ferrari key from her hand. "This one isn't."

"But—"

"You feel like spending the next five to ten in jail? You used up your hall pass earlier today, and that was before we killed McNair. I may have pulled the trigger, but you're my accomplice."

"But he was going to kill me."

"That's a lot of *buts* hanging out there in the wind."

"Dammit," said Mary.

"At least let me try to get us out of here."

Mary looked at Garza standing thirty feet away, gun aimed at her, and at the tow-truck drivers, positioned more prudently next to their vehicles. Her disdain for Mason returned, and with it her anger. If she stopped now, if she stopped before exhausting her every opportunity, she would have let them win. Ian Prince and Edward Mason and Fergus Keefe. Joe would be remembered as inept, or even a failure. Worse, his death would go unavenged.

"No shooting anyone," she repeated.

"Yes, ma'am. Now open the door. And remember—"

"On three, hit the ground."

Tank nodded. "Trust me."

Mary threw her legs from the car and stepped out. Without prompting, she raised her hands. It came to her that this was the third time in twenty-four hours that she'd had a gun pointed at her.

"Stay there," said Garza. Then she called to the drivers. "Ray, there's a pair of cuffs in my desk. Go get 'em and bring 'em to me."

"*One . . . ,*" said Tank.

"Open your jacket so I can see your weapon," said Garza. "Nice and slow. And tell your partner to get out, too."

"*Two.*"

Garza stepped closer, eyes narrowed, wary. Mary unbuttoned her blazer and opened it wide. "Tank, get out, please," she said.

"*Three.*"

Mary threw herself to the ground. From the corners of her eyes she caught Tank jumping from the car, pistol in hand. He wasn't aiming at Garza or at the drivers. He was pointing the gun at a cylindrical iron tank near the front gate. She spotted a diamond-shaped sticker on it and the word *flammable*, but only for a second. Then there was a gunshot and the tank exploded.

Mary dug her face into the dirt as the blast wave passed over her, the heat intense but fleeting. She peeked from beneath her arm and saw Tank running to the Ferrari. In front of her, Garza lay prone on the ground, unmoving. The tow-truck drivers had disappeared altogether. A fireball rose from the tank into the night sky like a giant roman candle.

She heard the Ferrari start. It was a sound like no other, a low-pitched, powerful rumble that resonated in her belly; the car was as much animal as machine. She pushed herself to her feet as Tank pulled up next to her.

He opened her door. "Get in."

"Is she . . ." Mary pointed at Garza.

"Unconscious."

"Are you sure?"

"Dammit, Mary, get in the car."

The car was so low to the ground that she fell into the seat. The interior was like nothing she'd ever seen. Dials and gauges and lights glowed electric shades of green and yellow.

The ringing of the explosion faded and she heard a siren.

"Police," said Tank, easing the car toward the exit. "Hold on."

The gate lay in the center of the street, a mangled, twisted sheet of metal. To their right, far away, a police car was speeding toward them, strobes flashing. To her horror, a second patrol car followed on its tail. "Go the other way," she said.

Tank looked to his left, where another squad car was approaching. "Must be a doughnut shop around here."

"Which way, then?"

"I'm thinking north."

"And then?"

"One step at a time." He pulled into the street and steered gingerly around the gate. The police cars were closing fast, yet he made no further move. They sat stationary in the middle of the street, lights extinguished, nose pointed directly at the sidewalk and the scrub beyond.

"Hold on to the armrest."

Mary wrapped her fingers around the leather grip. The lights from the police cars shone into the cabin, forcing her to look away.

Tank punched the gas, turning the car to the left and driving north. There was a squeal of rubber, an ungodly roar. Mary's head hit the seatback. Her fingers tightened on the grip. The road disappeared beneath the car, the lines a blur. She'd never accelerated so rapidly in her life. It wasn't a car; it was a rocket ship.

They passed the oncoming police car six seconds later, the speedometer reading 130 miles per hour. The headlights of the trailing cars dimmed. Tank ran a red and continued another few blocks, then braked and turned right before giving another burst of acceleration.

Two minutes later they were driving slowly through a quiet, sleeping neighborhood. Tank had one hand on the wheel and was slumped against the door.

"Are you all right?" Mary asked.

Tank touched his side and grimaced. "No, ma'am."

"What is it?" said Mary. "What's wrong?"

He held up a bloody hand. "I think I've been shot."

79

Southwest Airlines Flight 79 touched down at Las Vegas McCarran International Airport at 2:15 a.m. local time. Jessie and Garrett were first off the plane. They ran through the terminal and down the escalator, Jessie braking by an ATM at the exit and withdrawing her maximum daily limit of $800.

"Where did you get so much money?" asked Garrett.

Jessie stuffed the bills into her jeans. "Men are kind of sick. That's all I'm going to say."

Garrett held the phone to his ear. "There's a voicemail from your mother. She says that we need to go to the police station. We can't stay at DEF CON because we need to get away from the people who hurt your dad."

"She's just trying to scare us."

"I thought that an informant shot him." Garrett held out the phone. "You'd better listen."

"I don't want to."

"Jess . . ."

"Garrett, I came here to get Rudeboy to help figure out who hacked into my mom's phone. What part of that did you miss?"

"The part that says we might be in danger."

"You sure don't look like a wuss, Abercrombie."

"What?" protested Garrett. "Who's Abercrombie?"

Jessie walked outside and made her way to the head of the taxi line. "So you told your parents?"

"Are you kidding?" said Garrett. "My parents would have called out the National Guard by now if I wasn't home. My mom waits up by the door to make sure I walk in before midnight. I'm not joking. By the door. I may be disobedient, but I'm not cruel." Garrett caught himself. "Oh, sorry. I didn't mean it that way."

Jessie had never thought of herself as cruel. "My mom's just freaking out because I didn't tell her where I've gone. Once we get to DEF

CON, if you see any guys in dark shirts and sunglasses looking at us strangely, let me know and we'll get out of there."

Garrett cued up the voicemail. "Just listen to her."

"I don't want to."

"It's your mother. She loves you."

Jessie grabbed the phone out of his hand and deleted the message. "My mom thinks I'm a freak. She can't stand that I don't wear tight blue jeans or put on makeup or straighten my hair and that I hate Taylor Swift and that I'm fat and I don't like to run or go to the gym. Okay? She may care for me. And yes, I know that she's worried. But she doesn't love me. Not really. My dad loved me. That's why I'm here. You want to go, go. I'm staying." She climbed into a minivan with an advertisement for a strip club on top. "What are you looking at?" she said.

"Nothing . . . I mean . . . oh, forget it." Garrett climbed in and closed the door. "I'm staying."

"Take us to the Rio," said Jessie.

"DEF CON, right?" said the driver, an unlit cigarette dangling from his mouth. "You guys are getting younger each year. Pretty soon I'll be driving babies out there."

"Hey, buddy," said Jessie, "just drive."

"Punk." Meadows

They turned onto Las Vegas Boulevard and drove past the Mandalay Bay, the Mirage, the Bellagio, temples of neon. The lights reminded her of Bangkok, the night markets, the hotels lining the Chao Phraya River. The two cities were nothing alike, really. Maybe it was just being in another city where it was hot all day and all night, with so many tall buildings. All she knew was that it made her sad. Her dad had been alive in Bangkok. Mouse hadn't been sick yet. And she hadn't made her mom miss her dad's last message.

"You okay?" asked Garrett, his hand touching her arm.

Jessie wiped at her cheek. "Be quiet."

"Sorry."

"I didn't mean it. I'm just tired."

"Me, too."

Jessie leaned her head against Garrett's shoulder. "Thanks."

"For what?"

Jessie wanted to say for a thousand things, but the words tripped all over each other. "Just thanks."

The cab turned onto Flamingo Road and Jessie saw the hotel at the end of the block, towering before them like a brightly lit birthday cake. It was big and pretty, but it didn't look as glitzy as the others. That figured. Hackers and computer nerds weren't glitzy either. They were just smarter.

Another turn and the cab pulled beneath the hotel's porte cochere. Jessie paid the fare and added a dollar for a tip, getting out before the driver could call her a punk again. She led the way into a lobby the size of a football field and spotted the placards for DEF CON at the entry to the East Corridor.

"This is it." Excited, she jogged the length of the hall. A blue banner with the words *Capture the Flag* hung above the entrance to the Miranda Ballroom. Jessie dialed the number for Linus's former teammate and announced their arrival. A few minutes later a short, skinny guy with a few days' stubble and messy hair came out of the ballroom.

"You Jesse?" he said, looking at Garrett.

"Actually, I'm Garrett. She's Jessie."

Max shifted his gaze in her direction. "You're Jessie?"

"Didn't Linus tell you I was a girl?"

"Guess he forgot that part. He just said you were smart as a whip and we'd be idiots not to let you join our team."

"Guess you'll find out soon enough."

He stuck out a bony hand. "Max. Good to have you aboard. Here, put on your shirt." Max thrust an orange, yellow, and black T-shirt at her. "Welcome to the Ninjaneers. And here's your ID. Wear it around your neck at all times when you're on the playing floor."

Jessie pulled on her T-shirt and strung the ID over her head. Her sadness and anxiety fled. She was at DEF CON. She was a Ninjaneer, and she was about to play Capture the Flag against Rudeboy. It was pretty much the coolest moment of her life.

"What about Garrett?" she asked. "He's pretty good with code, too."

"Sorry," said Max. "Eight men to a team. Garrett, if you'd like to watch, there are stands all around the game floor. The room opens at seven-thirty, thirty minutes before start of play."

"No worries." Garrett thrust his hands into his pockets. "I'm going to get something to eat. I'll see you."

"See you." Jessie stared at him hard so that he wouldn't even think of doing something cheesy like try to kiss her.

"Later." Garrett headed off down the hall. Jessie adjusted her shirt, bending to get a look at the design of a cartoon ninja putting his samurai sword through a laptop. The drawing was lame, but she didn't care. She was a Ninjaneer now, too, and she wouldn't allow a word against her team.

"Come with me," said Max. "We're doing some warm-ups. Root-the-box problems. Standard stuff. You'll need to meet everyone and let them know what we can expect of you."

He pushed open the door and Jessie followed him into a cavernous ballroom. Only eight out of two thousand teams had qualified for the finals. Each team occupied a U-shaped configuration of tables arrayed around a central command square. A scoreboard on one wall listed the teams. Besides the Ninjaneers, there were the Plaid Purple Pioneers, Team Mutant X, Big Bad Daddies, the Mummies, Team Koo Teck Rai, Das Boot, and, finally, Rudeboy.

"New rules this year," said Max. "We've got a TV audience, so they've shortened the game. We've got eight hours to solve four problems. Each problem is broken up into parts—'flags' that you have to win."

"That's all?"

"Short and sweet. Fewer hacks, but harder."

Max arrived at the Ninjaneers' command post. Six guys in team T's were in various states of preparation—attaching network cables, plugging in laptops, lining up bottles of Red Bull for easy access. Max introduced Jessie to each member of the team. All were polite enough; none of them tried too hard to hide his skepticism. Jessie looked at the other teams. Of course she was the only girl. *Because girls can't compute*

"We divide our team into three squads," said Max. "Attack, Research, and Defense. Attack analyzes the problem we're given—usually it's an admin code—for vulnerabilities. Once we find one, we hand the problem over to Research and they figure out any possible ways of exploiting the vuln. Defense keeps a watch on our own board to stop the other guys from stealing our flags once we get them."

"I'm Attack," said Jessie.

"I'll make that decision." Max pulled up a problem on his laptop. "Show us your stuff, hotshot."

Jessie scanned the code. Within a minute she'd spotted three "vulns," or vulnerabilities, and called each out to Max. "How'd I do?"

"Like I said, you're Attack." Max pulled up a chair and sat down next to her. "Linus said you want to beat Rudeboy."

"I have to beat him."

"No one has ever beaten him," said Max. "But if you can spot vulns that quickly when the game starts, we just might have a chance."

80

Tank parked the Ferrari next to an old oak on a deserted side street in East Austin.

"Pull up your shirt," said Mary. "Let me take a look."

"I'm okay. Let's check that key."

"The key can wait."

Tank reached for the tablet on the rear console and Mary blocked him, pushing him gently back into his seat, raising a warning finger to let him know there would be hell to pay if he tried it again. She opened the glove compartment and freed the flashlight. The tan seat ran wet with blood.

"Gosh, Tank. You really are hurt."

Tank lifted the tails of his shirt, revealing a pale, corpulent midsection. Blood dribbled from a hole the circumference of a pencil eraser in one of his rolls of fat. She helped him lean forward. There was an exit wound on the opposite side of his love handle. "Went through."

"I knew there was a reason I decided to put off getting in shape till fall."

"You need to say a prayer tonight."

Mary opened the car's first aid kit and took out a roll of gauze, tape, scissors, and an antiseptic. Carefully she fashioned two bandages and put them on the center console. She cut another piece of gauze and doused it with disinfectant. "Sit still. This may hurt."

"I played ball, remember."

"One . . . two . . ."

Tank hollered and drove a fist against the armrest. "You didn't say *three*."

"Old trick. Now, relax. The second won't be as bad."

"The second?"

"I thought you played ball."

"That was a long time ago. Be gentle." Tank looked away, eyes watering, and bit back the pain as Mary finished dressing the wound.

"Try not to move too much. I'm not sure how secure the tape is."

Tank pulled his shirt over the wound. "Can we check the key now?"

Mary grabbed the tablet and plugged in the flash drive. An icon of a hard drive appeared on the screen. It was named Snitch. "Let's see what Mr. Stark has to offer the FBI."

She double-clicked on the icon. A directory listing three folders filled the screen.

"Merriweather, Orca, and Titan," said Tank.

"Merriweather. That's the guy who accused ONE of extortion."

"Your boy Fergus Keefe led the investigation that cleared ONE of any wrongdoing."

"He's not my boy."

Mary double-clicked on the folder. It contained a list of over one hundred documents, Word files, photographs, and spreadsheets. Her eye landed on one titled "Prince Directive to Briggs/Nov. 10." It was an internal e-mail from Ian Prince to a Peter Briggs, head of corporate security, and read: "Peter, pursuant to our conversation regarding M, follow up on attached list of target shareholders with a view to influencing positive outcome: our interests."

"Clever," said Tank. "Prince says everything and nothing. Doesn't specify who M is, doesn't come out and say, Extort the uncooperative bastards who won't get with the program."

Next Mary opened a file titled "Weekly update/Keefe to Prince." It was an e-mail sent from Fergus Keefe's private address to Ian Prince and offered a detailed summary of the latest developments in the FBI's investigation into ONE. "Keefe was in Ian Prince's pocket all along."

"I'm sorry," said Tank.

"You just might have your story."

Tank started the engine. "I'll need a lot more than that. One thing's for sure. We can't stay here and read it."

"Where are we going?"

Tank pulled away from the curb and drove down the street, lights dimmed. "Off the grid."

81

"Ed, this is Don Bennett."

"Don . . . hold on . . . Jesus, what time is it?"

"It's five o'clock here in Texas."

Edward Mason cleared the sleep from his throat. "Five o'clock. Yeah, all right. Give me a second."

Don Bennett stood on his back porch, gazing over his share of the American dream: a large, rolling square of crabgrass, dichondra, and dirt that made up the backyard of his home in Westlake Hills. Toys were scattered everywhere. In the dark he could make out a tricycle, a Big Wheel, baseball mitts, and a Slip 'N Slide that did double duty as the family pool.

He picked up his oldest son's mitt, a black Rawlings Gold Glove Gamer. In his day it had been a Steve Garvey with a webbed pocket. Don Bennett had bled Dodger Blue his entire life. Vin Scully had called the play-by-play of his youth, and though he hadn't lived in L.A. since he was eighteen, he was still a die-hard fan. He tapped the glove against his leg. $250 million contract

Garvey. Valenzuela. Kershaw.

It was all about loyalty.

"Hello, Don—sorry about that. I had to get clear of the wife. I don't imagine you're calling with good news at this time of night."

"It's about Mary Grant."

"Christ . . . what now? Did something happen to her?"

"She stopped by the impound yard where we were keeping the Ferrari, posing as an FBI agent."

"Asking about the car?"

"Yessir. Details are sketchy, but at some point there was an exchange of gunfire and a significant explosion. One woman was slightly injured."

"And?"

"She stole the Ferrari."

"Mary Grant stole the fucking Ferrari?"

"She was in the company of a tall, dark-haired male. We assume it's Tank Potter, the reporter who drove her to the airfield yesterday. Apparently his car was towed to the same yard after he was arrested for a DUI. He must have seen the Ferrari when he came to claim his vehicle."

"And this happened when?"

"Thirty minutes ago. I've been working with local police trying to locate the vehicle, but so far we've come up empty-handed."

"She came at three-thirty posing as an FBI agent to steal the car?"

"That's about all of it, sir."

"Shit," said Mason, almost to himself. "That's where it was. He must have told her."

"Excuse me?"

"Nothing, Don. Just thinking out loud."

"So you have an idea why she wanted the car?"

"This matter doesn't concern the Austin residency."

"A question of national security. Yessir. I remember."

"That's right."

"But you see, Stark worked at ONE. Even if it's a question of national security, as SAC here in Austin, I think I ought to know about a case involving one of the biggest corporate concerns in my area. At least about what angle Joe Grant was following."

"If you needed to know, we'd have told you already."

Don Bennett laid his son's mitt on the porch and set out across the lawn, the dew cold on his feet. He told himself that he was an obedient man. He believed in the chain of command. He was a reliable man. Above all, he was loyal to his own. And that included Joe Grant.

Bennett was thinking about the call Mary Grant had asked about when they'd met for lunch two days earlier. Who, she'd demanded, had called 911 to look after Joe?

Bennett hadn't answered, though he'd already heard the call himself. It was standard practice in a homicide to gather data from emergency responders. Since then he'd listened to it so many times he had it memorized.

"This is Special Agent Joseph Grant, FBI. Send an ambulance to the Flying V Ranch on Highway 290 exactly nine miles outside of Dripping Springs. I'm parked in a blue Chevy Tahoe. The victim is suffering from a gunshot wound."

"What is his age?"

"He's forty-two. Look, I don't have time. I have to make another call."

"Is the wound life-threatening?"

"I don't know yet . . . I mean, yes, it is—possibly fatal. Send someone. Hurry."

"Sir, do you know the victim's name?"

"It's me. Do you understand? Now do it. And hurry."

Bennett winced at the memory. Joe Grant had known he was about to be killed and had called in his own evac. And the other call? It was to his wife. The voice message that had been mysteriously erased from her phone. The message that Edward Mason had ordered him to do nothing to help restore. And that was what had Bennett so upset: why hadn't Joe called him or any one of the other agents at the Austin residency? Why had he called his wife instead?

Edward Mason went on. "Where are they now?"

"No idea. The police tried to follow them, but they didn't have any vehicles able to keep up."

"It's a fire-engine-red sports car. There can't be too many on the streets at this time of night. All right, then. Get a team out to her home, and to Potter's, too. I want both of them brought in for questioning."

"I doubt they're there. I mean, given the circumstances . . ."

"She's got to be somewhere. She's a mother, not a criminal mastermind. Just do your job. Find her."

"And the car, sir."

Bennett could just make out a mangled expletive before the phone went dead.

Inside his home, Don Bennett poured himself a shot of whiskey. He took the glass and sat at the kitchen table, drumming his fingers on the surface. A minute later his phone rang. He checked the number and answered.

"You get that?" he asked.

"Every word."

"And now?"

"Just do your job."

82

Seated in the cockpit of ONE 1, Ian Prince completed his preflight checklist. Takeoff was scheduled for 0630. Weather en route was calm and clear. He forecast flying time to be two and a half hours, so he'd be arriving in Utah at approximately 0800 local time. He put down his clipboard and watched the sun creep over the horizon.

Today was the day.

Serena, the chief flight attendant, poked her head into the cockpit. "Everyone present and accounted for."

"Mr. Briggs manage to find his way aboard?" It was a rhetorical question. Ian had seen Briggs arrive at the FBO and hurry across the tarmac, looking far worse for wear. Noticeably, Briggs had not come inside the cockpit to say good morning or to offer his usual briefing.

"He looks like he had a pretty rough night," said the attendant.

"Well, we all know Peter."

"Katarina is ready for you anytime after takeoff, but she says to hurry if you want to take all your fluids. Mr. Gold and Mr. Wolkowicz are sleeping in the guest compartment. Forward door is secured and ready for takeoff."

Ian taxied to the main runway and radioed the tower for clearance. He received it, and a moment later eased the thrusters forward. As the speedometer touched 120, he eased the yoke toward him. The nose rose effortlessly. The wheels left Earth's embrace. ONE 1 climbed into a cloudless blue sky.

Ian remained at the controls until the plane reached its cruising altitude of 38,000 feet, then handed off responsibilities to his copilot. "Stick is yours."

"I have the stick."

Ian made his way into the main compartment. Briggs sat upright in his seat, reading from his tablet.

"Interesting night?" asked Ian, taking the seat across from him.

"Had worse."

"And Mary Grant?"

"Nothing to report. The ball's in your court, right?"

"So it is. I don't anticipate having any more problems with her."

"If you say so."

"See you when we get to Utah." Ian patted Briggs on the shoulder and headed aft to his private quarters. He felt like a man whose vision had been restored after long years of blindness.

Finally he could see.

83

The cabin sat on a patch of grassland at the end of a dirt road, as lonely as the sole house on a Monopoly board. They'd passed the last dwelling several miles back, and that was already twenty miles due east of the highway.

"When you said 'off the grid,' you weren't kidding," said Mary as she got out of the car. "And you come here for what, exactly?"

"Quail hunting. I call it my lodge. Not much to look at this time of year, but in the spring the creek fills up and the grass grows waist-high."

"And no one knows about it?"

Tank hauled himself out of the car and walked unsteadily to the house. "Plenty of people do. But they're my buddies. There isn't any paperwork or court records or deeds that Ian Prince or Edward Mason can check to give them the idea we may be hiding out here. Water comes from our own well. Power from my generator. Nothing they can trace."

"I can see that."

Mary stood behind him as he fished his keys out of his shorts. She was thinking about the poster on Jessie's wall and its line about "information wanting to be free." She believed she understood what it meant. Words, ideas, expressions, all had a life of their own—if not a life exactly, some inchoate animus that screamed for attention. You might keep them quiet for a while, but their very existence militated toward exposure and dissemination. The same went for the evidence Stark had put on the flash drive.

Tank threw open the door. "After you."

Couch, table, potbellied stove, cabinets. "Nice," said Mary. "Abe Lincoln would have felt right at home. You're only missing a chamber pot."

"Facilities are out back. This isn't the Ritz-Carlton."

"I noticed that. Even have the half-moon painted on the door."

"We aim to please."

Tank locked the door behind them before collapsing on the couch. "Coffee and mugs are above the sink."

"You doing okay?"

"I'll make it."

Mary fed the stove with kindling and got a fire going, then heated a pot of water and made coffee while Potter sat with the tablet, immersing himself in Stark's files. "He delivered the goods. No question."

Mary sat beside him. There were the three folders, Merriweather, Orca, and Titan, each brimming with hundreds of files. They began with Merriweather.

The directory showed e-mails from Ian Prince to Edward Mason and from Mason to Prince; from Prince to Peter Briggs, and from Briggs to a Wm. McNair. (It was Briggs who'd texted McNair: "Done?") There were also e-mails from Prince to Harold Stark. Next came a dozen FBI case files that should never have appeared on a private corporation's server. Joe had worked the Merriweather case along with Randy Bell and Fergus Keefe, and it appeared that Ian Prince had obtained every witness interview, every progress report, every request for evidence the agents had ever filed.

A cursory examination showed that the Merriweather investigation had begun promisingly. Several key Merriweather shareholders gave sworn affidavits about intimidation tactics directed against them by individuals they suspected of working for ONE Technologies. Another shareholder spoke of an anonymous threat to expose his son's drug addiction if he did not vote his shares for ONE. There was an affidavit from Merriweather's chief financial officer that confidential sales data had been stolen from the company's servers, and laterally, a complaint by the chief technical officer about the theft of secret engineering data for a project called Titan (which Mary and Potter presumed was the subject matter of the folder of that name).

But then the investigation went sideways. One witness recanted his affidavit, claiming that he had been coerced into making a false statement. Another fell ill and could not be interviewed. Requests for information from ONE went unanswered. Subpoenas were challenged. It was a classic case of stonewalling. But instead of pressing harder, which was the FBI's normal modus operandi, the Bureau backed off. A memo from Fergus Keefe to Joe and Randy Bell requested that they terminate the investigation. Both men objected, but to no avail. A week later

John Merriweather perished in a plane crash and the case was officially closed. The sale to ONE Technologies was approved shortly thereafter.

There was more to it than that, as Harold Stark had made sure that Joe would find out. With a mixture of anger and disbelief, Mary read through a series of e-mails from Ian Prince to Edward Mason requesting that the FBI's deputy director "tamp down" the Merriweather investigation. Lobbying on Ian's behalf was the director of the NSA, who called ONE's acquisition of Merriweather and the forthcoming Titan supercomputer "paramount to ensuring the continued supremacy of United States intelligence- and data-gathering efforts around the world." Mason responded that so far the investigation had not turned up sufficient evidence to indicate criminal wrongdoing, and he would do his utmost to bring the case to a quick and favorable conclusion.

At this Mary offered a disgusted expletive. When did a sitting deputy director of the FBI offer any kind of comment to the CEO of a company it was investigating? she asked Tank. Let alone promise that he would aid in shutting the investigation down?

A moment later they discovered the reason. They found the smoking gun: an e-mail from Ian Prince to Edward Mason confirming the transfer of $10 million to a numbered account in Liechtenstein of which Mason was the sole beneficiary.

"Ten million," said Tank. "That buys a lot of margaritas."

"Ian Prince must have wanted Merriweather pretty badly."

"I'm beginning to guess why."

"Titan?"

He nodded grimly.

Setting the tablet on her lap, Mary opened the Titan folder. Not e-mails and documents this time, but complex computer engineering schematics. Diagrams showing the layout and manufacture of Titan's internal components, many with significant sections highlighted in yellow and words like *bypass*, *backdoor*, *override*. To a layman the plans were as incomprehensible as they were impressive. Aware of this, Hal Stark had provided a one-page explanation for the common man.

"It's the mother lode," said Tank after they'd finished reading. "He's got it all. Hook, line, and sinker."

"Do people in the government know he's modified their computers?"

"No chance. I don't think they'd appreciate Ian Prince looking over their shoulders."

Mary laid her head back and sighed.

"Look at this," said Tank after a minute. "From Mason to Prince. It's about Joe."

Mary snapped to attention. In the message Mason warned Prince that a secret task force had been established by Dylan Walsh, the chief of the FBI's Cyber Investigations Division, to look into ONE's hacking of the FBI's servers for six months during the company's takeover of Merriweather Systems. The task force was named Semaphore.

"Joe was investigating ONE all the time," said Tank. "He knew exactly what Prince was up to."

"You got your story."

"Story? I've got a book," said Tank. "But I'll start with a story. How's this for a lead: 'Last December, Edward Mason, deputy director of the FBI, received a ten-million-dollar payment from Ian Prince, founder and chief executive officer of ONE Technologies, to a numbered account at the National Bank of Liechtenstein in exchange for halting the FBI's investigation into charges against the company of extortion and shareholder intimidation relating to its takeover of Merriweather Systems'?"

"Sounds good."

"Front page. Above the fold."

Mary was looking back at the Merriweather folder. "There's something we missed."

"What is it?"

"Something a lot worse than extortion." Mary moved the cursor onto the icon for a document inside the Merriweather folder titled "Crash."

The document ran to one page and was a screenshot of computer code. At the top, a single line of clarification: "Malware used against John Merriweather's on-board navigation system (serial number XXX77899). Installed 12/15 by Ian Prince."

Mary looked up. "You said that John Merriweather flew his plane into the side of a mountain. Pilot error."

"Apparently not."

"Your story just got a lot better." She checked her watch and stood, shocked at the time. "I have to go. My flight leaves at seven-fifty-five."

"Hold on," said Tank. "You still have five minutes. Let's take a look at Orca."

And five minutes was all they needed to learn about Ian Prince's

plans to construct the largest supertanker ever built. Not even a supertanker, really, but an island, by the look of the elevations provided.
An island with homes for a few thousand people, factories, offices, an
airstrip, a beach, its own nuclear power plant, and, every bit as impressive, rising directly in its center, a mountain. An island or a ship or
something entirely new.

"Why did Stark name the file Orca?" Mary asked.

"Because he's a bit of a joker. Orca's the name of the shark fisher-
man's boat in *Jaws*," said Tank. "The movie. Don't you remember what
Roy Scheider says when he and Robert Shaw and Richard Dreyfuss are
way out in the middle of the ocean and he first sees the shark?"

"No," said Mary. "I don't."

"'You're going to need a bigger boat.'" Tank put down the tablet.
"Ian Prince built himself the biggest boat ever."

"What kind of shark is he afraid of?"

Tank shrugged and pulled himself off the couch. "Time for you to
skedaddle."

"I can't drive that thing. Even if I could, I couldn't. The police will
be looking everywhere for it."

"Take my truck. It's out in the shed. Keys are in the ignition."

"And you?"

"I'll find a way back into town."

Mary stood and walked with him to the door. "We did good," she
said.

"Your husband did good. But our work won't be done till we get that
story to the paper."

"Isn't there a way we can send over all the files?"

"No connection out here. No cell service. No wireless. Like I said—"

"'Off the grid.'"

"Yep."

Mary kissed Tank on the cheek. "Thank you."

"Don't thank me. I told you, I'm in this game for myself. Now go get
your daughter."

Mary stepped outside and crossed the yard to a ramshackle shed.
The truck was an old Ford, even more beat-up than the Jeep, with
manual transmission and springs pushing through the worn-out seats.
The engine turned over on the first try. She stopped in front of the
cabin. "Write your story."

"*Our* story," said Tank.

Mary put the truck into drive and headed down the dirt road. A wind had picked up and filled the cabin with the scent of thistle and loam. In the rearview mirror she saw Tank waving. She thought he was calling to her. She wasn't sure, but it sounded as if he was saying something about a buggy whip.

84

"Mine."

Its official name was the Intelligence Community Comprehensive National Cybersecurity Initiative, though it was better known as simply the Utah Data Center. And it sat on 240 acres carved from the hillside directly above Highway 71, between the town of Bluffdale and Salt Lake City.

No measures had been taken to hide the facility. Four data halls measuring 100,000 square feet and built parallel to one another housed the thousands of servers necessary to store the oceans of data it collected. The halls were serviced by a dedicated cooling station. An on-site power plant provided the compound's electricity. To the naked eye it looked like nothing more glamorous than a giant Walmart or Costco or Target distribution center, the kind of gargantuan bland warehouses that lined highways in rural areas all over the United States.

And it belonged to the National Security Agency, which was to say that it belonged to the combined intelligence establishment of the United States of America.

After the successful demonstration of ONE's Titan supercomputer, it would belong to Ian Prince.

"This is it," said Bob Goldfarb, the Emperor's gnomish assistant. "Time to see what all those exaflops get us."

"Like a hammer on a walnut," said Ian. "AES doesn't stand a chance."

"I hope you're right," said Goldfarb, eyes twinkling with dreams of world domination. "And so does the president."

Not all of the Utah Data Center was visible to the naked eye. The Operations Room sat inside a nuclear-hardened concrete bunker three hundred feet below the surface. It was a SCIF inside a SCIF, with floor-to-ceiling monitors on the walls, rows of analysts' workstations, flags standing in the corners.

This morning the Operations Room was filled to capacity, seats taken by a mix of government and military personnel, the overflow lining the walls. The briefing was beyond top-secret or ultra top-secret or whatever was the latest term for the highest security clearance in the land. The vice president was present and stood with his coterie next to General Terry Wolfe. Even the president was in attendance, if from two thousand miles away, joining them along with the national security adviser and the director of the CIA from the Situation Room beneath the White House.

Ian stood against the back wall, arms crossed. He'd left Briggs in the visitors' lounge, along with a dozen other high-ranking officers and officials who did not possess adequate clearance. Ian was part of the brain trust. General Wolfe called him his own Oppenheimer. While others theorized, Ian had built the damned thing.

Seventy years ago a similar group had gathered in the dunes of White Sands, New Mexico, to gaze at a round object perched atop a tall tower and bear witness to the first atomic explosion in the history of mankind. Fat Man and Little Boy were but a black-and-white memory. The new kid on the block was named Titan.

The NSA had purchased it for but one purpose: to decrypt information culled from the deep Web, or Deepnet—the part of the Internet invisible to the common man. The Deepnet included all password-protected data, both government and commercial; all U.S. and foreign government communications; and all noncommercial file sharing between trusted peers. The problem had never been collecting the information. With sieves at every transit point in every communications hub on earth, the NSA was capable of collecting all it wanted. The problem was decryption.

All data found on the Deepnet was encrypted according to the Advanced Encryption Standard, or AES, a theoretically unbreakable shell encasing each message to protect it from intruding eyes and to ensure that only the intended recipient read it. To date, no machine had been able to crack the AES in anything close to a quick and efficient manner.

Titan would change that.

Titan, with its enormous processing power, its gargantuan intellect, its unfathomable speed, could break any code within seconds. Titan was the hammer to AES's shell. One blow, and *crack*! The shell would disintegrate.

Ian could see by the skeptical expressions that few present this morning believed Titan would work. Ian had no doubt. He knew.

"Ladies and gentlemen, please." General Terry Wolfe stood at the front of the room, fussing with his eyeglasses. "We've gathered here today to witness the first operational test of the new Titan supercomputer. We're going to start with an intercept we pulled down from our friends in Moscow. Judging from the format, it looks like it's from FSB director Gromov to a counterpart in Kiev. We've been at it for two days now and we can't crack the shell." A nod to a technician. "Go ahead. Let's see what Titan can do."

The technician fed the intercept into Titan. Lines of encrypted code flooded the main screen: letters, symbols, numerals, a seemingly random mishmash. The word *Processing* flashed at the bottom as Titan ran the message through multiple decryption programs simultaneously.

"Two days and we can't make head nor tail of it," whispered Goldfarb. "Not all the bright Russians are working for Google."

Ian stared at the screen, hands clasped behind his back, as the seconds ticked by. A minute passed, and then another. Someone cleared his throat. A chair slid across the floor. There was a cough. Reports of Titan's superpowers had been overrated.

"At least you got the heat issue fixed," said Goldfarb. "That's a start."

Someone said, "Hey!"

A hush swept the room.

"Here we go," said the Emperor.

Ian didn't alter his expression as the mishmash of letters, symbols, and numerals was replaced line by line with a message, not only decrypted but translated into flawless English.

From: Yuri Gromov, Director, FSB
 Recipient: Boris Klitschko, President, Ukraine
 Text: In regards to the premier's upcoming visit, he has asked that you have ten kilos American dry-aged filet per day on hand to be prepared medium rare, sliced thinly, and served to Ivan at 6 a.m., 1 p.m., and 8 p.m. promptly. There will be an afternoon snack of one kilo steak tartare. Ivan also requires at least five cashmere blankets and two veal shank bones with marrow.

"Who the hell's Ivan?" It was the president, asking from the Situation Room.

"I believe it's his dog," said the CIA director. "An Irish wolfhound."

Laughter all around.

Ian felt a presence at his side. He looked over to see the vice president glaring at him. "So we built a one-and-a-half-billion-dollar data center employing the world's most advanced supercomputer to learn what the Russian premier's dog likes to eat."

The vice president had long opposed the expansion of the secret state and was a vocal opponent of the Utah Data Center.

The laughter died.

"Happy, Mr. Prince?" he whispered. "Get to add another zero to your fortune. You guys are all snake-oil salesmen. Only your gadget can save the world. Give me a break. What are we supposed to do with all this stuff, anyway?"

"I think you're missing the point," said Ian. "It isn't what's in the message, it's the fact that we were able to read it."

The vice president turned his attention to the Emperor. "Anything else up your sleeve, General Wolfe?" he barked.

The NSA director fidgeted as he adjusted his eyeglasses yet again. "Impress us, Dave," he said to an air force colonel seated nearby.

"Yessir." Dave punched away at his keys. Voices played over the loudspeaker. Ian recognized the language as Mandarin, but a northern dialect. A translation of the conversation appeared in real time on the main screen.

> *"The meeting began fifteen minutes ago,"* said someone identified only as Speaker 1. *"The vice president, the director of the National Security Agency, and many other government functionaries are in attendance. Pictures show that sixteen vehicles arrived at the site in the last hour. We believe they are testing the new hardware that was recently installed."*
>
> *"What is it?"* said Speaker 2. *"Titan?"*
>
> *"We are not yet certain, but most probably it is a more sophisticated processing apparatus."*
>
> *"Are we at risk?"*
>
> *"Absolutely not. No one can penetrate our systems."*

"Gentlemen, we are listening to a general at the Chinese Ministry of State Security in Beijing speaking to China's vice premier, over a secure, encrypted line. Normally it would take us several hours to break the encryption, if we could at all. As we are all witnesses, the translation is real-time. It seems, Mr. President, that the Chinese are talking about us. They are discussing the demonstration of Titan. *Here. Today. Now.* The pictures they are referring to come from one of their spy satellites looking down on us from a few hundred miles up. In effect we are spying on our enemies spying on us—and we are having a better time of it."

In the Situation Room, the president did nothing to hide his pride.

"And it's these new machines that are enabling this?" asked the vice president.

"Yessir," said Wolfe. "It is. Here's another we have queued up. This conversation began three minutes ago and is continuing."

This time it was Arabic voices, but the translation was as timely and accurate as before. Wolfe explained that the group was listening in on a conversation between the Saudi Arabian minister of defense and a man named Mohammed Fawzi, an Algerian who headed up Al-Qaeda in the Islamic Maghreb.

"My forces are being decimated," said Fawzi. *"We have nowhere to hide."*

"Patience, my friend," said the Saudi.

"Fuck patience. Time is an expensive commodity. We need money to purchase it, money for better communications equipment, for more safe houses, and to pay men to take the place of those martyred."

"The king will make his usual contribution."

"Five million dollars isn't enough. I need at least ten if we are to continue with Paris as the king wishes."

"The king does not like Paris. He was asked to leave a hotel there once. The Meurice. It is owned by Jews. You must continue with Paris."

Wolfe killed the feed. "Please be aware that the Central Intelligence Agency has been in the loop about Paris for some time now."

The vice president raised a hand to summon the room's attention. "Just one question," he said. "If you guys can listen to the Chinese all the way in Shanghai or Beijing or wherever the hell they are, and to Al-Qaeda wherever the hell they are, and everyone's talking on secure and encrypted links, what's to stop you from listening in on the president when he's talking to the British prime minister over our own secure encrypted link?"

"Yes," echoed the president. "How do I know you won't be listening to me?"

General Wolfe pulled at his cuffs, then adjusted his glasses. His eyes darted to Ian and Bob Goldfarb, then back to the screen. "Because, Mr. President," he said with a Boy Scout's solemnity, "that would be illegal."

These days, thought Ian, the law is the last refuge of a scoundrel.

One hour later Ian was back aboard ONE 1, seated in the aft lounge. Katarina had given him his supplements. His IV was dutifully administering his phosphatidylcholine, bathing his telomeres with life-extending nutrients. His laptop was open in front of him, his eyes keenly studying the screen.

Seven years running.

David Gold entered the cabin, slim, tanned, a force. "Ian, you wanted to see me."

Ian looked up, placing a mental bookmark to remind him where he was. "Yes, David. One question: are we getting all of it?"

"Oh yes," said the Israeli computer scientist. "Our machines capture everything that goes in and out of the Operations Room. That's what Clarus does."

"So I really can listen in on the president and the British PM on their secure line?"

Gold dug his chin into his throat, a man affronted. "Why, of course. Tell me, is there anything that Titan can help you with? Anything that's of pressing concern?"

Ian tapped his fingers on the table. A name came to mind. A fiery, red-headed Mick with a big mouth and dangerous opinions.

"As a matter of fact, there is."

85

Gordon May walked around his airplane, the *Battleax*, stopping here and there and standing on his tiptoes to polish its fire-engine-red fuselage. Three days remained until the last race of the season. Despite his vehement protests, the race stewards had denied his objection. He was baffled how they were unable to recognize that Ian Prince had cut to the inside and forced him out of his pattern, endangering his life. The ruling left the series between them tied at two wins apiece.

Come Sunday, it would be all or nothing.

May climbed into the cockpit and fired up the engine. The propeller stuttered, then caught, the eight-piston engine coming to life, roaring like a bull with its balls caught in the ringer. He taxied out of the hangar and onto the runway. It was another cloudless day in the high desert of northern Nevada.

He planned on a short flight. A run to put the engine through its paces and see if it was capable of holding a speed of 550 knots for prolonged periods.

He gazed at the instrument panel. He'd kitted out *Battleax* with the same state-of-the-art avionics that powered an F-16. Glass displays. Touch-screen monitors.

Additionally he strapped a tablet to his leg that linked wirelessly to the engine. In this manner he could adjust fuel flow, oxygen mix, and oil pressure, fine-tuning the motor's torque while in the air.

"Tower, this is Golf Bravo 415 requesting permission to take off."

"Roger that, Golf Bravo 415. You are number one for takeoff. Runway is yours."

"Roger, Tower."

Gordon May continued to the end of the runway, then made a 180-degree turn. He stopped to make a final check of his gauges, then began his rollout. At 90 knots he rotated the front wheel. The nose kicked into the sky and he shot upward like a screaming banshee.

He flew northeast, in the direction of Pyramid Lake. The air was calm. The updrafts and chop that often rolled off the Sierra Nevada to the west were nowhere to be found. At 15,000 feet he leveled off and took a few moments to enjoy the view toward Lake Tahoe to the west and the Oregon border to the north.

May tightened his harness and settled into his seat. Today was about speed. It was about pushing *Battleax* to her limits.

He made another check of his gauges. Oil pressure was normal, engine temp squarely in the black. Satisfied that his baby was ready to rumble, he laid his hand on the throttle and eased it forward, increasing his airspeed to 400 knots. He smiled. The engine had never sounded better. He felt as if he were strapped to a rocket. Ian Prince didn't stand a chance.

May increased the airspeed to 500 knots, then 520. The plane kept its nose, the frame as solid as a rock. He pushed the throttle further and the airspeed rose to 550. It was these last few knots he'd lacked during the last race, which had allowed Prince to pass him. He checked the tablet and enriched the fuel mix, adding high-grade test fuel and siphoning out some of the oxygen. The result was an increase of torque, the blast of acceleration an aircraft required to overtake a competitor.

The plane responded as he'd hoped.

Sunday couldn't come soon enough.

It was then that the nose dove. One moment he was flying level to the horizon, the next he was heading for the surface of Pyramid Lake.

Stunned, May hauled back on the stick, leveling the plane out. He looked at the tablet, but the screen was dark. He tapped on the glass, to no avail. The engine coughed and the plane jerked, as if something had hit it from below.

May took a breath, calming himself. Everything had been working marvelously ten seconds ago. His ground crew had signed off on all their modifications. It was a glitch. Nothing more.

He began an easy turn back to the south. It was time to go home and get *Battleax* back on the ground. He double-checked that his tablet was indeed dead. When he returned his attention to his controls, the avionics screen had gone dark. In fact, the entire display was black. Simultaneously the stick slammed forward and the plane went into a dive. May threw both hands around the stick and pulled back with all his might. The stick did not budge. The nose dipped further, and further still, until he was flying directly at the ground.

He cut the gas, but the engine didn't slow. In fact, he was certain that the rpm's were increasing. He played with the pedals, with the flaps, trying everything to pull out of the dive. Nothing worked. The plane was no longer his.

"Tower, this is Golf Bravo 415 declaring an emergency. Am in uncontrolled descent."

The tower didn't answer.

May felt his consciousness slipping away. The g's were mounting. He felt the pressure on his eyeballs and in his chest. It was difficult to breathe. For the first time he took his eyes entirely off his instruments and gazed out the windscreen. The water was approaching fast. He was below one thousand feet.

With a last effort he pulled back on the stick.

"Please," he shouted.

The stick gave. The nose rose. "Thank god," he said.

And then the stick dived forward and Gordon knew that all was lost.

As the water approached and his windscreen filled with blue, he realized that this was not an accident, that his avionics had not failed, but that somehow someone had taken control of his aircraft. He could think of only one person. And as the plane struck the water and disintegrated into a thousand pieces, he screamed his name.

"Prince!"

86

Jessie Grant sat in her assigned seat at the Ninjaneers post watching the clock tick down the seconds until Capture the Flag began. Her laptop was plugged in and fully charged. Her phone was charged, too, and ready for use should additional browsing be necessary.

"Two minutes," said the announcer. "If you have to go to the bathroom, too late. You'll just have to hold it."

Jessie rolled her eyes. Computer geeks. She'd bought plenty of provisions to get her through the game. Mountain Dew, Skittles, and a dozen pieces of Bazooka bubblegum, the kind with the comic wrapped inside. Bazooka was her dad's favorite.

The ballroom was packed to bursting. Grandstands erected against three walls were full. Two fixed television cameras were posted at opposite sides of the room. There was even a roving reporter going from one team to the next, interviewing players.

She gazed at the stands, looking for Garrett, but it was hard to see with the lights dimmed. Besides, Jessie was more interested in someone else. Her eyes sought out the solitary figure occupying the post farthest from the Ninjaneers. He wore a dark sweatshirt, its hood pulled far over his head. Even so he sat with his back to her and everyone else. While the other teams boasted a full complement of eight players, he sat alone. Even the sign bearing his team name was left intentionally blank. It didn't matter. Everyone in the ballroom knew who he was.

Max came over, looking as nervous as she felt. "You ready to go, kid?"

"I guess so."

"This can be our year. We're counting on you!"

Jessie kept her eyes on the laptop's screen, too embarrassed by the compliment to reply.

"All right," Max went on, "let's do it." He put out a bony fist. Reluctantly, Jessie met it with her own. If they actually won this thing, he might want to do a flying chest bump. Not going to happen, thought Jess.

"One minute."

All teams were to receive the first problem via the dedicated competition net (CTF.net) the minute the game began, but for the moment the screen continued to glow blue with the Capture the Flag logo. She drew a breath. *The team was counting on her.*

An air horn sounded.

The first hack appeared on the screen. It was a root-the-box problem similar to the one she'd done in Linus's class. Jess scoured the code, seeking out the vulns put there purposefully to act as the secret passageways into the heart of the code. Right away she spotted one.

"Got it," said Research. Once he received the vuln, he'd search through his toolbox to discover a means to exploit it.

Jessie smiled inwardly. The first problem was easiest. There was no time to be cocky. But still . . .

Hacking had always come easily. In many respects it was just like playing the "find what's hidden" game in those old *Highlights* magazines she used to read in the dentist's office. She remembered how she'd loved poring over the illustration—of a barnyard or a circus or a carnival—determined to spot the hidden comb, coin, tennis racket, or sailboat. Later she'd loved the Where's Waldo? books. No one could spot Waldo and his red knit cap faster. And not just Waldo—Jess was able to pinpoint Wenda; Woof, his dog; and all the other secret characters with a speed bordering on freakish. Among all the elaborate pictorial chaos, the hidden images seemed to pop out at her. There was really no explanation for her uncanny ability, other than that she was just programmed that way.

Hacking into a network was no different. It was a question of knowing what belonged and what didn't and having that special connection between your eye and your brain that allowed you to be the first to spot it.

"Gotcha!" Jess called out another vuln. A second later Research solved the first and the Ninjaneers captured their first flag. A cheer erupted from the spectators. Jessie looked up for a second and found Garrett looking back at her. She smiled, but was surprised at his grave demeanor. Didn't he see the scoreboard? The Ninjaneers had their first flag.

Garrett shook his head and pointed at the board. Rudeboy had three flags.

Jessie's heart sank. And then it sank further as Defense called out, "Shit. The bastard nabbed it already."

On the scoreboard, the Ninjaneers' flag disappeared.

Rudeboy had stolen it.

87

Mary bolted from her seat the moment the plane arrived at the gate and pushed her way through the packed cabin, ducking and dodging and begging her pardon all the way to the forward door.

"In a hurry, are we?" asked the flight attendant.

Mary swept past without a word and charged up the ramp. The flight to Las Vegas had landed thirty minutes late. It was ten. She'd left the last message with Garrett nearly four hours earlier. She had no idea how long Jessie had been at the police station, or if she'd continue to wait.

Inside the concourse, Mary ducked into the first electronics store she spotted and selected a prepaid cell phone costing $29.95. She placed the box on the counter along with her credit card and tapped her foot impatiently as the clerk rang up her purchase.

"Excuse me, ma'am, but this card has been declined."

"Run it again," said Mary. "Please."

The clerk zipped the card through the reader a second time. "I'm sorry, ma'am. The card's been declined."

"You're sure?"

"I'm sorry."

Of all times . . . Mary put the card back into her wallet and selected another. It was the machine, not her card. She kept her balances memorized the way baseball fans memorized batting averages. "This one should work."

She turned to survey the throngs walking in every direction. She'd never liked Las Vegas. The idea of the place ran against her Calvinist roots. It wasn't the sin or the iniquity. It was the wastefulness. Nearly all the people she saw appeared to be in need of saving money, not handing it over to a one-armed bandit.

She yawned. She'd been awake for more than twenty-four hours, but no matter how she'd tried, she'd been unable to nod off on the flight. She was too worried about Jess. About Grace. About everything.

"Ma'am?"

Mary knew from the young woman's tone that something was wrong. "Yes?"

"This card's been refused as well."

"Really? I never use it. It's my emergency card."

"I can only tell you what the machine says."

Mary took back the card, more angry than mystified. "Can I give you another? Really, I'm sure it has to be your machine."

"Ma'am, please." The clerk looked past Mary to where a line was forming. "We accept cash."

Mary paid for the phone with her last two twenties. A minute later she was heading down the escalator to the taxi stand, the phone pressed to her ear. The call to Garrett rang through to his voicemail. Kids, she thought crossly. They spend all day with their noses buried in their phones and refuse to answer when they actually receive a call. "This is Jessie's mom again. I hope you passed along my message. I just landed and I'm on my way to the police station. Please call me at this number the moment you listen to this."

She hurried past the baggage claim toward the exit. Through the windows she observed a monstrous line for cabs. She slowed, realizing that $9 and change was not enough to get her to the police station.

An ATM stood against a nearby wall.

Sliding her card into the machine, she felt a cold hand upon her shoulder, a dread voice whispering in her ear that it was no mistake that her cards were being declined. She dismissed it. Machines made mistakes all the time. There was nothing wrong with her credit.

She typed in her PIN and her screen came up without incident. Relieved, she selected a quick withdrawal of $60. The machine hummed for much too long. Finally it spit out her card and informed her that her request was denied due to insufficient funds.

This isn't right, she told herself, refusing to believe the machine's verdict or that the problem was in any way tied to her credit cards.

She slipped in her bank card again and navigated to her account balances. Her checking account stood at −$27.98.

Overdrawn.

It was not a word to her. Mary had never bounced a check in her life. Two days earlier the balance had stood at nearly $3,000. She would remember if a significant check was outstanding.

It was a mistake . . . yet it was no mistake.

For the first time she felt panic nipping at her heels.

She returned to the main menu and selected her savings account, which had a balance of $14,000 and change. It was an abysmally low sum for a couple in their forties with two children. Even then, it didn't take into account the stack of hospital bills yet to be paid.

The screen blinked.

0

Mary stared at the display transfixed, not entirely able to grasp the new reality the single empty digit conferred. Money was her responsibility. Joe earned it. She guarded it like a hawk.

No money. No credit cards. No savings.

Her eyes filled even as the admiral commanded her not to panic. The *Titanic* had not just hit an iceberg. There was not a giant gash in the Grant family vessel. Water was not pouring in at the rate of 50,000 gallons a minute.

Hand shaking, she checked recent transactions. The entire balance of $14,459 had been wired out to something called MJG Enterprises. No further information given.

MJG, for Mary, Jessie, and Grace.

A closer look at her checking account showed that all her money had been transferred to the same institution.

Mary ended her session and walked outside. It was controlled mayhem, the sidewalk jammed with tourists, taxis honking, cops blowing whistles. This wasn't fair, she told herself. It was hitting below the belt. Demoralized, she sat down on the curb and cradled her head in her hands. She was aware of people staring, but no one inquired as to her well-being. Desperation was just the flip side of joy. Both were on constant display in Sin City.

No mountain gets smaller for . . .

She stopped quoting the admiral. It was time to rely on herself.

After a minute she opened her purse and took stock of her situation. First some good news. She'd been wrong about having $9 to her name. In fact she had $10.80. Not a huge improvement, but when you're starting at zero, a buck's a big deal. She dropped her wallet back into her purse and saw something shimmer in the corner. A blink of brass or gold. She rooted through the Altoids and Kleenexes and carefully folded receipts until her fingers touched something round and smooth and polished.

To H.S. Thanks, I.

She closed the purse. The line for taxis had grown even longer during her pity party. She walked past the head of the line and crossed to the center island, where a dozen town cars sat parked, waiting for the big spenders.

"Morning, ma'am," said a liveried chauffeur as he opened the door. "You look like you're headed to the Strip. Let me guess . . . the Wynn."

"No, I'm sorry—"

"The Bellagio. I knew it."

"I'm not going to a hotel," said Mary.

"Oh? Where can I take you?"

"The Pawn Stars shop," said Mary as she slid into the air-conditioned back seat. "And step on it."

88

The Patek-Philippe wristwatch sat on a baize-lined tray atop a display housing necklaces, earrings, bracelets, and other wristwatches.

"It's not often we get a timepiece of this quality. Production is limited to five to six pieces a year. These are really quite rare."

His name was Al, and by his own admission he was the store's resident watch expert. Al was short and running to fat, with meaty forearms and an ungroomed black beard like that of the wacky pitcher of the San Francisco Giants. Cars, maybe. Motorcycles, for sure. Watches, no way.

"I'm glad you like it," said Mary.

"I know quality," said Al as he jotted down a number on a notepad and offered it for her inspection.

"I think you can do better."

"Thirty cents on the dollar is generous. However, given your item's pedigree, I can go a little higher. If you're interested in selling it, I can offer a more attractive sum."

"A loan will be fine."

Al picked up the watch and held it up for inspection, as an oenophile might study a glass of vintage Bordeaux. "Exceptional."

"It belonged to a friend."

"I'm sorry," said Al.

"Don't be. He was a prick."

Al returned the watch to the tray, crossed out his original figure, and wrote a new one. "My best offer."

Mary tore the paper from the pad. "Done."

"If you'll just fill out the paperwork, I'll be back with a cashier's check."

"I'd prefer cash."

Al gave a double-take, stroking his beard for good measure. "For the entire amount?"

Mary nodded. "You can't trust banks these days."

Al invited her into a private office. It took several minutes to fill out the paperwork and several more for it to be processed. The terms were straightforward enough. The watch was to act as collateral against the loan. She had sixty days to repay the full amount at 22.5 percent interest per annum. It wasn't loan sharking, but close.

A woman entered and placed a manila envelope on the desk. Al spilled the contents on the top. Crisp packets of $100 bills, still bundled from the bank. He counted the money with care, laying it in fans of $10,000 across his desk.

"Ten . . . twenty . . . thirty . . . thirty-six thousand dollars."

Mary signaled her approval and Al gathered the bills like a blackjack dealer gathering playing cards, then placed the entire stack in a smaller, more discreet envelope.

Slipping the envelope into her purse, Mary enjoyed a moment of relief. The money wasn't hers. The watch belonged to Hal Stark's family, and she'd return it as soon she'd gotten Jessie home and Tank had published his article.

Somehow, she prayed, she'd have gotten her savings back by then, too.

"Will there be anything else?" asked Al once they'd returned to the showroom.

Mary ambled toward a nearby display case. It did not contain necklaces, earrings, bracelets, or other wristwatches.

"Yes," she said, pointing at the item that had caught her fancy. "I'd like that one there. It is for sale, isn't it?"

89

Tank pulled the sheet of foolscap from his old Underwood typewriter and read the final paragraph of his article.

"The Titan supercomputer developed by John Merriweather and perfected by Ian Prince is said to be the cornerstone of the NSA's next-generation surveillance system, designed to decrypt even the most strenuously guarded messages of allies and enemies alike. Schematic data provided by ONE engineers show that 'backdoors' built into Titan (and nearly all machines designed and manufactured by ONE Technologies) allow unfettered access to these messages and to all information passing through it to anyone possessing the proper pass codes. Calls to the FBI and ONE Technologies have not been returned at this time."

He grabbed a pen and wrote 30 at the bottom: old-school newspaper shorthand for "The end. Take this to the typesetter."

With a groan, he stood and walked to the sink. He hadn't figured that a bullet passing through his side could cause so much pain. His torso ached as if he really had been in that car accident he'd lied about to Al Soletano. He drank a glass of water but, despite some momentary refreshment, felt no better.

Leaning against the counter, he looked across the cabin at the ancient Underwood typewriter. The machine was heavy, cumbersome, arthritic, and altogether a relic. It reminded him of someone he knew.

He returned to the desk and gathered up his papers. Running to some two thousand words, the article stated that Ian Prince had overseen a campaign of extortion and intimidation against Merriweather Systems' shareholders to convince them to vote in favor of a sale to ONE Technologies, that he had overseen the hacking of the FBI's mainframe in Washington, D.C., resulting in the theft of over one thousand confidential files, and that he had paid Edward Mason $10 million to end the FBI's investigation into ONE, all of it in a quest to take de facto control of the National Security Agency's Utah Data Center.

There was no need to speculate to what end Ian Prince would abuse his access. His track record spoke eloquently of his past deeds. Intimidation, theft, sabotage, and murder were only the beginning.

Finally there was the matter of the malware that Hal Stark had posited Ian Prince had introduced into the avionics system of John Merriweather's plane, which had led to Merriweather flying his aircraft into a mountainside. Short of getting into Prince's computers, there was no way of corroborating the speculation. He would give the evidence to the FBI and let them handle it.

The irony, he thought.

Even without accusations of murder, the article was enough to bag him a big prize. A Pulitzer at the least. Once it ran, all hell would break loose. Tank could count on being busy for months on end, years possibly, covering all the stories sure to fall out. He felt like a hero in a World War II movie, the intrepid soldier who finds a detonation cord hidden in the sand and, with no care for his welfare, laboriously pulls it clear and follows wherever it might lead.

He could already hear Al Soletano apologizing: "You know, Tank, I was out of line when I called you a has-been. You weren't ever just a decent reporter. You were a great one. Let's forget all this nonsense about downsizing. The paper wants you back."

Tank enjoyed the thought. Frankly, he wasn't so sure he wanted his job back. He might just freelance, pull down a hefty book contract, and hang out his shingle as a roving investigative journalist.

He limped to the closet and dug around for some clean clothes, settling for a pair of Wranglers with mud on the cuffs and a flannel shirt that smelled of mothballs. He splashed some water on his face and combed his hair. It had been a long couple of days. Even so, he was shocked at his appearance. He looked as if he'd been pulled through a cotton gin one inch at a time.

Averting his gaze, he finished buttoning up his shirt and picked up the article and his notes and laid them on the tablet. With care, he yanked the flash drive clear, popped it back into the key. Without the key, it was all hearsay. Without the key, Tank Potter was a dead man.

Still thirsty, he opened a cabinet hoping to find a Coke or a root beer. Something to pep him up. There were no soft drinks, but there on the top shelf, pushed almost out of his sight, rested two small wooden crates. He stood on his tiptoes, his heart racing. Tequila. And not the Cuervo Gold he kept in the Jeep as his backstop, but Jose Cuervo Reserva de la Familia, a royal elixir that went for over $100 a bottle.

Tank sank down to his feet. Suddenly the pain in his side was unbearable. The past days' travails weighed down on him. He thought of confronting Edward Mason at the airport, of discovering Carlos Cantu's disfigured body, and of firing two shells into McNair's chest. Any man would need a drink after going through all that.

Just one shot to steady his nerves and kill the pain in his gut.

And yet . . . He hesitated. As much as he desired a sip—just one—he knew he should walk out the door this second, climb into the Ferrari, and drive like hell into Austin. It was his job to get proof to the authorities. His life depended on it, and so did Mary's.

Go. Now.

Strangely, his feet had turned into lead weights.

He reminded himself that he was a journalist. He had an obligation to the truth.

Even so, his hand reached high and took hold of one of the wooden boxes. He lowered it carefully . . . *$100 a bottle* . . . and carried it to the sink. He was on autopilot now. He didn't think about getting proof to the authorities or about Mary. The fact that he was a journalist—*and a damned good one*—meant nothing to him.

He needed a few minutes to pry open the crate, free the bottle, and pop the cork. The smell nearly drove him to his knees. He found a glass and poured a sip, and then more than a sip, licking his lips greedily as the amber fluid filled the glass.

Reverently he raised the glass to his mouth. "Salud," he said, to Mary and Al Soletano and even Pedro. "We got 'em."

Only then did he hear a car driving across the scattered gravel. The engine quit. A car door slammed. Footsteps on the porch. A knock on the door.

"Mr. Potter. FBI. Please come out."

Tank looked around the cabin. There was nowhere to run. He hid the key in the only place he knew.

"Open up, Mr. Potter."

Tank opened the door. He recognized the agent at once. He'd seen him just the night before. Only then he hadn't been holding a pistol. "You?" he said.

Special Agent Fergus Keefe shot him in the right knee. Tank toppled to the floor, grasping his leg.

Keefe stepped over him into the cabin. "I believe that the automobile parked out front belongs to us."

90

Rudeboy 17, Ninjaneers 16.

With ten minutes remaining, it was down to two teams. First to capture twenty flags won. It had been back-and-forth the entire game. Every time Jess and her teammates captured a flag, Rudeboy would steal it back.

"Tell Defense to sharpen his game," said Jess. "There aren't enough vulns left to win if we keep losing our flags."

She cracked her knuckles and took a swig of Mountain Dew. She was beating Rudeboy on the attack, capturing two flags to his one. But her team was having little luck preventing him from stealing them back. She saw her dad in front of the TV watching a Celtics game. "It's defense that wins games," he always said.

A cheer went up from the crowd. Another flag for Rudeboy.

She caught Max looking expectantly at her. *We're counting on you.* A cameraman shined a light in her face. "Get lost," she shouted.

The last problem flashed onto her screen. Immediately she knew she was in trouble. It was like nothing she'd seen before. She needed a full minute just to read the entire code. Nothing clicked. She scanned it again, feeling more lost than before. None of it made sense.

She glanced up to find Garrett staring right at her, fists clenched, urging her on. She returned her attention to the screen and then she saw it . . . something familiar . . . She didn't know what it meant, but she felt as if she'd taken a step closer. And then she had it.

Jessie picked up her phone and pulled up the snippet of code left behind by the person who'd deleted her father's message. She compared it to the problem and saw that she was correct. The two codes matched exactly except for a sequence on the final line. There it was—the vuln.

"Got one," she called out, highlighting the error and sending it to Research.

"It's a variant on Linux," he said. "Did one like it at Caltech last year. Telecommunications protocol. We were hacking into the phone company."

Jessie jumped from her chair and took a seat with Defense. "Move it," she said, squeezing closer so she had a clear view of his screen. "Look," she said. "He's breaking in through the black matrix."

It was Rudeboy, infiltrating their system. She blocked him with a cross-dominant strix. Easy enough. While he was figuring out what had happened, she accessed his board and found a chink. A minute later she'd stolen one of his flags. "Got one back."

Ninjaneers 18, Rudeboy 18.

"Solved it," said Research.

For the first time their team took the lead.

Ninjaneers 19, Rudeboy 18.

But a second later another cheer erupted as Rudeboy picked up another flag.

"Hit me with some Skittles," said Jess.

Max dumped a mound in her palm and she threw them all into her mouth. Chewing ferociously, she went back to her original seat. "Steal one of his flags," she called over her shoulder.

"Working on it!"

There was one flag remaining to be won. It all came down to who would spot the last vuln first and solve it.

Jessie ran her fingernails across the desk as she studied the next batch of code. Telecommunications protocol wasn't her area of expertise. She didn't care about hacking into phones. She liked hacking into networks, mainframes.

"One minute," announced the referee over the loudspeaker.

If the game ended now, it would be a tie. A tie wasn't good enough. Not when she was so close to giving the Ninjaneers their first victory. Not when she was so close to beating Rudeboy.

"Did you get it?"

"He's blocking me. Did you?"

Jessie couldn't answer. She needed time to work it out. Stay calm. Concentrate. It'll come.

A cheer from the audience. She glanced up. Rudeboy had captured his twentieth flag. She ran back to Defense and shoved him out of his chair. Their only hope was to steal one of Rudeboy's flags back.

The crowd began to count down the last twenty seconds. "Twenty . . . nineteen . . ."

Jessie was aware of Max and the others huddled behind her. Time and again she attempted to penetrate Rudeboy's board, only to be blocked.

Ten . . . nine . . .

And there it was—wide open, a hole she could drive a truck through. She typed in the solution. Just a few more seconds . . .

Six . . . five . . .

She finished the last word and hit Return. She'd done it. She'd nailed Rudeboy. She'd stolen his flag. It would be a tie.

Two . . . one . . .

The air horn sounded, signifying the end of competition. Jessie stood from her chair. The scoreboard remained unchanged. Rudeboy 20, Ninjaneers 19.

"But I got it," she said. "I broke through his defense. I captured his flag."

"No," said Max. "Typo in the last word."

"What?" Jessie sat down and looked at her work. Max was right. She'd typed a *c* in place of an *x*. It was her fault all over again. "Crap!"

The Ninjaneers collapsed in their chairs, despondent. No one said a word to her. She'd made them believe they could win, and she'd let them down.

The crowd poured out of the stands. She glimpsed Rudeboy moving past the judges, disregarding the referee's outstretched hand, ignoring all attempts to congratulate him as he skirted the podium toward the exit.

Now or never.

Jess slid over the table and made her way through the crowd. She had to speak with him. She'd come so close. One flag. It was all because of a typo.

In the hall she saw the black hoodie again. She hurried toward him, breaking into a jog, carving a path through the spectators leaving the ballroom. She turned a corner and saw him by the elevator, hands in his pockets, back to her.

She stopped and steeled herself, squaring her shoulders. She had practiced what she was going to say a hundred times and now she couldn't remember a word. "Whatever, Jess, just talk to him," she muttered.

A hand landed on her shoulder.

"Jessie!"

She spun. Her stomach dropped. Not now. Not here. "Mom? You came?"

"I've been at the police station for hours. I keep calling Garrett, but he isn't answering. Didn't you get my messages? Are you okay?"

Jessie nodded. She wanted to say that she was fine and that she'd almost won Capture the Flag—*one stupid typo!*—but there wasn't time.

"We need to leave," said Mary. "I'm just so glad you're here and I found you." She put out her arms, and Jessie saw that she had tears in her eyes. Backpedaling, Jessie avoided the hug. She glanced over her shoulder to see the elevator opening and Rudeboy stepping inside.

"Not now. Sorry, but I have to—"

"Jess, stay—no!"

Jessie pushed her mother away and ran.

She made it into the packed elevator as the doors closed.

91

"Where is it?" demanded Keefe.

Lying on his side, Tank stared at the swirls in the wood floor. Shot twice in one day, he was thinking. My luck has got to get better.

"Was it in the car?" Keefe went on. "Mr. Mason can't see any other reason for you and Grant's wife to do something so patently stupid as steal a piece of government property in the middle of the night. He thinks the files Stark stole were hidden in the car key. He said it had to be on a flash drive or something similar. Where is she, by the way?"

"I don't know. Gone. An hour ago."

"We'll come back to that. Right now I need the key or whatever device Stark put the stolen information onto."

"How did you find me?" asked Tank.

"Newfangled invention called LoJack. Just about every car over twenty grand has been carrying one for the past ten years."

"I haven't been in the market lately."

Keefe shut and locked the door, then knelt to pat down Tank, removing his wallet and dropping all his credit cards on the floor. Finding nothing, he stood and walked the perimeter of the cabin. He stopped at the kitchen table, where he read the article. "Nice work," he said. "Joe Grant would have had a field day with this. He'd finally have gotten the promotion to D.C. he wanted. Then again, maybe not. He was too good at his job to be put behind a desk." Keefe studied the tablet on which Tank had backed up all of Stark's files. "And here you are, way out here without an Internet connection."

"Not even dial-up," said Tank.

Keefe picked up the glass of tequila and drank half of it down. "A little early, but then again, I don't usually shoot anyone before noon." Then he was kneeling in front of Tank again. "So are you going to cooperate or not?"

Tank closed his eyes and pressed his forehead to the floor. "Not."

Keefe put the gun to Tank's left knee and fired. "IRA used to do that. They call it kneecapping someone. Hurts, doesn't it?"

Tank couldn't speak. He knew only agony.

Keefe finished the tequila and put the glass in the sink. "You know," he said, "it doesn't really matter whether I get the key or not. It only matters that no one else finds it. But if I do leave without it, everyone upstairs is going to think Mary Grant has it. We don't know where she is at the moment, but I don't imagine she can stay hidden for long. So if you don't have the information Stark stole, we'll have no choice but to assume she does."

Tank began to cry. It wasn't the pain so much as the disappointment— the despair of it all.

"In the typewriter," he said. "The key is in the typewriter."

Keefe retrieved the key to the LaFerrari. "Clever bastard," he said as he popped the flash drive. "Just so you know, we're going to kill Mary and her daughters anyway. Mr. Mason doesn't like loose ends. Neither does Ian Prince."

"Don't you dare!"

Keefe stood over Tank and pointed the gun at his head. "And how do you propose to stop us?"

92

The elevator was hot and crowded. Jessie stood with her face pressed against the door, hemmed in on all sides. She was aware of Rudeboy somewhere behind her, but there were too many people to speak to him here. The elevator stopped repeatedly, disgorging passengers. The last two left at the twenty-first floor. The doors closed and she had her wish. She was alone with Rudeboy.

"Um . . . ," she began, facing him, smiling. "Good game."

Rudeboy kept his head lowered, saying nothing.

"I was on the Ninjaneers. We needed better defense."

Still no response.

Jess turned back toward the front, every atom of her wanting to shrivel up and die.

The elevator continued to the penthouses. The door opened and Rudeboy brushed past her. Jess followed. "I was wondering if I could talk to you for a second. I don't know how you manage to do attack, research, and defense all at once. That's awesome."

Jessie cringed. She sounded like a total fangirl.

"I actually came to play against you," she went on blindly, hurrying to keep up. "I thought if I won, you might talk to me. You see, I have this problem. It's about a hack. I can't figure it out on my own. Even my TA couldn't make sense of it. Whoever did it is, like, super-smart. In fact, I don't know who else to ask."

They'd come to the end of the hall.

The presidential suite.

Jessie stood back as Rudeboy slid his card key through the lock and opened the door. She caught a glimpse of marble and lots of plants and an aquarium that looked like Sea World. Rudeboy walked inside, leaving the door open. Jessie poked her head into the suite, not daring to enter. "Please," she said, begging but not begging. "It's about my family. My dad, really. I need your help."

Rudeboy turned around. For the first time she got a clear look at his face. Dark, deep-set eyes; a small twitchy mouth, the lips sickeningly red, inflamed.

"Come in," he said. "Shut the door."

Jessie stepped inside and closed the door. The aquarium formed a wall between the entry and a living area that looked as large as her home on Pickfair Drive. Floor-to-ceiling windows offered a view over the Las Vegas strip and beyond.

"So you want to talk to Rudeboy?" he said.

Jessie nodded. Weird question. Obviously.

"He's in there." Rudeboy, or the person she'd thought was Rudeboy, pointed to a doorway.

"But aren't you—"

The door opened. A man she'd seen a thousand times on television and on the Net walked toward her. "Hello, Jessie," he said. "Brilliant play. You almost had me."

"One letter," said Jess.

"Sometimes that's all it takes," said Ian Prince.

"You're Rudeboy?"

"Seven years running."

"But you weren't on the floor."

"It's difficult. Too much attention. My associate takes my place. He helps a bit, but I feed him the answers. You're a gifted player, young lady. Maybe one day you'll work for me."

"That would be cool."

"After all, we both live in Austin."

Jessie was confused, off balance. It was too much to take in. Ian Prince was five feet away, talking to her. The hotel suite was insane, and there was a shark in the aquarium. "How did you know my name?"

"I know all about you. I know you love Led Zeppelin. Me, too. Favorite song?"

"'Heartbreaker.'"

"Mine's 'Stairway to Heaven.'" over the hills and far away

Weak answer, but Jessie wasn't going to say anything.

Prince went on. "I know that you're taking a summer school class at UT and that you have a younger sister named Grace. I also know that you both adore sloths."

"Sorry, but you're kind of creeping me out."

"And I know that you recently lost your father. I'm sorry."

Before Jessie could say anything, there was a sharp knock on the door. Ian Prince said, "Excuse me," then walked to the entryway. "Come in," he said, opening the door and throwing out a welcoming arm. "This is a surprise."

Jessie's mom entered the suite. Behind her was a slim, rough-looking man with a blond crew cut.

"Mom? What are you doing up here?"

Mary Grant didn't answer. "Let her go," she said to Ian Prince.

"So nice to finally meet you. I feel as though I know you already."

Jessie looked back and forth between the two of them. "Mom, what is this? How do you know Ian Prince?"

"Your father did. Be quiet now, Jessie."

Jessie backed up a step. She had no idea what was going on, only that she'd never seen her mother look so upset.

Ian Prince dropped his hand. "Close the door, Peter," he said to the tough-looking blond guy. "Mary and I need to have a chat."

93

"This doesn't have to end badly. As long as I have what I need, I see no reason why we can't go back to how things were."

Mary sat in a low-backed leather chair facing Ian Prince in the library on the second floor of the presidential suite. "My husband is dead. You had him killed. Things can't go back to how they were."

"You have no money. No savings. Your credit is ruined. You have a stack of medical bills as high as a mountain. And now Grace is back in hospital in the company of a guardian—a Mrs. Kramer, whose credit card you used to book your flight to Las Vegas. Don't ask me how I know."

Mary contained her fear. He knew because he knew everything. She looked into Prince's eyes, part of her questioning whether he was even human. The easy smile, the flawless complexion, the sparkling eyes and lustrous hair. He radiated health, well-being, yet it was somehow artificial, not entirely lifelike.

"I'm prepared to rectify these unfortunate reversals," he went on. "Your checking account will be refunded. Ditto your savings. Additionally, I'll pay Grace's hospital bills to the penny. I'll even provide you with a generous cushion to find your footing after so difficult a loss." He put out a hand to touch her knee. "I only want the best for you."

Mary knocked the hand away. "You should have thought of that before you had Joe killed."

Ian Prince chuckled, as if this were a misunderstanding between friends. "Edward Mason told me you were stubborn."

"He has no idea."

The look in Ian Prince's eyes changed. A light went out. "Of course, there's also the matter of your husband's pension," he said.

"What about it?" With all their money stolen from the bank, Joe's pension was all they had. Mary had calculated it to be a little more than $3,000 a month. If Edward Mason made good on his promise of a posthumous raise to Senior Executive Service, the amount would rise to nearly $5,000. The pension was their only remaining safety net.

"If I'm to understand correctly, the FBI considers drug or alcohol use in the course of duty as a punishable offense. Joe spent some time at Hazelden, did he not? A sixty-day course of treatment, lengthened to ninety owing to the severity of his addictions . . . *plural*. Alcohol. Prescription drugs. Even marijuana."

"Joe hadn't drunk or used in two and a half years. It started because of an accident at work. He ruptured a verterbra—" Joe liked to party

"Lifting a filing cabinet while removing evidence," said Ian Prince. "I know, I know. These things often start in the most innocuous ways. Still, Edward Mason informed me that an analysis of his blood work at the time of death is standard. Should the FBI find any abnormalities, they'll be well within their rights to decrease his pension, if not to cancel it altogether."

"Are you threatening me?"

"We're far past threats, Mary." And then Ian smiled. The light in his eyes went back on. "Regarding Grace, I nearly forgot to tell you. I've found a promising physician in Houston who can look after her, a Dr. Shender, at the MD Anderson clinic. A leader in his field. Brilliant."

"Grace is fine."

"So you told me. And I'd love for Jessie to come work for us at ONE. She's a natural. Just like I was at her age. We can start with an internship next summer. Of course we'll pay her college tuition and for any graduate studies she might wish to pursue. A full ride. Expenses, too."

"No, thank you," said Mary. "That won't be necessary."

Ian narrowed his eyes. "I don't know that you're in a position to turn me down."

"I believe I am."

"Really?"

Mary leaned closer. "Another thing the FBI frowns upon is bribery. You paid Edward Mason ten million dollars to stop my husband's investigation into Merriweather Systems. And then there's the matter of your hacking into the FBI's mainframes, not to mention the original accusations of extortion against Merriweather shareholders. Don't ask me how I know."

"Are you threatening me?"

"We're far past threats, Ian. I have all of Hal Stark's files. Everything he copied from your computers to give to Joe. Any minute my associate will deliver an article to the newspaper, along with copies of the files detailing the crimes you committed." Mary stood and picked up her purse. "I would advise Edward Mason to leave my husband's blood as it is and not to mess with it in any way, shape, or form. Now, if you'll excuse me, I'm going downstairs and taking my daughter."

As Mary left the room, Ian Prince's head of security entered. "I believe we've met," said Mary as he passed her. "Last night. My place. I was the one with the steel bowl."

"I'll see you soon."

"Doubtful."

Mary continued downstairs to where Jessie sat on the couch, working on her laptop alongside the man with the deep-set eyes. "Come on, peanut. We're out of here."

"We're just talking about the code I found on your phone. This is Greg. He went to MIT. He totally explained it to me."

"Hello, Greg. I'm impressed." Mary took Jessie's hand and yanked her off the couch. "We're going home."

Jessie pulled her hand free. "Okay. You don't have to be so aggro." She looked at Greg from MIT. "Thanks for showing me that. I didn't see it on GitHub anywhere."

"Too bad about the typo." Greg smiled, and Mary thought he looked like a hyena. More than ever she wanted to get away from Ian Prince.

"I have to get my laptop," said Jessie. "I left it in the ballroom. I hope Garrett is taking care of it."

"Fine. Let's just go."

Ian Prince had come down the stairs and was standing near the aquarium. His bodyguard walked past him toward Mary. "You should have kept your mouth closed," he said in the South African accent she'd heard the night before.

Mary didn't see the blow coming. She felt something hard and unyielding strike her jaw. Her vision blurred. The next thing she knew she was lying on the floor, blood filling her mouth. Jessie was shouting and then she wasn't. Strong hands pulled Mary to her feet. She saw Jess on the couch, doubled over, clutching her stomach. Her "friend," Greg from MIT, stood above her.

"Bad news, I'm afraid," said Ian Prince. "Mr. Mason informs me that your friend Mr. Potter has been killed. The FBI is in possession of the evidence you alluded to. A car key. Points to Hal Stark for thinking of it—or was it your husband's idea? Either way, very clever indeed." He looked at his bodyguard. "Mr. Briggs, I believe we're done here." He approached Mary. "You should have taken my offer while you had the chance. I'm afraid it's off the table now."

Mary spat a wad of blood and saliva into his face. "That's what I think of your offer."

Ian recoiled, brushing the spit from his face. "You could never have stopped my work," he said. "I'm the future."

"God, I hope not."

Ian walked from the suite.

Briggs guided Mary to a chair and sat her down. He drew a pair of flex cuffs from his jacket and fastened her wrists in front of her, then placed a length of duct tape over her mouth. Jess bolted from the couch, trying for the door. Greg tackled her and held her until Briggs cuffed and taped her, too.

"Wait until dark," said Briggs to Greg from MIT. "We'll send someone to help out. Until then, they're yours. Just don't make a mess."

94

Tank Potter was not dead yet. He lay on the floor of his cabin in a netherworld of pain.

Standing above him, Fergus Keefe finished his call. "Hear that, Potter? Directions from the boss himself. Eliminate all loose ends. That means you, my friend."

Tank turned onto his back. "A drink. One last one."

"You wouldn't rather say your prayers?"

"He and I aren't on speaking terms."

Keefe poured two fingers of tequila into the glass and returned. "This is good stuff. I won't argue with you there."

"A buck a bottle."

"No shit. Hope you don't mind if I help myself to the other one." Keefe propped Tank up and put the glass to his mouth. Tank tried to take a sip, but the tequila no longer smelled so enticing. It came to him that if he hadn't stopped to take a drink, he would have gotten away. Right now he'd be driving somewhere near Hutto with the article on the seat beside him and Hal Stark's files safe and sound on the key and the tablet. He thought of Mary and her girls and knew that Keefe, or someone like him, would be visiting them very soon.

With the last of his strength, he pushed the glass away.

"What is it?" said Keefe.

"I can't," said Tank.

Keefe shrugged. "Suit yourself." He drank down the tequila with relish, then stood. "You ready?"

Tank laid his head down. For the first time in many a year, he prayed. He prayed for Mary and her girls. He prayed that Ian Prince and Edward Mason would die terrible deaths. And he prayed for forgiveness. It didn't take long.

"Now's as good a time as any."

There was the hollow thump of footsteps on the porch. Keefe moved eagerly toward the door. "Who's that? Mary Grant still here?"

Keefe raised his pistol and yanked the door open. Tank saw his eyes widen. There was a terrific, ear-splitting noise. Fergus Keefe dropped to the floor as a hail of machine-gun bullets tore up his chest.

Don Bennett advanced into the cabin, firing a second burst into Keefe's prone body.

"Not you, too," said Tank, his heart sinking.

Bennett knelt at Tank's side. "Hang on," he said. "We'll have an ambulance here soon."

An older man with shaggy gray hair and a belly followed. He picked up the key to the LaFerrari off the floor. "This it?" asked Randy Bell.

"Is it, Potter?"

Tank nodded. "It's all there."

Bennett shouted for Bell to get a first-aid kit out of the car, then returned his attention to Tank. "I'm sure we'll read about it in the paper."

But by then Tank wasn't interested in the paper or in writing an article that would win him the Pulitzer Prize or in pulling down a hefty book contract. He took hold of Bennett's arm. "Find Mary."

95

The Mole touched the blade to the pouch of flesh below Jessie's eye. Her skin was so smooth. She was pure. Untouched.

"Stand up. I don't want to embarrass you in front of your mother."

He saw the hate in her eyes and he felt himself stir. The Mole pushed the point against the skin. He saw fear, too, and this excited him more.

Jessie stood.

"Go into the bedroom."

Mary Grant rose to her feet and charged. The Mole kicked her and she fell backward over the coffee table. He was on her in a second, the knife puncturing her neck, a rivulet of blood besmirching the blade. "Stay here. Don't move. Don't make a sound. If I hear you, I'll bury my knife in your baby girl's belly so deep it won't ever come out. And then I'll bury it in yours."

The Mole flipped the knife in his hand and brought the weighted handle down on her forehead, shutting those pleading eyes. He had plans for Mary, too.

He stood and pushed Jessie forward toward the bed.

He closed the door behind them. But not all the way. If Mary Grant made a noise, he'd be listening.

Seconds after the door closed, Mary struggled to her feet. She was dazed, nothing more. If anything, the pain acted as a prod. She slid off her shoes and glided soundlessly across the room to where her purse lay on the floor. She got to her knees and opened it, and her bound hands delved inside, pushing aside her wallet, the envelope containing $36,000 before finding the grip of the nickel-plated .38 revolver. An old-fashioned Saturday night special—$295 at the Pawn Stars shop.

She freed the pistol and, using both thumbs, cocked the hammer. Step by step she advanced toward the bedroom. Her neck was bleeding terribly, leaving a crimson trail on the marble floor. The door stood open an inch. She saw his naked buttocks. She moved faster. She would not allow anyone to hurt her daughter.

She was beautiful.

She was his.

The Mole held his phone in his left hand and the knife in his right. He wanted to film his first time. He looked forward to watching it again and again. Watching was better.

Jessie lay on the bed as he'd told her. He approached warily, ready for any outburst. He slipped the knife beneath the Ninjaneers T-shirt and cut it open down the center of her chest.

"That's right," he said. "Stay still and look at the camera."

He drew nearer, smelling her, wanting all of her.

Jessie kicked out at him. He dodged her blows easily, pressing the knife against her.

"Now take the other shirt off," he said.

He wanted to kiss her, too, but he couldn't risk taking off the tape. He'd kiss her later, when she was still warm.

Jessie didn't move, and he nicked her cheek.

"Next time it'll hurt more."

Jessie pulled off her shirt and looked away.

"Eyes open, Jess," he said. "I want you to see everything."

Later, when he watched, he wanted to see the life drain out of her eyes.

The Mole laid the knife against her bra, then slid it lower, against her jeans. He felt powerful, in control. He was in charge, no one else. Not Briggs. Not Ian Prince. The world was doing as he commanded, no differently than if he'd programmed its every action.

"Now these."

Jessie tugged off her pants. He looked into her eyes as he touched her. A flicker of fear, of apprehension. And then the fear vanished. He caught a reflection in her iris, a flash of movement behind him.

Jessie wrenched her head to one side and squeezed her eyes shut.

Something hard and cold touched the base of his skull.

The Mole began to protest, desperately needing to see who was behind him, who was disobeying his program.

There was a bright light. The sun.

Then darkness.

96

Mary held Jessie in her arms and let her cry until there were no more tears.

"How's Grace?" was the first thing her daughter asked. "She sent me a message saying she was going to the hospital."

"We don't know yet."

"But you're here with me."

Mary nodded. "Of course I am."

At this, Jessie began crying anew. "I love you, Mama," she said.

"I love you, too."

Mary had moved Jess back to the living area. The door to the bedroom was closed.

Jessie sobbed a last time and wiped at her eyes. "I'm sorry. I should have told you I was coming. I knew you'd say no."

"You were right. But we can talk about that later, okay?"

"Okay."

"And about that e-cigarette, young lady . . ."

Jessie drew back. "You looked in my desk?"

"Jess."

"It's okay. I know you were just worried." She sat up straighter. "So why are you here? Why does Ian Prince want to hurt us? Is this because of Dad?"

"Dad was investigating him," said Mary. "Ian Prince had your father killed to stop him."

It took Mary ten minutes to tell Jessie everything that had happened over the past forty-eight hours. She left nothing out. She spoke to Jessie as if she were an adult because that's the way the admiral would have spoken to her. In a few months Jessie would be sixteen. If she was anything like her mother, she was as good as gone the moment she passed her driver's test. There comes a point when you have to let go. Mary wasn't ready yet, but she didn't have a say in the matter.

"Tank really killed that guy?" Jessie asked afterward, needing to process all she'd heard.

"He had to. That guy was going to kill me."

"And you really hit Briggs over the head with our steel bowl?"

"I had to."

"Holy crap," said Jessie. "My mom's Wonder Woman."

"No," said Mary, "just your mom. That's enough."

"But how does Ian Prince know so much about me?"

"Somehow he hacked into our computer and got hold of our passwords. I guess he was able to see everything."

"He took all our money."

"For now, at least."

"That's fucked," said Jessie. "Sorry, but it is."

"You're right," said Mary. "It's really fucked."

"Mom!"

"I thought I was Wonder Woman."

"Wonder Woman does not have a potty mouth." Jessie buried her head in Mary's shoulder. After a minute or so, she began to laugh.

"What is it?" asked Mary.

"I have an idea."

"What about?"

"I know how he hacked into our computer."

"Oh?"

"I told Grace not to open messages from people she didn't know." Jessie got up off the couch, moved to a desk, took a seat, and tapped away at Greg from MIT's laptop.

"What are you doing?" asked Mary.

Jessie didn't look up. "Getting even."

97

Ian Prince was exultant.

Semaphore was behind him. Mary Grant was no longer a worry. As important, Titan was up and running.

Back in Austin and seated contentedly at his desk, he opened the software designed by David Gold and Menachem Wolkowicz and the brain trust at Clarus, his Praetorian Guard. He logged in for the first time, creating a username and password. Seconds later he was inside.

Clarus was already hard at work, shadowing Titan's every iteration. The NSA had wasted no time in feeding intercepts for decryption. Ian counted over fifty thousand documents in the queue. The intercepts were grouped by geopolitical source and prioritized from one to three stars, three being the most important. There were requests from Europe, Asia, the Middle East. The requests came from all the NSA's "customers": the Pentagon, the CIA, the FBI, MI6, and many, many more.

Ian went directly to the economics directorate, specifically, to the U.S. corporate subsection, and then to "Internet." He was rewarded with a cornucopia of intercepts from his largest competitors. There was news of pending mergers, of contracts with foreign governments, of new product development. It was an all-seeing eye into every CEO's suite, their research laboratories, their strategic planning.

Ian knew better than to act rashly. For now there was nothing to do except harvest, store, and study. He planned on remaining invisible for years to come. Knowledge, even for its own sake, was power.

He gazed across the office at the black satchel. Nearly twenty-six years ago to the day, his father had disappeared. As soon as he familiarized himself with the system, he could peek into British intelligence's files. He had little hope of finding anything within the files of the British Foreign Office. Documents dating from 1989 would be far down the list to be digitized and placed on the Net. Records from secondary consulates in Bruges and Leipzig would figure at the bottom of those.

MI6 was a different story. Ian knew he'd find everything he needed there. The problem was that the U.K. was the United States' sacrosanct partner. The countries exchanged information on a "per request" basis. MI6 was a customer of the NSA, just as the CIA was a customer of GCHQ, the Government Communications Headquarters, the NSA's counterpart in Cheltenham, England. They did not spy on each other. Getting into MI6 would merely be a question of learning proper protocol for these exchanges. Nothing beyond his skill set. Not with Titan at his beck and call.

Ian pushed his chair back, crossed his office, and took a seat next to the satchel. He made an oath to his father that he would uncover his service record and let the world know of his accomplishments.

"Boss." He glanced up to find Peter Briggs in his office. "You wanted to see me."

"It won't take long. Everything under control?"

"Last I heard from Mason, his man had recovered the flash drive. I have confirmation that the Mole took care of our problem in Vegas. Our men should be at the hotel presently. The situation is tied off, once and for all."

"Good," said Ian. "Seems like the right moment, then. I'm letting you go, Peter."

"Pardon me?"

"I can't have my chief of security going behind my back and disobeying me. Your job is to protect me, not get me into trouble."

"What are you referring to?"

"That nasty knot on your head, to begin with. As I was doing some work last night, I happened to see you at Mary Grant's home. You know how that works. I heard you speaking to the Mole about Mr. McNair. I told you to leave her alone."

"I was only trying to cover your back. You're a busy man. Sometimes you get . . . removed from how things really are."

"I ordered you not to lay a finger on Mary Grant or her children. You disobeyed me. There's nothing more to say except goodbye."

"You're letting me go—with all I know?"

"You've been paid handsomely. A call to Edward Mason will quiet any accusations should you be that stupid."

"I took care of Merriweather and Joe Grant. Without me, you'd never have gotten the contract with the NSA."

"Goodbye, Peter."

But Briggs didn't leave. He unbuttoned his jacket and advanced on

Ian, his ruddy face flushed nearly crimson. He eyed the satchel mockingly. "Find anything about your father yet?"

"That's none of your concern."

"Or is it that you don't want to look too hard?"

"What are you getting at?"

"All the time you spend staring at this silly case, daydreaming about him. Come off it, Ian, you know better. He wasn't a secret agent. He was a drunk. He drowned facedown in his own puke in a gutter outside a Brussels whorehouse."

"That's ridiculous."

"Ask your mother."

"We don't speak."

"She told you the truth twenty years ago."

"She was lying. She hated him."

"With good reason." Briggs picked up the satchel. "I looked, too. On my own. I wanted to help you find out the truth. She told me everything. About the gambling. The fights. Mostly about the drinking. Still, I wanted to believe you. Most women are skags anyway. But it's all there in the Belgian police's files. I'll be sure to leave you copies on my way out."

Ian grabbed the satchel away from Briggs. "He wasn't a drunk. It was cover. He was an agent with MI6. He was killed while on duty. They never found the body."

Briggs was laughing at him. "Of course they did, only your mother refused to claim it. The British government refused as well. Do you know why? Because your father had been sacked six months before. Your dear old dad's buried in an unmarked grave in a potter's field, or whatever they call it over there."

"You're lying."

"Am I?" Briggs jabbed his finger into Ian's chest. "I'm going to tell the world, Ian. I'm going to tell everyone the truth about Peter fucking Prince. Everyone's going to know what a drunken lowlife your father was."

"No, you're not."

"Yes, I am. Bank on it."

Ian shot him. Peter Briggs staggered back a step. Ian dropped the satchel, the Walther gripped in his right hand. He fired again. Briggs fell. He was dead before he hit the floor. "Banked."

The crack of the gunshots brought Ian to his senses. His rage vanished. Self-preservation took hold. He kneeled and freed Briggs's pistol from his holster and placed it in his hand. It was a matter of self-defense. Anyone could see it.

He waited for his assistants to come running to his aid, but it was nearly eight and everyone had gone home. No one had heard the shots. He walked to his desk and called Edward Mason. He would tell him that Briggs had been threatening to go to the authorities. Mason would send someone. They were all in this together. There was no other choice.

The call rolled to voicemail. "Ed, this is Ian. Call me. It's an emergency."

Ian put his pistol in his top drawer, then returned to the body. Briggs was single. He had no family in the city. No one would miss him for days. Maybe it wouldn't come to self-defense. There was ample time to dispose of the body. Maybe he could even tie it to Mary Grant somehow.

His personal line rang. Eight o'clock meant it was the daily call from his children in Los Angeles. The timing couldn't be better. He would say he had been talking with his family when Briggs was killed. Ian turned the camera away from Briggs and positioned himself in front of the lens.

"Hello there," he said with false merriment.

The screen came to life. He saw his boys, Tristan and Trevor, in the kitchen of the home in Bel-Air.

"Dad, Dad," Tristan, the younger boy, was shouting. "We've got a surprise."

Ian did his best to smile. "Really? What's that?"

"We know you said no more animals, but this one was special."

"Another one? What is it this time? Not another dog?"

"Just wait, Dad," said Trevor. "You're going to freak. It's so cool."

"Take a guess," said Tristan.

"I don't know . . . a cat."

"Of course not."

"A snake?"

"It's easy, Dad. I mean, you sent us that video for a reason."

"Did I? Which one was that?"

Just then Tristan picked up the animal and held it in his arms. It was large and furry, with great big claws and sad black eyes. "Say hi to Joey. He's a three-toed South American tree sloth."

"A sloth?" said Ian, blinking, sure he was imagining this.

"Don't be mad," Tristan went on. "Isn't that why you sent us the video of the sloth trying to climb out of the crib? You knew we couldn't resist."

It was the video he'd sent to the Grant girls, to which he'd attached the malware. But how in the world had his sons received it?

"You're sure I sent it to you?"

"Yeah, Dad," said Trevor. "We know better than to open messages that come from strangers."

"I made Mom go to the exotic pet store in Beverly Hills. Don't you think he's cute?"

Ian dashed to his computer. If they'd downloaded the video of the sloth, they'd imported the malware. The family's machines were networked. The malware would grant a user free rein inside all of them—desktops, laptops, tablets. It would be simplicity itself to locate his passwords and access his files, both personal and professional. There was no telling what someone might find.

Ian logged on to his e-mail and saw that it was true: he had sent them the video. Or rather, the person who had hacked into his computer had sent it from Ian's account.

He drew a breath, wondering how this had happened. How all of it had happened.

A shriek came from somewhere in the kitchen behind the boys. "Ian!"

It was his wife, Wendy. She came through the butler's pantry, clutching her laptop, the screen open. "What have you done? It's everywhere."

"What are you talking about?"

"Is it real? Tell me, Ian, is it?" Wendy aimed the laptop at the camera, but he could see the images only faintly.

"I have no idea what you're talking about," he said.

"Did you shoot him? Did you?"

"Shoot who?"

"Briggs! Did you?" Wendy was bawling hysterically, screaming at the boys to get out of the kitchen.

Ian brought up Rivalfox, a website devoted to the highest-trending topics and personalities on the Web. To his horror, his name was ranked first. He double-clicked on his name and was given a link to a video on YouTube titled "Ian Prince Murders Peter Briggs in cold blood."

He hit Play, and there he was, standing in his office, speaking with Peter Briggs only five minutes earlier.

"*He wasn't a spy,*" Briggs was saying. "*He was a drunk.*"

Ian froze as the rest of the encounter played out, filmed in high definition by the camera in his desktop.

"*Your dear old dad's buried in an unmarked grave in a potter's field, or whatever they call it over there.*"

"*You're lying.*"

"*Am I?*" Briggs jabbed his finger into Ian's chest. "*I'm going to tell the world, Ian. I'm going to tell everyone the truth about Peter fucking Prince. Everyone's going to know what a drunken lowlife your father was.*"

"*No, you're not.*"

"*Yes, I am. Bank on it.*"

Ian shot him. Peter Briggs staggered back a step. Ian dropped the satchel, the Walther gripped in his right hand. He fired again. Briggs fell. He was dead before he hit the floor.

"*Banked,*" said Ian.

He looked away from the screen. Only one person could have done this: Jessie Grant. He'd sent her the sloth video, too. She possessed the skills. She'd nearly defeated him at Capture the Flag. But she was dead in a Vegas hotel room. Briggs had confirmed it.

Or was she?

Ian refreshed the page. The views were increasing exponentially.

2,000 . . . 10,000 . . . 100,000.

The video was going viral.

The entire world was watching.

"Ian, is this real?" Wendy Prince continued to shout. "Ian!"

He ended the call.

From afar he heard a siren, and then another. He hurried to the window. A dozen unmarked cars were barreling over the Meadow toward his office.

His phone rang. Edward Mason.

"Ed, hello, thank God you called. There are—"

"Mr. Prince, my name is Dylan Walsh. I'm chief of the Cyber Investigations Division at the FBI. Edward Mason is presently in custody. Our agents have surrounded your office. We ask that you surrender yourself immediately. Please walk out the front door with your hands up."

Ian hung up the phone. Mason was in custody. The FBI had Stark's files. They knew everything. His office was surrounded.

The number of views continued to spiral upward.

500,000. . . . 600,000.

He'd be at a million soon, and that was only the beginning. He was looking at what was certain to become the most-watched video of all time.

Ian opened the drawer and stared at his father's pistol.

JANUARY

The outrigger canoe bobbed on the early-morning swell.

"Is this the place?" asked Grace.

"It better be," said Jessie. "I'm done paddling."

Mary gazed out over the sea toward the green slopes of Maui. A gentle breeze blew off the island, bringing the scent of gardenias and frangipani. Across the channel the rising sun gilded Lanai's coast with a rich golden warmth. She stowed her paddle. "I think your father will like it here."

"What do we do now?" asked Jessie.

Mary opened her rucksack and took out a small iron box. Five months had passed since Joe's death and the events that followed. There had been a service in Boston, but she'd decided against a formal burial. Joe needed to be where he was happiest, and he'd always been happiest on a beach somewhere with his girls. She handed Grace the box. "Remember, not all at once."

Grace held the box over the side and carefully shook loose the ash. She put her hand in the water and laughed at some private thought. "Bye, Daddy."

Jess took the box next. She held it in her lap for a long while, saying nothing, staring into the fine dust. Then, abruptly, she thrust the box over the ocean and tipped it, sprinkling the ash in a circle. As abruptly she handed the box to Mary.

Mary held it in both hands. She'd said her goodbyes long ago. She lifted her eyes to her daughters, Jessie, now sixteen, and Grace, twelve . . . *her husband's daughters* . . . and thanked him for such a wonderful blessing. Then she poured the remainder of Joe's ashes into the Pacific Ocean.

"Okay, you guys, the flowers."

Jessie took off her lei and dropped it into the ocean. Grace followed suit, then Mary. A fourth lei flew high into the air and landed amid the disappearing ash.

"Nice shot, Tank," said Grace.

Tank Potter smiled. His hair was cut short, and he'd lost fifty pounds during his stay in the hospital. Mary had visited him often, and they'd grown close. The girls adored him. He was family.

"Can we go now?" said Jessie. "There's no cell service out here."

"You brought your phone?" asked Grace.

"Why wouldn't I?"

Mary stared out across the ocean. She wanted to believe that everything was going to be perfect. Grace would stay in remission. Jessie would come to terms with the ordeal she'd suffered. Tank would learn to walk without a cane one day, and maybe even win the Pulitzer for his series about Ian Prince and ONE. The future held promise and mystery in equal parts.

For the moment, though, she was thinking only about the present. Ian Prince was dead. ONE Technologies was under investigation for a litany of crimes. Edward Mason was in prison. In recognition of Joe's (and Mary's) services, the FBI had awarded her his salary through retirement. And some unknown party had restored the family's checking and savings accounts to their previous levels and paid off their hospital debt. Mary refused to take more, though she did allow the unknown party to buy herself a brand-new laptop and iPhone and to give her little sister a new pet: a three-toed South American tree sloth. Grace named him Sleepy.

All that mattered right now was that Mary was with her daughters and a man she cared for.

It really was a beautiful morning.

"Yes," said Mary. "We can go."

Tank dropped his paddle into the water and began to stroke.

Mary matched his timing, and together they began the journey to land.

ACKNOWLEDGMENTS

I would like to thank the following people for their invaluable assistance: Stephen Kahn, Steve Elefant, Phil Trubey, Mat Honan, Sally Anne McCartin, Kris Bergen, Dr. Douglas Fischer, Stan Scheuffler, Jon Lee, David Yorkin, Pradeep Tarbat, Esq., Ed Antak, Gary Burdick, and Dr. Jon Shafqat.

At Doubleday, my thanks go to John Pitts, Rob Bloom, Bette Alexander, Todd Doughty, Bill Thomas, the entire Random House sales team, and, finally, to my editor and friend, Jason Kaufman. It's been a great run, and I couldn't be more grateful for all the incredible effort expended on my behalf.

Last, and most important, I want to give a heartfelt "shout-out" to my team at Inkwell Management. Hugs to Charlie Olsen, Eliza Rothstein, Michael Carlisle, and, of course, to my agent, Richard Pine. *Invasion of Privacy* is our tenth book together. I still remember the day in May 1996, when Richard called from New York saying he'd read the manuscript of my first novel, *Numbered Account*, and asking if he could represent me. I'm pretty sure I said yes before falling off my chair. Thank you, Richard, for taking a chance. Here's to ten more!

A NOTE ABOUT THE AUTHOR

Christopher Reich is the *New York Times* best-selling author of *The Prince of Risk, Rules of Deception, Rules of Vengeance, Rules of Betrayal, Numbered Account,* and *The Runner.* His novel *The Patriots Club* won the International Thriller Writers Award for Best Novel in 2006. He lives in Encinitas, California.